HOUSE OF CARDS

Praise for *House of Cards*

"This blood-and-thunder tale, lifelike and thoroughly cynical, carries the ring of authenticity…a great triumph."

—Independent

"*House of Cards* is fast-moving, revelatory, and brilliant."

—Daily Express

"With a friend like Michael Dobbs, who on earth needs enemies? His timing is again impeccable. Gloriously cheeky."

—The Times

"Razor-sharp and merciless."

—Daily Mail

"Francis Urquhart is one of the great characters of modern fiction."

—York Evening Press

"*House of Cards* is a work of genius."

—Sunday Post

HOUSE OF CARDS

MICHAEL DOBBS

sourcebooks
landmark

Published by Sourcebooks Landmark, an imprint of Sourcebooks, Inc.
P.O. Box 4410, Naperville, Illinois 60567-4410
(630) 961-3900
Fax: (630) 961-2168
www.sourcebooks.com

Originally published in 1989 in the United Kingdom by Collins, an imprint of HarperCollins.

Library of Congress Cataloging-in-Publication data is on file with the publisher.

Printed and bound in the United States of America.
VP 10 9 8 7 6 5 4 3 2 1

PART ONE
THE SHUFFLE

*N*othing lasts, not forever. Not laughter, not lust, not even life itself. Not forever. Which is why we make the most of what we have.

Why waste a life in search of an epitaph? "Fondly Remembered." Who other than a half-wit has that chiseled above his head? It is nothing but sentimental incontinence. Let's face facts, life is a zero-sum game and politics is how we decide who wins, who loses. And whether we like it or not, we are all players.

"Respected By All Who Knew Him." Another monumental whimper. Not for my gravestone. It's not respect but fear that motivates a man; that's how empires are built and revolutions begin. It is the secret of great men. When a man is afraid you will crush him, utterly destroy him, his respect will always follow. Base fear is intoxicating, overwhelming, liberating. Always stronger than respect.

Always.

ONE

It seemed scarcely a moment since she had made it back home, stumbling up the last step in exhaustion, yet already the morning sun was sticking thumbs in her eyes as it crept around the curtain and began to nestle on her pillow. She turned over irritably. Her head was thick, her feet sore, and the bed beside her empty. Helping finish off that second bottle of Liebfraumilch had been a lousy idea. She'd let down her defenses, got herself stuck in a corner with some creep from the *Sun* who was all acne and innuendo. She'd had to spill the last of the wine down his shirt before he'd backed off. She took a quick peek under the duvet, just to make sure she hadn't screwed up completely and he wasn't lurking there. She sighed; she hadn't even got round to taking off her socks.

Mattie Storin beat her pillow into submission and lay back once again. She deserved a few extra moments in bed; she knew she wouldn't get any sleep tonight. Election night. Day of Damnation. Voters' Vengeance. The past few weeks had been ferocious for Mattie, under siege from her editor, stretched too tightly between deadlines, tossed between excitement and exhaustion. Maybe after this evening she could take a few days off, sort her life out, find a better quality of both wine and man to spend her evening with. She pulled the duvet more closely around her. Even in the glare of the early summer sun she felt a chill.

It had been like that ever since she had left Yorkshire almost a year before. She'd hoped she could leave all the accusations and the anger behind her, but they still cast a cold shadow that followed her everywhere, particularly into her bed. She shivered, buried her face in the lumpy pillow.

She tried to be philosophical. After all, she no longer had any emotional distractions, nothing to get in the way of discovering whether she really had what it took to become the best political correspondent in a fiercely masculine world. Only herself to bother about, not even a cat. But it was difficult to be philosophical when your feet were freezing. And when you didn't have any clean laundry. She threw back the duvet and clambered out of bed, only to discover that her underwear drawer was bare. She'd miscalculated, forgotten, too much to do and so little time to do any of it, least of all the bloody washing. She searched other drawers, every corner, made a mess but found nothing. Damn, she was glad no man had to watch her do this. She dived into her laundry basket, ferreted around and came up with a pair of knickers a week old but only a day worn. She turned them inside out, stepped into them. Ready for battle. With a sigh Mattie Storin threw open the bathroom door and got on with her day.

❖ ❖ ❖

As dusk began to settle across the June skies, four sets of HMI mercury oxide television lamps clicked on with a dull thud, painting the front of the building with high intensity power. The brilliant light pierced deep behind the mock Georgian façade of the Party's headquarters. A curtain fluttered at a third floor window as someone took a quick glance at the scene outside.

The moth also saw the lamps. It was waiting for the approaching night, resting in a crevice of one of the nearby towers of St. John, the graceful church built by Wren in the middle of Smith Square. The church had long been deconsecrated, St. John dismissed, but its four limestone towers still dominated this now godless square in the heart of Westminster. They stared down, frowning in disapproval. But not the moth. It began to tingle with excitement. It stretched its wings, drawn by ten thousand watts and a million years of instinct.

The moth strained in the early evening air, forcing its body along the river of light. It flew above the heads of the growing crowd, beyond the bustle and gathering pace of preparations. Nearer and nearer it flew, eager, passionate, erratic, ambitious, heedless of everything other than the power it was being drawn to, power beyond dreams, beyond resistance. It had no choice.

There was a bright flash as the moth's body hit the lens a millisecond before its wings wrapped around the searing glass and vaporized. Its charred and blackened carcass gave off little vapors of despair as it tumbled toward the ground. The night had gained its first victim.

❖ ❖ ❖

Another of the night's early victims was propping up the varnished bar at the Marquis of Granby, just around the corner from the growing commotion. The original Marquis of Granby had been a popular military figure more than two hundred years earlier and had more pubs named after him than any other figure in the land, but the marquis had succumbed to politics, lost his way, and died in debt and distress. Much the same fate lay in store for Charles Collingridge, according to his many tolerant friends. Not that Charlie Collingridge had ever been elected, but neither had the marquis, it wasn't the done thing in those early days. Collingridge was in his midfifties, looked older, worn, and hadn't had a particularly glorious

military career, two years of national service that had left him
with little more than a sense of his own inadequacy in the order
of life. Charlie had always tried to do the decent thing but he
was accident prone. It happens when you have a drinking habit.

His day had started early with a shave and a tie, but now
the stubble was beginning to show and the tie was hanging at
half-mast. The eyes told the barman that the large vodka he
had served two glasses ago hadn't been the first of the day.
But Charlie was a genial drunk, always ready with a smile
and a generous word. He pushed his empty glass back across
the counter.

"Another?" The barman asked, dubious.

"And one for yourself, my good man," Charlie replied,
reaching for his wallet. "Ah, but it seems I'm a little short," he
muttered, staring at a solitary note in disbelief. He searched
through his pocket and pulled out keys, a gray handkerchief,
and a few coins. "I'm sure, somewhere…"

"The note will do," the barman replied. "Nothing for me,
thanks. It's going to be a long night."

"Yes. It will. My younger brother, Hal, you know him?"

The barman shook his head, pushed the drink across the
varnish, glad the old drunk was out of money and soon out of
his bar.

"You don't know Hal?" Charlie asked in surprise. "You
must." He sipped. "Everyone knows Hal." Another sip. "He's
the Prime Minister."

TWO

It's a very good idea for a politician to have vision. Yes, the Vision Thing, just the ticket. Really useful, don't you think? Why, on a clear day most politicians can see as far as—well, I know some who can see almost as far as Battersea.

Francis Ewan Urquhart was a man of many parts, a Member of Parliament, a Privy Councilor that gave him the prefix of Right Honorable, a Minister of the Crown, and a Commander of the Most Excellent Order of the British Empire. He was all these things and this was his night, yet still he wasn't enjoying himself. He was squashed into the corner of a small and stuffy living room, pressed hard up against a hideous 1960s standard lamp that showed every sign of toppling over. He was hemmed in by a posse of matrons who doubled as his constituency workers and who had cut off his means of escape as they chattered proudly about their last-minute mail drops and pinched shoes. He wondered why they bothered. This was suburban Surrey, the land of the A and B social classes in the terminology of pollsters, where passports lay at the ready and Range Rovers stood in the driveway. Range Rovers? The only time they ever encountered mud was when being driven care- lessly over front lawns late on a Friday night or when dropping off their little Johnnies and Emmas at their private schools. Canvassing in these parts was held to be almost vulgar. They didn't count votes here, they weighed them.

"Another vol-au-vent, Mr. Urquhart?" A plate of sagging pastry was thrust in front of him by an overweight woman whose bosom was clad in large floral print and seemed to be hiding two fractious cats.

"No, thank you, Mrs. Morecombe. I fear I shall explode!"

With impatience. It was a fault, one that stretched back many generations. The Urquharts were a proud warrior family from the Highlands of Scotland, their castle on the banks of Loch Ness, but the MacDonalds had arrived and the castle now lay in ruins. Urquhart's childhood memories were of the bracing, crystal air of the moors, in the company of an old gillie, lying for hours in the damp peat and sweetly scented bracken waiting for the right buck to appear, just as he had imagined his older brother Alastair was doing, waiting for the Germans in the hedgerows outside Dunkirk. His brother had called him FU, a nickname that had often got them both a clout from their father, even though it was years before Francis understood why. He didn't mind, happy to tag along behind his big brother. But Alastair hadn't come home. His mother had crumbled, never recovered, lived in memory of her lost son and neglect of Francis, so FU had eventually come south, to London. To Westminster. To Surrey. Abandoned his duties. His mother had never spoken to him again. To have sold his heritage for the whole of Scotland would have been unforgivable, but for Surrey?

He sighed, even as he smiled. This was the eighteenth committee room of the day, and the enthusiasm that had knitted together the early morning humor had long since unraveled and turned to thread. It was still forty minutes before the polling booths closed and the last vote was cast. Urquhart's shirt was wringing wet. He was tired, uncomfortable, penned in by the posse of women who pursued him with spaniel-like persistence.

Yet still he kept his smile afloat, because his life was about to change, whatever the result. Urquhart had spent years climbing the political ladder, from backbencher through Junior Ministerial jobs and now attending Cabinet as Chief Whip, one of the two dozen most powerful posts in the Government. It provided him with splendid offices at 12 Downing Street, just yards from the Prime Minister's own. It was behind the door of Number 12 that two of the most celebrated Britons of all time, Wellington and Nelson, had met for the first and only time. The walls echoed with history and with an authority that was now his.

Yet Urquhart's power didn't stem directly from his public office. The role of Chief Whip didn't carry full Cabinet rank. Urquhart had no great Department of State or massive civil service machine to command; his was a faceless task, toiling ceaselessly behind the scenes, making no public speeches and giving no television interviews. A man of the shadows.

And also a man of discipline. He was the Enforcer, the one whose job it was to put a bit of stick about. That meant he was not simply respected but also a little feared. He was the minister with the most acute political antennae in government. In order to deliver the vote, day after day, night after night, he needed to know where his Members of Parliament were likely to be found, which meant he needed to know their secrets— with whom they were conspiring, with whom they might be sleeping, whether they would be sober enough to vote, whether they had their hands in someone else's pocket or on someone else's wife. All these secrets with their sharp little edges were gathered together and kept in a black book, locked inside a safe, and not even the Prime Minister had access to the keys.

In Westminster, such information is power. Many in Urquhart's Parliamentary Party owed their continuing position to the ability of the Whips' Office to sort out and occasionally cover up their personal problems. Backbenchers intent on

rebellion or frontbenchers distracted by ambition found themselves changing their minds when reminded of some earlier
indiscretion that had been forgiven by the Party, but never
forgotten. It was astonishing how pliable politicians became
when confronted by the possibility of a collision between their
public and private lives. Why, even that dyspeptic Staffordshire
soul, the Transport Secretary, a man who had planned to make
a conference speech way outside his remit and far too close to
the Prime Minister's home turf, had come to his senses. All it
had taken was a phone call to his mistress's mews house rather
than the marital home.

"Francis, how the fuck did you find me here?"

"Oh, Keith, have I made some terrible mistake? I'm so sorry, I
wanted to have a quick chat with you about your little speech, but
it seems I looked for your number in the wrong set of accounts."

"What the bloody hell do you mean?"

"Oh, don't you know? We keep two sets of books. One is the
official tally, the other…Well, don't worry, we keep our little
black book under very careful control. It won't happen again."
A pause before: "Will it?"

The Transport Secretary had sighed, a sound full of melan-
choly and guilt. "No, Francis, it bloody well won't." Another
sinner came to rapid repentance.

The Party owed Francis Urquhart, everyone knew that. And,
after this election, it would be time for the debt to be called in.

Suddenly Urquhart was brought back to the moment by one
of his devoted ladies. Her eyes were excited, her cheeks flushed,
her breath heavy with the sour afterlife of egg and watercress
sandwiches, her sense of coyness and discretion overcome by
the heat and excitement of the day.

"Tell us, Mr. Urquhart, what are your plans? Will you still
stand at the next election?" she inquired brashly.

"What do you mean?" he replied, taken aback, his eyes flaring in affront.

"Are you thinking of retiring? You're sixty-one, aren't you? Sixty-five or more at the next election," she persisted.

He bent his tall and angular figure low in order to look her directly in the face. "Mrs. Bailey, I still have my wits about me and in many societies I would just be entering my political prime," he responded through lips that no longer carried any trace of good nature. "I still have a lot of work to do. Things I want to achieve."

He turned away from her, not bothering to hide his impatience, even while deep down he knew she was right. The strong red hues of his youth had long since vanished, gold turned to silver, as he liked to joke. He wore his hair over-long, as if to compensate. His spare frame no longer filled the traditionally cut suits as amply as in earlier years, and his blue eyes had grown colder with the passing of so many winters. His height and upright bearing presented a distinguished image in the crowded room, but one minister, a man he had crossed, had once told him he had a smile like the handle on an urn of cold ashes. "And may those ashes soon be yours, you old bastard," the man had snapped. Urquhart was no longer in the first flush of middle age and he couldn't hide it, even from himself. Experience was no longer an ally.

How many years had he watched younger and less gifted men finding more rapid advancement? How many times had he dried their eyes, wiped their arses, buried their secrets deep from view in order to clear their way? Yes, they owed him! He still had time to make his mark, but both he and Mrs. Bailey knew he hadn't so much of it.

Yet even as he turned from her she pursued him, haranguing him about the proposed one-way system for the High Street shopping center. He raised his eyes in supplication and managed to catch the attention of his wife, Mortima, busily engaged in platitudes on the far side of the room. One glance told her that his rescue was long overdue and she hurried to his side.

"Ladies, you will have to excuse us, we have to go back to the hotel and change before the count. I can't thank you enough for all your help. You know how indispensable you are to Francis."

Urquhart even managed a smile for Mrs. Bailey; it was like a mayfly, so brief it almost died before it could be seen but enough to repair relations. He made quickly for the door. He was saying good-bye to the hostess when he was waved to a halt by his election agent who was busily scribbling down notes while talking into the telephone.

"Just getting the final canvass returns together, Francis," she explained.

"And there was me wondering why that hadn't been done an hour ago." Again the faintest of amused expressions that died long before it reached the eyes.

"It doesn't look quite as cheerful as last time," she said, blushing from the rebuke. "A lot of our supporters seem to be staying at home. It's difficult to read but I suspect the majority will be down. I can't tell how much."

"Damn them. They deserve a dose of the Opposition for a few years. Maybe that would get them off their rumps."

"Darling," his wife soothed as she had done on countless previous occasions, "that's scarcely generous. With a majority of nearly twenty-two thousand we could allow for just the tiniest of little dips, couldn't we?"

"Mortima, I'm not feeling generous. I'm feeling hot, I am tired, and I've had about as much chatter about doorstep opinion as I can take. For God's sake get me out of here."

He strode on as she turned round to wave thanks and farewell to the packed room. She was just in time to see the standard lamp go crashing to the floor.

❖ ❖ ❖

The air of controlled menace that usually filled the editor's office had vanished, replaced by a brooding sense of panic that was threatening to get out of hand. The first edition had long since gone to press, complete with a bold front page headline proclaiming: "Home and dry!" But that had been at 6:00 p.m., four hours before the polls closed. The editor of the *Daily Chronicle* had taken his chance on the election result in order to make his first edition of even marginal interest by the time it hit the streets. If he was right, he would be first with the news. If he got it wrong, he'd be up to his neck in it with the alligators circling.

This was Greville Preston's first election as an editor and he wasn't feeling comfortable. His nervousness showed in his constant change of headlines, his insatiable demand for updates from his political staff, and his increasingly lurid language. He'd been brought in just a few months earlier by the new owner of Chronicle Newspapers with one simple and irreducible instruction: "Succeed." Failure wasn't an option in his contract, and he knew he wouldn't be given a second chance—any more than he showed any hint of remorse for the others who worked at the *Chronicle*. The demands of the accountants for instant financial gratification had required ruthless pruning, and a large number of senior personnel had found themselves being "rationalized" and replaced by less experienced and considerably less expensive substitutes. It was great for the bottom line but had kicked the crap out of morale. The purge left the remaining staff insecure, the loyal readers confused and Preston with a perpetual sense of impending doom, a condition that his proprietor was determined to do nothing to dispel.

Preston's strategy for increasing the circulation had taken the paper down-market, but it had yet to reap the promised harvest. He was a small man who had arrived at the paper with the air of a new Napoleon but who had lost weight until he required braces to haul up his trousers and a tide of coffee to keep open his eyes. The once smooth and dapper appearance had begun to be washed away by countless beads of perspiration that

collected on his brow and made his heavy rimmed glasses slip
down his nose. Fingers that had once drummed in thought now
snapped in impatience. The carefully manufactured attempt
at outward authority had been eaten away by the insecurity
within, and he was no longer certain he could rise to the occasion, any occasion. He'd even stopped screwing his secretary.

Now he turned away from the bank of flickering television
monitors piled against one wall of his office to face the member
of staff who had been giving him such a hard time. "How the
hell do you know it's going wrong?" he shouted.

Mattie Storin refused to flinch. At twenty-eight she was the
youngest recruit to the paper's political staff, replacing one of
the senior correspondents who had fallen foul of the accountants for his habit of conducting interviews over extended
lunches at the Savoy. Yet despite her relative youth and recent
arrival, Mattie had a confidence about her judgment that inadequate men mistook for stubbornness. She was used to being
shouted at and no stranger at yelling back. Anyway, she was as
tall as Preston, "and almost as beautiful" as she often quipped
at his expense. What did it matter if he spent most of his time
staring at her breasts? It had gotten her the job and occasionally won her a few of their arguments. She didn't find him a
sexual threat. She knew his secretary too well for that, and
being harassed by short men in lurid red braces was the price
she had chosen to pay by coming south. Survive here and she
could make her career anywhere.

She turned to face him with her hands thrust defensively into
the pockets of her fashionably baggy trousers. She spoke slowly,
hoping her voice wouldn't betray her nervousness. "Grev, every
single Government MP I've been able to talk to in the past
two hours is downgrading their forecast. I've telephoned the
returning officer in the Prime Minister's constituency who says
the poll looks like it's down by five percent. That's scarcely an
overwhelming vote of confidence. Something is going on out

there, you can feel it. The Government aren't home and certainly not bloody dry."

"So?"

"So our story's too strong."

"Crap. Every poll during the election has talked of the Government getting home by a sodding mile, yet you want me to change the front page on the basis of—what? Feminine instinct?"

Mattie knew his hostility was built on nerves. All editors live on the edge; the secret is not to show it. Preston showed it.

"OK," he demanded, "they had a majority of over a hundred at the last election. So you tell me what your feminine instinct suggests it's going to be tomorrow. The opinion polls are predicting around seventy seats. What does little Mattie Storin think?"

She went up on tiptoes, just so she could look down on him. "You trust the polls if you want, Grev, but it's not what's going on in the streets. There's no enthusiasm among Government supporters. They won't turn out. It'll drag the majority down."

"Come on," he bullied. "How much?"

She couldn't stand on tiptoe forever. She shook her head slowly to emphasize her caution, her blond hair brushing around her shoulders. "A week ago I'd have said about fifty. Now—I reckon less," she responded. "Perhaps much less."

"Jesus, it can't be less. We've backed those bastards all the way. They've got to deliver."

And you've got to deliver, too, she mused. They all knew where their editor stood, in the middle of one of the largest swamps in Fleet Street. Preston's only firm political view was that his newspaper couldn't afford to be on the losing side, and that wasn't even his own view but one thrust on him by the paper's new cockney proprietor, Benjamin Landless. It was one of his few attractive aspects that he didn't bother being coy and trying to hide his true opinions, he wore them in full public view. As he constantly reminded his already insecure staff, thanks to the Government's competition policy it was easier to buy ten new editors than one new newspaper, "so we don't piss off the Government by supporting the other fucking side."

Landless had been as good as his word. He had delivered his growing army of newspapers into the Government camp, and all he expected in return was for the Government to deliver the proper election result. It wasn't reasonable, of course, but Landless had never found being reasonable helped get the best out of his employees.

Preston had gone over to stare at the bank of television screens, hoping for better news. Mattie tried again. She sat herself on the corner of the editor's vast desk, obliterating the pile of opinion polls on which he so blindly relied, and marshaled her case. "Look, Grev, put it in perspective. When Margaret Thatcher at last ran out of handbag time and was forced to retire, they were desperate for a change of style. They wanted a new fashion. Something less abrasive, less domineering; they'd had enough of trial by ordeal and being shown up by a bloody woman." You of all people should understand that, she thought. "So in their wisdom they chose Collingridge, for no better reason than he was confident on TV, smooth with little old ladies, and likely to be uncontroversial." She shrugged her shoulders dismissively. "But they've lost their cutting edge. It's rice pudding politics and there's no energy or enthusiasm left. He's campaigned with as much vigor as a Sunday school teacher. Another seven days of listening to him mouthing platitudes and I think even his wife would have voted for the other lot. Anything for a change."

Preston had turned from the television screens and was stroking his chin. At last he seemed to be paying attention. For the tenth time that evening Mattie wondered if he used lacquer to keep his carefully coiffured hair so immaculate. She suspected a bald patch was developing. She was certain he used eyebrow tweezers.

He returned to the charge. "OK, let's dispense with the mysticism and stick to hard numbers, shall we? What's the majority going to be? Are they going to get back in, or not?"

"It would be a rash man who said they wouldn't," she replied.

"And I have no goddamned intention of being rash, Mattie. Any sort of majority will be good enough for me. Hell, in the circumstances it would be quite an achievement. Historic, in fact. Four straight wins, never been done before. So the front page stays."

Preston quickly brought his instructions to an end by pouring out a glass of champagne from a bottle that was standing on his bookcase. He didn't offer her any. He started scrabbling through papers in dismissal but Mattie was not to be so easily put off. Her grandfather had been a modern Viking who in the stormy early months of 1941 had sailed across the North Sea in a waterlogged fishing boat to escape from Nazi-occupied Norway and join the RAF. Mattie had inherited from him not only her natural Scandinavian looks but also a stubbornness of spirit that didn't always commend itself to inadequate men, but what the hell.

"Just stop for a moment and ask yourself what we could expect from another four years of Collingridge," Maddie challenged. "Maybe he's too nice to be Prime Minister. His manifesto was so lightweight it got blown away in the first week of the campaign. He's developed no new ideas. His only plan is to cross his fingers and hope that neither the Russians nor the trade unions break wind too loudly. Is that what you think the country really wants?"

"Daintily put, as always, Mattie," he taunted, patronizing once more. "But you're wrong. The punters want consolidation, not upheaval. They don't want the toys being thrown out of the pram every time the baby's taken for a walk." He wagged his finger in the air like a conductor bringing an errant player back to the score. "So a couple of years of warm beer and cricket will be no bad thing. And our chum Collingridge back in Downing Street will be a marvelous thing!"

"It'll be bloody murder," she muttered, turning to leave.

THREE

Jesus told us to forgive our enemies, and who am I to second-guess the Almighty? But in his infinite wisdom he didn't mention a damned thing about forgiving our friends, and least of all our families. I'm happy to take his advice on the matter. In any case, when it comes to it, I find it much easier to forgive myself.

It was the Number 88 bus thundering past and rattling the apartment windows that eventually caused Charles Collingridge to wake up. The small one-bedroom flat above the travel agency in Clapham was not what most people would have expected of the Prime Minister's brother, but reduced needs must. Since he had run out of money at the pub he had come home to regroup. Now he lay slumped in the armchair, still in his crumpled suit, although his tie was now completely missing.

He looked at his old wristwatch and cursed. He'd been asleep for hours yet still he felt exhausted. He'd miss the party if he didn't hurry, but first he needed a drink to pick himself up. He poured himself a large measure of vodka, not even Smirnoff any more, just the local supermarket brand. Still, it didn't hang on the breath or smell when you spilled it.

He took his glass to the bathroom and soaked in the tub, giving the hot water time to work its wonders on those tired limbs. Nowadays they often seemed to belong to an entirely different person. He must be getting old, he told himself.

He stood in front of the mirror, trying to repair the damage of his latest binge. He saw his father's face, reproachful as ever, urging him on to goals that were always just beyond him, demanding to know why he never managed to do things quite like his younger brother Henry. They both had the same advantages, went to the same school, but somehow Hal always had the edge, and gradually had overshadowed him in his career and his marriage. Charles didn't feel bitter about it, was a generous soul, far too generous, and indulgent. But Hal had always been there to help when he needed it, to offer advice and to give him a shoulder to cry on after Mary had left him. Yes, particularly when Mary had left him. But hadn't even she thrown Hal's success in his face? "You're not up to it. Not up to anything!" And Hal had much less time to worry about any other chap's problems since he had gone to Downing Street.

As young boys they had shared everything; as young men they still shared much, even an occasional girlfriend or two. And a car, one of the early Minis, before Charlie had driven it into a ditch, staggering away, persuading the young police-man it was shock and bruising rather than alcohol that made him so unsteady. But these days there was little room left in Hal's life for his younger brother, and Charlie felt—what did he feel, deep down, when he allowed himself to be honest? Angry, stinking bloody one-bottle-a-time furious—not with Hal, of course, but with life. It hadn't worked out for him, and he didn't understand why.

He guided the razor past the old cuts on his baggy face and began putting the pieces back together. The hair brushed over the thinning pate, the fresh shirt, and a new, clean tie. He would be ready soon for the election night festivities to which his family links still gave him passage. A tea towel over his shoes gave them back a little shine, and he was almost ready. Another glance at the wristwatch. Oh, it was all right after all. Just time for one more drink.

❖ ❖ ❖

North of the river a taxi was stuck in traffic on the outskirts of Soho. It was always a bottleneck and election night seemed to have brought an additional throng of revelers onto the streets. In the back of the taxi Roger O'Neill cracked his knuckles in impatience, watching helplessly as bikes and pedestrians flashed past. He was growing agitated, he didn't have much time. He'd had his instructions. "Get over here quick, Rog," they had said. "We can't wait all fucking night, not even for you. And we ain't back till Tuesday."

O'Neill neither expected nor received preferential treatment, he'd never tried to pull rank. He was the Party's Director of Publicity but he hoped to Christ they knew nothing of that. There were times when he thought they must have recognized him, seen his photo in the papers, but when he was less paranoid he realized they probably never read a newspaper, let alone voted. What did politics matter to these people? Bloody Hitler could take over for all they cared. What did it matter who was in government when there was so much loose tax-free money to make?

The taxi at last managed to make it across Shaftesbury Avenue and into Wardour Street, only to be met by another wall of solid traffic. Shit, he would miss them. He flung open the door.

"I'll walk," he shouted at the driver.

"Sorry, mate. It's not my fault. Costs me a fortune stuck in jams like this," the driver replied, hoping that his passenger's impatience wouldn't lead him to forget a tip.

O'Neill jumped out into the road, jammed a note into the

driver's hand, and dodged another motorcyclist as he made his way past the endless huddle of peep shows and Chinese restaurants into a narrow, Dickensian alley piled high with rubbish. He squeezed past the plastic bin liners and cardboard boxes and broke into a run. He wasn't fit and it hurt, but he didn't have far to go. As he reached Dean Street he turned left, and a hundred yards further down ducked into the narrow opening to one of those Soho mews which most people miss as they concentrate on finding fun and dodging traffic. Off the main street the mews opened out into a small yard, surrounded on all sides by workshops and garages that had been carved out of the old Victorian warehouses. The yard was empty and the shadows deep. His footsteps rang out on the cobbles as he hurried toward a small green door set in the far, gloomiest corner of the yard. He stopped only to look around once before entering. He didn't knock.

It took less than three minutes before he re-emerged. Without glancing to either side he hurried back into the crowds of Dean Street. Whatever he had come for, it evidently hadn't been sex.

❖ ❖ ❖

Behind the brick façade of Party Headquarters in Smith Square, opposite the limestone towers of St. John's, the atmosphere was strangely subdued. For the past weeks this had been a place of ceaseless activity, but on election day itself most of the troops had disappeared, heading for the constituencies, those far outposts of the political world where they had tried to drum up the last few converts for the cause. By this hour most of those who remained were taking an early supper at nearby restaurants or clubs, trying to exude confidence but lapsing repeatedly into insecure discussion of the latest rumors about voter turnout and exit polls and critical seats. Few of them had much appetite and they soon began drifting back, pushing their way through the ever-growing crowds of spectators, beyond the cordons of police and past the mounting piles of scorched moths.

During the last month these offices had grown overcrowded, overheated, and impossibly cluttered, but tomorrow everything would be different. Elections are a time of change, and of human sacrifice. By the weekend, no matter what the result, many of them would be out of a job, but almost all of them would be back for more, sucking at the nipple of power. For now they settled in for what would seem an interminable wait.

Big Ben struck ten o'clock. It was over. The polling booths had closed and no further appeal, explanation, attack, insinuation, libel, or god-awful cock-up could now affect the outcome. As the final chime of the old clock tower faded into the night air a few of the Party workers shook each other's hand in silent reassurance and respect for the job well done. Just how well done they would discover very shortly. As on so many previous evenings, like a religious ritual they turned their attention to the news screens and the familiar voice of Sir Alastair Burnet. He appeared like a latter-day Moses, with his reassuring tones and ruddy cheeks, his flowing silver hair with just enough backlighting to give him a halo effect.

"Good evening," he began in a voice like a gently flowing stream. "The election campaign is over. Just seconds ago thousands of polling booths across the country closed their doors, and now we await the people's verdict. The first result is expected in just forty-five minutes. We shall shortly be going over live for interviews with the Prime Minister, Henry Collingridge, in his Warwickshire constituency and the Opposition leader in South Wales. But, first, ITN's exclusive exit poll conducted by Harris Research International outside one hundred and fifty-three polling booths across the country during today's voting. It gives the following prediction…"

The country's most senior newsreader opened a large envelope in front of him, as reverently as if the A4 manila contained his own death certificate. He extracted a large card from within the envelope, and glanced at it. Not too quickly, not too slowly he raised his eyes once more to the cameras, holding his congregation of thirty million in the palm of his hand, teasing them gently. He was entitled to his moment. After twenty-eight years and nine general elections as a television broadcaster, he had already announced that this was to be his last.

"ITN's exclusive exit poll forecast—and I emphasize this is a forecast, not a result—is…" He glanced once more at the card, just to check he hadn't misread it.

"Get on with it, you old sod!" a voice was heard to cry from somewhere within the Smith Square complex; from elsewhere came the sound of a champagne cork being loosened in premature celebration, but for the most part they stood in profound silence. History was being made and they were part of it. Sir Alastair stared at them, kept them waiting a heartbeat longer.

"…that the Government will be re-elected with a majority of thirty-four."

The building itself seemed to tremble as a roar of triumph mixed with relief erupted from within. Thirty-bloody-four! It was victory, and when you are in a game to the death it's really only the winning that matters, not how the game has been played or how close the result. Time enough later for sober reflection, for history to reach its verdict, but to hell with history—for the moment it was enough to have survived. In every corner there were tears of joy, of exhaustion, and of release that many found almost as good as orgasm and, in the view of a few old hands, considerably better.

The screen divided briefly between mute shots of the Party leaders taking in the prediction. Collingridge was seen nodding, in acceptance, his smile thinner than satisfaction, while the broad grin and shake of his opponent's head left viewers in no doubt that the Opposition had yet to concede. "Wait and see," he was mouthing, in triumph. Then his lips moved again, saying something that lip readers later thought had been in Welsh. Two words, both very inappropriate.

❖ ❖ ❖

"Bollocks!" Preston was shouting, his hair falling into his eyes, revealing the secrets of the shiny scalp beneath. "What the fuck have they done?" He looked at the ruins of his first edition and began furiously scribbling on his notepad. "Government Majority Slashed!" he tried. It was hurled into the bin.

"'Too close to call,'" Mattie suggested, trying to hide any hint of satisfaction.

"'Collingridge squeaks in,'" the editor tried once more.

They all ended up in the bin.

He looked around desperately for some help and inspiration.

"Let's wait," Mattie advised. "It's only thirty minutes to the first result."

FOUR

The crowd is vulgar. Always play to the crowd, praise the common man, and let him think he is a prince.

Without waiting for the first result, celebrations were already well under way at the Party's advertising agency. With the confidence shown by all positive thinkers, the staff of Merrill Grant & Jones Company PLC had been squashed for nearly three hours in the agency's reception area to witness history in the making and every wrinkle of it projected on two vast TV screens. A river of champagne was flowing, washing down an endless supply of deep pan pizzas and Big Macs, and predictions of a drastically reduced majority only served to spur the party-goers on to more feverish efforts. Even at this early hour it was clear that two ornamental fig trees that had graced the reception area for several years wouldn't survive the night; it seemed probable that several young secretaries wouldn't either. Most of the wiser heads were pacing themselves, but there seemed little reason to exercise excessive restraint. Ad men don't do restraint. Anyway, the client was setting a fearsome example.

Like many expatriate Dublin adventurers, Roger O'Neill was renowned for his quick wit, his irresistible capacity for exaggeration and his unquenchable determination to be involved in everything. So overwhelming were his energies and so varied his enthusiasms that no one could be entirely certain what he had done before he joined the Party—it was something in public relations or television, they thought, and there were rumors about a problem with the Inland Revenue, or was it the Irish Garda—but he had been available when the post of Publicity Director became vacant and he'd filled it with both charm and ability, fueled by a ceaseless supply of Gauloises and vodka tonics.

As a young man he had shown great promise as a fly-half on the rugby field but it was a talent that was never to be fulfilled, his highly individualistic style making him ill-suited for team games. "With him on the field," complained his coach, "I've got two teams out there, Roger and fourteen others. Screw him." And so Roger had been duly screwed, in many areas of his life, until Fortune had smiled and brought him to Smith Square. At the age of forty he sported an unruly shock of dark hair that was now perceptibly graying and his muscle tone had long since gone, but O'Neill refused to acknowledge the evidence of his middle age, hiding it beneath a carefully selected wardrobe worn with a deliberate casualness that displayed the designers' labels to their best advantage. His non-conformist approach and the lingering traces of an Irish accent hadn't always endeared him to the Party's grandees—"All bullshit and no bottom," one of them had loudly observed—but others were simply overwhelmed by his unusual vigor.

His path through the thicket had been made much easier by his secretary. Penelope—"Hi, I'm Penny"—Guy. Five foot ten, an exciting choice of clothes and a devastating figure on which to hang them. There was that other aspect that made her stand out from the Westminster crowd. She was black. Not just dusky or dark but a polished hue of midnight that made her eyes twinkle and her smile fill the entire room. She had a

university degree in the History of Art and 120 wpm shorthand and was ruthlessly practical. Inevitably there had been a
riptide of gossip when she'd first arrived with O'Neill, but her
sheer efficiency had silenced, if not won over, the Doubting
Thomases, of which there were still many.

She was also totally discreet. "I have a private life," she
explained when asked. "And that's just how it's going to stay."

Right now at Merrill Grant & Jones—Grunt & Groans, as
Penny preferred to call them—she was effortlessly providing
the center of attention for several red-blooded media buyers
plus the deputy creative director while at the same time managing to ensure that O'Neill's glass and cigarettes were always
available but closely rationed. She didn't want him going over
the top, not tonight of all nights. For the moment he was dug
in deep with the agency's managing director.

"The future starts right here, Jeremy. Let's not lose sight of
that. We need that marketing analysis as soon as possible. It's
got to show just how effective our efforts have been, how brilliant the ads, how much impact they've had, how we hit our
target voters. If we win, I want everyone to know they owe it to
us. If we lose, God help us…" Suddenly he sneezed with great
violence. "Shit! Excuse me. Damned hay fever. But if we lose I
want to be able to show the entire bloody world that we beat
the other side hands down at our communications game and
it was only the politics which blew it." He drew close so they
were almost touching foreheads. "You know what's needed,
Jeremy. It's our reputations on the line, not just the politicians',
so don't screw it up. Make sure it's ready by Saturday morning
at the latest. I want it in the Sunday papers and I want it as
prominent as an actress's arse."

"And I thought I was supposed to be the creative one,"
Jeremy reflected, sipping more champagne. "But that doesn't
give us much time."

O'Neill lowered his voice, drew closer still so that the ad man could smell the sourness of French tobacco on his breath. "If you can't get the figures, make the bloody things up. They'll all be too exhausted to look at them closely, and if we get in there first and loudest we'll be fine." He paused only to blow his nose, which did nothing to ease the other man's visible discomfort. "And don't forget the flowers. I want you to send the most enormous bouquet around to the PM's wife in Downing Street first thing in the morning. In the shape of a gigantic letter 'C.' Make sure she gets them as soon as she wakes up."

"From you, of course."

"She'll get in a twist if they don't arrive because I've already told her they're coming. I want the TV cameras to film them going in."

"And to know who's sent them," the other man added.

"We're all in this together, Jeremy."

Yet with only your name on the card, Jeremy almost added, but didn't. It was possible to take sincerity too far. He was used to his client's breathless monologues by now, and to the irregular instructions and accounting procedures demanded by O'Neill. A political party wasn't like any other client; it played by different and sometimes dangerous rules. But the last two years working on the account had given Jeremy and his youthful agency more than enough publicity to stifle the lingering doubts. Yet, as they waited nervously for the results, a silent fear struck him as he thought of what would happen if they lost. Despite O'Neill's assurances that they were all in this together, he had no doubts the agency would be made the scapegoat. It had all looked rather different when they'd started their work, with the opinion polls predicting a comfortable win, but his confidence had begun to evaporate with the exit polls. His was an industry of images where reputations withered like yesterday's flowers.

O'Neill rattled on, effervescent, irrepressible, until their attention was grabbed by the six-foot image of Sir Alastair, who was now holding his ear with his head cocked to one side. Something was coming through his earpiece.

"And now I believe we are ready for the first result of the evening. Torbay once again, I'm told. Breaking all records. Just forty-three minutes after the polls have closed and already I see the candidates are gathering behind the returning officer. It's time to go over live…"

❖ ❖ ❖

The Assembly Room, Torbay. Victorian, crowded, humid, desperately hot, crackling with tension. Bundles of counted votes stretched out along trestle tables, empty black tin ballot boxes stacked to one side. On the stage at one end, amid the banks of hyacinths and spider plants, the rosettes and mayoral regalia, the candidates were gathered. The first result was about to be announced, yet the scene resembled more a village pantomime than an election; the promise of nationwide media coverage had attracted more than the usual number of crank candidates who were now doing their best to capture the moment by waving balloons and brightly colored hats to attract the cameras' attention.

The Sunshine Candidate, dressed from head to toe in a searing yellow leotard and waving a plastic sunflower as ludicrous as it was large, was standing directly and deliberately in front of the sober-suited Tory. The Tory, his suit pressed and hair cut for the occasion, tried to move to his left to escape from the embarrassment but succeeded only in bumping into the man from the National Front, who was inciting a minor riot in the crowd by displaying a clenched fist and an armful of tattoos. The Tory, desperate to do the right thing and uncertain what his candidate's manual prescribed in such circumstances, retreated with reluctance back behind the sunflower. Meanwhile, a young woman representing the Keep Our Seas Clean party and who was clad in blue and green chiffon, walked back and forth in front of everyone, trailing yards of cloth that billowed like an incoming tide.

The mayor coughed into his microphone. "Thank you, ladies and gentlemen. I, as returning officer for the constituency of Torbay, hereby declare that the votes cast in the election were as follows…"

❖ ❖ ❖

"So there we have it from colorful Torbay," Sir Alastair's sepulchral tones intervened. "The Government hold the first seat of the night but with a reduced majority and a swing against them of, the computer says, nearly eight percent. What does that mean, Peter?" the newscaster asked as the screen cut to the channel's academic commentator. A bespectacled, rather tussled figure in Oxford tweeds was given on the screen.

"It means the exit poll is just about right, Alastair."

FIVE

Politics requires sacrifice. The sacrifice of others, of course. Whatever a man can achieve by sacrificing himself for his country, there's always more to be gained by allowing others to do it first. Timing, as my wife always says, is everything.

Great show, Roger, isn't it? Another majority. I can't tell you how absolutely thrilled I am. Relieved. Delighted. All of that. Well done. Well done, indeed!" The breathless enthusiasm of the chairman of one of Grunt & Groans's major retail clients poured into O'Neill's face without any visible effect. The thick-waisted industrialist was enjoying himself, sweating, smiling; the evening was turning into a full-fledged victory party irrespective of the fact that the Government had just lost its first two seats of the night.

"That's very kind of you, Harold. Yes, I think a thirty- or forty-seat majority will be enough. But you must take some of the credit," O'Neill replied. "I was reminding the Prime Minister just the other day how your support goes way beyond the corporate donation. I remember the speech you gave at the Industrial Society lunch last March. By God it was good, so it was, if you'll forgive a touch of blasphemy, you really banged the message home. Surely you've had professional training?"

Without waiting for an answer, O'Neill rushed on. "I told Henry—I'm sorry, the PM!—told him how good you were, that we need to find more platforms for captains of industry like you. Giving us the view from the coal face."

"There was no need for that, I'm sure," replied the captain without the slightest trace of sincerity. The champagne had already overcome his natural caution and images of ermine and the House of Lords began to materialize in front of his eyes. "Look, when this is all over perhaps you and I could do lunch together. Somewhere a little quieter, eh? I've several other ideas he might find interesting, on which I'd very much welcome your views." The eyes bulged expectantly. He took another huge mouthful of wine. "And talking of banging home the message, Roger, tell me, that little secretary of yours—"

Before the thought could be pursued any further, O'Neill burst into a series of volcanic sneezes that bent him almost double, leaving his eyes bloodshot and rendering any hope of continued conversation impossible. "Sorry," he spluttered, struggling to recover. "Hay fever. Always seem to get it early." As if to emphasize the point he blew his nose with the sound of many trumpets and what seemed like a few bass drums. The moment gone, the industrialist backed off.

The Government lost another seat, a junior minister with responsibility for transport, a callow man who'd spent the last four years rushing to every major motorway crash scene in the country, dragging the media behind him. He had developed an almost religious conviction that the human race's capacity for violent self-sacrifice was unquenchable; it didn't seem to be helping him very much to accept his own. His chin jutted forward to meet adversity while his wife dissolved in tears.

"More bad news for the Government," commented Sir Alastair, "and we'll see how the Prime Minister is taking it when we go over live for his result in just a few minutes. In the meantime, what is the computer predicting now?" He punched a button and turned to look at a large computer screen behind his shoulder. "Nearer thirty than forty, by the look of it."

A studio discussion began as to whether a majority of thirty was enough to see a government through a full term of office, but the commentators were constantly interrupted as more results began to pour in. Back at the agency, O'Neill excused himself from the group of overheated businessmen and fought his way through a growing and steadily more voluble group of admirers that was pressing in on Penny. In spite of their protests he drew her quickly to one side and whispered briefly in her ear. Meanwhile the ruddy face of Sir Alastair intruded once more to announce that the Prime Minister's own result would soon be declared. A respectful silence took hold of the revelers. O'Neill returned to the industrial captains. All eyes were fixed on the screen. No one noticed Penny gathering her bag and slipping quietly out.

In the studio an Opposition gain from the Government was announced. A less than splendid night. Then it was Collingridge's turn. His appearance brought forth a roar of loyal approval from the Grunt & Groans staff, most of whom had by now lost whatever political convictions they'd brought with them beneath the tidal wave of celebration. Hell, it was only an election.

As they stared, Henry Collingridge waved back from the screen, his stretched smile suggesting he was taking the result rather more seriously than was his audience. His speech of thanks was formal rather than polemical, his face gray with exhaustion beneath the makeup. For a moment they watched somberly, almost soberly, as he hurried from the platform to begin his long drive back to London. Then they set to celebrating once more.

It was a few minutes later that a shout pierced the party atmosphere. "Mr. O'Neill! Mr. O'Neill! There's a call for you." The security guard who was presiding over the reception desk held the telephone up in the air and gesticulated dramatically at the mouthpiece.

"Who is it?" mouthed O'Neill back across the room.

"What?" queried the guard, looking nervous.

"Who is it?" O'Neill mouthed again.

"Can't hear you," the guard yelled above the hubbub.

O'Neill cupped his hands to his mouth and once more demanded to know who it was in a voice and with a volume that would have done justice to a winning try at Lansdowne Road.

"It's the Prime Minister's Office!" screamed the frustrated guard, unable to restrain himself and not quite sure whether he should be standing to attention.

His words had an immediate effect. The room fell an expectant hush. An avenue to the telephone suddenly opened up in front of O'Neill. Obediently he stepped forward, trying to look modest and matter-of-fact.

"It's one of his secretaries. She'll put you through," the guard said, in awe, grateful to hand over the awesome responsibility.

"Hello. Hello. Yes, this is Roger." A brief pause. "Prime Minister! How very good to hear from you. Many, many congratulations. The result is really excellent in the circumstances. My old father used to say that a victory is sweet whether you win 5–0 or 5–4..." His eyes darted around the room; every face was turned to him. "What did you say? Oh, yes. Yes! That's so kind. I'm at the advertising agency right this moment as it happens."

The room was now hushed to a point where they could hear the fig trees weeping.

"I think they've performed marvelously, and I certainly couldn't have done it without their support...May I tell them that?"

O'Neill placed his hand over the mouthpiece and turned to the audience, which was held in total rapture. "The Prime Minister just wants me to thank you all on his behalf for helping run such a fantastic campaign. He says it made all the difference." He went back to the phone and listened for a few seconds more. "And he's not going to demand the money back!"

The room erupted into a great roar of applause and cheers. O'Neill held the phone aloft to catch every last sound.

"Yes, Prime Minister. I want to tell you that I'm totally thrilled, overwhelmed to receive your first telephone call after your own election…I look forward to seeing you, too. Yes, I shall be at Smith Square later…Of course, of course. See you then. And congratulations once again."

He replaced the telephone gently in its cradle, his expression heavy with the honor that had been done him. He turned to face the room. Suddenly his face burst into a broad smile and the gathering broke into a series of resounding cheers and everyone attempted to shake his hand at once.

They were still saluting him with a chorus of "For He's a Jolly Good Fellow" as, in the next street, Penny replaced the car phone in its cradle and began to adjust her lipstick in the mirror.

SIX

It was my old gillie who taught me a lesson, up on the moor, one I've always remembered. I was a child—what, eight years old? But cast your own mind back; it's at that sort of age the lessons sink in, take hold.

He said this to me: "If you must inflict pain, make sure it is irresistible and overwhelming, so that he knows you will always do him more harm than he can ever do to you." The gillie was talking about wild dogs, of course. But it's been a good lesson in politics, too.

Friday, June 11

The crowd in Smith Square had increased dramatically in size as supporters, opponents, and the merely curious waited for the Prime Minister's arrival. Midnight had long since tolled but this was a night when biological clocks would be stretched to the limit. The onlookers could see from the TV technicians' monitors that his convoy, escorted by police outriders and pursued by camera cars, had long since left the M1 and was now approaching Marble Arch. It would be less than ten minutes before they arrived, and three youthful cheerleaders employed by the Party were encouraging the crowd to warm up with a mixture of patriotic songs and shouts.

They were having to work harder than at previous elections. While people appeared more than happy to wave enormous Union Jacks there seemed to be less enthusiasm to brandish the large mounted photographs of Henry Collingridge that had just appeared through the doorway of Party Headquarters. Several members of the crowd were wearing personal radios and informing those around them of the results. It didn't seem to lift spirits. Even the cheerleaders would stop occasionally to form a huddle and discuss the latest news. There was also an element of competition because several Opposition supporters, emboldened by what they'd heard, had decided to infiltrate and were now proceeding to wave their own banners and chant slogans. Half a dozen policemen moved in to ensure that emotions on both sides didn't bubble over. A coach with a dozen more was parked around the corner in Tufton Street. Appear, don't interfere, was the instruction.

The computers were now forecasting a majority of twenty-eight. Two of the cheerleaders broke away from their work to engage in an earnest discussion as to whether this constituted an adequate working majority. They concluded that it probably was and returned to their task, but spirits were flagging, the early enthusiasm increasingly deflated with concern, and they decided to save their effort until Henry Collingridge arrived.

Inside the building, Charles Collingridge was getting increasingly drunk. One of the senior members of the Party had put him in the Chairman's office with a comfortable chair where he could sit beneath a portrait of his brother, and somehow Charlie had found a bottle. His capillaried face was covered in perspiration, his eyes were liquid and bloodshot. "A good man, brother Hal. A great Prime Minister," he was babbling. There was no denying the alcoholic lisp that had begun to take control of his voice as he repeated the familiar family history.

"Could have taken over the family business, you know, made it one of the country's truly great companies, but he always preferred politics. Mind you, manufacturing bath fittings was never my cup of tea, either, but it kept Father happy. D'you know they even import the ruddy stuff from Poland nowadays? Or is it Romania...?"

He interrupted his own monologue by knocking what was left of his glass of whiskey over his trousers. Amidst the fluster of apologies the Party Chairman, Lord Williams, took the opportunity to move well out of range. His wise old eyes revealed none of it but he resented having to extend hospitality to the Prime Minister's brother. Charlie Collingridge wasn't a bad man, never that, but he was a weak man who was becoming a bloody nuisance on a regular basis, and Williams liked to run a tight ship. Yet the aging apparatchik was an experienced navigator and knew there was little point in trying to throw the admiral's brother overboard. He had once raised the problem directly with the Prime Minister, tried to discuss the increasing rumors and the growing number of snide references to his brother in the gossip columns. As one of the few men left who had been a prominent sailor even in the pre-Thatcher days, he had the seniority, and some would argue even the responsibility, to do so. But it had been to no avail.

"I spend half my time spilling blood, that's the job I do," the Prime Minister had pleaded. "Please don't ask me to spill my own brother's."

The Prime Minister had vowed he would get Charlie to watch his behavior, or rather that he would watch Charlie's behavior himself, but of course he never had the time, not to babysit. And he knew Charlie would promise anything even while he became increasingly incapable of delivering. Henry wouldn't moralize or be angry, he knew it was always the other members of the family who suffered most from the pressures of politics. In part it was his fault. Williams understood that, too, for hadn't he gone through three marriages since he'd first arrived in Westminster nearly forty years ago? There was always plenty of collateral damage; politics left a trail of pain and tortured families in its wake. Williams watched Collingridge stumble from the room and felt a twinge of sorrow, but quickly stifled it. Emotion was no basis on which to run a Party.

Michael Samuel, the Secretary of State for the Environment and one of the newest and most telegenic members of the Cabinet, came over to greet the old statesman. He was young enough to be the Chairman's son and he was something of a protégé; he'd been given his first major step up the greasy ministerial pole by Williams when, as a young Member of Parliament and on Williams's recommendation, he'd been made a Parliamentary Private Secretary. It was the most meager of parliamentary accolades, an unpaid job as skivvy to a senior minister, to fetch, to carry, to do so without complaint and without question—qualities designed to impress prime ministers when selecting candidates for promotion. Williams's help had ignited a spectacular rise through ministerial ranks for Samuel and the two men remained firm friends.

"Problem, Teddy?" Samuel inquired.

"A prime minister can choose his friends and his Cabinet," the old man sighed, "but not his relatives."

"Any more than we get to choose our bedfellows."

Samuel nodded toward the door. Urquhart had just entered with his wife after driving up from his constituency. Samuel's glance was cold. He didn't care for Urquhart, who hadn't supported his promotion to Cabinet and who on more than one occasion had been heard to describe Samuel as "a latter-day Disraeli, too good looking and too clever for his own good."

The veneer over the traditional and still lingering anti-Semitism wore very thin at times, but Williams had offered the brilliant young lawyer good counsel. "Francis is right," he had said. "Don't be too intellectual, don't look too successful. Don't be too liberal on social matters or too prominent on financial matters."

"You mean I should stop being Jewish."

"And for God's sake watch your back."

"Don't worry, we've been doing that for two thousand years."

Now Samuel watched unenthusiastically as Urquhart and his wife were forced by the crush of people toward him. "Good evening, Francis. Hello, Mortima." Samuel forced a smile. "Congratulations. A seventeen thousand majority. I know about six hundred MPs who are going to be very jealous of you in the morning with a victory like that."

"Michael! Well, I'm delighted you managed to hypnotize the female voters of Surbiton once more. Why, if only you could pick up their husbands' votes as well, you too could have a majority like mine!"

They laughed gently at the banter, accustomed to hiding the fact that they did not enjoy each other's company, but it quickly passed to silence as neither of them could think of a suitable means for disengaging from the conversation.

They were rescued by Williams, who had just put down the phone. "Don't let me interrupt, but Henry will be here any minute."

"I'll come down with you," Urquhart volunteered immediately.

"And you, Michael?" asked Williams.

"I'll wait here. There will be a rush when he arrives. I don't want to get trampled, from behind."

Urquhart wondered whether Samuel was having a gentle dig at him but chose to ignore it and accompanied Williams down the stairs, which had become crowded with excited office staff. Word of the Prime Minister's imminent arrival had spread and the appearance of the Party Chairman and Chief Whip outside on the pavement galvanized the crowd. An organized cheer went up as the armored black Daimler with its battalion of escorts swung around the square, appearing from behind the skirts of St. John's to be greeted by the brilliance of television lights and a thousand flaring flashguns as cameramen, both professional and amateur, tried to capture the scene.

As the car drew to a halt, Collingridge emerged from the rear seat and turned to wave to the crowd and the cameras. Urquhart pushed forward, tried just a little too hard to shake his hand and instead managed to get in the way. He retreated apologetically. On the other side of the car Lord Williams, with the chivalry and familiarity that comes of many years, carefully assisted the Prime Minister's wife out of the car and planted an avuncular kiss on her cheek. A bouquet appeared from somewhere along with two dozen party officials and dignitaries, all of whom were struggling to get in on the act. It seemed a minor miracle that the heaving throng managed to squeeze through the swing doors and into the building without casualties.

Similar scenes of confusion and congestion were repeated inside as the Prime Minister's party pushed its way upstairs, pausing only for a traditional word of thanks to the staff. It had to be repeated because the press photographers hadn't been assembled quickly enough. Through it all, the delay, the gentle pushing, the noise, the Prime Minister smiled.

Yet once upstairs in the relative safety of Lord Williams's suite, the signs of strain that had been so well hidden all evening began to appear. The television set in the corner was just announcing that the computer was predicting a still lower majority, and Collingridge let out a long, low sigh. "Turn the bloody thing off," he whispered. Then his eyes wandered slowly round the room.

"Has Charlie been around this evening?" he asked.

"Yes, he's been here, but…"

"But what?"

"We seem to have lost him."

The Prime Minister's eyes met those of the Chairman.

"I'm sorry," the older man added, so softly that it almost required the Prime Minister to lip read.

Sorry for what? The fact that my brother's a drunk? Sorry that I've almost thrown away this election, put so many of our colleagues to the sword, done more damage than Goering? Sorry that you'll have to wade through the sewage that's about to hit us along with me? But anyway, thanks for caring, old friend.

The adrenalin had ceased flowing and suddenly he was desperately tired. After weeks of being hemmed in on all sides and without a single private moment to himself, he felt an overwhelming need to be on his own. He turned away to find somewhere a little quieter and more private but he found his way blocked by Urquhart who was standing right by his shoulder. The Chief Whip was thrusting an envelope at him.

"I've been giving some thought to the reshuffle," Urquhart said, his eyes lowered, his voice betraying a mixture of discomfiture and hesitation. "While this is hardly the time, I know you will be giving it some thought over the weekend, so I've prepared a few suggestions. I know you prefer positive ideas rather than a blank sheet of paper, so…" He held out his handwritten note. "I hope you find this of use." He was demanding his place at the top table, and by right rather than invitation.

Collingridge looked at the envelope and something inside him broke, the little wall that keeps politeness and honesty well apart. He raised his exhausted eyes to his colleague. "You're right, Francis. This is scarcely the time. Perhaps we should be thinking about securing our majority before we start sacking our colleagues."

Urquhart froze in embarrassment. The sarcasm had cut deep, deeper than the Prime Minister had intended, and he realized he had gone too far.

"I'm sorry, Francis. I'm afraid I am a little tired. Of course you're quite right to think ahead. Look, I'd like you and Teddy to come round on Sunday afternoon to discuss it. Perhaps you'd be kind enough to let Teddy have a copy of your letter now, and send one round to me at Downing Street tomorrow—or, rather, later this morning."

Urquhart's face refused to betray the turmoil that was growing within. He had been too anxious about the reshuffle and cursed himself for his folly. Somehow his natural assurance deserted him when it came to Collingridge, the product of a grammar school who in social terms would have had trouble gaining membership to any of Urquhart's clubs. The role reversal in Government unnerved him, unsettled him; he found himself acting out of character when he was in the other man's presence. He had made a mistake and he blamed Collingridge for that more than he blamed himself, but now was not the time to reclaim the ground he had lost. Instead, he retreated into affability, bowing his head in acceptance. "Of course, Prime Minister. I will let Teddy have a copy straight away."

"Better copy it yourself. Wouldn't do to have that list getting around here tonight." Collingridge smiled as he tried to bring Urquhart back into the conspiracy of power that always hovers around Downing Street. "In any event, I think it's time for me to depart. The BBC will want me bright and sparkling in four hours' time, so I shall wait for the rest of the results in Downing Street."

He turned to Williams. "By the way, what is the wretched computer predicting now?"

"It's been stuck on twenty-four for about half an hour now. I think that's it." There was no sense of victory in his voice. He had just presided over the Party's worst election result in nearly two decades.

"Never mind, Teddy. A majority is a majority. And it will give the Chief Whip something to do instead of sitting idly around with a majority of over a hundred. Eh, Francis?" And

with that he strode out of the room, leaving Urquhart forlornly
clutching his envelope.

❖ ❖ ❖

Within minutes of the Prime Minister's departure the crowds
both inside and outside the building began perceptibly to melt.
Urquhart, still feeling bruised and not in a mood either to celebrate or to sympathize, made his way to the back of the first
floor where he knew the photocopying office could be found.
Except that Room 132A was scarcely an office at all, little
more than a windowless closet barely six feet across and kept
for supplies and confidential photocopying. Urquhart opened
the door and the smell hit him before he had time to find the
light switch. Slumped on the floor by the narrow metal storage
shelves was Charles Collingridge. He had soiled his clothes
even as he slept. There was no glass or bottle anywhere to be
seen but the smell of whiskey was heavy in the air. Charlie, it
seemed, had crawled away to find the least embarrassing place
to collapse.

Urquhart reached for his handkerchief and held it to his face,
trying to ward off the stench. He stepped over to the body and
turned it on its back. A shake of the shoulders did little other
than disrupt the fitful heavy breathing for a moment. A firmer
shake gave nothing more, and a gentle slap across the cheeks
produced equally little result.

He gazed with disgust at what he saw. Suddenly Urquhart's
body stiffened, his contempt mingled with the lingering
humiliation he had suffered at the Prime Minister's hands.
And here, surely, was an opportunity for repayment of the
slight. He grabbed at the lapels of Charlie's jacket, hauled him
up, drew back his arm, ready to strike, to lash the back of his
hand across this pathetic wretch's face, to release his humiliation and anger at all the Collingridges. Urquhart was trembling
now, poised.

Then an envelope fell from Charlie's jacket pocket, an unpaid electricity bill by the look of it, a final demand, covered in red, and suddenly Urquhart realized there was another way to even up the scales of injustice, to tilt them back and over to his side. He wouldn't hit Charlie after all, not out of any particular sense of fastidiousness, nor any feeling that Charlie was entirely innocent of any offense against him, apart from the smell. Urquhart knew he could hurt Henry Collingridge by inflicting pain upon his brother, of that there was no doubt, but the hurt wouldn't be enough, wouldn't last. Anyway, this wasn't the way, not in some noisome cupboard, nor was it the time. Francis Urquhart was better than this, much better. Better than them all.

He allowed the sleeping form of Charles Collingridge to fall back gently to the floor, straightened the lapels, left him to rest. "You and I, Charlie, we're going to become very close. Great friends. Not right this moment, of course. After you've cleaned yourself up a bit, eh?"

He turned to the photocopier, took the letter from his pocket, made one copy, after which he took the bill from Charlie's pocket and made a copy of that, too. Then he left the drunken form of his new friend to sleep it off.

SEVEN

Wasn't it that fellow Clausewitz who once said that war is the continuation of politics by other means? He was wrong, of course, ridiculously wrong. Politics? War? As my dear wife Mortima constantly reminds me, there is no distinction.

Sunday, June 13

Urquhart's official car turned from Whitehall into Downing Street to be greeted by a policeman's starched salute and a hundred exploding flashguns. It was Sunday, shortly before four. He had left Mortima at home in Pimlico with their guests, eight of them, more than usual for a Sunday but this was the anniversary of his father's death and he was in the habit of filling it with distraction. The men and handful of women of the press were gathered behind the barriers on the far side of the street from the world's most famous front door, which stood wide open as the car drew up—like a political black hole, Urquhart had often thought, into which new prime ministers disappeared and rarely if ever emerged without being surrounded by protective hordes of civil servants, and only after they had sucked the life out of them.

Urquhart had made sure to travel on the left-hand side of the car's rear seat so that as he climbed out in front of Number Ten, he would provide an unimpeded view of himself for the TV and press cameras. He stretched himself to his full height and was greeted by a chorus of shouted questions from the press huddle, providing him with an excuse to walk over for a few words. He spotted Manny Goodchild, the legendary Press Association figure, firmly planted under his battered trilby and conveniently wedged between ITN and BBC news camera crews.

"Well, Manny, did you have any money on the result?" he inquired.

"Mr. Urquhart, you know my editor would frown on putting his money where my mouth is."

"Nevertheless." Urquhart raised an eyebrow.

The old press man's lips wriggled like two unrelated caterpillars. "Put it this way, Mrs. Goodchild has already booked her holiday in Majorca, and thanks to Mr. Collingridge I'm going with her, too."

Urquhart sighed theatrically. "'Tis an ill wind."

"And talking of ill winds, Mr. Urquhart"—his colleagues pressed closer as Manny got into his stride—"are you here to advise the Prime Minister about the reshuffle? Won't there have to be a pretty good clear out after a disappointing result like that? And does it all mean a new job for you?"

"Well, I'm here to discuss a number of things, but I suppose the reshuffle might come into it," Urquhart responded coyly. "And we won, remember. Don't be so downbeat, Manny."

"It's rumored that you're expecting a major new post."

Urquhart smiled. "Can't comment on rumors, Manny, and anyway you know that's one for the PM to decide. I'm here simply to give him some moral support."

"You'll be going to advise the PM along with Lord Williams, will you then?"

The smile struggled to survive. "Lord Williams, has he arrived yet?"

"More than an hour ago. We were wondering when someone else was going to turn up."

It took every ounce of experience gathered through Urquhart's
many years in politics not to let his surprise show. "Then I must
go," he announced. "Can't keep them waiting." He gave a cour-
teous nod of his head, turned on his heel, and strode back across
the road, ditching his plan to wave at the cameras from the
doorstep of Number Ten, just in case it looked presumptuous.

On the other side of the black-and-white tiled hallway, a
carpeted corridor led toward the Cabinet Room. The Prime
Minister's youthful political secretary was waiting for him at
the end. As Urquhart approached, he sensed that the young
man was uneasy.

"The Prime Minister is expecting you, Chief Whip."

"Yes, that's why I'm here."

The secretary flinched. "He's in the study upstairs. I'll let
him know you've arrived." Duty done, and not waiting for any
further hint of sarcasm, he bounded off up the stairs.

It was twelve knuckle-cracking, watch-tapping minutes
before he reappeared, leaving Urquhart to stare distractedly
at the portraits of previous prime ministers that adorned the
famous staircase. He could never get over the feeling of how
inconsequential so many of the recent holders of the office had
been. Uninspiring, unfitted for the task. By contrast, the likes
of Lloyd George and Churchill had been magnificent natural
leaders, but would they be allowed to rise to the top nowadays?
One had been promiscuous and had sold peerages, the other
had spent far too much time in drink, debt, and hot temper;
both were giants, yet neither man would have made it past the
modern media. Instead the world had been left to the pygmies,
men of small stature and still less ambition, men chosen not
because they were exceptional but because they didn't offend,
men who followed the rules rather than making their own,
men…Well, men like Henry Collingridge.

The return of the political secretary interrupted his thoughts. "Sorry to keep you waiting, Chief Whip. He's ready for you now."

The room used by Collingridge as his study was on the first floor, overlooking the Downing Street garden to St. James's Park. A modest room, as so much else in this jumble of spaces that made up the second most important address in the country. As Urquhart entered he could see that, in spite of efforts to tidy up the large desk, there had been much shuffling of paper and scribbling of notes in the previous hour or so. An empty bottle of claret stared out of the waste bin and plates covered with crumbs and a withered leaf of lettuce lurked on the windowsill. The Party Chairman sat to the right of the Prime Minister, his notes spilling over the green leather top. Beside them stood a large pile of manila folders containing MPs' biographies.

Urquhart brought up a chair, one without arms, and sat in front of the other two, feeling rather like a schoolboy in the headmaster's study. Collingridge and Williams were silhouetted against the windows. Urquhart squinted into the light, balancing his own folder of notes uneasily on his knee.

"Francis, you were kind enough to let me have some thoughts on the reshuffle," the Prime Minister began. No ceremony, straight down to business. "I am very grateful; you know how useful such suggestions are in stimulating my own thoughts."

Urquhart inclined his head in silent gratitude.

"You've obviously put a lot of work into them. But before we get down to specifics I thought we should chat about the broad objectives first. You've suggested—well, what shall I call it?—a rather radical reshuffle." Collingridge peered at the sheet of paper in front of him, through reading glasses he kept only for private occasions. His finger ran down the list. "Six new members for the Cabinet, some extensive swapping of portfolios among the rest." He sighed, sat back in his chair, as though distancing himself from it all. "Tell me why. Why such a heavy hand? What do you think it would achieve?"

Urquhart's senses were on alert. He didn't care for this. He had hoped to be brought in at the earliest stage but the other two were already well ahead of him and he didn't know where. He'd found no chance to sniff out the Prime Minister's own views, to read his mind; it was an unhealthy place for a Chief Whip to be in. He wondered whether he was being set up.

As he blinked against the sunlight that was streaming in from behind the Prime Minister's head, he could read nothing of the expression. He wished now that he hadn't committed his thoughts to paper—it left him no wriggle room, no escape route—but it was too late for regrets. Williams was staring at him like a hawk. He spoke slowly, so as not to raise alarm, searching for words that might cover his tracks.

"Of course, Prime Minister, they are only suggestions, indications really, of what you might be able to do. I thought, in general, in the round, that it might be better to err on the side of action, as it were, to undertake more rather than fewer changes, simply to indicate that you are firmly in charge. That you are expecting a lot of new ideas and new thinking from your ministers. And a chance to retire just a few of our older colleagues; regrettable, but necessary if you are to bring in some new blood."

Damn, he thought suddenly, what a bloody inept thing to say with that ancient bastard Williams sitting on the PM's right hand. But it had been said, there was no means of retreat.

"We've been in power for longer than any Party since the war, which presents a new challenge," he continued. "Boredom. We need to ensure we have a fresh image for the Government team. We must guard against going stale."

The room fell silent. Then, slowly, the Prime Minister began tapping his pencil on the desk.

"That's very interesting, Francis, and I agree with you—to a large extent."

Oh, that hesitation, that little pause, what might that denote? Urquhart found that his hands were clasped, the nails digging into the flesh.

"Teddy and I have been discussing just that sort of problem," the Prime Minister continued. "Bring on a new generation of talent, find new impetus, put new men in new places. And I find many of your suggestions for changes at the lower ministerial levels below Cabinet very persuasive."

But they were not the ones that mattered, they all knew that. And the Prime Minister's tone had changed, grown more somber.

"The trouble is that too much change at the top can be very disruptive. It takes most cabinet ministers a year to find their feet in a new Department, and right now a year is a long time without being able to show positive signs of progress. Rather than your Cabinet changes helping to implement our new program, Teddy's view is that on balance it would more likely delay the program."

What new program? Urquhart was screaming inside his skull. The manifesto had about as much backbone as a sack of seaweed.

"But, with respect, Prime Minister, don't you think that by cutting our majority the electorate was telling us of its desire for some degree of change?"

"An interesting point. But as you yourself said, no government in our lifetimes has been in office as long as we have. Without in any way being complacent, Francis, I don't think we could have rewritten the history books if the voters believed we'd run out of steam. On balance, I think it suggests they are content with what we offer."

It was time to change tack. "You may very well be right, Prime Minister."

"There's another point, pretty damned vital in the circumstances," Collingridge continued. "We have to avoid giving the impression that we're panicking. That would send entirely the wrong signal. Remember that Macmillan destroyed his own Government by sacking a third of his Cabinet. They took it as a sign of weakness. He was out of office inside a year. I'm not anxious for a repeat performance." He gave one final beat with the pencil, then put it aside. "I'm thinking of a much more controlled approach myself."

Collingridge slipped a piece of paper across the desk toward his Chief Whip. On it was printed a list of Cabinet positions, twenty-two in all, with names alongside them.

"As you see, Francis, I am suggesting no Cabinet changes at all. I hope it will be seen as a sign of strength. We have a job to do, I think we should show we want to get straight on with it."

Urquhart quickly returned the paper to the desk, anxious that the tremble in his hand might betray his inner feelings. "If that is what you want, Prime Minister."

"It is." There was the slightest pause. "And of course I assume I have your full support?"

"Of course, Prime Minister."

Urquhart scarcely recognized his own voice, it sounded as though it came from an entirely different part of the room. Not his words. But he had no choice: it was either support or suicide through instant resignation. Yet he couldn't leave it there. "I have to say that I…was rather looking for a change myself. A bit of new experience…a new challenge." His words faltered as he found his mouth suddenly dry. "You may remember, Prime Minister, we had discussed the possibility…"

"Francis," the Prime Minister interrupted, but not unkindly, "if I move you, I have to move others. The whole pile of dominoes begins to tumble. And I need you where you are. You are an excellent Chief Whip. You have devoted yourself to burrowing right into the heart and soul of the Parliamentary Party. You know them so well. We have to face up to the fact that with such a small majority there are bound to be one or

two sticky patches over the next few years. I need to have a
Chief Whip who is strong enough to handle them. I need you,
Francis. You're so good behind the scenes. We can leave it to
others to do the job out front."

Urquhart lowered his eyes, not wanting them to see the turmoil of betrayal that flushed through them. Collingridge took
it as an expression of acceptance.

"I am truly grateful for your understanding and support,
Francis."

Urquhart felt the cell door slam shut. He thanked them both,
took his farewell. Williams hadn't uttered a single word.

He left by the back route through the basement of Number
Ten. It took him past the ruins of the old Tudor tennis court
where Henry VIII had played, then to the Cabinet Office that
fronted onto Whitehall, along the road from the entrance to
Downing Street and well out of sight of the waiting press. He
couldn't face them. He had been with the Prime Minister less
than half an hour and he couldn't trust his face to back up the
lies he would have to tell them. He got a security guard at the
Cabinet Office to telephone for his car to be brought round. He
didn't bother with small talk.

EIGHT

The truth is like a good wine. You often find it tucked away in the darkest corner of a cellar. It needs turning occasionally. And given a gentle dusting, too, before you bring it out into the light and start using it.

The battered BMW had been standing outside the house in Cambridge Street, Pimlico for almost a quarter of an hour. The vacant seats were smothered in a chaos of discarded newspapers and granola bar wrappers that only a truly busy single woman could produce, and in the middle of it all Mattie Storin sat biting her lip. The announcement of the reshuffle late that afternoon had led to febrile discussion as to whether the Prime Minister had been brilliant and audacious, or simply lost his nerve. She needed the views of the men who had helped shape the decisions. Williams had been persuasive and supportive as usual, but Urquhart's phone had rung and rung, unanswered.

Without fully understanding why, after her shift at the *Chronicle* had finished Mattie had decided to drive past Urquhart's London home, just ten minutes from the House of Commons in one of the elegant side streets that adorn the better parts of Pimlico. She expected to find it dark and empty but instead she discovered the lights were burning and there were signs of movement. She telephoned once more, yet still there was no answer.

The world of Westminster is a club of many unwritten rules and is guarded jealously by both politicians and press—and particularly the press, the so-called "lobby" of correspondents that quietly and discretely regulates media activity in the Palace of Westminster. It allows, for instance, briefings and interviews to take place on the strict understanding that the source will never be identified, not even a hint, everything in the shadows. This encourages politicians to be wildly indiscreet and to break confidences; in turn it allows the lobby correspondents to meet their deadlines and create the most remarkable headlines. The code of *omertà* is the lobby correspondent's passport; without it he—or she—would find all doors closed and mouths firmly shut. Revealing sources is a hanging offense, banging on a minister's private door only slightly lower down the list of contemptible behavior designed to cut off all forms of useful contact. Political correspondents don't pursue their quarry back to their homes; it's bad form, black marks and bollockings all round.

Mattie gave the inside of her cheek another bite. She was nervous. She didn't lightly bend the rules but why was the bloody man not answering his phone? What on earth was he up to?

A thick Northern voice whispered in her ear, the voice she had so often missed since leaving the *Yorkshire Post* and the wise old editor who had given Mattie her first proper job. What had he said? "Rules, my girl, are nothing more than a comfort blanket for old men, something to wrap themselves up in against the cold. They exist for the guidance of the wise and the emasculation of the foolish. Don't you ever dare come into my office and tell me you missed out on a good story because of somebody else's sodding rules."

"OK, OK, you miserable bugger, get off my back," Mattie

said out loud. She checked her hair in the mirror, running a hand through it to restore some life, opened the car door, stepped out onto the pavement and instantly wished she were somewhere else. Twenty seconds later the house echoed to the sound of the front door's ornate brass knocker.

Urquhart answered the door. He was alone, casually dressed, not expecting visitors. His wife had returned to the country and the maid didn't work weekends. As his eyes fell on Mattie they were filled with impatience; in the darkness of the street he didn't immediately recognize the caller.

"Mr. Urquhart, I've been trying to contact you all afternoon. I hope it's not inconvenient."

"Ten thirty at night? Not *inconvenient?*" The impatience had turned to exasperation.

"Forgive me, but I need some help. No Cabinet changes, not one. It's extraordinary. I'm trying to understand the thinking behind it."

"The *thinking* behind it?" Urquhart's voice dipped deeper into sarcasm. "I'm sorry but I have nothing to say." He began to close the door only to see his unwanted visitor take a stubborn step forward. Surely the silly girl wasn't going to put her foot in the door, it would be too comic for words. But Mattie spoke calmly and quietly.

"Mr. Urquhart. That's a great story. But I don't think you'd want me to print it."

Urquhart paused, intrigued. What on earth did she mean? Mattie saw the hesitation, and threw a little more bait in the water.

"The story would read, 'There were signs last night of deep Cabinet divisions over the non-shuffle. The Chief Whip, long believed to have harbored ambitions for a move to a new post, refused to defend the Prime Minister's decision.' How would you care for that?"

Only now, as his eyes adjusted to the shadows beyond his

doorstep, did Urquhart recognize the *Chronicle*'s new correspondent. He knew her only slightly but had seen and read enough of her in action to suspect she was no fool. It made him all the more astonished that she was now camped on his doorstep trying to intimidate him. "You cannot be serious," Urquhart said slowly.

Mattie broke into a broad smile. "Of course I'm not. But what's a girl supposed to do? You won't answer your telephone or talk face-to-face."

Her honesty disarmed him. And, as she stood beneath the light from the lamp above his door, highlights glinting in her short, blond hair, he had to admit that he'd come across less attractive sights in the lobby.

"I'd really like your help, Mr. Urquhart. I need something of substance, something I can get my teeth into, otherwise all I've got is thin air. And that's all you're leaving me at the moment. Please—help me."

Urquhart sniffed, stared. "I ought to be bloody furious. On the phone to that editor of yours demanding an apology for such blatant harassment."

"But you won't. Will you?" She was being deliberately coquettish. While their previous encounters had been minimal, she remembered the glance he had thrown at her one day as they'd passed in the Central Lobby, the discreet male glint in the eye that had taken in all of her without for a moment appearing to deviate from the direct.

"Perhaps you had better come in after all—Miss Storin, isn't it?"

"Please, call me Mattie."

"The sitting room is upstairs," he said. He made it sound like a small confession. He led the way to a tasteful if very traditionally decorated room, its mustard walls covered in oil paintings of horses and country scenes, the furniture inlaid and elegant. There were tall shelves of books, family photos in frames, a white marble fireplace. The shades were silk, the lighting sparse, the atmosphere intense. He poured himself a large single malt, an old Glenfiddich, and without asking did the same for her before settling into a dark leather armchair. A book with a cracked spine was balanced on the arm, plays by Molière. Mattie sat opposite, nervously perching on the edge of the sofa. She retrieved a small notebook from her shoulder bag but Urquhart waved it away.

"I'm tired, Miss Storin—Mattie. It's been a long campaign and I'm not sure I would express myself particularly well. So no notes, if you don't mind."

"Of course. Lobby terms. I can use what you tell me but I can't attribute it to you in any way. No fingerprints."

"Precisely."

He put away Molière, she her notebook and settled back on the sofa. She was wearing a white cotton blouse; it was tight. He noticed, but not in a predatory fashion. He seemed to have eyes that absorbed things, penetrated deeper than most. They both knew they were playing a game.

He took a cigarette from a silver cigarette box, lit it and inhaled deeply, then he began. "What would you say if I told you, Mattie, that the Prime Minister sees this as the best way of getting on with the job? Not letting ministers get confused with new responsibilities? Full steam ahead?"

"I would say, Mr. Urquhart, that we would scarcely have to go off the record for that!"

Urquhart chuckled at the young journalist's bluntness. Drew deep on the nicotine. The combination seemed to satisfy him.

"I would also say," Mattie continued, "that in many people's eyes the election showed the need for some new blood and some new thinking. You lost a lot of seats. Your endorsement by the voters wasn't exactly gushing, was it?"

"We have a clear majority and won many more seats than the main opposition party. Not too bad after so many years in office...Wouldn't you say?"

"I'm here for your views, not mine."

"Indulge me."

"But not really full of promise for the next election, is it? More of the same. Steady as she sinks."

"I think that's a little harsh," Urquhart said, knowing he should be protesting more.

"I came to one of your election rallies."

"Did you, Mattie? I'm flattered."

"You spoke about new energy, new ideas, new enterprise. The whole thrust of what you were saying was that there would be change—and some new players." She paused but Urquhart didn't seem keen to respond. "Your own election address—I have it here…" She fished a glossy leaflet from a wad of papers that were stuffed into her shoulder bag. "It speaks about 'the exciting challenges ahead.' All this is about as exciting as last week's newspapers. And I'm doing too much of the talking."

He smiled, sipped. Stayed silent.

"Let me ask you bluntly, Mr. Urquhart. Do you really think this is the best the Prime Minister could do?"

Urquhart didn't answer directly but raised his glass slowly once more to his lips, staring at her across the crystal rim.

"Do you think Henry Collingridge is the best this country can do?" she persisted, more softly.

"Mattie, how on earth do you expect me to reply to a question like that? I am the Chief Whip, I am totally loyal to the Prime Minister—and his shuffle. Or rather non-shuffle." The edge of sarcasm was back in his voice.

"Yes, but what about Francis Urquhart, a man who is very ambitious for his party and is desperately anxious for its success. Does he support it?"

There was no reply.

"Mr. Urquhart, in my piece tomorrow I shall faithfully record your public loyalty to the reshuffle and your justification of it. But…"

"But?"

"We're speaking on lobby terms. All my instincts suggest you don't care for what's happening. I want to know. You want to ensure that your private thoughts don't get back to my colleagues, or your colleagues, or become common Westminster gossip. I give you my word on that. This is just for me, because all this might be important in the months ahead. And by the way, no one else knows I came to see you tonight."

"You are offering me a deal?" he muttered softly.

"Yes. I think you want one. Someone like me. A mouthpiece."

"And why do you think I would want that?"

"Because you let me in."

He stared with blue eyes that seemed to dig deep inside her, stirring excitement.

"You want to be a player, not simply a pawn," she said.

"Better a man of any reputation than a forgotten one, eh?"

"I think so," she said, returning the stare, holding his eyes, smiling.

"Let us try this, Mattie. A simple tale. Of a Prime Minister surrounded by ambition, not his own but the ambition of others. Those ambitions have grown since the election. He needs to keep them in check, to stifle them, otherwise they might escape and completely obliterate him."

"Are you telling me that there's a lot of rivalry and dissent within the Cabinet?"

He paused to consider his words carefully before continuing in a slow, deliberate voice. "A great elm waiting to rot. And once that rot has taken hold it is only a matter of time. So there are some who, you might suppose, are wondering what life might be like in another eighteen months, or two years, what position they want to be in if—when—the tree comes crashing down. As they all do in the end."

"So why doesn't he get rid of the troublesome ones?"

"Because he can't risk having disgruntled former Cabinet ministers rampaging all over the backbenches when he's got a majority of only twenty-four which could disappear at the first parliamentary cock-up. He has to keep everything as quiet, as low key as possible. He can't even move the Awkward Brigade to new Cabinet posts because every time you send a new minister to a new Department they get a rush of enthusiasm and want to make their mark. They become of renewed interest to important people in the media, like you. Suddenly we find that ministers aren't simply doing their jobs but also promoting themselves for a leadership race that must inevitably come. It's a cancer. Government thrown into chaos, everyone looking over their shoulders, confusion, disharmony, accusations of lack of grip—and suddenly we have a leadership crisis."

"So everyone has to remain where they are. Do you think that's a sound strategy?"

He took a deep mouthful of whiskey. "If I were the captain of the *Titanic* and I saw a bloody great iceberg dead ahead, I think I'd want a change of course."

"Did you tell this to the Prime Minister this afternoon?"

"Mattie," he scolded, "you take me too far. I am thoroughly enjoying our conversation but I fear I would be going too far if I started divulging the details of private discussions. That's a shooting offense."

"Then let me ask you about Lord Williams. He was with the PM an extraordinarily long time this afternoon if all they were deciding was to do nothing."

"A man grown gray in the service of his party. Have you heard the phrase, 'Beware of an old man in a hurry'?"

"He surely can't think he could become Party Leader. Not from the Lords!"

"No, of course not. Even dear Teddy isn't that egotistical. But he's an elder statesman, he would like to make sure the leadership found its way into suitable hands."

"Whose hands?"

"If not him, then one of his young acolytes."

"Like who?"

"Don't you have thoughts of your own?"

"Samuel. You mean Michael Samuel," she said excitedly, pursing her lips.

"You might think that, Mattie."

"How do you know that?"

"I couldn't possibly comment." Urquhart smiled, finished his whiskey. "I think I have allowed you to speculate enough. We should call this conversation to a halt."

Mattie nodded reluctantly. "Thank you, Mr. Urquhart."

"For what? I have said nothing," he said, rising.

Her mind was buzzing with theories as she tried to place the pieces of the jigsaw puzzle together. They were shaking hands by the front door before she spoke again.

"Mrs. Urquhart?"

"Isn't here. She is in the country."

Their hands were still linked.

"Please give her my best wishes."

"I shall, Mattie. I shall."

She let go of his hand and turned to leave, before hesitating. "One last question. A leadership election. If there were to be one, would you be part of it?"

"Good night, Mattie," Urquhart said, closing the front door.

❖   ❖   ❖

Daily Chronicle. Monday, June 14. Page 1.

———❖———

The Prime Minister shocked many observers yesterday by announcing there were to be no Cabinet changes. After conferring for several hours with his Party Chairman, Lord Williams, and also with the Chief Whip Francis Urquhart, Henry Collingridge issued a "steady as she goes" message to his party.

However, senior Westminster sources last night expressed astonishment at the decision. It was seen in some quarters as revealing the weakness of the Prime Minister's position after what was seen as a lackluster campaign.

There was growing speculation that Collingridge is unlikely to fight another election, and some senior ministers already appear to be maneuvering for position in the event of an early leadership contest. One Cabinet minister compared the Prime Minister to "the captain of the Titanic as it was entering the ice pack."

The decision not to make any Cabinet changes, the first time since the war that an election has not been followed by some senior reshuffle, was interpreted as being the most effective way for Collingridge to keep the simmering rivalries of his Cabinet colleagues under control. Last night the Chief Whip defended the decision as being "the best means of getting on with the job" but speculation is already beginning about likely contenders in a leadership race.

Contacted late last night, Lord Williams described any suggestion of an imminent leadership election as "nonsense." He said, "The Prime Minister has gained for the Party an historic fourth election victory. We are in excellent shape." Williams's position of the Party Chairman would be crucial during a leadership race and he is known to be close to Michael Samuel, the Environment Secretary, who could be one of the contenders.

Opponents were quick to pounce on what they saw as the Prime Minister's indecisiveness. The Opposition Leader said: "The fires of discontent are glowing within the Government. I don't think Mr. Collingridge has the strength or the support to put them out. I am already looking forward to the next election."

A senior source within the Government described the situation as being like "a great elm waiting to rot."

NINE

Some men never manage to live with their principles. In Westminster it helps to be seen lunching with them occasionally, but not too often, in case you find yourself mistaken for a prude.

Tuesday, June 22

O'Neill had been delighted and, at first, a little surprised to get an invitation from Urquhart to lunch at his St. James's Street club. The Chief Whip had never shown much warmth toward the Party's communications man in the past, but now he suggested they "celebrate the splendid work you did for us all throughout the campaign." O'Neill took it as recognition of his rising eminence in the Party.

It had been a damned good lunch, too, all the trimmings. O'Neill, hypertense as always, had fortified himself with a couple of mighty vodka tonics before he'd arrived, but they hadn't been necessary. Two bottles of Château Talbot '78 and a couple of large cognacs were enough, even for his Irish appetites. He had talked too much, he knew, always did, but he couldn't help it. In the past Urquhart had made him feel nervous. It was something about the cool reserve of the man, and the fact that Urquhart had once been overheard talking about him as "a marketing johnny," but he had proved an attentive host as the other man babbled on. Now they were sitting in the substantial cracked leather armchairs that surrounded the snooker tables in the back room at White's. When the tables were not in use the seats offered a quiet and confidential spot for members to take their guests.

"Tell me, Roger, what are your plans now the election is over? Are you going to stay on with the Party? We can't afford to lose good men like you."

O'Neill flashed yet another winning smile, stubbed out the cigarette he was smoking in the hope that a decent Havana might be in the offing, and assured his host that he would stay on as long as the Prime Minister wanted him.

"But how can you afford to, Roger? May I be just a little indiscreet? I know how little the Party pays its employees, and money is always tight after an election. The next couple of years are likely to be tough. Your salary will get frozen, your budget cut. It's always the same, we politicians being our typical short-sighted selves. Aren't you tempted by some of the more handsome offers you must be getting from outside?"

"Well, it's not always easy, Francis, as you've already guessed. It's not so much the salary, you understand. I work in politics because I'm fascinated by it and love to play a part. But it would be a tragedy if the budget gets cut. So much work still to do." His smile was broad, his eyes bright, but they began dancing in agitation as he considered what the other man had said. He began to fidget nervously with his glass. "We should start working for the next election now. Particularly with all these ridiculous rumors flooding round about splits within the Party. We need some positive publicity, and I need a budget to create it."

"An interesting point. Is the Chairman receptive to all this?" Urquhart raised an inquiring eyebrow.

"Are chairmen ever?"

"Perhaps there's something I can do about that, Roger. I would like to be able to help you. Very much. I could go in to bat with the Chairman about your budget, if you want."

"Really? That'd be astonishingly kind of you, Francis."

"But there is something I must ask you first, Roger. And I must be blunt."

The older man's ice eyes looked directly into O'Neill's, taking in their habitual flicker. Then O'Neill blew his nose loudly. Another habit, Urquhart knew, as was the constant tapping of the two middle fingers on his right hand. It was as if there were another life going on within O'Neill that was quite separate from the rest of the world, and that communicated itself only through O'Neill's hyperactive mannerisms and twitching eyes.

"Had a visit the other day, Roger, from an old acquaintance I used to know in the days when I held directorships in the City. He's one of the financial people at the Party's advertising agency. And he was very troubled. Very discreet, but very troubled. He said you were in the habit of asking the agency for considerable sums of cash to cover your expenses."

The twitching stopped for a moment. Urquhart reflected just how rarely he had ever seen O'Neill stop moving.

"Roger, let me assure you I am not trying to trap you or trick you. This is strictly between us. But if I am to help you, I must be sure of the facts."

The face and the eyes started up again, as O'Neill's ready laugh made a nervous reappearance. "Francis, let me assure you there's nothing wrong, nothing at all. It's silly, of course, but I'm grateful that you raised it with me. It's simply that there are times when I incur expenses on the publicity side which are easier for the agency to meet rather than putting them through the Party machine. Like buying a drink for a journalist or taking a Party contributor out for a meal." O'Neill was speeding on with his explanation, which showed signs of having been practiced. "You see, if I pay for them myself I have to claim back from the Party. Which takes its own sweet time writing the bloody check—two months or more. You know what they're like, takes forever for the ink to dry. Frankly, with the way they pay me, I can't afford it. So I charge them through the agency, I get the money back immediately while they put them through their own accounts. It's like an interest-free loan for the Party. And in the meantime I can get on with my job. The amounts are really very small."

O'Neill reached for his glass while Urquhart steepled his fingers and watched the other man empty his glass.

"Like £22,300 in the last ten months small, Roger?"

O'Neill all but choked. His face contorted as he struggled simultaneously to gulp down air and blurt out the required denial. "It's nothing like that amount," he protested. His jaw dropped as he debated what to say next. This part of the explanation he hadn't practiced. O'Neill's twitching now resembled a fly caught in a spider's web. Urquhart spun more silken threads.

"Roger, you have been charging regular expenses to the agency without clearly accounting for those amounts to the tune of precisely £22,300 since the beginning of September last year. What began as relatively small amounts have in recent months grown to £4,000 a month. You don't get through that many drinks and dinners even during an election campaign."

"I assure you, Francis, that any expenses I've charged have all been entirely legitimate!"

"Expensive, isn't it? Cocaine."

O'Neill's glazed eyes had frozen in horror.

"Roger, as Chief Whip I have to become familiar with every problem known to man. I've had to deal with cases of wife beating, adultery, fraud, mental illness. I've even had a case of incest. No, it's all right, we didn't let him stand for re-election, of course, but there was nothing to be gained by making a public fuss. That's why you almost never hear about them.

Incest I draw the line at, Roger, but in general we don't moralize. In my book every man is allowed one indulgence—so long as it remains a private one."

He paused; a flicker was returning to O'Neill's eyes, one of desperation.

"One of my Junior Whips is a doctor. I appointed him specifically to help me spot the signs of strain. After all, we have well over three hundred MPs to look after, all of whom are living under immense pressure. You'd be surprised, too, how many cases of drug abuse we get. There's a charming and utterly private drying-out farm just outside Dover where we send them, sometimes for a couple of months. Most of them recover completely, one of them is even a senior Minister." He leaned forward to close the gap between them. "But it helps to catch them early, Roger. And cocaine has become a real problem recently. They tell me it's fashionable—whatever that means—and too damned easy to obtain. Makes a good man brilliant, so they say. Pity it's so addictive. And expensive."

Urquhart hadn't taken his eyes off O'Neill for a second during his narrative. He found something exquisite and compelling in the agony that was stripping the flesh off O'Neill. Any doubt he might have had about the diagnosis was swept aside by the trembling hands and the lips that parted but could not speak. When, at last, O'Neill found words, they came as a whimper.

"What are you saying? I am not a drug addict. I don't do drugs!"

"No, of course not, Roger." Urquhart adopted his most reassuring tone. "But I think you must accept that there might be some people who could jump to the most unfortunate conclusions about you. And the Prime Minister, you know, particularly in his present mood, is not a man to take chances. Please believe me it's not a matter of condemning a man without trial, simply of opting for a quiet life."

"Henry can't believe this! You haven't told him surely…" O'Neill gasped as if he had been butted by a charging bull.

"Of course not, Roger. I want you to regard me as a friend. But the Party Chairman…"

"Williams? What has he said?"

"About drugs? Nothing. But I'm afraid the dear Lord isn't one of your greatest fans. He wasn't very helpful with the Prime Minister. Seems to think you should be blamed for the election result rather than himself."

"What?" The word emerged as a squeak.

"Don't worry, Roger, I spoke up for you. There's nothing to fear. As long as you have my support."

Urquhart knew what he was doing, understood full well the paranoia that grips the mind of a cocaine addict and the impact his invented story about the Chairman's disaffection would leave on O'Neill's tender emotions. The man had a lust for notoriety that could only be met through the continued patronage of the Prime Minister; it was something he couldn't bear to lose. "As long as you have my support." The words rang in O'Neill's ears. "One slip and you are dead," it was saying. The web of fear had closed around O'Neill. Now was the time to offer him a way out.

"Roger, I've seen gossip destroy so many men. The corridors around Westminster can become a killing field. It would be a tragedy for which I could never forgive myself if you were placed upon the rack either because of Teddy Williams's hostility toward you or simply because people misunderstood your arrangement about expenses and your—hay fever."

"What should I do?" The voice was plaintive.

"Do? Why, Roger, I would suggest that you trust me. You need a strong supporter in the inner circles of the Party, particularly right now. There's a swell on the water, it's growing, the Prime Minister's boat is taking on water, he won't give a second thought to throwing someone like you overboard if it might help save himself. People like that think you're little more than ballast."

The words were having the desired effect. O'Neill was writhing in his chair, sipping blindly at a crystal glass that was already empty, the old leather groaning beneath him. Urquhart paused for a moment to take in every detail.

"Help me, Francis."

"That's why I invited you, Roger."

The other man wept. Tears were falling down his face.

"I will not let them push out a good man like you, Roger." His tone was that of a vicar reading out a psalm. "Every penny of your expenses is legitimate. That is what I shall tell the agency. I shall advise them to continue with the arrangement, and keep it confidential, so as to avoid unhelpful jealousy from those within the Party who want to slash the advertising budget. But there is more to be done. We shall make sure the Prime Minister is fully informed of the good works you are doing. And I shall advise him not to drop his guard, to continue with a high level of campaigning if he's to get through the difficult months ahead. Your budget will survive. And so will you, Roger."

"Francis, you know I would be most grateful..." O'Neill mumbled.

"But there is something I will need in return, Roger."

"Anything."

"If I'm to guard your back I shall need to know everything that's going on at Party Headquarters."

"Of course."

"And in particular what the Chairman is up to. He's a very ambitious and dangerous man, playing his own game while professing loyalty to the Prime Minister. You must be my eyes and ears, Roger, and you will have to let me know immediately of anything you hear of the Chairman's plans. Your future could depend upon it."

O'Neill was drying his eyes, blowing his nose, his handkerchief an appalling mess.

"You and I, Roger, must work together on this. You will have to help steer the Party through some difficult times ahead. Horatio at the bridge."

"Francis, I don't know how to thank you."

"You will, Roger, you will."

❖ ❖ ❖

A door slammed. Mortima was back. She scurried up the stairs, searching for him in every room, until she found him on their roof terrace, gazing out across the London night to the Victoria Tower that stood in spot-lit splendor at the southern end of the Parliament building. The Union flag was unfurling in the gentle currents of air thrown up from the hot streets. The building seemed as though it had been carved from honeycomb. Urquhart was smoking, a rare sight.

"Francis, are you OK?"

He turned, startled, as though surprised to see her, then went back to searching out across the rooftops of Westminster to the Victoria Tower.

"When you called and said something had happened I thought you might be sick. You scared me and…"

"They have Charles I's death warrant in there, in the tower. And the Bill of Rights. Acts of Parliament dating back more than five hundred years." He spoke as though he had not heard her or noticed her concern.

"Something *has* happened." She drew close, took his arm. His eyes seemed held by an apparition or prospect that only he could see and that lay somewhere out in the night.

"If you listen carefully, Mortima, you can hear the cries of the mob outside the gates."

"Can you?"

"I can."

"Francis?" Her voice still trembled with concern.

Only then did he come back to her. He squeezed her hand. "It was kind of you to rush back. I'm so sorry if I caused you concern. No, I'm not sick, I am fine. In fact I feel better than I have for a long while."

"I don't understand. You were so disappointed not to have been moved."

"Nothing lasts. Not great empires, least of all weak prime ministers." His voice was riddled with contempt. He held out his cigarette to her; she drew deeply on the strong vapors.

"You will need helpers," she whispered, returning the cigarette.

"I think I may have found some."

"That young journalist you mentioned?"

"Perhaps."

She didn't reply for a while. They stood in the darkness, sharing the night, the muffled sounds of the lives that were going on beneath them, the air of conspiracy.

"Will she be loyal?"

"Loyalty among journalists?"

"You must bind her in, Francis."

He looked at her sharply, offered a thin smile that vanished quickly. There was no humor in it. "She is far too young, Mortima."

"Too young? Too beautiful? Too intelligent? Too ambitious? I think not, Francis. Not for a man like you."

His smile returned, warmer now. "As so often, Mortima, I am in your debt."

She was twelve years younger than he was, still vibrant, and wore the few extra pounds the years had put on her with elegance. She was his closest friend, the only one he allowed to dig inside him, on whom he could rely without question. They had their different lives, of course, his in Westminster and hers…Well, she loved Wagner. Never one of his enthusiasms. She would disappear for days, travel abroad, with others, to share the passions of the *Ring* cycle. He never questioned her loyalty, nor she his.

"This will not be easy," he said.

"Neither is failure."

"Are there any limits?" he asked, as gently as such a question would allow.

She rose on tiptoe to kiss his cheek, then returned inside, leaving him with the night.

TEN

I knew a man once whose memory was so desiccated that he quite forgot he'd hung a Howard Hodgkin on its side for three years without realizing, yet who remembered he'd been a trustee of the Tate, which he never was. He became Minister for the Arts, of course. I wonder what ever happened to him after that?

Wednesday, June 30

The Strangers' Bar in the House of Commons is a small room of dark paneling and quiet corners overlooking the Thames where Members of Parliament may take their "Stranger" or non-Member guests. It's usually crowded and noisy with rumor and gossip, occasionally with moral violence, sometimes physical violence, too. Some politicians just don't do sober.

O'Neill was propped up on one elbow against the bar while struggling with the other to avoid knocking the drink out of his host's hand. "Another one, Steve?" he asked of his immaculately dressed companion.

Stephen Kendrick was a newly-elected Opposition MP who had yet to find his place. He gave off a mixture of messages, his light gray Armani mohair suit and pearl white cuffs contrasting with the pint of Federation bitter that he clasped in his immaculately manicured hand. "You know better than me that Strangers can't buy drinks here. Anyway, since I've only been in this place a couple of weeks I think it's a little early to ruin my career by being caught spending too long with the Prime Minister's pet Irish wolfhound. Some of my more dogmatic colleagues would treat that as treachery. One more and that's my limit!" He grinned and winked at the barmaid. Another pint of dark bitter and a double vodka tonic appeared in front of them.

"You know, Rog, I'm still pinching myself. I never really expected to get here. Still can't decide whether it's a dream or just a bloody awful nightmare." His voice was thick with the back streets of Blackburn. "Funny thing, fate, ain't it? When we worked together at that little PR shop seven years ago, who'd have guessed you would now be the Prime Minister's chief grunter and I'd be the Opposition's newest and most talented MP?"

"Not that little blond telephonist we used to take turns with."

"Dear little Annie."

"I thought her name was Jennie."

"Rog, I never remember you being fussy about what they were called."

The banter finally broke the ice. When O'Neill had telephoned the new MP to suggest a drink for old times' sake they had both found it difficult to revive the easy familiarity they had known in earlier years. Throughout the first couple of rounds they had sparred gently, avoiding the subject of politics that now dominated their lives. Now O'Neill decided it was time to take the plunge.

"Steve, as far as I'm concerned I don't mind you buying the drinks all night. Christ, the way my masters are going at the moment I think a saint would be driven to drink."

Kendrick accepted the opening. "It's got bloody messy, bloody quick, that's for sure. Your lot do seem to have lost the elastic in their knickers. Hell's bells, I can't believe the gossip. Samuel furious with Williams for putting his head on the block with the PM, Williams hacked off with Collingridge for screwing up the election, Collingridge raging about everything and just about everyone. Bloody brilliant!"

"They're all knackered, can't wait to get away on holiday. Squabbling about how to pack the car."

"You'll not mind me saying, old chum, but your gaffer's going to have to put an end to all the bickering pretty damned quick, or else. I may be wet behind the ears but once rumors like that start, they begin to gain a life of their own. They become reality. Still, that's where you and your mighty publicity machine come to the rescue, I suppose, like the Seventh Cavalry over the hill."

"More like Custer's last stand," O'Neill said with some bitterness.

"What's the matter, Rog, Uncle Teddy run off with all your toy soldiers or something?"

O'Neill emptied his glass with a savage flick of his wrist. Kendrick, his caution overcome by curiosity, ordered another round.

"Since you ask, Steve—between you and me, as old friends— our ancient and vastly overrated Chairman has decided to retreat behind the barricades. Just when we need to come out fighting."

"Ah, do I detect the cries of a frustrated Publicity Director who's been told to shut up shop for a while?"

O'Neill banged his glass down on the bar in exasperation. "I shouldn't tell you this, I suppose, but you'll know about it soon enough. You know the hospital expansion program we promised at the election, matching Government funds for any money raised locally? Brilliant idea. And we had a wonderful promotional campaign ready to go throughout the summer while you cloth-capped bastards were off on the Costa del Cuba or wherever it is you go."

"But?"

"Not going to happen, is it? I had everything in place, Steve, ready to go. And by the time your lot had packed away their buckets and spades and come back in October, I would have won the hearts and minds of voters in every marginal seat in the country. We had the campaign all set. Advertising, ten million leaflets, direct mail. 'Nursing Hospitals Back to Health.' But…The old bastard's pulled the plug. Just like that."

"Why?" Kendrick asked consolingly. "Money problems after the election?"

"That's what's so ruddy ridiculous about it, Steve. The money's in the budget and the leaflets have already been printed, but he won't let us deliver them. He just came back from Number Ten this morning and said the thing was off. Lost their nerve, they have. Then he had the balls to ask whether the bloody leaflets would be out of date by next year. It's so amateurish!"

He took another large mouthful of vodka and stared into the bottom of his glass. O'Neill prayed he had followed Urquhart's instructions not to show too much disloyalty, nothing more than professional pique and a little gentle alcoholic excess. He was still puzzled. He had no idea why Urquhart had told him to concoct an entirely spurious story about a non-existent publicity campaign to pass on in the Strangers' Bar, but if it involved landing Williams in the shit, he was all for it. As he swirled the slice of lemon around his glass he saw Kendrick give him a long and deliberate glance.

"What's going on, Rog?"

"If only I knew, old chum. Complete bloody mystery. Total fucking mess."

Thursday, July 1

The Chamber of the House of Commons is of relatively modern construction, rebuilt following the war after one of the Luftwaffe's bombs had missed the docks and carelessly scored a direct hit on the Mother of Parliaments instead. Yet in spite of its relative youth the Chamber has an atmosphere centuries old. If you sit quietly in the corner of the empty Chamber on one of the narrow green benches, the freshness fades and the ghosts of Chatham, Walpole, Fox, and Disraeli pace the gangways once again.

It is a place of character rather than convenience. There are seats for only around four hundred of the six hundred and fifty Members, who cannot listen to the rudimentary loudspeakers built into the backs of the benches without slumping to one side and giving the appearance of being sound asleep. Which sometimes they are.

The design is based on the old St. Stephen's Chapel, where the earliest parliamentarians sat, like choirboys in facing pews, yet there is little that is angelic in the modern set-up. Members face each other in confrontation, as antagonists. They are separated by two red lines on the carpet, whose distance apart represents the distance of two sword lengths, yet this is misleading, for the most imminent danger is never more than a dagger's distance away, on the benches behind.

Almost all prime ministers end up being hacked, chopped, or forced bloodily from office. More than half the members of the Government's Parliamentary Party usually believe they can do the job far better. Those who have been sacked, or who have never been offered a job, sit behind their leader measuring the width between his or her shoulder blades. The pressure is relentless. Every week prime ministers are called to account at Prime Minister's Question Time, an institution honored only for its excess. In principle it gives Members of Parliament the opportunity to seek information from the leader of Her Majesty's Government; in practice it is an exercise in survival that owes more to the Roman arena of Nero and Claudius than to the ideals of parliamentary democracy. The questions from Opposition Members usually don't even pretend to seek information, they seek only to criticize, to inflict damage. Will this pathetic excuse for a Prime Minister fuck off?—or words to that effect. Similarly the answers given rarely seek to give information but are intended to retaliate and to cause pain and humiliation. And prime ministers always have the last word, it gives them the advantage in combat, like the gladiator allowed the final thrust. That is why a prime minister is expected to win. Woe betide the prime minister who does not. Tension and terror are never far behind the confident smile. It made Macmillan sick with tension, caused Wilson to lose sleep and Thatcher to lose her temper. And Henry Collingridge was never quite up to any of their standards.

The day following O'Neill's evening foray into the Strangers' Bar hadn't been running smoothly for the Prime Minister. The Downing Street press secretary had been laid low by his children's chicken pox so the normal daily press briefing was of inferior quality and, even worse to the impatient Collingridge, was late. So was Cabinet, which had gathered at its accustomed time of 10:00 a.m. on Thursday but had dragged on in confusion as the Chancellor of the Exchequer sought to explain, without any evident offense to Collingridge, how the Government's reduced majority had taken the edge off the financial markets, making it impossible in this financial year to implement the hospital expansion program they had promised so enthusiastically during the election campaign. The Prime Minister should have kept a grip on the discussion, but it rambled on and ended in embarrassment.

"A pity, perhaps, that the Chancellor wasn't a little more cautious before allowing us to run off and make rash commitments," the Education Secretary commented, dripping acid.

The Chancellor muttered darkly that it wasn't his fault the election results were worse than even the cynics in the Stock Market had expected, a comment he had instantly regretted. Collingridge tried to knock heads together and instructed the Health Secretary to prepare a suitable explanation for the change of plans. It was also decided that this change of course would be announced in a fortnight's time, during the last week before Parliament ran away for recess.

"Let us hope," said the septuagenarian Lord Chancellor, "that by then minds will be on the follies of summer."

So Cabinet overran by twenty-five minutes, which meant that the Prime Minister's briefing meeting with officials for Question Time was also late, and his ill-temper ensured that he took in little of what they were saying. When he strode into a packed Chamber just before the appointed time for questions, he was neither as well armed nor as alert as usual.

This didn't seem to matter much as Collingridge batted back questions from the Opposition and accepted plaudits from his own party with adequate if not inspired ease. Business as usual. The Speaker of the House, the man in charge of parliamentary proceedings, glanced at the clock and decided that with just over a minute left of the session there might be time for just one more outing to round off the session. The next question on the Order Paper was from one of the new members; a good moment, he decided, to initiate new blood.

"Stephen Kendrick," he called across the Chamber.

"Number Six, sir." Kendrick rose briefly to his feet to indicate the question from the Order Paper that stood in his name: "To ask the Prime Minister if he will list his official engagements for the day." It was a hollow question, identical to Questions One, Two, and Four, which had already preceded it.

Collingridge rose ponderously and glanced at the red briefing folder already open on the Dispatch Box in front of him. He read in a dull monotone. They'd heard it all before. "I refer the Honorable Member to the reply I gave some moments ago to Questions One, Two, and Four." Since his earlier reply had said no more than that he would spend the day holding meetings with ministerial colleagues and hosting a dinner for the visiting

Belgian Prime Minister, no one had yet learned anything of interest about the Prime Minister's activities—but that was not the intention. The gladiatorial courtesies were now over and battle was about to commence. Kendrick rose to his feet from the Opposition benches.

Steve Kendrick was a gambler, a man who had found professional success in an industry that rewarded chutzpah and oversized balls. No one had been more surprised than he had been, apart from perhaps his ex-wife, that he'd decided to risk the expense account and sports car by fighting a marginal parliamentary seat. Not that he had expected or indeed wanted to win; after all, the Government had been sitting on a pretty reasonable majority, but fighting the seat would help establish his brand name and help him both socially and professionally. He'd spent several weeks on the front pages of the PR trade magazines. "The man with the social conscience" always made good copy in such an aggressively commercial industry.

His majority of seventy-six, after three recounts, had come as an unpleasant shock. It meant a considerably reduced income and a creaking private life put under close scrutiny, and chances were he'd get thrown out at the next election anyway. So what was the point in caution? He had nothing to lose except his anonymity.

Kendrick had spent a fractured night and frustrated morning wrestling with what O'Neill had said. Why cancel a publicity campaign promoting a vote-winning policy? It made no bloody sense unless…Unless it was the policy rather than the publicity campaign that was in trouble. That must surely be it. Wasn't it? What else could it be? Or was he simply too wet behind the ears to understand what was going on? The more he grappled with the puzzle, the more it wriggled. Should he inquire or accuse? Question or condemn? He knew that if he got it wrong, the first and lasting impression he made would be that of the House fool.

Doubts were still buzzing around his mind like hornets as he rose to his feet. His momentary uncertainty caused the general commotion of the House to die away as MPs sensed his indecision. Had the new Member frozen? Kendrick took a deep breath and decided there was no point trying to stand on his dignity. He jumped.

"Will the Prime Minister explain to the House why he has canceled the promised hospital expansion program?"

No criticism. No elaboration. No added phrase or rambling comment that would give time to the Prime Minister to dodge or duck. A murmur went up as the new backbencher resumed his seat. The hospital program? Canceled? The sport had taken an interesting new turn, and the three hundred-odd spectators turned as one to look toward Collingridge. He clambered to his feet, feeling as he did so that the blood supply to his brain had been left behind. He knew there was nothing in his red briefing folder from which to draw inspiration, no prop, no straw at which he might grasp. It had leaked, been stolen, was ruined, he was fucked. He smiled broadly. It's what you had to do. Only those sitting very close to him could see the whites of his knuckles as he gripped the Dispatch Box.

"I hope that the Honorable Gentleman will be careful to avoid being carried away by the summer silly season, at least before August arrives. As he is a new Member, it's a good opportunity for me to remind him that in the last four years under this Government, the health service has enjoyed a substantial real increase in spending of some six to eight percent." Collingridge knew he was being inexcusably patronizing but he couldn't find the right words. What else could he do? "The health service has benefited more than any other Government service from our success in defeating inflation, which compares..."

From his perch a little higher up on the bank of green leather benches, Kendrick stared. The Prime Minister wasn't looking him in the eye, was casting around. He was lost. "Answer the bloody question," he growled, in a Northern accent that some-how makes such indelicacy acceptable or at least expected. Several other Members echoed the suggestion.

"I shall answer the question in my own way and in my own time," the Prime Minister snapped. "It is a pathetic sham for the Opposition to whine when they know that electors have reached their own conclusions and only recently voted with their feet for this Government. They support us and I can repeat our determination to protect them and their hospital service."

Rude shouts of disapproval from the Opposition benches grew louder. Most of them would go unrecorded by Hansard, whose editors at times had a remarkably deaf ear, but they were clearly audible to the Prime Minister, every syllable. His own backbenchers began to stir uneasily, uncertain as to why Collingridge didn't simply reaffirm the policy and shove it deep down Kendrick's throat.

Collingridge ploughed on against a backdrop of interrup-tions. "The House will be aware…that it is not the custom of governments…to discuss the specifics of new spending plans in advance…We shall make an announcement about our inten-tions at the appropriate time."

"You have. You've bloody dropped it, haven't you?" the Honorable and usually disrespectful Member for Newcastle West erupted from his position below the gangway, so loudly that not even Hansard could claim to have missed it.

The faces on the Opposition Front Bench broke into smiles, at last catching up with the game. Their Leader, not six feet from where Collingridge stood, turned to his nearest col-league and gave the loudest of Welsh whispers. "You know I think he's fluffed it. He's running away!" He began waving his Order Paper, as did all his colleagues. It seemed like the sails of ancient galleons sailing into battle.

The pain of a thousand encounters in the House welled up inside Collingridge. He was unprepared for this. He couldn't bring himself to admit the truth yet neither could he lie to the House, and he could find no form of words that would tread that delicate line between honesty and outright deceit. As he observed the smugness on the faces in front of him and listened to their jeers, he remembered all the many lies they had told about him over the years, the cruelty they had shown and the tears they had caused his wife to shed. As he gazed at contorted faces just a few feet in front of him, his patience vanished. He had to bring it to an end, and he no longer cared how. He threw his hands in the air.

"I don't have to take comments like that from a pack of dogs," he snarled, and sat down. Like a bear backing out of the baiting ring.

Even before the shout of triumph and rage had a chance to rise from the Opposition benches, Kendrick was back on his feet. "On a point of order, Mr. Speaker. The Prime Minister's remarks are an absolute disgrace. I asked a perfectly straightforward question about why the Prime Minister had reneged on his election promise and all I've got are insults and evasion. While I understand the Prime Minister's reluctance to admit that he's perpetrated a gigantic and disgraceful fraud on the electorate, is there nothing you can do to protect the right of Members of this House so that we get a straight answer to a straight question? I know I'm new in this place but there must be something in the Trade Descriptions Act that covers this."

Waves of approval washed across the Opposition benches as the Speaker struggled to be heard above the commotion. "The Honorable Member may be new, but he seems already to have developed a sharp eye for parliamentary procedure, in which case he will know that I am no more responsible for the content or tone of the Prime Minister's replies than I am for the questions which are put to him. Next business!"

As the Speaker tried to move matters on, a red-faced Collingridge rose and strode angrily out of the Chamber, gesticulating for the Chief Whip to follow him. The very unparliamentary taunt of "Coward!" rang after him across the floor. From the Government benches there was nothing but an uncertain silence.

❖   ❖   ❖

"How in Christ's name did he know? How did that son-of-a-bitch know?"

The door had barely been slammed upon the Prime Minister's office, which stood just off the rear of the Chamber before the tirade began. The normally suave exterior of Her Majesty's First Minister had been cast aside to reveal a wild Warwickshire ferret. "Francis, it's simply not good enough. It's not bloody good enough I tell you. We get the Chancellor's report in Cabinet Committee yesterday, the full Cabinet discusses it for the first time today, and by this afternoon it's known to every sniveling little shit in the Opposition. Less than two dozen Cabinet ministers knew, only a handful of civil servants were in the loop. Who leaked it, Francis? Who? You're Chief Whip. I want you to find the bastard and I want him hanged from the clock tower by his balls!"

Urquhart breathed a huge sigh of relief. Until the Prime Minister's outburst he'd had no idea if the finger of blame was already pointing at him. He smiled, but only on the inside. "It simply astonishes me, Henry, that one of our Cabinet colleagues would want deliberately to leak something like this," he began, implicitly ruling out the possibility of a civil service leak, narrowing the circle of suspicion to include each and every one of his Cabinet colleagues.

"Whoever is responsible has humiliated me. I want him out, Francis. I want—I insist—that you find the worm. And then I want him fed to the crows."

"Henry, as a friend?"

"Of course!"

"I'm afraid there's been too much bickering among our colleagues since the election. Too many of them want someone else's job."

"They all want my job, I know that, but who would be so—so cretinous, so calculating, such a cock-artist as to deliberately leak something like that?"

"I can't say"—the smallest of hesitations—"for sure."

Collingridge picked up on the inflection. "An educated guess, for Chrissake."

"That would scarcely be fair."

"Fair? You think what just happened was fair, having my arse used as a letterbox?"

"But…"

"No 'buts,' Francis. If it's happened once it can happen again and almost certainly will. Accuse, imply, whatever you damned well like. There are no minutes being taken here. But I want some names!" Collingridge's fist came down on his desk so hard it made the reading lamp jump.

"If you insist, I'll speculate. I know nothing for sure, you understand…let's work from deduction. Given the timescale involved, it seems more likely to have leaked from yesterday's Cabinet Committee rather than from today's full Cabinet. Agreed?"

Collingridge nodded his assent.

"And apart from you and me, who is on that Committee?"

"Chancellor of the Exchequer, Financial Secretary, Health, Education, Environment, Trade, and Industry." The Prime Minister reeled off those Cabinet ministers who had attended.

Urquhart remained silent, forcing Collingridge to finish off the logic himself. "Well, the two Treasury Ministers were scarcely likely to leak the fact that they'd screwed it up. But Health bitterly opposed it, so Paul McKenzie had a reason to leak it. Harold Earle at Education has always had a loose lip. And Michael Samuel has a habit of enjoying the company of the media rather too much for my liking."

The suspicions and insecurities that lurk in the darker recesses of a Prime Minister's mind were being dragged into the light.

"There are other possibilities, Henry, but I think them unlikely," Urquhart joined in. "As you know Michael is very close to Teddy Williams. They discuss everything together. It could have come out of Party Headquarters. Not from Teddy, I'm sure, he'd never...But one of the officials there might have leaked it. Some of them spend their lives pissing into paper pots."

Collingridge pondered for some moments in silence. "Could it really have been Teddy?" he mused. "He was never my greatest supporter—different generations—but I brought him in from the scrap heap, made him one of the team. And he repays me with this?"

"It is only a suspicion, Henry..."

The Prime Minister threw himself into his chair, exhausted, no longer willing to fight the thought. "Perhaps I've relied on Teddy too much recently. I thought he had no ax to grind, no ambition left, not in the House of Lords. One of the old guard. Loyal. Was I wrong, Francis?"

"I don't know. You asked me to speculate."

"Make sure, Francis. Do whatever you need to do. I want him, whoever he is. I want his balls dragged out through his ears and I want the whole of Westminster to hear the screams."

Urquhart nodded and lowered his eyes, as a servant might, not wanting the Prime Minister to see the delight dancing within them. Collingridge had announced open season. Urquhart was back on the moors, his feet planted firmly in the heather, waiting for the birds to rise.

ELEVEN

Christopher Columbus was a huge disappointment. When he set out he had no idea where he was going, and when he'd arrived he had no idea where he was. If you want to screw the natives, much better to stay at home.

Friday, July 16—Thursday, July 22

Life in the House of Commons can be exhilarating, occasionally historic, but that is not the norm. The norm is crap. Long hours, heavy workloads, too much entertaining and too little respite all ensure that the long summer break beckons to Members like an oasis in a desert. And while they wait, patience thins and tempers fray. During the days before the recess, Urquhart moved around the corridors and bars of the House, trying to bolster morale and calm the doubts of many Government backbenchers who were growing uneasy about Collingridge's increasingly scratchy performance. Morale is easier to shatter than to rebuild and some old hands thought Urquhart was trying perhaps a little too hard, his strenuous efforts serving to remind many that the Prime Minister had gotten himself into surprisingly choppy waters, but if it were a fault on the part of the Chief Whip, it was one that was generally recognized as exceptional if occasionally aggressive loyalty. But what did it all matter? The breezes of the South of France beckoned and would soon be washing away many of the parliamentary cares.

August was a safety valve, which was why governments had a knack of trying to bury difficult announcements in the final dog days of the session, often slipping out the details by means of a Written Answer published in Hansard, the voluminous official report of parliamentary proceedings. It meant that the matter had been placed openly and clearly on the public record, but at a time when most Members were packing up their desks and trying to remember where they had hidden their passports. Even if one or two did spot the detail, there was scarcely time or opportunity to make much of a fuss. It was the truth, the whole truth and nothing but the truth—so long as you read the fine print.

Which was why it was unfortunate that a photocopy of a draft Written Answer from the Secretary of State for Defense should have been found a full ten days before it was due to be published, lying under a chair in Annie's Bar, where Members and journalists congregated to gossip. It was an added embarrassment that the Written Answer announced the intention to impose substantial cuts on the Territorial Army on the grounds that the TA was increasingly less relevant to government plans in the nuclear era. What made the matter all the more exquisitely awkward was that the draft was found by the lobby correspondent of the *Independent*. Everybody liked the man, respected him, he knew how to check out a story. So when it became the page one lead item in his newspaper four days later, at what was the start of the final full week before the summer recess, people knew it was reliable. Cock-up soon became chaos.

Retribution arrived from an unusual source. The pay of the Territorial Army wasn't large but its numbers were great and influential. Considerable prestige was involved. In constituency parties up and down the country there were senior members who proudly added the initials "TD" after their names— "Territorial Decoration"—someone who had served in and would defend the Terrors to their last drop of writing ink.

So when the House gathered to wrap up some of the final business of the session with the Leader of the House, the air was heavy not simply with midsummer heat but with accusations of betrayal and emotional appeals for a change of course, almost all of which came from the Government benches. The Opposition scarcely had to break sweat, sitting back like contented Roman lions watching the Christians do all the work for them.

Sir Jasper Grainger, OBE, JP, and very much TD, was on his feet. The old man proudly sported a carefully ironed regimental tie along with a heavy three-piece tweed suit, refusing to compromise his personal standards in spite of the inadequate air-conditioning. He was a senior backbencher and the elected Chairman of the Backbench Defense Committee. His words carried weight.

"May I return to the point raised by several of my Honorable Friends about these unnecessary and deeply damaging cuts? Will the Leader of the House be in no doubt about the depth of feeling among his own supporters on this matter?" As his anger grew, white flecks of spittle gathered at the corners of his mouth. "Has he any idea of the damage that this will do to the Government over the coming months? Will he even now allow the House time to debate and reverse this decision, because if he doesn't, he will leave the government defenseless to accusations of bad faith just as he will leave the country defenseless against bad friends?"

Roars of manly support came from all sides, apart from the government Front Bench. The Leader of the House, Simon Lloyd, straightened and readied himself once again to come to the Dispatch Box; he was beginning to feel it should have been constructed with sandbags. He was a sound man, plenty of "bottom," but it had been a torrid twenty minutes and he had grown tetchy as he found the response he had prepared earlier affording increasingly less protection from the grenades being thrown at him by his own side. He was glad his Prime Minister and the Defense Secretary were sitting beside him on the Front Bench. Why should he suffer on his own? He hopped from foot to foot, as did his argument.

"My Honorable Friend misses the point. The document published in the newspapers was stolen Government property. Stolen! And that's an issue which rises high above the details of the document itself. If there is to be a debate, it should be about such flagrant breaches of honesty. He's a man of both honor and experience and frankly I would have expected him to join me in wholeheartedly condemning the theft of important Government documents. He must realize that by going on about its details he's as good as condoning the activity of common theft."

It sounded good, for a moment, until Sir Jasper rose to seek permission to pursue the point. It would not normally be granted but these circumstances weren't normal. Amidst waving of Order Papers throughout the Chamber, the Speaker consented. The old soldier gathered himself up to his full height, back straight, mustache bristling and face flushed with genuine anger.

"It's my Right Honorable Friend who is missing the point," he thundered. "Doesn't he understand that I would rather live alongside a common British thief than a common Russian soldier, which is precisely the fate his policy is threatening us with?"

Uproar followed, which took the Speaker a full minute to quell. During that time the Leader of the House turned and offered a look of sheer desperation to the Prime Minister and the Defense Secretary. They huddled, heads locked, until Collingridge gave a curt nod to the Leader of the House. He rose slowly to his feet once more.

"Mr. Speaker," he began, and paused to clear his throat, which was by now parched. "Mr. Speaker, my Right Honorable Friends and I have listened carefully to the mood of the House. I have the permission of the Prime Minister and the Secretary of State for Defense to say that, in light of the representations put from all sides today, the Government will look once again at this important matter to see…"

What he could see seemed of little interest to others; his words were lost amidst a huge outcry. He had run up the white flag. Colleagues slapped Sir Jasper's back, the Opposition jeered, the parliamentary correspondents scribbled in their notebooks. Amidst the hubbub and confusion on all sides, the lonely figure of Henry Collingridge sat forlorn and shrunken, staring at his socks.

❖ ❖ ❖

"Kebabed, wouldn't you say? Done to a bloody crisp," the PA's Manny Goodchild announced as Mattie pushed her way through the crowd jostling in the lobby outside the Chamber. She didn't stop. In every corner there was argument: Opposition Members gloating, claiming victory for themselves while Government supporters with considerably less conviction tried to claim victory for common sense. Yet no one was in any doubt that they had witnessed a Prime Minister on the rack.

Mattie pursued her quarry. Above the mêlée she saw the tall figure of Urquhart, stony-faced, moving, avoiding the questions of several agitated backbenchers. He disappeared through a convenient door. Mattie charged after him. She found him striding two steps at a time up the marbled stairs that led to the upper galleries.

"Mr. Urquhart," she shouted breathlessly after the fleeing minister. "Please! I need your view."

"I'm not sure I have one today, Miss Storin." Urquhart threw his reply over his shoulder; he didn't stop.

"Oh, surely we're not back on the 'Chief Whip refuses to endorse Prime Minister' game again?"

Suddenly Urquhart stopped and turned, bringing him face to face with the panting Mattie. His eyes burned bright, there was no humor in them. "Yes, Mattie, I suppose you have a right to expect something. Well, what do you think?"

"Skewered. That's the official view. If Collingridge's feet were in the fire before this, then the more sensitive parts of his anatomy seem about to follow."

"Yes, you might say that. It's not unusual for a prime minister to have to discard his clothes, of course. But to have them stripped off him quite so publicly…"

Mattie waited in vain for Urquhart to finish. He wasn't about to condemn his Prime Minister, not openly on the stairs. But if there were no condemnation, neither was there any attempt at justification.

"But this is the second major leak in as many weeks. Where are they coming from?"

He stared at her in his hawk-like manner that she found so compelling, and just a little scary. "As Chief Whip I am responsible only for discipline on the Government backbenches. You can scarcely expect me to play headmaster to my own Cabinet colleagues as well."

Her lips trembled, she gasped. "It's coming from Cabinet?"

He arched an eyebrow. "Did I say that?"

"But who? And why?"

He drew closer. "Oh, you see right through me, so you do, Miss Mattie Storin." He was laughing at her now, and so close she could feel the heat of his body. "In answer to your question, I simply don't know," he continued, "but doubtless the Prime Minister will instruct me to find out."

"Formally or informally?"

"I think I've probably said enough already," he said, and continued up the stairs.

But Mattie wasn't to be thrown off. "Fascinating. Thank you. Lobby terms, of course."

"But I have told you nothing."

"The Prime Minister is about to launch an inquiry into which of his own Cabinet colleagues is leaking sensitive information."

He stopped once more, turned. "Oh, Mattie, I couldn't possibly comment. But you are so much more sensitive than most of your dull-witted colleagues. It seems to me that your logic rather than my words has led you to your conclusions."

"I wouldn't want to get you into any trouble."

"But, Mattie, I think that's precisely what you *would* like to do." He was playing with her, almost flirting.

She stared back at him, her voice little more than a whisper. "You know far more about trouble than I do. You'd find me a willing pupil."

She wasn't entirely sure why she had said that. She should have blushed, but didn't. He should have deflected the innuendo, but held it, savored it with his eyes.

Suddenly, she grasped his sleeve. "If we're going to be wicked together we have to learn to trust each other, so just let me get one thing perfectly clear. You are not denying that the Prime Minister will order an investigation into his Cabinet members' conduct. And by not denying it, you are confirming it."

It was his turn to lower his voice. "You might say that, Mattie. I couldn't possibly comment."

"That's the story I'm going to write. If it's wrong, I beg you, stop me now."

Her grip on him had tightened. His hand was on top of hers.

"Stop you, Mattie? Why, we've only just started."

TWELVE

A life of extended credit, Indian cooking, and English boys is never likely to keep a man comfortable for long. But of all those three, I would recommend extended credit.

Wickedness. Was that what he was up to? Yes, it probably was, Urquhart decided as he continued up the stairs. He leaned against the wall and laughed out loud, much to the consternation of two passing colleagues who scurried past, shaking their heads. Eventually he found himself at the Strangers' Gallery, where members of the public squeeze themselves into rows of narrow benches to view the proceedings of the House below them. He caught the eye of a small and impeccably dressed Indian gentleman for whom he had obtained a seat in the Gallery, and signaled to him. The man struggled to extract himself from the packed public benches, squeezing past knees, mouthing apologies as he went, until he found himself standing before his host. Urquhart motioned him to silence and led him toward the small hallway behind the Gallery.

"Mr. Urquhart, sir, it has been a most exciting and highly educational ninety minutes. I am deeply indebted to you for assisting me to obtain such a comfortable position." The man's accent was thick with the subcontinent and his head weaved from side to side in the mannered Indian way as he spoke.

Urquhart knew this was balderdash, that even small Indian gentlemen such as Firdaus Jhabwala found the seating arrangement acutely uncomfortable, but he nodded in gratitude. They chatted politely while Jhabwala secured the release of his black hide attaché case from the attendant's desk. When he had arrived he had firmly refused to hand it over until told that his entry to the Gallery would be forbidden unless he lodged it with the security desk.

"I am so glad that we British can still trust ordinary working chaps with our possessions," he stated very seriously, patting the case for comfort.

"Quite," replied Urquhart, who trusted neither the ordinary working chap nor Jhabwala. Still, he was a constituent who seemed to have various flourishing local businesses and had provided a £500 donation toward his campaign expenses, asking for nothing in return except a personal interview in the House of Commons. "Not in the constituency," he had explained to Urquhart's secretary on the phone. "It's a national rather than local matter."

At £500 for a cup of tea it seemed a bargain. As Urquhart led the way he gave his guest a short tour—the glorious Pugin mosaics of Central Lobby, the frescoes of St. Stephen's Chapel, the vaulted oak ceiling of Westminster Hall that soared so high and so dark it was almost lost to view. Those rafters were a thousand years old, the most ancient part of the palace. It was here that Jhabwala asked to stand for a while. "I would be grateful for a silent moment in this spot where King Charles was condemned and Winston Churchill lay in state."

The Chief Whip arched his brow in surprise.

"Mr. Urquhart, please do not think me pretentious," the Indian insisted. "My family associations with British institutions go back nearly two hundred and fifty years to the days of the Honorable

East India Company and Lord Clive, whom my ancestors advised and to whom they loaned considerable funds. Both before that time and since my family has occupied prestigious positions in the judicial and administrative branches of Indian government." There was no mistaking the pride, but, even as the words rang out in Jhabwala's trilling voice, the eyes lowered in sadness. "Yet since Independence, Mr. Urquhart, that once great subcontinent has slowly crumbled into a new dark age. The modern Gandhi dynasty has shown itself to be far more corrupt than any my family ever served in colonial days. I am a Parsee, a cultural minority which has found little comfort under the new Raj. That is why I moved to Great Britain. My dear Mr. Urquhart, please believe me when I tell you that I feel more a part of this country and its culture than ever I could back in modern India. I wake up grateful every day that I can call myself a British citizen and educate my children in British universities."

"That is…so touching," responded Urquhart, who had never been particularly keen on foreigners taking up places at British universities and had said so on several public occasions. He hurried his guest on toward the interview rooms beneath the Great Hall, their shoes clipping across the worn flagstones as the sun slanted through the ancient windows and staircases of light reached down to the floor.

"And what precisely is it that you do, Mr. Jhabwala?" asked Urquhart hesitantly, afraid his inquiry might spark another monologue.

"I, sir, am a trader, not an educated man, not like my sons. I left behind any hope of that during the great turmoil of Indian Independence. I have therefore had to find my way not with my brain but by diligence and hard work. I am happy to say that I have been moderately successful."

"What sort of trade?"

"I have several business interests, Mr. Urquhart. Property. Wholesaling. A little local finance. But I am no narrow-minded capitalist. I am well aware of my duty to the community. It is about that I wished to speak with you."

They had arrived at the interview room and, at Urquhart's invitation, Jhabwala seated himself in one of the green chairs, his fingers running with delight over the gold embossed portcullis that embellished the upright leather back.

"So, Mr. Jhabwala, how might I help you?" Urquhart began.

"But no, my dear Mr. Urquhart, it is I who wish to help you."

A furrow of puzzlement planted itself on Urquhart's forehead.

"Mr. Urquhart, I was not born in this country. That means that of necessity I am required to work particularly hard to gain respectability in the community. So I try. The local Rotary Club, various charities. And, as you know, I am a most enthusiastic supporter of the Prime Minister."

"I'm afraid you did not see him to best advantage this afternoon."

"Then I suspect he needs his friends and supporters more than ever," Jhabwala declared, slapping the palm of his hand on the hide case that lay on the table in front of him.

The furrows deepened on Urquhart's brow as he struggled to find the meaning and direction behind his guest's remarks.

"Mr. Urquhart. You know that I have great admiration for you."

"Ye-e-e-s," Urquhart said cautiously.

"I was happy to assist in a modest way with your election appeal and would be happy to do so again. For you, Mr. Urquhart. And our Prime Minister!"

"You wish…to make…a donation?"

The head was wobbling from side to side once more. Urquhart found it disconcerting.

"Election campaigns must be so very expensive, my dear Mr. Urquhart. I wonder, would it be permissible for me to make a small donation? To replenish the coffers?"

When it came to donations from foreign sources, Urquhart

was well outside his comfort zone. Time and again such matters had dragged politicians into trouble, sometimes even into jail. "Well, I'm sure that…As you say, such things are costly…I believe we could…" For pity's sake, Urquhart, pull yourself together! "Mr. Jhabwala, could I ask how much you were thinking of giving?"

In reply Jhabwala twirled the combination lock on his case and flipped the two brass catches. The lid sprang open and he turned the case to face Urquhart.

"Would £50,000 be an acceptable gesture of support?"

Urquhart resisted the ferocious temptation to pick up one of the bundles of notes and start counting. He noticed that all the wads were of used £20 notes and were tied with rubber bands rather than bank wrappers. He had little doubt that none of this money had passed through formal accounts.

"This is…most generous, Mr. Jhabwala. Yes, certainly, as I say, most very generous. But…it is a little unusual, for such a large donation to the Party, to come—in cash."

"My dear Mr. Urquhart, you will understand that during the civil war in India my family lost everything. Our house and business were destroyed, we only narrowly escaped with our lives. A mob burned my local bank to the ground—with all its deposits and records. The bank's head office apologized, of course, but without any records they could only provide my father with their regrets rather than the funds he had deposited with them. It may seem a little old fashioned of me, I know, but I still prefer to trust cash rather than cashiers."

The businessman's teeth sparkled in reassurance. Urquhart was convinced this was trouble. He took a deep breath. "May I be blunt, Mr. Jhabwala?"

"But of course."

"It is sometimes the case with first-time donors that they believe there is something the Party can do for them, when in reality our powers are very limited…"

Jhabwala nodded in understanding even as his head weaved from side to side. "There is nothing I wish to do other than to be a firm supporter of the Prime Minister. And yourself, Mr. Urquhart. You will understand as a local MP that my business interests occasionally bring me into most friendly contact with local authorities on matters such as planning permission or tendering for contracts. I may at some point ask for your advice but I assure you I am looking for no favors. I want nothing in exchange. Absolutely nothing, no, no! Except, perhaps, to request that I and my wife have the honor of meeting with the Prime Minister at some suitable time, particularly if he should ever come to the constituency. Might that be acceptable? It would mean a very great deal to my wife."

£500 for a cup of tea, £50,000 for a photograph. The man struck a generous bargain.

"I am sure that could be arranged. Perhaps you and your wife would like to attend a reception at Downing Street."

"It would be an honor, of course, and perhaps to be able to have just a few private words with him, to express my great personal enthusiasm?"

A little more than a mere photograph, then, but that was only to be expected. "You will understand that the Prime Minister himself couldn't personally accept your donation. It would not be—how should I put it?—delicate for him to be involved with such matters."

"Of course, of course, Mr. Urquhart. Which is why I want you to accept the money on his behalf."

"I'm afraid I can only give you a rudimentary receipt. Perhaps it would be better if you delivered the money directly to the Party treasurers."

Jhabwala threw up his hands in horror. "Mr. Urquhart, sir, I do not require a receipt. Not from you. You are my friend. I have even taken the liberty of engraving your initials on this case. Look, Mr. Urquhart." He tapped the initials with his fingertip. FU stood out in bold capitals of gold. "It is a small gesture which I hope you will accept for all your wonderful work in Surrey."

You crafty, ingratiating little sod, thought Urquhart, all the while returning Jhabwala's broad smile and wondering how long it would be before he got the first call about planning permission. He should have thrown the Indian out but instead he reached across the table and shook Jhabwala's hand warmly. An idea was forming in his mind. This man and his money were undoubtedly trouble, of that there was no longer a shred of doubt. The question was, trouble for whom?

THIRTEEN

Westminster was once a riverside swamp. Then they transformed it, built a palace and a great abbey, piled it high with noble architecture and insatiable ambition.
But deep down it is still a swamp.

Friday, July 23

Praed Street, Paddington. A scruffy newsagent's in a street that was modest by day and, in the view of the local constabulary, far too ambitious by night. A young black woman hesitated on the pavement, took a breath of west London air, and stepped inside. Behind the security grille and dirty windows, the shop was dark and musty. The shopkeeper, an overweight middle-aged Italian in a tight T-shirt with a cigarette hanging from his lip, was bent over a magazine, the sort that had few words. He raised his eyes reluctantly. She asked about the cost of accommodation address facilities that he advertised on a card in the window, explaining that she had a friend who needed a private address for some of his personal mail. The shopkeeper brushed away the cigarette ash he had spilled over the counter.

"This friend of yours, he got a name?"

In reply she pushed across a copy of an old utility bill.

"No credit. I work only in cash," he said.

"So do I," she replied.

He offered her a fleshy smile, leered. "You do discounts?"

She stared at his midriff. "I'd have to charge you double."

He raised a lip, sneered, scribbled a quick note. She paid the fee for the minimum period of three months, put the receipt she would need for identification in her purse, and left. The shopkeeper stared at the retreating and delicately curved backside before being distracted by the complaints of an old age pensioner about the lack of her morning newspaper. He didn't see the young woman get into the taxi that had been waiting for her outside.

"All right, Pen?" O'Neill asked as she slammed the door behind her and settled into the seat beside him.

"No problem, Rog," his assistant answered. "But why the hell couldn't he do it himself?"

"Look, I told you. He has some delicate personal problems to sort out and needs some privacy for his mail. Dirty magazines for all I know. So no questions, and not a word to anyone. OK?"

O'Neill was irritable, felt uncomfortable. Urquhart had sworn him to secrecy and he suspected the Chief Whip would be furious if he discovered that O'Neill had pushed the envelope and got Penny Guy to do his dirty work. But he knew he could trust Penny. And he resented the way Urquhart seemed to regard him as a dogsbody and made him feel so ridiculously insignificant.

As the taxi pulled away he settled back in the seat while his fingers toyed nervously until they touched the small plastic packet in his pocket. That would soon settle things for him. Make him feel himself once again.

❖   ❖   ❖

The day was growing ever hotter by the time the man in the sports jacket and trilby hat ventured into the north London branch of the Union Bank of Turkey on the Seven Sisters Road. He presented himself to the Cypriot counter clerk and inquired about opening an account. His eyes were hidden behind tinted glasses and he spoke with a slight but perceptible regional accent that the clerk couldn't quite place.

It took only a few minutes before the manager became available and the prospective new client was ushered into an inner sanctum. They exchanged pleasantries before the man explained that he lived in Kenya but was visiting the United Kingdom for a few months to develop his holiday and property portfolio. He was interested in investing in a hotel that was being built outside the Turkish resort of Antalya, on the southern Mediterranean coast.

The manager responded that he did not know Antalya personally but had heard that it was a beautiful spot and, of course, the bank would be delighted to help him in whatever way possible. He offered the prospective customer a simple registration form, requiring details of his name, address, previous banking reference, and other details. The customer apologized for being able to provide a banking reference only from Kenya but explained that this was his first trip to London in nearly twenty years. The manager assured the older man that the bank was very accustomed to dealing with overseas inquiries and a banking reference from Kenya did not pose any particular problem.

The customer smiled. The system operated in its own sweet time. It would take at least four weeks for the reference to be checked and would probably take another four before it would be established that the reference was false. Time enough for what he had in mind.

"And how would you like to open your account, sir?" the manager inquired.

The man pulled open a brown corduroy holdall and placed it on the desk between them. "I would like to make an initial deposit of £50,000—in cash."

"But, of course…" the manager said, struggling to contain his delight.

Francis Urquhart leaned back in his chair and, without removing his glasses, rubbed his eyes. The spectacles were years old, at least two prescriptions behind his current contacts, and were making his eyes ache. A simple disguise, but one he thought was more than adequate to avoid recognition by any but his closest colleagues. There was, after all, some benefit in being the most faceless senior member of Her Majesty's Government.

While Urquhart signed the necessary forms with a scrawl, the manager finished counting the money and began filling out a receipt. Banks are like plumbers, Urquhart thought; cash in hand and no questions asked.

"One other thing," Urquhart said.

"But of course."

"I don't want the cash sitting idle in a current account. I'd like you to purchase some shares for me. Can you arrange that?"

The manager was nodding delightedly. More commission.

"I'd like you to purchase twenty thousand ordinary shares in the Renox Chemical Company PLC. They're currently trading at just over 240p per share, I believe."

The manager consulted his screen and assured his client that the order would be completed by 4:00 p.m. that afternoon, at a cost of £49,288.40 including stamp duties and brokers' fees. It would leave precisely £711.60 in the new account. Urquhart signed yet more forms with a flourish and the same illegible signature.

The manager smiled as he pushed the receipt across the desktop to his new client. "It is a great pleasure doing business with you, Mr. Collingridge."

Monday, July 26—Wednesday, July 28

End of term. The final week before the start of the summer recess. And a heat wave. Many MPs had already abandoned Westminster and those who had stayed at their posts were left distracted and impatient. Surviving eighty degree temperatures inside a building where the idea of air conditioning was to open a window and flap an Order Paper was an ordeal. But it would soon be over. Only seventy-two hours of bickering left.

The Government didn't mind the sense of distraction. The record would show that they, at least, had stuck to their posts, issuing wodges of Written Answers and press releases while others wilted. Ministers from the Department of Health were particularly grateful for the diversion since one of the many Written Answers they issued concerned the postponement of the hospital expansion program. Thanks to the leak it was already old news, but now it was on the record they could at least come out in daylight and not run for the shadows every time anyone asked.

The Department had other issues to deal with, too. Hospital waiting lists. A press release about the latest outbreak of mumps in Wales. And a routine announcement about three new drugs that the Government, on the advice of their Chief Medical Officer and the Committee on the Safety of Medicines, were licensing for general use. One of the drugs was Cybernox, a new medication developed by the Renox Chemical Company PLC that had proved startlingly effective in controlling the craving for nicotine when fed in small doses to addicted rats and beagles. The same excellent results had been obtained during extensive testing on humans, and now the entire population could get it under doctor's prescription.

The announcement caused a flurry of activity at Renox Chemicals. A press conference was called for the following day. The Marketing Director pressed the button on a pre-planned mail shot to every single general practitioner in the country, and the company's broker informed the Stock Exchange of the new license.

The response was immediate. Shares in the Renox Chemical Company PLC jumped from 244p to 295p. The twenty thousand ordinary shares purchased two days before by the Union Bank of Turkey's brokers were now worth £59,000, give or take a little loose change.

Shortly before noon the following day, a telephone call to the manager of the Union Bank of Turkey instructed him to sell the shares and credit the amount to the appropriate account. The caller also explained that regrettably the hotel venture in Antalya was not proceeding and the account holder was returning to Kenya. Would the bank be kind enough to close the account and expect a visit from the account holder later that afternoon?

It was just before the bank closed at 3:00 p.m. that the same man in the hat and sports jacket and tinted glasses walked into the branch on Seven Sisters Road. He was invited into the manager's office, where tea was waiting, but he declined. He watched as the manager and an assistant placed bundles of £20 notes on his desk to the value of £58,250.00, plus another £92.16 in other denominations, which the customer placed in the bottom of his brown corduroy bag. He eyebrows arched at the £742.00 in charges the bank had levied on his short-lived and simple account but, as the manager had suspected, he chose not to make a fuss. He asked for a closing statement to be sent to him at his address in Paddington and thanked the clerk for his courtesy.

The following morning and less than one week after Firdaus Jhabwala had met with Urquhart, the Chief Whip delivered £50,000 in cash to the Party treasurer. Substantial payments in cash were not unknown and the treasurer expressed delight at discovering a new source of funds. Urquhart suggested that the treasurer's office make the usual arrangements to ensure that the donor and his wife were invited to a charity reception or two at Downing Street, and asked to be informed when this happened so that he could make a specific arrangement with the Prime Minister's political secretary to ensure that Mr. and Mrs. Jhabwala had ten minutes alone with the Prime Minister beforehand.

The treasurer made a careful note of the donor's address, said that he would write an immediate and suitably cryptic letter of thanks, and locked the money in a safe.

Uniquely among the fellowship of Cabinet ministers, Urquhart left for holiday that evening feeling utterly relaxed.

PART TWO
THE CUT

FOURTEEN

I once won second prize at school. I got a Bible, bound in leather. A note inside the cover, written in copperplate, said it was a prize for achievement. Achievement? For coming second?

I read that Bible from cover to cover. I noticed that St. Luke said that we should forgive our enemies. I read the rest of his words, and the words of all the saints, truly I did. Nowhere did any of them mention a thing about forgiving our friends.

August

A time of respite, of pushing cares to one side, of summer showers and freshness, of ice cream and strawberries and lollipops and laughter, of remembering all those things that life should be about. Except the newspapers during August were bloody dreadful.

With politicians and the main political correspondents all away, second-string lobby correspondents struggled to fill the vacuum and cement their careers. So they chased every passing whisper. What was on Tuesday only a minor piece of speculation on page five had by Friday sometimes led the paper.

The August crowd wanted to make their mark, and the mark they chose all too frequently to make was on the reputation of Henry Collingridge. Backbenchers who had been left to molder and whom time had forgotten suddenly were honored with significant pieces describing them as "senior party figures," those who were new to the game were called "up and coming," and they were all given space so long as their views were salacious and spiced. Rumors about the Prime Minister's distrust of his Cabinet colleagues abounded, as did reports of their dissatisfaction with him, and since there was no one around to authoritatively deny the rumors the silence was taken as authoritative consent. The speculation fed on itself and ran riot.

Mattie's report sparked rumors about an "official inquisition" into Cabinet leaks. Soon after, they had grown into predictions that there would after all be a reshuffle in the autumn. The word around Westminster had it that Henry Collingridge's temper was getting increasingly erratic, even though he was enjoying a secluded holiday on a private estate many hundreds of miles away near Cannes.

It was during these dog days of August that the Prime Minister's brother also became the subject of a spate of press stories, mostly in the gossip columns. The Downing Street Press Office was repeatedly called upon to comment on suggestions that the Prime Minister was bailing out "dear old Charlie" from the increasingly close attentions of his creditors, including the Inland Revenue. Of course, Downing Street wouldn't offer any comment—it was personal, not official—so the formal "no comment" that was given to the most fanciful of accusations was recorded in the news coverage, usually with a twist and innuendo that left it bathed in the most damaging light.

August tied the Prime Minister ever more closely to his impecunious brother. Not that Charlie was saying anything stupid; he had the common sense to keep well out of the way. But an anonymous telephone call to one of the sensationalist

Sunday newspapers helped track him down to a cheap hotel in rural Bordeaux. A reporter was sent to pour enough wine down him to encourage a few vintage "Charlie-isms," but instead succeeded only in making Charlie violently sick over the reporter and his notebook. Then he passed out. The reporter promptly paid £50 to a big-busted girl to lean over the slumbering form while a photographer captured the tender moment for posterity and the newspaper's eleven million readers.

"'I'M BROKE AND BUSTED,' SAYS CHARLIE," the headline screamed while the copy beneath it reported that the Prime Minister's brother was nearly destitute and cracking under the pressure of a failed marriage and a famous brother. In the circumstances Downing Street's "absolutely no comment" seemed even more uncaring than usual.

The next weekend the same photograph was run alongside one of the Prime Minister holidaying in considerable comfort in the South of France—to English eyes a mere stone's throw from his ailing brother. The implication was clear. Henry couldn't be bothered to leave his poolside to help. The fact that the same newspaper a week earlier had been reporting how deeply Henry was involved in sorting out Charlie's financial affairs seemed to have been forgotten—until the Downing Street Press Office called the editor to complain.

"What the hell do you expect?" came the reply. "We always give both sides of the story. We backed him warts and all through the election campaign. Now it's time to restore the balance a bit."

Yes, the newspapers during August were dreadful. Truly bloody dreadful.

September–October

It got worse. As the new month of September opened, the Leader of the Opposition announced he was resigning to make

way for "a stronger arm with which to hold our banner aloft."
He had always been a little too verbose for his own good,
that was one of the reasons why he'd been pushed—that, and
losing the election, of course. He was killed off by the younger
men around him who had more energy and more ambition,
who made their moves quietly, almost without his knowing
until it was too late. He announced his intention to resign in
an emotional late-night interview from his constituency in the
heartland of Wales, but by the weekend almost seemed to
have changed his mind under pressure from his still intensely
ambitious wife, until he discovered that he could no longer
rely on a single vote in his Shadow Cabinet. Yet, once he had
gone, they were eloquent in praise of their fallen leader. His
death united his party more effectively than anything he had
achieved in office.

The arrival of a new political leader electrified the media
and gave them raw meat on which to feast. It wasn't enough to
satisfy them, of course. It did nothing but whet their appetite
for more. One down, more to follow?

When Mattie received her summons to hurry back to the
office she was with her mother in the kitchen of the old stone
cottage outside Catterick.

"But you've only just got here, love," her widowed mother
protested.

"They can't do without me," Mattie replied.

It seemed to mollify her mother. "Your da would be so proud
of you," she said as Mattie scraped charcoal from the slice of
toast she had just scorched. "You sure there's not a young man
you're missing?" she added gaily, teasing.

"It's work, Mum."

"But…Is there anyone you've found in London, caught your
eye, sort of thing?" her mother pressed, eying her daughter with
curiosity as she served up a plate of bacon and eggs fresh from
the pan. Mattie had been remarkably quiet since she'd arrived

a couple of days earlier. Something was going on. "I were so worried for you when you broke up with Whassisname."

"Tony, Mum. He has a name. Tony."

"Not since he was silly enough to give up on you."

"*I* gave up on *him*, Mum, you know that." Not a bad sort, Tony, far from it, but no ambition to go South, not even with Mattie.

"So," her mother muttered, wiping her hands on a tea towel, "is there anyone? In London?"

Mattie didn't speak. She stared out of the window, ignored the breakfast. It was answer enough for her mother.

"Early days, is it, pet? Well, that's good. You know, I was so worried when you went down to London. Such a lonely, unfriendly place. But if you've found your bit of happiness then that's all right wi' me." She stirred a spoonful of sugar into her mug of tea. "Perhaps it's not fair for me to say, but you know what your da thought about you. Nothing would've given him greater pleasure than to be around to watch you settle down."

"I know, Mum."

"Does he have a name?"

Mattie shook her head. "It's not like that, Mum."

But her mother knew better, could see it in her face, in the way her daughter's thoughts had been elsewhere, back in London, ever since she'd arrived. She put her hand on Mattie's shoulder.

"All in good time. Your da would be ever so proud of you, pet."

Would he? Mattie doubted that. She'd done no more than touch the sleeve of this man but had spent the weeks since then fixated with him, lying awake, jumping when the phone rang, hoping it was him. Conjuring up thoughts she should never have about someone who was three years older than her father would have been. No, her dad would never have understood, least of all approved. Mattie didn't understand it, either. So she said nothing and went back to her plate of cooling breakfast.

FIFTEEN

Party conferences can be such fun. They resemble a nest of cuckoos. Sit back and enjoy watching everyone trying to push the others out.

The Opposition elected its new leader shortly before the Party's annual conference in early October. The process of selecting a replacement front face seemed to galvanize them, gave them new hope, resurrection, and redemption wrapped in a bright red ribbon. The party that gathered together for its conference was unrecognizable as the rabble that had lost the election only a few months before. It celebrated beneath a banner that was as enormous as it was simple: VICTORY.

What took place the following week, as Collingridge's flock was gathered for its own conference, was in complete contrast. The conference center at Bournemouth could be uplifting when filled with four thousand enthusiastic supporters, but something was missing. Spirit. Ambition. Balls. The bare brick walls and chromium-plated fitments served only to emphasize the sullenness of those who gathered.

Which posed a considerable challenge for O'Neill. As Publicity Director he was charged with the task of packaging the conference and raising spirits; instead, he could be seen talking with increasing agitation to individual members of the media scrum, apologizing, justifying, explaining—and blaming. In particular, and when in alcohol, he blamed Lord Williams. The Chairman had cut the budget, delayed decisions, not got a grip on things. Rumors were circulating that he wanted the conference to be low key because he expected that the Prime Minister was likely to get a rough ride. "PARTY DOUBTS COLLINGRIDGE LEADERSHIP" was the first *Guardian* report to come out of Bournemouth.

In the conference hall, the debates proceeded according to a rigid pre-set schedule. An enormous sign hung above the platform—"FINDING THE RIGHT WAY." To many eyes it seemed ambivalent. The speeches struggled to obey its command and a distracting buzz took hold in margins of the hall that the stewards were quite incapable of quelling. Journalists and politicians gathered in little huddles in the coffee shops and rest areas, stirring tea and discontent. Everywhere they listened, the men from the media heard criticism. Former MPs who had recently lost their seats voiced their frustration, although most asked not to be quoted for fear of screwing up their chances of being selected for safer seats at the next election. However, their constituency chairmen showed no such caution. They'd not only lost their MPs but also faced several years of the Opposition in control of their local councils, nominating the mayor and committee chairmen, disposing of the fruits of local office.

And, as a previous prime minister had wistfully acknowledged, there were "events, dear, events" to reduce the hardiest of men to tantrums and despair. One of the most compelling events of the week was to be a by-election, due on Thursday. The Member for Dorset East, Sir Anthony Jenkins, had suffered a stroke just four days before the general election. He had been elected while in intensive care and buried on the day he should have been taking the Oath of Allegiance. Dorset East would have to do battle all over again. His seat, just a few miles from those gathering at Bournemouth, had a government majority of nearly twenty thousand, so the Prime Minister had decided to hold the by-election during conference week. There were those who had advised against it but he argued that, on balance, it was worth the risk. The conference publicity would provide a good campaigning background, and there would be a strong sympathy vote for Sir Anthony (not by those who knew the old sod, his agent had muttered). Party workers at the conference could take a few hours off and get in some much-needed canvassing, and, when they had finished their task and success was won, the Prime Minister would enjoy the enormous satisfaction (and cheap publicity) of being able to welcome the victorious candidate during his own conference speech. It was a plan. Of sorts.

Yet the busloads of conference-goers returning from their morning's canvass were bringing back reports of a coolness and complaint on the doorstep. The seat would be held, of course, nobody doubted that, it had been in the Party since the war, but the thumping victory that Collingridge had demanded was beginning to look more distant with every day.

Bugger. It was going to be a difficult week, not quite the victory celebration the Party managers had planned.

Wednesday, October 13

Mattie woke with a pounding headache. She looked out of the window at the sheet of grayness that had been pulled across the sky. A cold wet wind was blowing off the sea, tormenting seagulls and rattling her window. "Another day in paradise," she muttered, throwing back the covers.

She had little cause to be ungrateful. As the representative of a major national newspaper she was one of the few journalists fortunate enough to be offered accommodation in the headquarters hotel. Others fended for themselves in more distant venues and would get a damned good soaking by the time they made it to the conference center. Mattie, however, was one of the chosen few, accommodated in a hotel where she could mix freely with politicians and party officials. That was what accounted for her headache; she'd mixed a little too freely the previous evening. She'd been propositioned twice, once by a colleague and much later that evening by a Cabinet minister, who had gotten over Mattie's rejection by turning his attention to a young woman from a PR company. They had last been seen wandering off in the direction of the car park.

Mattie wasn't prudish about such matters. She and her colleagues deliberately stoked politicians with alcohol and there was a price to pay when the furnace grew overheated. A politician in a bar usually had one of two objectives—sex or slander—and such encounters provided a wonderful opportunity for Mattie to pick up gossip. The biggest problem was how many of the pieces her befuddled mind could pull together in the morning. She stretched her legs, trying to force the blood around her system, and made a tentative start on some calisthenics. Every limb screamed that this was a rotten way to cure a hangover so she opted instead for an open window—a move that she immediately recognized as the second bad decision of the day. The small hotel was perched high on the cliff tops, ideal for catching the summer sun but exposed on an autumn morning of scudding clouds and sea storms. Her overheated room turned into an icebox in seconds, so Mattie decided she would make no more decisions until after a gentle breakfast.

It was as she wandered out of the shower that she heard a scuffling noise outside in the corridor. A delivery. She pulled a towel around her and crossed to the door. Work, in the form of the morning newspapers, was piled outside on the hallway carpet. She gathered them up and threw them carelessly toward the bed. As they spread chaotically over the rumpled duvet, a sheet of paper fluttered free and fell to the floor. She rubbed her eyes when she picked it up, then rubbed them again. The morning mists were slow to disperse. When they did she read the words emblazoned across the top of the sheet: "Opinion Research Survey No. 40, October 6." Even more prominent, in bold capital letters, was the word: "SECRET."

She sat down on the bed, rubbed her eyes once again to make sure. They've surely not started giving them away with the *Mirror*, she thought. She knew the Party conducted weekly surveys of public opinion but these had a highly restricted distribution, Cabinet ministers and a handful of top Party officials. She'd been shown copies on rare occasions, but only when they contained good news that the Party wanted to spread about a bit; otherwise they were kept under strictest security. Two questions immediately sprang into Mattie's mind, which was quickly recovering its edge. What good news could possibly be found in the latest survey? And why had it been delivered wrapped up like a serving of cod and chips?

As she read, her hand began to tremble in disbelief. The Party had won the election weeks ago with 43 percent of the vote. Now its popularity rating was down to 31 percent, a full 14 percent behind the Opposition. Avalanche and earthquake. Yet there was worse to come. The figures on the Prime Minister's popularity were appalling. He was miles behind the new Leader of the Opposition. About as popular as an intestinal worm. Collingridge was more disliked than any prime minister since Anthony Eden in his mad phase.

Mattie reknotted the towel around her and squatted on her bed. She no longer needed to ask why she had been sent the information. It was dynamite, and all she had to do was light the touch paper. The damage it would do if it exploded in the middle of the Party conference would be catastrophic. This was a deliberate act of sabotage and a brilliant story—*her* story, so long as she got it in first.

She grabbed for the telephone and dialed.

"What?" a sleepy woman's voice yawned.

"Hello, Mrs. Preston? It's Mattie Storin. Sorry, so sorry if I woke you. Is Grev there, please?"

There was some subdued muttering before her editor came on the phone. "Who's died?" he snapped.

"What?"

"Who's bloody died? Why else would you call me at such a bloody stupid time?"

"Nobody died. I mean…I'm sorry. I forgot what time it was."

"Shit."

"But it doesn't matter what time it is," she bit back. "It's a brilliant story."

"What is?"

"I found it with my morning newspapers."

"Well, that's a relief. We're now only a day behind the rest."

"No, Grev. Listen will you? I've got hold of the Party's latest polling figures. They're sensational!"

"How did you get them?"

"They were left outside my door."

"Gift wrapped, were they?" The editor never made much attempt to hide his sarcasm, and none at all at this hour of the morning.

"But they're really unbelievable, Grev."

"I bet they bloody are. So who left this little present outside the door, Santa Claus?"

"Er, I don't know." For the first time a hint of doubt crept into her voice. Her towel had slipped and she was sitting there naked. She felt as if her boss were staring at her. She was waking up very rapidly now.

"Well, I don't suppose it was Henry Collingridge who left them there. So who do you think wanted to leak them to you?"

Mattie's silence confessed her confusion.

"I don't suppose you were out on the town with any of your colleagues last night, were you?"

"Grev, what the hell's that got to do with it?"

"You've been set up, little girl. They're probably sitting in the bar right now with the hair of the dog pissing themselves with laughter. Which is more than can be said for me."

"But how do you know?"

"I don't bloody know. But the point is, Wonder Woman, neither do you!"

There was another embarrassed silence from Mattie as she tried in vain to retrieve her fallen towel and before she made a last, despairing attempt to persuade her editor. "Don't you even want to know what they say?"

"No. Not if you don't know where they came from. And remember, the more sensational they look, the more certain it is you're being set up. A bloody hoax!"

The sound of the telephone being slammed down exploded in her ear. It would have hurt even had she not been hung over. The page one headlines she had conjured up in her mind dissolved back into the gray morning mists. Her hangover was a million times more malevolent. She needed a cup of black coffee. Badly. She'd made a fool of herself. Not for the first time. But normally she didn't do it stark naked.

SIXTEEN

What is the point of drawing a line in the sand? The wind blows and before you know it you're right back where you started.

Mattie cursed her editor under her breath as she slipped down the broad stairs of the hotel and found her way into the breakfast room. It was still early, only a handful of enthusiasts yet about. She sat down at a table on her own praying she wouldn't be disturbed. She needed recovery time. She hid herself in an alcove behind a copy of the *Express* and hoped people would conclude she was working rather than fixing a hangover.

The first cup of coffee bounced off her like a pebble skimming water but the second helped, a little. Slowly her depression began to loosen its grip and she began to take some interest in the rest of the world. Her gaze worked its way round the small Victorian room. In a far corner she spotted another political correspondent in a huddle of conversation with a minister. Elsewhere a senior party figure with his wife, a television newscaster, an editor of one of the Sundays, two other people she thought she recognized but couldn't yet place. The young man on the next table she definitely didn't know. He sat, rather like Mattie, almost hiding from the rest of the room. He had a pile of papers and folders on the chair next to him and an air of academic scruffiness. A party researcher, she concluded, not because her intellect was yet working but because squeezed onto the table between the tea and toast was a folder with a prominent party logo, and a name. K. J. Spence.

Her professional instincts began gradually to reassert themselves under the steady bombardment of caffeine, and she reached inside her ever-present shoulder bag for a copy of the Party's internal telephone list that at some point she had begged or stolen—she couldn't remember which.

"Spence. Kevin. Extension 371. Opinion Research."

She rechecked the name on top of the folder, taking things one step at a time. She'd already waded through enough crap. She didn't want to make a fool of herself yet again, not before lunchtime at least. Her editor's sarcasm had undermined her faith in the leaked poll's statistics but it also left her wanting to rescue something from the fiasco. Maybe she could find out what the real figures were. She caught the man's eye.

"Kevin Spence, isn't it? From Party Headquarters? I'm Mattie Storin of the *Chronicle.*"

"Oh, I know who you are," he replied, flustered, but also delighted to have been recognized.

"Can I join you for a cup of coffee, Kevin?" she asked, and without waiting for a reply moved across to his table.

Kevin Spence was aged thirty-two but looked older, was unmarried and a life-long creature of the Party machine with a salary of £10,200 (no perks). He was shy, bespectacled, awkward, bobbed up and down, not knowing whether it was the done thing to rise to a young woman at the breakfast table. Mattie shook his hand and smiled, and soon he was explaining with enthusiasm and in detail about the regular reports he'd given during the election to the Prime Minister and the Party's War Committee.

"They spent the entire campaign claiming that they took almost no notice of opinion polls," she prodded, "that the only poll that mattered—"

"—was the one on election day," he interrupted, delighted they were on a wavelength. "Yes, it's a little fiction we have. My job depends on them taking things seriously, although between you and me, Miss Storin—"

"Mattie."

"Some of them might be said to take the polls too seriously."

"How could that be, Kevin?"

"There's always a margin of error. And a rogue poll, just when you don't need it! Those wicked little creatures still sneak their way through from time to time."

"Like the one I've just seen," Mattie remarked with a twinge, still tender from her earlier embarrassment.

"What do you mean?" Spence inquired, suddenly cautious, returning his tea to its saucer.

As Mattie stared at him she saw that the affable official had become formal, his hands clasped together on the tablecloth. A flush was spreading upwards from the collar to the eyes, and the eyes themselves had lost their eagerness. Spence wasn't a trained politician and had no skill at hiding his feelings. His confusion was flowing through, yet why was he so flustered? Suddenly, Mattie mentally kicked herself. Surely the damned figures couldn't be right after all? But why not hoist them up the flagpole and see if someone saluted? She'd already jumped several somersaults that morning and made a fool of herself in the process; one more leap could scarcely dent her professional pride any further.

"I understand, Kevin, that your latest figures are quite disappointing. Particularly those about the Prime Minister."

"I don't know what you're talking about." His hands were still clasped together, in prayer, or was it to stop them trembling? Then, in distraction, he made a grab for his cup but succeeded only in spilling it. In despair, he tried to mop up the mess with his napkin.

Meanwhile Mattie had reached once more inside her bag and pulled out the mysterious sheet of paper, which she proceeded to smooth out on the tablecloth. As she did so, she noticed for the first time the initials KJS typed along the bottom. The last dregs of her hangover vanished.

"Aren't these your latest figures, Kevin?"

Spence tried to push the paper away from him as though it had some deep infestation. "Where on earth did you get that?" He looked around desperately to see whether anyone had noticed the exchange.

Mattie picked up the note and began reading it out loud. "Opinion Research Survey Number Forty—"

"Please, Miss Storin!"

He wasn't a man used to dissembling, far too transparent to travel in safety, and he knew it. He could see no way of escape from his dilemma and decided that his only means of survival was to throw himself on the mercy of his breakfast companion. In a hushed voice he pleaded with her. "I'm not supposed to talk to you. It's strictly confidential."

"But Kevin, it's only one piece of paper."

His eyes darted once more around the room. "You don't know what it's like. If these figures get out, and I'm the one thought to have given them to you, I'd be ruined. Shafted. Absolutely stuffed. Everyone's looking for scapegoats. There are so many rumors flooding around. The PM doesn't trust the Chairman, the Chairman doesn't trust us, and nobody's going to take pity on a guy like me. I like my job, Miss Storin. I can't afford to be blamed for leaking confidential figures to you."

"I didn't realize morale was so bad."

Spence looked utterly miserable. "You can't imagine. I've never known it worse. Frankly, all most of us are trying to do is to keep our heads down so that when it hits the fan we get as little of it as possible." He looked at her eye-to-eye for the first time. "Please, Mattie, don't drag me into this."

Sometimes she hated her job, and herself. This was one of those moments. She had to squeeze him until the pips squeaked. "Kevin, you didn't leak this report. You know it, I know it, and I'll confirm that to anyone who wants to know. But if I'm to help you, I shall need a little help myself. This is your latest polling report, right?"

She pushed the paper back across the table. Spence took another anguished look at it and nodded.

"They are prepared by you and circulated on a tightly restricted basis."

Another nod.

"All I need to know from you, Kevin, is who gets them. That can't be a state secret, can it?"

There was no more fight left in the man. He seemed to hold his breath for a long time before replying. "Numbered copies are circulated in double-sealed envelopes solely to Cabinet ministers and five senior headquarters personnel: the Deputy Chairman and four senior directors." He tried to moisten his mouth with another drink of tea but discovered he had already spilled most of it. "How on earth did you get hold of it?" he demanded wretchedly.

"Let's just say someone got a little careless, shall we?"

"Not my office? Tell me it wasn't my office!"

"No, Kevin. Do the arithmetic. You've just given me the names of more than two dozen people who get to see these figures. Add in their secretaries or assistants and that brings the possible number of sources to well over fifty." She gave him one of her most reassuring, warm smiles. "Don't worry, I won't involve you."

Relief flooded his face.

"But let's keep in touch," she added.

Mattie left the breakfast room with Spence's gratitude, which made her feel better, and his home phone number, which made her feel better still. Part of her felt elated about the front page story she was now able to write, and the sense of satisfaction she would get when she watched her editor eat his version of humble pie. The news desk would wine out on that for a week. Yet through it all cut another, altogether more powerful consideration. Any one of fifty-odd people could have been the turncoat, setting up Collingridge by leaking this piece of paper. So who the hell was it?

❖　❖　❖

Room 561 in the hotel could not be described as five-star. It was one of the smallest rooms, far away from the main entrance at the end of the top floor corridor and squeezed under the eaves. This wasn't where the Party hierarchy stayed, it was definitely a room for the workers.

Penny Guy was taken unawares. She hadn't heard any sound of approaching steps before the door burst open. She sat bolt upright in bed, startled, exposing two perfectly formed breasts.

"Shit, Roger, don't you ever bloody knock?" She threw a pillow at the intruder in exasperation more than anger. "And what the hell are you doing up so early? You don't normally surface until lunchtime." She didn't bother covering herself as O'Neill sat down at the end of the bed. There was an ease between them suggesting an absence of any sexual threat, which would have startled most people. O'Neill constantly flirted with her, particularly in public, could be proprietorial when other men came on the scene; yet on the two occasions when Penny had mistaken the signals and offered more than secretarial service, O'Neill had been very affectionate and warm and muttered about being too exhausted. She guessed it wasn't her, it was his way with all women, that he had a deep streak of sexual insecurity running through him which he hid beneath flattery and innuendo. He'd been married once, way back, a pain that still pursued him through the mists of years, another part of his private life he was keen to cover up. Penny had worked for O'Neill for nearly three years and was devoted to him, longing to ease his insecurities, but he never seemed willing to drop his guard. To those who didn't know him well he was extrovert, amusing, full of charm, ideas, and energy, but Penny had watched him become increasingly erratic. His caution, even paranoia, about relationships had grown worse in recent months as he found the pressures of political life increasingly infatuating, even as he found them steadily more difficult to cope with. Nowadays he rarely came into the office before noon; he had started making many private phone calls, getting agitated, disappearing suddenly. Penny wasn't in any respect naive but she did love him, and her devotion made her blind. She knew he depended on her and, if he didn't need her in his bed, he needed her practically every other moment of his day. The bond between them was strong, and while it wasn't all that she wanted, she was willing to wait.

"You got up this early just to come and woo me, didn't you?" she teased, pouting in her bed.

"Cover yourself up, you little tart. That's not fair. *They're* not fair!" he exclaimed, gesturing at her body.

Playfully, provocatively, she threw back the bedclothes. She was starkly, stunningly naked.

"Oh, Pen, my darling, I wish I had this moment captured forever, in oils and on my wall."

"But not in your bed."

"Pen, please! You know I'm not at my best this early in the morning."

Reluctantly, she reached for her gown. "Yes, it is rather early for you, Rog. You haven't been up all night, have you?"

"Well, there was this incredibly beautiful Brazilian gymnast who's been teaching me a whole series of new exercises. We didn't have any gymnastic rings, so we used the chandelier. OK?"

"Shut up, Rog," she said firmly, her mood grown gray like the morning sky. "What's going on?"

"So young and yet so cynical?"

"It's never let me down."

"Which? Youth or cynicism?"

"Both. Particularly where you are concerned. So tell me the real reason you're here."

"OK, OK. I had to make a delivery. In the vicinity. So…I thought I'd come and say good morning." It was almost the truth, as close as he got nowadays, but not all the truth. He didn't mention that Mattie Storin had nearly caught him as he was putting the document among her newspapers and needed a place to lie for a while. Oh, he'd scuttled down that corridor as though he were sidestepping his way through the entire English defense toward the try line. What fun! So it would cause the Party Chairman trouble. Brilliant. The cantankerous old sod had been particularly short with him these last few weeks, as Urquhart had pointed out. The paranoia that possessed O'Neill's mind completely failed to capture the fact that Williams had been short with almost everyone.

"Let's just say I believe you," Penny said. "But for pity's sake, Rog, next time you come to say good morning, try knocking first. And make it after eight-thirty."

"Don't give me a hard time. You know I can't live without you."

"Enough passion, Rog. What do you want? You have to want something, don't you, even if not my body?"

His eyes darted, like a guilty secret exposed. "Actually, I did come to ask you something. It's a bit delicate really…" He gathered together his salesman's charms and started upon the story that Urquhart had drummed into him the previous evening. "Pen, you remember Patrick Woolton, the Foreign Secretary. You typed a couple of his speeches during the election and he certainly remembers you. He, er, asked after you when I saw him last night. I think he's rather smitten with you. Anyway, he wondered if you would be interested in dinner with him but he didn't want to upset or offend you by asking direct, so I sort of offered, you know, to have a quiet word as it might be easier for you to say no to me rather than to him personally. You see that, don't you, Pen?"

"Oh, Rog." There were tears in her voice.

"What's the matter, Pen?"

"Pimping for him." Her tone was bitter, an accusation.

"No, no at all, Pen, it's only dinner."

"It's never been just dinner. Ever since the age of fourteen it's never been just dinner." She was second-generation immigrant, had been brought up in a crowded tenement off Ladbroke Grove and knew all the compromises required of a young black girl in a white male world. That didn't distress her unduly; it gave her opportunity, but she wouldn't have her dignity stripped away, not like this.

"He's the Foreign Secretary, Pen," O'Neill protested.

"With a reputation as long as the Channel Tunnel."

"But what have you got to lose?"

"My self-esteem."

"Oh, come on, Pen. This is important. You know I wouldn't ask if it weren't."

"What the hell do you think of me?"

"I think you are beautiful, truly I do. I see you every day and you're the one thing that brings laughter into my life. But I'm desperate. Please, Pen, don't ask but…you've got to help me on this. Just dinner, I swear."

They were both in tears, and in love with each other. She knew it hurt him to ask this of her, that for some reason he found himself with no choice. And because she loved him, she didn't want to know why.

"OK. Just dinner," she whispered, lying to herself.

And he threw himself at her and kissed her with joy before he rushed out as breathlessly as he had barged in.

Five minutes later he was back in his own room and on the phone to Urquhart. "Delivery made and dinner fixed, Francis."

"Splendid, Roger. You've been most helpful. I hope the Foreign Secretary will be grateful too."

"But I still don't see how you're going to get him to invite Penny to dinner. What's the point of all this?"

"The point, dear Roger, is that he won't have to invite her to dinner at all. He is coming to my reception this evening. You will bring Penny, I shall introduce them over a glass of champagne or two, and see what develops. If I know Patrick Woolton—which as Chief Whip I do—it won't take more than twenty minutes before he's suggesting that he might help her improve her French etiquette."

"But I still don't see where that gets us."

"Whatever happens, Roger, and that we must leave in the hands of two consenting adults, you and I will know about it."

"I still don't see what use that is," O'Neill protested, still hoping the other man might change his mind.

"Trust me, Roger. You must trust me."

"I do. I have to. I don't really get much choice, do I?"

"That's right, Roger. Now you are beginning to see. Knowledge is power."

The phone went dead. O'Neill thought he understood but still wasn't absolutely sure. He was still struggling to figure out whether he was Urquhart's partner or prisoner. Unable to decide, he rummaged in his bedside cabinet and took out a small carton. He swallowed a couple of sleeping pills and collapsed fully clothed on the bed.

SEVENTEEN

Political office is like life. Your attitude toward it is usually determined by whether you are arriving or departing.

P atrick. Thanks for the time," Urquhart greeted as the Foreign Secretary opened the door.

"You sounded serious on the phone. When the Chief Whip says he want an urgent private word with you, it usually means he's got the photographs under lock and key but unfortunately the *News of the World* has got the negatives!"

Urquhart smiled and slipped through the open door into Woolton's suite. It was late afternoon, the gale had stopped blowing but the umbrella standing in a puddle in Woolton's hallway spoke of a tormenting day. Urquhart hadn't come far, indeed only a few yards from his own suite in a series of luxury bungalows that stood in the hotel grounds. They had been set aside for Cabinet ministers, all of whom had a twenty-four-hour rotation of police guards running up huge bills. The local constabulary had christened it "Overtime Alley."

"Drink?" the genial Lancastrian offered.

"Thanks, Patrick. Scotch."

The Right Honorable Patrick Woolton, Her Majesty's Principal Secretary for Foreign and Commonwealth Affairs and one of Merseyside's many successful emigrés, busied himself at a small drinks cabinet that bore the signs of already having been put to use that afternoon, while Urquhart placed the ministerial red box he was carrying beside the four belonging to his overworked host, close to the edge of the puddle of rainwater. These brightly colored leather-clad boxes were the mark of any minister, their almost constant companions that guarded the official papers, speeches, and other confidential items. A Foreign Secretary requires several red boxes; the Chief Whip, with no conference speech to make and no foreign crises to handle, had arrived in Bournemouth with his box filled with three bottles of twelve-year-old malt whiskey. Hotel drink prices are always staggering, he explained to his wife, even when you can find the brand you want.

Now he faced Woolton across a paper-strewn coffee table, and dispensed with the small talk. "Patrick, I need to get your opinion. In the strictest confidence. As far as I am concerned, this has to be one of those meetings which never took place."

"Christ, you do have some bloody photographs!" exclaimed Woolton, now only half joking. His eye for attractive young women had led him down a few perilous paths. Ten years earlier when he was just starting his ministerial career, he had spent several painful hours answering questions from the Louisiana State Police about a weekend he'd just spent in a New Orleans motel with a young American girl who looked twenty, acted as if she were thirty and turned out to be just a few days over sixteen. The incident had been brushed over but Woolton had never forgotten the tiny difference between a glittering political future and a charge of statutory rape.

"Something which could be rather more serious," Urquhart muttered. "I've been picking up some unhealthy vibrations in the last few weeks. About Henry. You've sensed the irritation with him around the Cabinet table, and the media seem to be falling out of love with him in a very big way."

"Well, there was no reason to expect an extended honeymoon after the election, I suppose, but the storm clouds have been remarkably quick to gather."

"Patrick, in confidence, I've been approached by two of the most influential grassroots party members. They say that feeling at local level is getting very bad. We lost two more important local council by-elections last week in what should have been very safe seats, and we're going to lose quite a few more in the weeks ahead."

"Bloody East Dorset by-election tomorrow. We're going to get kicked in the crotch on that one, too, you mark my words. We'd have trouble winning a vote for local dog-catcher at the moment."

"There is a view, Patrick," Urquhart continued in a tone of considerable discomfort, "that Henry's personal unpopularity is dragging the whole Party down."

"It's a view I share, frankly," Woolton said, sipping his whiskey.

"The question is, how much time does he have to sort it out?"

"With a majority of only twenty-four, not much." Woolton was cupping his hands around his glass for comfort. "A few lost by-elections and we'd be facing an early election." He stared into the peaty liquid, then up at his colleague. "So what's your view, Francis?"

"As Chief Whip I don't have a view."

"You always were a canny bugger, Francis."

"But as Chief Whip I have been asked by one or two of our senior colleagues to take some gentle soundings about how deep the problem actually goes. In short, Patrick, and you will appreciate this isn't easy…"

"You haven't touched your bloody drink."

"Give me one more moment. I've been asked to find out how much trouble colleagues think we are in. Cards on the table. Is Henry any longer the right leader for us?" He raised his glass,

stared hard at Woolton, then took a deep draught before settling back in his chair.

The silence settled around the Foreign Secretary, impal-
ing him on the point of the question. "Well, bugger me,
it's come to that already, has it?" A pipe appeared from his
pocket, followed by a tobacco pouch and a box of matches.
He made an elaborate ceremony of filling the bowl, tamping
down the fresh tobacco with his thumb, before taking out a
match. The striking of the match seemed very loud in the
silence. Smoke began to rise from around Woolton as he
drew on the pipe stem until the sweet smelling tobacco was
well alight and his face was almost obscured from view by a
clinging blue fog. He waved his hand to disperse it, coming
out of hiding. "You'll have to forgive me, Francis. Four years
in the Foreign Office hasn't prepared me particularly well for
handling direct questions like that. Maybe I'm not used any
more to people coming straight to the point. You've knocked
me out of my stride."

This was nonsense, of course. Woolton was renowned for
his direct, often combative political style, which had found an
uneasy home in the Foreign Office. He was simply playing for
time while he collected his thoughts.

"Let's try to put aside any subjective views"—he blew
another enormous cloud of smoke to hide the patent insincer-
ity of the remark—"and analyze the problem like a civil service
position paper."

Urquhart nodded, and smiled inwardly. He knew Woolton's
personal views, he already knew the conclusion their hypo-
thetical civil servant was going to arrive at.

"First, have we got a problem? Yes, and it's a serious one.
My lads back in Lancashire are hopping mad. I think it's right
that you should be taking soundings. Second, is there a pain-
less solution to the problem? Let's not forget we did win the
bloody election. But we didn't win it like we should've. And

that's down to Henry. But"—he waved the stem of his pipe for emphasis—"if there was any move to replace him—which is essentially what we are discussing…"

Urquhart contrived to look pained at Woolton's bluntness.

"It would raise hell inside the party and those bastards in the Opposition would have a field day. It could get very messy, Francis. There's no guarantee Henry would go quietly. And it would look like an act of desperation. It would take a new leader at least a year to glue together the cracks. So we shouldn't fool ourselves that getting rid of Henry represents an easy option. No, sir. But, third, when all is said and done, can Henry find the solution to the problem himself? Well, you know my views on that. I stood against him for the leadership when Margaret went, and I've not changed my mind that his selection was a mistake."

Urquhart lowered his head, stony faced, as though in gratitude for the candor, but in celebration. He had read his man well.

Woolton was refilling their glasses while continuing his analysis. "Margaret managed an extraordinary balance of personal toughness and sense of direction. She was ruthless when she had to be and often when she *didn't* have to be as well. She always seemed to be in such a bloody hurry to get where she was going that she had no time to take prisoners and didn't mind trampling on a few friends, either. It didn't matter so much because she led from in front. You've got to give that to the girl. But Henry doesn't have a sense of direction, only a love of office. And, without that sense of direction, we're lost. He tries to mimic Margaret but he hasn't got the balls." He banged a large glass down in front of his colleague. "So there we have it. If we try to get rid of him we're in trouble. But if we keep him, we're in shit." He raised his glass. "Confusion to the enemy, Francis." And he drank.

Urquhart hadn't spoken for nearly ten minutes. The tip of his middle finger was running slowly around the rim of his glass setting up a discordant wailing. His eyes came up, blue, penetrating. "But who is the enemy, Patrick?"

The stare was returned. "Whoever is most likely to bring us to defeat at the next election. The Leader of the sodding Opposition? Or Henry?"

"And your view? What *precisely* is it you are saying, Patrick?"

Woolton roared with laughter. "I'm sorry, Francis. Too much diplomatic claptrap. You know I can't even kiss the wife good morning without her wondering what my intentions are. You want a direct answer? OK. Our majority is too small. At the rate we're going we'll get wiped out next time around. We can't go on as we are."

"So what is the solution? We have to find one."

"We bide our time, that's what we should do. A few months. Prepare the public perception, put pressure on Henry to stand down, so that when he does we'll be seen to be bowing to what the public wants rather than indulging in private squabbles. Perceptions are crucial, Francis, and we'll need time to get our ducks in a row."

And you need a little time to prepare your own pitch, thought Urquhart. You old fraud. You want the job just as badly as ever.

He knew Woolton. The man was no fool, not in all things. He would already be planning to spend as many evenings as possible in the corridors and bars of the House of Commons, strengthening established relationships, making new friends, eating rubber chicken on the constituency circuit, chatting up newspaper editors and columnists, building up his credentials. His official diary would get cleared, he would spend less time traveling abroad and much, much more time dashing around Britain making speeches about the challenges facing the country in the next decade.

"That's your job, Francis, and a damned difficult one it is, too. To help us decide when the time is right. Too early and we'll all look like assassins. Too late and the Party'll be in pieces. You will have to keep your ear damned close to the ground. I assume you're taking soundings elsewhere?"

Urquhart nodded carefully in silent assent. He's nominated me as Cassius, he thought, put the dagger in my hand. Urquhart was exhilarated to discover that he didn't mind the sensation, not one bit.

"Patrick, I'm honored that you've been so frank with me. Deeply grateful for the confidence you've shown in me. The next few months are going to be difficult for all of us, and I will need your continuing counsel. You will always find in me a firm friend."

"I know I will, Francis."

Urquhart rose. "And, of course, not a word of this will pass outside this room."

"My Special Branch team are all going on at me about how walls have ears. I'm glad it's you who's got the bungalow next door!" Woolton exclaimed, thumping Urquhart playfully and a little patronizingly between the shoulder blades as his visitor strode over to retrieve his red box.

"I'm holding my conference reception this evening, Patrick. Everyone will be there, a most useful gathering. You won't forget, will you?"

"Course not. Always enjoy your parties. Be rude of me to refuse your champagne!"

"I'll see you in a few hours then," replied Urquhart, picking up a red box.

As Woolton closed the door behind his visitor, he poured himself another drink. He would skip the afternoon's debates in the conference hall. Instead he'd have a bath and a short sleep to prepare himself for the evening's heavy schedule. As he reflected on the conversation he'd just had he began to wonder whether the whiskey had dulled his senses. He was trying to remember how Urquhart had voiced his own opposition to

Collingridge, but couldn't. "Crafty sod. Let me do all the talking." Still, that's what was expected of a Chief Whip, and he could trust Francis Urquhart, couldn't he? As he sat there wondering whether he had been just a little too frank, he failed to notice that Urquhart had walked off with the wrong red box.

❖ ❖ ❖

Mattie had been in high spirits ever since sending through her copy shortly after lunch. Opinion poll shocker. A front page exclusive, at a moment when she was surrounded by every single one of her competitors. She had won bragging rights for this conference, that was for sure. She had spent much of the afternoon wistfully thinking about the new doors that were slowly beginning to open for her. She had just celebrated her first anniversary at the *Chronicle* and her abilities were getting recognition. Another year of this and maybe she'd be ready to make the next step, perhaps as an assistant editor or even as a columnist with room to write serious political analysis and not just daily potboilers. And with friends like Francis Urquhart she'd never be short of an inside story.

There was a price to be paid, of course. Her mother was still under the impression that she had found someone in London, a partner to share her life, but it was a hard and often lonely life, once she had gotten back to her apartment late at night and scrabbled yet again through her laundry bin in the morning. She had needs, not just professional vanity, and they were becoming increasingly difficult to ignore.

Neither could she ignore the urgent message to call her office that she got shortly before five o'clock. She had just finished chatting over tea on the terrace with the Home Secretary—he was keen to get the *Chronicle* to puff his speech the following day and in any event much preferred an hour chatting with a young blond than sitting through another interminable afternoon of his colleagues' speeches—when a receptionist thrust the message into her hand. The hotel lobby was crowded but one of the public telephones was free and she decided to put up with the noise. When she got through, Preston's secretary explained that he was engaged on the phone and connected her with the deputy editor, John Krajewski, a gentle giant of a man she had begun to spend a little time with during the long summer months, spurred on by a shared enjoyment of good wine and the fact that his father, like her grandfather, had been a wartime refugee from Europe. Nothing sexual, not yet, although he'd made it clear he wanted to swap more than office gossip. But his tone was suddenly awkward.

"Hi, Mattie. Look, er…Oh, fuck it, I'm not going to cover this in three yards of bullshit. We're not—he's not—running your story. I'm really sorry."

There was a stunned silence over the phone as she turned over the words to make sure she had understood correctly. But, whichever way she turned them, they still came out the same.

"What the hell do you mean you're not running it?"

"Just what I say, Mattie. It's not going to happen." Krajewski was clearly having grave difficulty with the conversation. "Look, I'm sorry I can't give you all the details because Grev has been dealing with it personally—I haven't touched it myself, please believe me on that—but apparently it's such a hot story that our esteemed editor feels he can't run it without being absolutely sure of our ground. He says we've always supported this Government and he's not about to throw editorial policy out of the window on the basis of an anonymous piece of paper. We have to be absolutely certain before we move, and we can't be if we don't know where this information came from."

"For God's sake, it doesn't matter where the bloody paper came from. Whoever sent it to me wouldn't have done it if he thought his identity was going to be spread all over our news-room. All that matters is that it's genuine, and I've confirmed that."

He sighed. "Trust me, I know how you must feel about this,

Mattie. I wish I were a million miles away from this one. All I can tell you is that Grev is adamant. It's not running."

Mattie wanted to scream long, hard, and very coarsely. Suddenly she regretted making the call from a crowded lobby. "Let me talk to Grev."

"Sorry. I think he's busy on the phone."

"I'll hold!"

"In fact," said the deputy editor in a voice heaped with embarrassment, "I know he's going to be busy for a long time and insisted that I had to be the one to explain it to you. I know he wants to talk to you, Mattie—but tomorrow. There's no point in trying to beat him into submission tonight."

"Tomorrow's no bloody good! Since when do we risk losing an exclusive because Grev's got his phone stuck up his arse?" Mattie spat out her contempt. "What sort of newspaper are we running, Johnnie?"

She could hear the deputy editor clearing his throat, unable to find suitable words. "Sorry, Mattie," was the best he could do.

"And screw you, Johnnie!" was all she was able to hiss down the line before slamming the phone back into its cradle. He didn't deserve it, but neither did she. She picked up the phone once again to see whether he was still on the end and was going to tell her it was all a stupid prank, but all she got was the disinterested buzzing of the dial tone. "Fuck!" she snapped, slamming the phone down once more. A conference steward on the next phone flashed her a tart look. She glared at him. "Fuck!" she said again, deliberately, just to make sure he'd heard, before stalking across the foyer toward the bar.

The steward was just raising the grille over the counter when Mattie arrived and slapped her bag and a five-pound note down on the bar. "I need a drink!" she declared, still in such a blind rage that she knocked the arm of another patron who was already lined up at the varnished counter and clearly intent on being served with the first drink of the night.

"Sorry," she apologized huffily without sounding as if she meant it.

The other drinker turned to face her. "Young lady, you say you need a drink. You look as if you need a drink. My doctor tells me there is no such thing as needing a drink, but what does he know? Would you mind if a man old enough to be your father joins you? By the way, the name's Collingridge, Mr. Charles Collingridge. But please call me Charlie. Everyone calls me Charlie."

"Well, Charlie, so long as we don't talk politics, it'll be my pleasure. Allow my editor to do the first decent thing he's managed today and buy you a very large one!"

EIGHTEEN

The world of Westminster is driven by ambition and exhaustion and alcohol. And lust. Especially lust.

The room had a low ceiling and was packed with people. Even with the windows wide open, "Overtime Alley" had come to resemble a Third World airport terminal. As a consequence the chilled champagne being dispensed by Urquhart's constituency secretary was in ever greater demand. The heat and alcohol cut through the formality and the occasion was already on its way to being one of the Chief Whip's more relaxed conference receptions.

Urquhart, however, was not in a position to circulate and accept his guests' thanks. He was effectively pinned in one corner by the enormous bulk of Benjamin Landless. The East End newspaper magnate was sweating heavily and he had his jacket off and collar undone, displaying his thick green braces like parachute webbing that were holding up his vast, flowing trousers. Landless refused to take any notice of his discomfort; his full attention was concentrated on his trapped prey.

"But that's all bloody bollocks, Frankie, and you know it. I put my whole newspaper chain behind you lot at the last election. I've moved my entire worldwide headquarters to

London. I've invested millions in the country. The way I see it, you owe me. But if Henry don't pull his fingers out the whole bloody circus is going down the drain at the next election. And because I've been so good to you, those buggers in the Opposition will crucify me if they get in. So stop pratting around, for God's sake!"

He paused to produce a large silk handkerchief from within the folds of his trousers and wipe his brow, while Urquhart goaded him on.

"Surely it's not as bad as that, Ben. All governments go through sticky patches. We've been through all this before. We'll pull out of it."

"Bollocks! That's complacent crap and you know it, Frankie. Haven't you seen your own latest poll? They phoned it through to me earlier this afternoon. Cata-bleedin'-strophic! If you held the election today you'd get thrashed. Bloody annihilated!"

Urquhart felt a rush of comfort as he envisaged the *Chronicle*'s headline in the morning, but couldn't afford to show it. "Damn. How on earth did you get hold of that? That will really hurt us at the by-election tomorrow."

"Don't mess your pants, Frankie. I've told Preston to pull it. It'll leak, of course, eventually, but that'll be after the by-election." He stuck a thick finger into his own chest. "I've saved your conference from being turned into a bear pit." He sighed deeply. "It's more than you bloody deserve."

"I know Henry will be grateful, Ben," Urquhart said, feeling sick with disappointment.

"Course he will," Landless growled, his finger now prodding into Urquhart's chest, "but the gratitude of the most unpopular Prime Minister since Christ was crucified isn't something you can put in the bank."

"What do you mean?"

"Get real, Frankie. Political popularity is cash. While you lot are in, I should be able to get on with my business and do what

I do best—make money. That's why I've supported you. But as soon as your boat starts taking in water everybody panics. The Stock Market sinks. People don't want to invest. Unions get bolshy. I can't look ahead. And that's what's been happening ever since June. The PM couldn't organize an arse-cracking contest right now. If he kissed a baby he'd be done for common assault. He's dragging the whole Party down, and my business with it. Unless you do something about it, we're all going to disappear down a bloody great hole."

"Do you really feel like that?"

Landless paused, just to let Urquhart know it wasn't the champagne speaking. "Passionately," he growled.

"Then it looks as if we have a problem."

"Damn right."

"What would you have us do, Ben?"

"Frankie, if my shareholders saw me screwing around like this, I wouldn't last till lunchtime. I'd be gone."

"You mean…?"

"Sure. Get rid of him. The Big Bye-Bye!"

Urquhart raised his eyebrows sharply but Landless was the sort of man who, once he mounted a horse and charged, had difficulty in turning the beast. "Life's too short to spend it propping up losers, Frankie. I haven't spent the last twenty years working my guts out just to watch your boss piss it all away."

Urquhart found his arm gripped painfully by his guest's huge fingers. There was real strength behind the man's enormous girth and Urquhart began to understand how Landless always seemed to get his way. Those he couldn't dominate with his wealth or commercial muscle he would trap with his physical strength and whip with his sharp tongue. Urquhart had always hated being called Frankie and this was the only man in the world who insisted on using it. But tonight, of all nights, he wouldn't object. This was one argument he was going to enjoy losing.

Landless drew nearer, conspiratorial, pinning Urquhart ever more tightly in the corner. "Let me give you an example, in confidence. OK, Frankie?" He glanced around to ensure no one was eavesdropping. "A little bird has told me that very shortly United Newspapers will be up for sale. If it is, I want to buy it. In fact, I've already had some serious discussions with them. But the limp-wrist lawyers are telling me that I already own one newspaper group and that the Government isn't going to allow me to buy another. I said to them, you are telling me that I can't become the biggest newspaper owner in the country, even if I commit all of the titles to supporting the Government!" Perspiration was slipping freely from his face but he ignored it. "You know what they said, Frankie? You know what those numb-nuts told me? That it's precisely because I *do* support the Government that I'm in trouble. If I so much as wink at United the Opposition's going to go apeshit. Kick up the most god-awful stink. And no one would have the guts to stand up and defend me, that's what they said. The takeover would be referred to the Monopolies and Mergers Commission, it'd get bogged down for months with a herd of expensive lawyers stuck in some bloody committee room, with me having to listen to a bunch of closet queens lecturing me on how to run my own business. And you know what makes me really fucking mad, Frankie?"

Urquhart blinked. Up close the man really was rather frightening. "I have no idea, Ben. Please tell me."

"What makes me really fucking mad"—the prodding finger again—"is that whatever arguments I use, whatever I say, in the end the Government will refuse to let the deal to go through. Why? Because they don't have the balls for a fight." He blew cigar smoke in Urquhart's face. "And because your Government doesn't have the balls, my dick's going to be shoved through the wringer. It's not enough that you're buggering up your own business, you're going to bugger up mine as well!"

Only then did Landless remove his finger from his host's

chest. It had been digging in painfully; Urquhart was sure he would find a bruise in the morning. His words came slowly.

"Ben, you have been a great friend of the Party. I, for one, very much appreciate what you have done. It would be unforgivable if we weren't able to repay that friendship. I can't speak for the Prime Minister on this—in fact, I find myself increasingly unable to speak for him on anything nowadays—but I would do everything I can to support you when you need it."

Landless was nodding. "That's good to know, Frankie. I like what you say, very much. If only Henry could be so decisive."

"I fear that's not his nature. But I know he'll be enormously grateful."

"For what?"

"For burying that opinion poll. I can't imagine what damage it would do to him if it were published. It would turn the entire conference into a bear fight."

"Yeah. It would, wouldn't it?"

"Mind you, there are those who believe that progress is never made without a little discomfort."

The frowns of frustration that had covered the Landless brow now gave way to a smile. His skin was remarkably pink and soft, his grin enormous. "I think I see your point, Frankie."

"What point was that, Ben?"

"Hah! I think we understand each other, you and me."

"Yes, Ben, I think we do."

Landless squeezed the Chief Whip's arm once more, but gently, in gratitude. Then he looked at his watch. "Tickle my tits, is that the time? I have work to do, Frankie. The first edition is closing in less than thirty minutes. I need to make a telephone call." He grabbed his jacket and draped it over his arm. "Thanks for the party. It's been fun. Won't forget it, Frankie."

Urquhart watched as the industrialist, damp shirt sticking closely to his broad back, pushed his way across the crowded room and disappeared through the door.

❖ ❖ ❖

Across the other side of the crowded room, hidden behind the squash of bodies, Roger O'Neill was huddled on a small sofa with a young and attractive conference-goer. He was in a state of considerable excitement. He fingers fidgeted incessantly, his eyes danced as though scalded, his words rattled out at an alarming pace. The young girl from Rotherham had already been overwhelmed with the names O'Neill had dropped and the secrets he had shared, an innocent bystander in a one-way conversation.

"The Prime Minister's under constant surveillance by our security men, of course. There's always a threat. Irish. Arabs. Black Militants. They're trying to get me, too. Been trying for months. The Special Branch boys insisted on giving me protection throughout the election. Found both our names on a hit list, Henry and me. So they gave me twenty-four-hour cover. Not public knowledge, of course, but all the journos know." He dragged furiously at a cigarette and started coughing. He took out a soiled handkerchief and blew his nose loudly, inspecting the result before returning it to his pocket.

"But why you, Roger?" his young companion ventured.

"Soft target. Easy access. High publicity hit," he rattled. "If they can't get the PM, they'll go for someone like me." He looked around nervously, his eyes not settling. "Can you keep a confidence? A real secret?" He took another deep drag. "This morning I found my car had been tampered with. Bomb Squad boys went over it with a fine tooth comb. They found the wheel nuts on one of the front wheels had been undone. Straight home on the motorway, the wheel comes off at eighty and—more work for the road sweepers! They think it was deliberate. The Murder Squad are on their way over to interview me right now."

"Roger, that's awful," she gasped.

"Mustn't tell anyone. The SB don't want to frighten them off if there's a chance of catching them unawares."

"I hadn't realized you were so close to the Prime Minister," she said with growing awe. "What a terrible time for…" She suddenly gasped. "Are you all right, Roger? You're looking very upset. Your, your eyes…" she stammered.

O'Neill's eyes were rotating wildly, sucking still further lurid hallucinations into his brain. His attention seemed to have strayed elsewhere; he was no longer with the young woman but in some other world, with some other conversation. His eyes wavered back to her but they were gone again in an instant. They were bloodshot and watering, had no focus, his nose was dribbling like an old man's in winter; he gave it a cursory and unsuccessful wipe with the back of his hand. As she watched, his face turned to an ashen gray, his body twitched and he stood up sharply. He appeared terrified, as if the walls were falling in on him.

She looked on helplessly, unsure what he needed, too embarrassed to make a public scene. She moved to take his arm and support him, but as she did so he turned on her and lost his balance. He grabbed at her to steady himself, caught her blouse, and a couple of buttons popped.

"Get out of my way, get out of my way," he snarled.

He thrust her violently backwards and she fell into a table laden with glasses before sprawling back onto the sofa. The crash of glass onto the floor stopped all conversation as everyone in the room turned to see what was going on. More buttons had gone and her left breast stood exposed.

There was absolute silence as O'Neill stumbled toward the door, pushing still more people out of the way before he tumbled into the night, leaving behind a room of shocked faces and a young girl clutching at her tattered clothing and fighting back tears of humiliation. An elderly female guest began helping her rearrange herself and shepherding her toward the bathroom. As the bathroom door shut behind them, the room instantly flooded with speculation that quickly grew into a broad sea of gossip that would keep them engaged and entertained all evening.

Penny Guy did not join in the gossip. A moment before, she had been laughing merrily, thoroughly enjoying the engaging wit and Merseyside charm of Patrick Woolton. Urquhart had introduced them more than an hour earlier and had ensured that the champagne flowed as easily as their conversation. But the moment of magic had dissolved in the uproar and Penny's bright smile withered into an expression of abject misery. She fought a losing battle to control the tears, which spilled down her cheeks and seemed unstoppable despite the encouragement and large white handkerchief that Woolton had provided. Her pain was all too real.

"He's really a kind man, brilliant at what he does," she explained. "But sometimes it all seems to get too much for him and he goes a little crazy. It's so out of character." As she pleaded for him the tears flowed still faster.

"Penny. I'm so sorry, love. Look, you need to get out of this bloody place. My bungalow's next door. What say you we go and dry you off there, OK?"

She knew what would happen. But it no longer seemed to matter very much. She nodded in gratitude and the couple squeezed their way through the crowd. No one seemed to notice as they eased their way out of the room, except Urquhart. His eyes followed them through the door where Landless and O'Neill had gone before. He felt deeply content. This was turning out to be a party to remember.

NINETEEN

Most by-election candidates are little more than legal necessities, required to make the victor feel he has done something worthwhile. Which he rarely has.

Thursday, October 14

Y ou're not going to make a bloody habit of getting me out of bed every morning, are you?" Even down the telephone line, Preston made it clear that he saw this as an instruction rather than a question.

Mattie was feeling even worse than she had managed the previous morning after several hours of alcoholic flagellation with Charles Collingridge. She was having considerable difficulty grasping the finer points of what was going on.

"Hell, Grev. I go to bed thinking I want to kill you because you won't run the opinion poll story. Then I wake up this morning and find a bastardized version of it all over the front page with a byline by someone called 'Our Political Staff.' I'm not *thinking* I want to kill you any more, I *know* I want to kill you. But first I want to find out why you're screwing around with my story. Why did you change your mind? Who's rewritten my copy? And who the hell is 'Our Political Staff' if it's not me?"

"Steady on, Mattie. Take a breath before you pop your corsets."

"I don't do corsets, Grev!"

"And you weren't doing much last night, were you? What were you up to, flashing your eyes at some eligible peer or burning your bra at some feminist coven? But *nada*. I tried to call. No bloody answer. If only you'd hung around, you'd have heard all about it."

Mattie began to recall the events of last night. It was a considerable effort, through a haze. Her distraction gave Preston time to continue.

"As I think Krajewski told you, last night some of the editorial staff here didn't believe there was enough substantiation on your piece for it to run today."

He heard Mattie snort with indignation.

"Frankly, I liked the piece, right from the start," he added, trying to sound as if he meant it. "I wanted to make it work, but we needed more corroboration before we tore the country's Prime Minister apart on the day of an important by-election. A single anonymous piece of paper wasn't enough."

"*I* didn't tear the Prime Minister apart, *you* did!" Mattie wanted to interject but Preston was already ahead of her.

"So I had a chat with some of my senior contacts in the Party, and late last night we got the backing we needed. Just before our deadline."

"But my copy—"

"The copy needed to be adapted, the story was moving on. I tried to reach you but since I couldn't, I rewrote it myself. Didn't want anyone else touching it, the story's too good. So 'Our Political Staff' in this instance is me."

"I wrote a piece about an opinion poll. You've turned it into the crucifixion of Collingridge. These quotes from 'leading party sources,' these criticisms and condemnations. Who else do you have working in Bournemouth apart from me?"

"My sources are my own business, Mattie, you should know that."

"Bullshit, Grev. I'm supposed to be your political correspondent at this bloody conference. You can't keep me in the dark like this. The paper's done a complete somersault over my story and another somersault over Collingridge. A few weeks ago the sun shone out of his backside as far as you were concerned and now he's—what does it say?—'a catastrophe threatening to engulf the Government at any moment.' I shall be about as popular as a witch's armpit around here this morning. You've got to tell me what's going on!"

Preston had tried. He'd offered an explanation. It wasn't the truth, but so what? Now he decided it was time to pull a little rank. "I'll tell you what's going on. A brilliant bloody exclusive, that's what's going on. And it may have passed your notice, Mattie, but I'm editor of this newspaper, which means I don't have to spend my day justifying myself to every cub reporter stuck out in the provinces. You do as you're told, I do as I'm told, and we both get on with the job. All right?"

"So who the hell tells you what to do, Grev?" Mattie demanded. But all she got in return was a dial tone. The phone had gone dead. She pounded the arm of her chair in frustration. She couldn't—wouldn't—take much more of this. She'd thought new doors were opening up to her; instead, her editor kept slamming them shut on her fingers. It made no sense to her.

It still made no sense a good thirty minutes later as she was trying to clear her thoughts with yet another cup of coffee in the breakfast room. She was relieved there was no sign of Kevin Spence. A pile of the morning's newspapers lay on the floor at her feet and she had to admit that Preston was right—it was a fine exclusive, the best front page of the lot. Great figures, great quotes. Too good for Greville Preston to have done it on a phone from London. As she scratched away at the puzzle she felt a shadow stretching across the room and looked up to see the vast bulk of Benjamin Landless lumbering across to a window table for a chat with Lord Peterson, the Party Treasurer. The proprietor settled his girth into a completely inadequate chair and leaned across as far as his belly would allow him. He smiled at Peterson, shook his hand, ignored Mattie completely. Suddenly she thought things were beginning to make a little more sense.

❖ ❖ ❖

The Prime Minister's political secretary winced. For the third time the press secretary had thrust the morning newspaper across the table at him, and for the third time he had tried to thrust it back. He knew how St. Peter must have felt.

"For God's sake, Grahame," the press secretary snapped, raising his voice, "we can't hide every damned copy of the *Chronicle* in Bournemouth. He's got to know, and you've got to show it to him. Now!"

"Why did it have to be today?" the political secretary groaned. "A by-election just down the road and we've been up all night finishing his speech for tomorrow. Now he'll want to rewrite the entire bloody thing, and where are we going to find the time? He'll blow a gasket." He slammed his briefcase shut in uncharacteristic frustration. "All the pressure of the last few weeks, and now this. There just doesn't seem to be any break, does there?"

His companion chose not to answer, preferring to study the view out of the hotel window across the bay. It was raining again.

The political secretary picked up the newspaper, rolled it up tight and threw it across the room. It landed with a crash in the waste bin, overturning it and strewing the contents across the carpet. The discarded pages of speech draft mixed with cigarette ash and several empty cans of beer and tomato juice.

"He deserves his bloody breakfast, for pity's sake. I'll tell him after that," he said.

It was not to be his best decision.

❖ ❖ ❖

Henry Collingridge was enjoying his eggs. He had finished his conference speech in the early hours of the morning and had left his staff to tidy it up and have it typed while he went to bed. He had slept soundly if briefly; it seemed for the first time in weeks.

The end-of-conference speech always hung over his head like a dark cloud. He disliked conferences and the small talk, the week away from home, the over-indulgence around the dinner tables—and the speech. Most of all the speech. Long hours of anguished discussion in a smoke-filled hotel room, breaking off just when progress seemed in sight in order to attend some ball-breaking function or reception, resuming a considerable time later and trying to pick up where they had left off, only more tired and less inspired. If the speech went well, it was only what they expected and required. If it was poor, they would still applaud but go away muttering about how the strain of office was beginning to show. Sod's Law.

Still, almost over, bar the delivery. The Prime Minister was relaxed enough to have suggested a stroll along the promenade with his wife before breakfast, blow the cobwebs away, to hell with the patchy rain. His Special Branch detectives followed a few paces behind. As they strolled, Collingridge was discussing the merits of a winter holiday in Antigua or Sri Lanka. "I think Sri Lanka this year," he said. "You can stay on the beach if you want, Sarah, but I'd rather like to take a couple of trips into the mountains. They've got some ancient Buddhist monasteries there, and the wildlife reserves are supposed to be quite spectacular. The Sri Lankan President was telling me about them last year and they sounded really...Darling, you're not listening!"

"Sorry, Henry. I was…just looking at that gentleman's news-paper." She nodded at a man, another conference-goer, who was struggling to hold his newspaper in the sea breeze.

"More interesting than me, is it?"

Yet his light-heartedness died on the wind as he began to feel ill at ease, remembering that no one had yet given him his daily press cuttings. Someone would surely have told him had there been anything that important, but… He'd made a mistake, a few months back, when his staff had persuaded him that he didn't need to spend his time reading the daily newspapers, that an edited summary would be more efficient. But civil servants had their own narrow views on what was important for a Prime Minister's day and he'd found increasingly that their summaries had holes in them, particularly when it came to political matters, even more so when there was bad news. They were trying to protect him, of course, but he'd always feared the cocoon they spun around him would eventually stifle him.

He remembered the first time he'd stepped inside 10 Downing Street as Prime Minister after the drive back from the Palace. He had left the crowds and the television crews outside and, as the great black door closed behind him, he had discovered an extraordinary sight. On one side of the large hallway lead-ing away from the door had gathered some two hundred civil servants, who were applauding him loudly—just as they had done Thatcher, Callaghan, Wilson, and Heath, and just as they would his successor. On the other side of the hallway facing the host of civil servants stood his political staff, the team of loyal supporters he had hurriedly assembled around him as his cam-paign to succeed Margaret Thatcher had begun to take off, and whom he had invited to Downing Street to enjoy this historic moment. There were just seven of them, dwarfed in their new surroundings. An impossibly unequal struggle. He'd scarcely seen his party advisers for the next six months as they were effectively squeezed out by the official machine, and none of the original band was still left. No, it wasn't a good idea to rely so completely on officials, he'd decided. He had also decided to do away with the press summaries and go back to reading real news, but he hadn't yet got round to it. Next week, for sure.

His attention returned to the newspaper being shaken back into shape by its owner. It was several yards away and at such a distance he had great difficulty in bringing it fully into focus. He tried hard not to stare too hard. Slowly the words came into some form of focus.

"POLL CRISIS HITS GOVERNMENT," it screamed.

He walked the five paces and snatched the newspaper from the startled man.

"PM's FUTURE IN DOUBT AS PERSONAL SLUMP HITS PARTY," he read. "BY-ELECTION DISASTER FEARED."

"Henry!" his wife shouted in alarm.

"What the bloody—" the man spluttered before his words froze as he recognized his assailant.

"Are you all right, Prime Minister?" one of the detectives asked, putting his body protectively between them.

Collingridge's head sank. "Forgive me, I didn't mean…I'm so sorry," he muttered in apology.

"No, Prime Minister, I'm the one who's sorry," the man said, recovering his wits. "You deserve better than this."

"I do, don't I?" Collingridge muttered before turning and striding back to the hotel.

❖ ❖ ❖

It did nothing to improve the Prime Minister's temper when he had to retrieve the copy of the *Chronicle* from among the cigarette ash in the waste bin.

"From a complete bloody stranger, Grahame. May I, just occasionally, not be the last to know?"

"I am sorry, Prime Minister. We were going to show it to you just as soon as you'd finished breakfast," came the meek response.

"You think I have any appetite left after this? Look at this rubbish! It's not good enough, Grahame, it's just not bloody—"

He stopped. He had arrived at the point in the *Chronicle's* report when the hard news had been superseded by speculation and hype.

> *The latest slump revealed in the Party's private polls is bound to put intense pressure on the Prime Minister. He makes his conference speech tomorrow in Bournemouth, and it will be seen as of still greater importance, perhaps even decisive. Rumblings about the style and effectiveness of Collingridge's leadership have grown since the election, when his performance disappointed many of his colleagues. These doubts are certain to be fueled by the latest poll, which gives him the lowest personal rating any Prime Minister has achieved since these polls began nearly forty years ago.*

"Oh, shit," Collingridge mouthed silently as he read on.

> *Last night, a leading Minister commented, "There is a lack of grip around the Cabinet table and in the House of Commons. The Party is restive. Our basically excellent position is being undermined by the leader's lack of appeal." Harsher views were being expressed in some Government quarters. Senior party sources were speculating that the Party was fast coming to a crossroad. "We have to decide between making a new start or sliding gently into decline and defeat," one senior source said. "We have had too many unnecessary setbacks since the election. We cannot afford any more." A less sanguine view was that Collingridge is "like a catastrophe threatening to engulf the Government at any moment."*

"Shit!" Collingridge exclaimed out loud, no longer bothering to whisper.

Today's parliamentary by-election in Dorset East, reckoned to be a safe Government seat, is now being seen as crucial to the Prime Minister's future.

❖ ❖ ❖

A man can spend half a lifetime at the top of the political ladder learning how to cope with his fear of heights, but sometimes he grows dizzy and it can all get too much for him.

"Find the sewer scum behind this, Grahame!" Collingridge snarled, throttling the newspaper in two hands like a Christmas chicken. "I want to know who wrote it. Who spoke to them. Who leaked the poll. And for breakfast tomorrow I want their balls on toast!"

"Shall I give Lord Williams a call?" the political secretary offered.

"Williams!" Collingridge exploded. "It's his fucking poll that's leaked! I don't want apologies, I want answers. Get me the Chief Whip. Find him, and whatever he is doing get him here. Right now."

The secretary summoned up his courage for the next hurdle. "Before he arrives, Prime Minister, could I suggest that we have another look at your speech? There may be various things you want to change—as a result of the morning press—and we don't have too much time…"

"The speech stays, just as it is. Every word. I'm not ripping up a perfectly good speech just because those half-wits of the press have gone out shit spreading. So find Urquhart. And find him now!"

❖ ❖ ❖

When the phone rang for Urquhart, who was sitting in his bungalow, it wasn't the Prime Minister but the Foreign Secretary on the end of the line. Much to Urquhart's relief, Woolton was chuckling.

"Francis, you're a damned fool!"

"My dear Patrick, I can't—"

"I'm going to have to put more water in your whiskey next time. You walked off with one of my boxes yesterday and left yours behind. I've got your sandwiches and you've got a copy of the latest secret plans to invade Papua New Guinea or whatever damn fool nonsense they're trying to get me to sign up to this week. I suggest we swap before I get myself arrested for losing confidential Government property. I'll be round in twenty seconds."

Soon Urquhart was smiling his way through an apology to his Ministerial colleague but Woolton brushed it aside.

"No matter, Francis. Truth is, I wouldn't have gotten round to reading the bloody stuff, not last night. Fact is, I've got to thank you. Turned out to be an exceptionally stimulating evening."

"I'm so glad, Patrick. These conferences can be such fun."

Yet as soon as Woolton had left, still chuckling, Urquhart's mood changed. He became serious, his brow furrowed with concern as he locked the door from the inside, testing the handle to make absolutely certain it was closed. He wasted no time in pulling the blinds down over the windows and, only when he was certain that there was no chance of his being observed, did he place the red box gingerly on the desk. He examined the box carefully for any signs of tampering, then selected a key from the large bunch he produced from his pocket, sliding it carefully into the lock. As the lid came up, it exposed neither papers nor sandwiches but a thick slab of polystyrene packing that entirely filled the box. He extracted the polystyrene and laid it to one side before turning the box on its end. Delicately he eased up the corner of the red leather, peeling a strip of it back until it revealed a small hole that had been carved right through the wall of the box. The recess measured no more than two inches square, and snuggling neatly in its middle was a radio transmitter complete with its own miniaturized mercury power pack, compliments of its Japanese manufacturer.

The manager of the security shop just off the Tottenham Court Road he had visited two weeks earlier had displayed a mask of utter indifference as Urquhart had explained his need to check up on a dishonest employee. "Happens," was all he said. He'd shown considerably more enthusiasm in describing the full capabilities of the equipment he could supply. This was one of the simplest yet most sensitive transmitters on the market, he'd explained, which was guaranteed to pick up almost any unobstructed sound within a distance of fifty meters and relay it back to the custom-built receiver and voice-activated tape recorder. "Just make sure the microphone is pointing generally toward the source of the sound, and I guarantee it'll sound like a Mahler symphony."

Urquhart went over to his wardrobe and pulled out yet another ministerial red box. Inside, nestling in another protective wrapping of polystyrene, sat a modified FM portable radio with built-in cassette recorder that was tuned to the wavelength of the transmitter. Urquhart noticed with satisfaction that the long-playing tape he had installed was all but exhausted. Plenty of noise to activate the recorder, then.

"I trust it's not simply because you snore, Patrick," Urquhart joked with himself. As he did so, the equipment clicked once more into action, ran for ten seconds, and stopped.

He pressed the rewind button and was watching the twin reels spin round when the telephone rang again, summoning him to the Prime Minister. Urgently. Another plumbing lesson.

"Never mind," he said, running his fingers over both red leather boxes, "you'll wait."

He was laughing as he went out the door.

TWENTY

Some politicians think of high office like a sailor thinks of the sea, as a great adventure, full of unpredictability and excitement. They see it as the way to their destiny. I see it as something they will probably drown in.

Saturday, October 16

It wasn't just the *Chronicle* that, the day after the Prime Minister's speech, declared it to be a disaster. Almost all the other newspapers joined in, as did several Government backbenchers and the Leader of the Opposition.

The loss of the Dorset East by-election, when the news had burst upon the conference in the early hours of Friday morning, had at first numbed the Party faithful, but the feeling had worn off by breakfast. Over their muesli or full English they began to vent their frustration, and there could be only one target. Henry Collingridge.

By lunchtime, correspondents in Bournemouth seemed to have been inundated with nameless senior Party officials, each of whom claimed to have warned the Prime Minister not to hold the by-election in conference week and who were now absolving themselves of responsibility for defeat. In turn, and in desperation, the Prime Minister's office retaliated—off the record, of course. They said the blame was down to Party Headquarters for which, of course, Lord Williams was responsible. The explanation, however, fell largely on deaf ears. The pack instinct had taken hold.

As one traditionally pro-government newspaper put it:

> *The Prime Minister failed yet again yesterday. He should have used his speech to quell growing doubts about his leadership, yet one Cabinet colleague described the speech as "inept and inappropriate." Following the disastrous opinion poll and the humiliating by-election defeat in one of its safest seats, the party was looking for a realistic analysis and reassurance. Instead, in the words of one representative, "we got a stale rehash of an old election speech."*
>
> *The criticism of Collingridge has become more open. Peter Bearstead, MP for marginal seat of Leicester North, said last night: "The electorate gave us a warning slap across the knuckles at the election. It's not going to be satisfied with clichés and suffocating complacency. It may be time for the Prime Minister to think about handing over."*

In an office tower on the South Bank of the Thames, the editor of *Weekend Watch*, the leading current affairs program, studied the newspapers and called a hurried conference of his staff. Twenty minutes later, the program planned for the following day on racketeering landlords had been shelved and the entire sixty-minute slot had been recast. Bearstead was invited to participate, as were several opinion pollsters and pundits. The new program was entitled "Time To Go?"

From his home in the leafy suburbs near Epsom, the senior manager of market makers Barclays de Zoete Wedd telephoned two colleagues. They agreed to be in the office particularly early on Monday. "All this political bollocks is going to upset the markets. Time to shift a little stock before the other bastards start selling."

The defeated candidate in the East Dorset by-election was contacted by the *Mail on Sunday*. The paper had deliberately waited until after he'd finished a lunch spent drowning his sorrows. The candidate's animus about his party leader was intense. "HE COST ME MY SEAT. CAN HE FEEL SAFE IN HIS?" Great headline.

In his magnificent Palladian country home in the New Forest of Hampshire, Urquhart was telephoned by several Cabinet colleagues and senior backbenchers expressing their concerns. The chairman of the Party's grassroots executive committee also called him from Yorkshire reporting similar worries. "You know I'd normally pass these on to the Party Chairman, Francis," the bluff Yorkshireman explained, "but it looks like open warfare between Party Headquarters and Downing Street. Damned if I'm going to get caught in the middle of that."

Meanwhile, at Chequers, the Prime Minister's official country residence set amidst rolling lawns and massive security in rural Buckinghamshire, Collingridge just sat, ignoring his official papers and devoid of inspiration. The rock had begun to roll downhill, and he hadn't the slightest idea how to stop it.

❖ ❖ ❖

The next blow, when it fell later that afternoon, caught almost everyone by surprise. Even Urquhart. He'd expected the *Observer* to take at least a couple more weeks checking the bundle of papers and photostats he had sent them, entirely anonymously. A bit of due diligence with the lawyers was the least he'd expected but it seemed the *Observer* feared that a competitor might also be on the trail. "Damned if we don't publish, damned if we do. So let's go!" the editor had shouted at his newsroom.

Urquhart was in his garage where he kept his 1933 Rover Speed Pilot when the call came. The Rover was a car he used for hurtling carelessly through the lanes of the New Forest "like a pink-skinned version of Mr. Toad," as his wife would say, safe in the knowledge that no policeman was going to be petty enough to book such a beautiful British classic, and in any event the chief constable was a member of the same golf club. Urquhart was adjusting the triple carburetors when Mortima called from inside the house. "Francis! Chequers on the phone!" He picked up the extension on the garage wall, wiping his hands carefully on a greasy rag. "Francis Urquhart here."

"Chief Whip, please hold. I have the Prime Minister for you," a female voice instructed.

The voice that stumbled down the phone was almost unrecognizable. It was faded, uncertain, drained. "Francis, I am afraid I've had some bad news. The *Observer* has been in touch. Bastards. They say they're running a story tomorrow. Can't explain it, but they say my brother Charles has been buying shares in companies with inside information—government information. Making a killing on them. They say they've got documentary evidence—bank statements, brokers' receipts, the lot. He bought nearly £50,000 worth of Renox, they say, a couple of days before we approved a new drug of theirs. Sold them a day later for a substantial profit. Did it all from a false address in Paddington, they say. It's going to be the lead story." There was an exhausted pause, as if he no longer had the energy to continue. "Francis, everyone's going to assume he got the information from me. What on earth do I do?"

Urquhart settled himself comfortably in the old leather seat of the car before replying. It was a seat from which he was used to taking risks. "Have you said anything to the *Observer*, Henry?"

"No. I don't think they were expecting a comment from me. They were really trying to find Charlie."

"Where is he?"

"Gone to ground, I hope. I managed to get hold of him. He…was drunk. I just told him to take the phone off the hook and not to answer the door."

Urquhart gripped the steering wheel, staring ahead. He felt strangely detached. He had set in motion a machine that was far more powerful than his ability to control it. He could no longer be certain what lay around the next bend, only that he was speeding much faster than could ever be considered safe. He couldn't stop, didn't want to. It was already too late for second thoughts.

"Where is Charlie?"

"At home in London."

"You must get someone down there to take care of him. He can't be trusted on his own, Henry. Look, I know it must be painful but there's a drying-out clinic outside Dover which the Whips' Office has used for the occasional backbencher. Very confidential, very kind. Dr. Christian, the head of the clinic, is excellent. I'll give him a call and get him to come to Charlie. I'm afraid you'll have to arrange for someone else from the family to be there, too, in case Charlie cuts up rough. Who do you think? Your wife, perhaps? We've got to move fast, Henry, because in a few hours the *Observer* will hit the streets and your brother's home is going to be under siege. We have to beat those bastards to the punch. With Charlie in his present state there's no knowing what he might say or do."

"But what do we do then? I can't hide Charlie forever. He's got to face up to it sooner or later, hasn't he?"

"Forgive me for asking, Henry, but did he do it? The shares?"

The sigh that came down the phone was like old air escaping from a long-buried coffin. "I don't know. I simply don't know. But…" The hesitation stank of doubt and defeat. "Apparently we did license a new Renox drug. Anyone holding any of their shares would have made a handsome profit. But Charlie hasn't got any money to pay his basic bills, let alone to splash around on shares. And how would he know about Renox?"

Urquhart came back in a tone that brooked no argument. "We worry about that when we've taken care of him. He needs help, whether he wants it or not, and we've got to get him some breathing space. You and I, Henry, we've got to take care of him. And you in particular will have to be very careful, Henry." There was a short pause for the words to sink in. "You can't afford to get this one wrong."

Collingridge's wearied assent was mumbled down the phone. He had neither the will nor the capacity to argue, and he was glad for his Chief Whip's authoritativeness, even if it stripped away both his family pride and the dignity of his office.

"What else do I do, Francis?"

"Nothing. Not once we've got Charlie away. We keep our powder dry. Let's see precisely what the *Observer* says, then we can come out to do battle. In the meantime, we say nothing."

"Thank you, Francis. Please, call your Dr. Christian, ask if he will help. Sarah can be at my brother's home in just under two hours if she leaves right now. Take care of things. Oh…damn."

Urquhart could hear the emotion ripping through the Prime Minister's voice.

"Don't worry, Henry. Everything will work out," he encouraged. "Trust me."

❖ ❖ ❖

Charles Collingridge didn't object at first when his sister-in-law let herself into the flat with the spare key. She found him snoring in an armchair, the clutter of an afternoon's heavy indulgence spread around him. She spent five frustrating minutes trying to shake him awake, to little effect, until she resorted to ice wrapped in a tea towel. That was when he started to object. His protests grew louder when he began to understand what Sarah was saying, persuading him to "come away for a few days," but the dialogue became totally incoherent when she began to question him about shares. She could get no sense out of him, and neither could she persuade him to move.

It took the arrival of Dr. Christian and a junior Whip almost an hour later before the situation made progress. An overnight bag was packed and the three of them bundled the still-protesting brother into the back of Dr. Christian's car, which was parked out of sight at the back of the building.

It was fortunate for them that Charlie had lost the physical coordination to offer much resistance. Unfortunately, however, the whole matter had taken time, too much time, so that when the doctor's black Ford Granada swept out from behind the building into the high street with Sarah and Charles in the back, the whole scene was witnessed by an ITN camera crew that had just arrived on the scene.

The videotape of a fleeing Charles cowering in the back seat of the car, accompanied by the Prime Minister's distressed wife, was the lead item of the late evening news.

TWENTY-ONE

Loyalty may be good news, but it is rarely good advice.

Sunday, October 17

The scenes of the fugitive Charles Collingridge were still the lead news item as *Weekend Watch* came on the air. The program had been thrown together in frantic haste and there were many untidy ends. The control room reeked of sweat and stale tobacco, there had been no time for a proper run-through and the autocue script for the later parts was still being typed as the presenter welcomed his viewers.

They hadn't been able to persuade a single minister to appear; the harder they'd tried, the more belligerent the refusals had been. One of the tame pundits had still not arrived at the studio. The sound man was desperately searching for fresh batteries even as the studio manager counted down with his fingers and the studio went live. An overnight opinion poll had been commissioned through Gallup and the polling company's chief executive, Gordon Heald, was presenting the results himself. He'd been kicking his computer all morning and was looking slightly flushed. It wasn't just the lights, it was what his polling agents had found. Another fall in the Prime Minister's popularity. Yes, a significant fall, Heald admitted. No, there was no example of a previous prime minister who'd ever won an election after being so unpopular.

The gloomy prognostications were supported by two senior newspaper analysts and made all the more Stygian by an economist who predicted turmoil in the financial markets in the days ahead. He was cut off mid-ramble as the presenter switched his attention to Peter Bearstead. Normally the East Midlands MP would have been videotaped beforehand but there had been no time for recording, so he went live. He was scheduled on the director's log for no more than two minutes fifty seconds but that took no account of the fact that, once started, the Honorable, garrulous, and diminutive Member for Leicester North was more difficult to put down than a bad-tempered badger.

"Well, Mr. Bearstead, how much trouble do you think the Party is in?"

"That depends."

"On what?"

"On how long we have to struggle on with the present Prime Minister."

"So you're standing by your comment of earlier in the week that perhaps the Prime Minister should be considering his position?"

"No, not exactly. I'm saying he should resign. He's destroying our Party and now he's got himself wrapped up in what looks like a family scandal. It can't go on. It just can't!"

"But do you think the Prime Minister is likely to resign? After all, we've only just had an election. It might be almost five years before the next. That must leave enormous scope for recovering lost ground."

"We will not—not, I tell you—survive another five years with this Prime Minister!" The MP was agitated, passionate, rocking back and forth in his studio chair. "It is time for clear heads, not faint hearts, and I'm determined that the Party must come to a decision on the matter. If he doesn't resign, then we'll have to make him."

"But how?"

"Force a leadership contest."

"Against who?"

"Well, I'll bloomin' stand if no one else will."

"You're going to challenge Henry Collingridge for the Party leadership?" the presenter spluttered in surprise. "But surely you can't win?"

"Course I can't win," Bearstead responded, almost contemptuous. "But it'll focus the minds of the big beasts in our jungle. They're all griping about the PM but none of them has the guts to do anything. So, if they won't, then I will. Flush it all into the open."

The presenter's lower lip was wobbling as he tried to decide the right place to intervene. "I don't want to interrupt but I do want to be clear about this, Mr. Bearstead. You are saying that the Prime Minister must resign, or else you will stand against him for leadership of the Party?"

"There has to be a leadership election no later than Christmas: it's Party rules after an election. I know it's normally nothing but a formality, but this time around it's going to be a real contest. My colleagues are going to have to make up their minds."

An expression of pain seemed to have taken hold of the presenter's features. He was holding his earpiece, listening to a shouting match underway in the gallery. The director was demanding that the dramatic interview should continue and to hell with the schedule; the editor was shouting that they should get away from it before the bloody fool changed his mind and ruined a sensational story. An ashtray crashed to the floor, someone cursed very crudely.

"We're going for a short commercial break," the presenter declared.

TWENTY-TWO

Politics. The word is taken from the Ancient Greek. "Poly"
means "many."
 And ticks are tiny, bloodsucking insects.

Monday, October 18—Friday, October 22

Sterling began to be marked down heavily as soon as
the Tokyo financial markets opened. It was shortly
before midnight in London. By 9:00 a.m. and with all
the Monday newspapers screaming about the challenge to
Collingridge, the *FT* All Share Index was down 63 points. It
fell a further 44 points by lunchtime. The money men don't
like surprises.

The Prime Minister wasn't feeling on top form, either. He
hadn't slept and had scarcely talked since Saturday evening,
gripped by a strong depression. Rather than allow him to return
to Downing Street that morning, Sarah kept him at Chequers
and called the doctor. Dr. Wynne-Jones, Collingridge's loyal
and highly experienced physician, prescribed a sedative and
rest. The sedative gave some immediate release; Collingridge
had his first lengthy spell of sleep since the start of the Party
conference a week earlier, but his wife could still detect the

tension fluttering behind his closed eyelids. Even as he slept, his fingers remained firmly clamped onto the bedclothes.

Late on Monday afternoon, after he had emerged from his drugged sleep, he instructed the besieged Downing Street Press Office to make it known that, of course, he would be contesting the leadership election and was confident of victory, that he was too busy getting on with Government business to give any interviews but would have something to say later in the week. Charlie wasn't giving any interviews, either. He still wasn't making a word of sense about the shares, and the resulting official "No comment" was never going to be enough to steady the family boat.

Over at Party Headquarters Lord Williams ordered some more polling, and in a hurry. He wanted to know what the country really thought. The rest of the Party machinery moved less quickly. The rules for a contested leadership election were dusted off and found to be less than straightforward. The process was under the control of the Chairman of the Parliamentary Party's Backbench Committee, Sir Humphrey Newlands, while the choice of timing was left in the hands of the Party Leader. The confusion only grew when it emerged that Sir Humphrey, displaying an acutely poor sense of timing, had left the previous weekend for a holiday on a private island in the West Indies and was proving extraordinarily difficult to contact. This resulted in a flurry of speculation among the scribblers that he was deliberately keeping his head low, playing for time while the awesome powers of the Party hierarchy were mobilized to persuade "the Lion of Leicester," as Bearstead had been dubbed, to withdraw. By Wednesday, however, the *Sun* had discovered Sir Humphrey on a silver stretch of beach somewhere near St. Lucia along with several friends, including at least three scantily clad young women who were obviously nearly half a century younger than he. It was announced that he would be returning to London as soon as flights could be arranged. Like Charlie Collingridge, his wife was offering no public comment.

In such a stormy sea Henry Collingridge began to find himself drifting, cut off from the advice of his wise and wily Party Chairman. He had no specific reason to distrust Williams, of course, but the constant media prattle of a growing gulf between the two began to make a reality of what previously had been little more than irresponsible gossip. Distrust is a matter of mind, not fact. The proud and aging Party Chairman felt he couldn't offer advice without being asked, while Collingridge took his silence as evidence of disloyalty.

Sarah went to visit Charlie and came back late and very depressed. "He looks awful, Henry. I never realized quite how ill he was making himself. So much alcohol. The doctors say he was close to killing himself."

"I blame myself," Henry muttered. "I could have stopped him. If only I hadn't been so preoccupied...Did he say anything about the shares?"

"He's scarcely coherent; he just kept saying '£50,000? What £50,000?' He swore he'd never been anywhere near a Turkish bank."

"Bugger!"

"Darling..." She was biting her lip, struggling with the words. "Is it possible...?"

"That he's guilty? I simply don't know. But what choice do I have? He has to be innocent because if he did buy those shares, then who but a total fool is going to believe that I didn't tell him to do so. If Charlie is guilty, I'm going down, too."

She gripped his arm in alarm. "Couldn't you say that Charlie was ill, didn't know what he was doing, that he somehow... found the information without your knowing..." Her excuse faded away. Even she couldn't believe it.

He took her in his arms, surrounding her, reassuring her with his body in a way that his words could not. He kissed her forehead and felt the warmth of tears on his chest. He knew he was close to tears, too, and felt no shame in it.

"Sarah, I'm not going to be the one to finish off Charlie. God knows he's been trying hard enough to do that himself, but I am still his brother. Will always be that. On this one we'll either survive, or sink if we must. But, whatever happens, we'll do it as a family. Together."

❖ ❖ ❖

The party conference season had been six weeks of sleep deprivation and sweat, and it had been Mattie's intention to take a little time off to recover. A long weekend had been enough. No matter how much exotic Chilean wine she drank or how many old films she watched, her thoughts kept straying back to her job. And Collingridge. And Urquhart. And Preston. Particularly Preston. She picked up several sheets of sandpaper and began rubbing down the woodwork of her Victorian apartment, but it didn't help, no matter how much she attacked the old paint. She was still mad as hell with her editor.

The following morning at 9:30 she found herself back in the office, rooted to the leather armchair in front of Preston's desk, laying siege. He wasn't going to put the phone down on her this time. But it didn't help.

She'd been there nearly an hour when his secretary peered apologetically round the door. "Sorry, Matts, the Big Man's just called to say he's got an outside appointment and won't be in until after lunch."

The world was conspiring against Mattie, spreading sauce on her shirt. She wanted to scream and was building up to do so. It wasn't brilliant timing, therefore, when John Krajewski chose that moment to come looking for his editor.

"I didn't know you were in, Mattie."

"I'm not. At least, not for much longer." She stood up to go. Krajewski stood ill at ease; he often was in her company, liked her just a shade too much for comfort. "Look, Mattie, I've picked up the phone a dozen times to call you since last week, but…"

"But what?" she snapped.

"I guess I couldn't be bothered getting my head bitten off."

"Then you were…" She hesitated, about to snap and suggest he was correct in his assumption, but she bit it back. It wasn't his fault. "You were wise," she said, her voice softening.

Since his wife had died in a traffic accident two years earlier, Krajewski had lost much of his self-confidence, both about women and about his professional abilities. He was able, had survived, but the protective shell he had built around himself was only slowly cracking. Several women had tried, attracted by his tall, slightly gangly frame and sad eyes, but he wanted more than their sympathy and a mercy fuck. He wanted something—someone—to shake him up and kick-start his life once again. He wanted Mattie.

"You want to talk about it, Mattie? Over dinner, maybe? Away from all this?" He made an irritated gesture in the direction of the editor's desk.

"Are you putting the squeeze on me?" The slightest trace of a smile began to appear at the corners of her mouth.

"A gentle tickle, perhaps."

She grabbed her bag and swung it over her shoulder. "Eight o'clock. The Ganges," she instructed, trying in vain to look severe as she walked past him and out of the office.

"I'll be there," he shouted after her. "I must be a masochist, but I'll be there."

And he was. In fact he got there ten minutes early in order to get a beer down him before she arrived, five minutes late. He knew he would need a little artificial courage. The Ganges, just around the corner from Mattie's flat in Notting Hill, was a tiny Bangladeshi restaurant with a big clay oven and a propri-etor who ran an excellent kitchen during the time he allowed

himself away from trying to overthrow the Government back
home. When Mattie arrived she ordered a beer and kept pace
with Krajewski until the last of the tikka had been scraped
from the plate. She pushed it away from her, as though clearing space.

"I think I've made a terrible mistake, Johnnie."

"Too much garlic in the naan?"

"I want to be a journalist. A good journalist. Deep down I
think I have the makings of a great journalist. But it's not going
to happen with an arsehole as an editor, is it?"

"Grev does have his less attractive side, I suppose."

"I gave up a lot to come down to London."

"Funny, we blokes from Essex always think of it as coming
up to London."

"I've decided. Made up my mind. I'm not taking any more of
Greville Preston's crap. I'm quitting."

He looked deep into her eyes, saw the turmoil. He reached
out and took her hand. "Don't rush it, Mattie. The political
world is falling apart, you need a job, a ringside seat, to be part
of the action. Don't jump before you're ready."

"Johnnie, you surprise me. That's not the impassioned plea
to stay on as part of the team that I was expecting from my
deputy editor."

"I'm not speaking as the deputy editor, Mattie." He squeezed
her hand. "Anyway, you're right. Grev is a shit. His only
redeeming factor is that he's totally uncomplicated about being
a shit. Never lets you down. You know, the other night…"

"Tell me before I rip your balls off."

The waiter arrived with yet another round of beers. He took
the head off his before he replied.

"OK, newsroom shortly before the first edition deadline.
A quiet night, not much late breaking news. Grev's holding
forth, spinning us some yarn about how he'd been drinking
with Denis Thatcher the night of the Brighton bomb. No one

believed it; DT wouldn't be seen dead with Grev Preston, let
alone drinking with him, and Lorraine in Features swears she
was shagging him in Hove at the time. Anyway, he's halfway
through his pitch when his secretary shouts at him. A phone
call. So he disappears into his office to take it. Ten minutes
later he's back in the newsroom and very flustered. Someone's
lit a fire under him. 'Hold everything,' he shouts. 'We're going
to change the front page.' We all think, Jesus, they must have
shot the President, because he's in a real state, nervous. Then
he asks for your story to be put up on one of the screens and
announces that we're going to lead with it. But we're going to
have to beef it up."

"It doesn't make sense. The reason he spiked it in the first
place was because he said it was too strong!" she protested.

"Shut up and listen. It gets better. So there he is, looking over
the shoulder of one of our general reporters who's sitting at the
screen, dictating changes directly to him. Twisting it, hyping
it, turning everything into a personal attack on Collingridge.
'We've got to make the bastard squirm,' he says. And you
remember the quotes from senior Cabinet sources on which
the whole rewrite was based? I think he made them up, on the
spot. Every single one of them. Didn't have notes, just dictated
them straight onto the screen. Fiction from beginning to end.
Mattie, believe me, you should be over the bloody moon your
name wasn't on it."

"But why? Why on earth invent a story like that? What made
him change his mind in such a hurry? *Who* made him change?
Who was he talking to on the phone? Who was this so-called
source in Bournemouth?"

"I don't know."

"Oh, but I think I do," she whispered. "It has to be. Could
only be. Benjamin Bloody Landless."

"We don't work for a newspaper anymore; it's little more than
a lynch mob run for the personal amusement of our proprietor."

They both went back to their beers for a moment as they tried to drown their miseries.

"Oh, but it's not just Landless, is it?" Mattie said, as though the beer had refreshed her mind.

"Isn't it?" Krajewski had taken the opportunity of diving into his drink to run his eye yet again across Mattie. He was growing distracted, while she was growing more intent.

"Look, Grev couldn't have concocted that article without my copy, and I couldn't have written it without the leaked opinion poll. Believe in coincidence if you want, but there's somebody else, someone on the inside of the Party who's leaking polls and pulling strings."

"What, leaking all that other material since the election, too?"

"Of course!" She finished the rest of her beer in triumph. The adrenalin was pouring into her veins. This was going to make the best story of all. It was what she had come south for.

"Johnnie, you're right!"

"Am I?" he said, bewildered. He'd lost track of this one a couple of beers ago.

"This is definitely not the time to throw in the towel and resign. I'm going to get to the bottom of this even if I have to kill someone. Will you help me?"

"If that's what you want—of course."

"Don't sound so bloody despondent."

"It's just that…" Oh, to hell with hesitation. "You remember you said you'd rip my balls off if I didn't tell you everything."

"But you have."

"Could you do it all the same?"

"You mean…" Yes, he did, she could see it in his eyes. "Johnnie, I don't do office romances."

"Romance? Who's talking romance? We've both had far too much beer for that. I'd be quite happy with a good old fashioned shag for now."

She laughed.

"I think we both deserve it," he insisted.

She was still laughing as they left the restaurant hand in hand.

❖ ❖ ❖

The Downing Street statement—or briefing, in fact, because it wasn't issued in the form of a press release but through the words of the press secretary, Freddie Redfern—was simple. "The Prime Minister has never provided his brother with any form of commercially sensitive Government information. He has never discussed any aspect of Renox Chemicals with him. The Prime Minister's brother is extremely ill and is currently under medical supervision. His doctors have stated that he is not in a fit state to give interviews or answer questions. However, I can assure you that he categorically denies purchasing any Renox shares, having a false address in Paddington, or being involved in this matter in any way whatsoever. That's all I can tell you at the moment. And that's all you're getting on the record."

"Come on, Freddie," one of the assembled correspondents carped, "you can't get away with just that. How on earth do you explain the *Observer* story if the Collingridges are innocent?"

"I can't. Mistaken identity, getting confused with another Charles Collingridge, how do I know? But I've known Henry Collingridge for many years, just as you've known me, and I know he's incapable of stooping to such sordid depths. My man is innocent. You have my word on that!"

He spoke with the vehemence of a professional placing his own reputation on the line along with that of his boss, and the lobby's respect for one of their former colleagues swung the day for Collingridge—just.

"WE'RE INNOCENT!" bawled the front page of the *Daily Mail* the following day. Since no one had been able to unearth any fresh incriminating evidence, most of the other newspapers followed a similar line. For the moment.

❖ ❖ ❖

"Francis, you're the only smiling face I see at the moment."

"Henry, it will improve. I promise. The hounds will scatter once they lose the scent."

They were sitting together in the Cabinet Room, newspapers scattered across the brown cloth.

"Thank you for your loyalty, Francis. It means a great deal to me right now."

"The storm clouds are passing."

But the Prime Minister was shaking his head. "I wish that were so, but you and I know this is only a breathing space." He sighed. "I don't know how much firm support I still have among colleagues."

Urquhart didn't contest the point.

"I can't afford to run away. I have to give them something to hold onto, show I've nothing to hide. It's time to take the initiative once again."

"What do you intend to do?"

The Prime Minister sat quietly at his place, chewing the end of his pen. He glanced up at the towering oil painting of Robert Walpole, his longest-serving predecessor, that stood above the marble fireplace. "How many scandals and crises did he survive, Francis?"

"More than you will ever have to."

"Or be able to," Collingridge whispered, searching the dark, too clever eyes for inspiration. Suddenly he was distracted as the sun burst through the gray autumn skies, flooding the room with light. It seemed to give him hope. Life would go on.

"I've had an invitation from those bastards at *Weekend Watch*. They want me to appear this Sunday and put my own case—to restore the balance."

"I trust them like I do a nest of adders."

"Nevertheless, I think I must do it—and do it damned well! They've promised no more than ten minutes on the *Observer* nonsense, the rest on broad policy and our ambitions for the fourth term. Raising sights, lifting the argument out of the gutter. What do you think?"

"Me, think, Prime Minister? But I'm the Chief Whip, you don't pay me to think."

"I know I disappointed you, Francis, but right now I couldn't ask for a better man than you at my side. After this is over, I promise—you'll get what you want."

Urquhart nodded his head slowly in gratitude.

"Would you do it? If you were standing in my shoes?" Collingridge pressed. "Freddie Redfern says it's too dangerous."

"There are also dangers in doing nothing."

"So?"

"At times like these, with so much at stake, I believe a man must follow his heart."

"Excellent!" Collingridge exclaimed, clapping his hands. "I'm glad you think that way. Because I've already accepted."

Urquhart nodded in approval, yet suddenly the Prime Minister swore. He was staring at his hands. The pen had leaked. His hands were filthy, he was covered in ink.

❖ ❖ ❖

Penny Guy had been expecting a call from Patrick Woolton. Somehow he'd found the direct line number and had been using it, trying to invite her out once again. He'd been persistent but she had been adamant. It was a party conference thing, nothing more, although she had to admit that he had been fun and remarkably athletic for his age. A mistake, but a memory that hadn't hurt anyone. Yet the call, when it came, was from Urquhart wanting to speak to her boss. She put the call through and a few seconds later the door to his office was carefully closed.

It was some minutes later that Penny heard the sound of O'Neill's raised voice, although she couldn't decipher what he was shouting about. And when the light on the extension phone flashed off to indicate the call was finished, there was no sound of any kind from O'Neill's office. She hesitated for another few minutes but, pressed on by a mixture of curiosity and concern, she knocked gently on his door and opened it cautiously.

O'Neill was sitting on the floor in the corner of the room, propped up by the angle of two walls. His head was in his hands.

"Rog…?"

He looked up, startled, his eyes full of chaos and pain. His voice croaked and his speech was disjointed.

"He…threatened me, Pen. Fucking…threatened me. Said if I don't he would…I've got to alter the file…"

She knelt down beside him, his head on her breast. She had never seen him like this. "What file, Rog? What have you got to do?"

He tried to shake his head, wouldn't answer.

"Let me help you, Rog. Please."

His head jerked up, his expression wild. "No one can help me!"

"Let me take you home," she said, trying to lift him.

He shoved her away. "Get away from me!" he snarled. "Don't touch me!" Then he saw the look of pain in her eyes and some of the fire inside him seemed to die. He collapsed in the corner, like a little boy, hiding his head in shame. "I'm fucked, you see. Totally fucked. Nothing you can do. Anyone can do. Go away."

"No, Rog—"

But he pushed her away again, so savagely that she fell over backwards. "Fuck off, you little slut! Just…leave."

In tearful confusion she climbed to her feet. He was hiding his head from her again, wouldn't talk. She left. She heard the door slam behind her and the sound of it being locked from the inside.

TWENTY-THREE

The dust of exploded ambition makes for a fine sunset. And I love walking out in the evening.

Sunday, October 24

*W*eekend Watch. An entire nation watching. Lions and Christians—or one Christian, at least. Collingridge was beginning to relax as the program unfolded. He had rehearsed hard for the previous two days and the questions were much as expected, giving him an opportunity to talk with genuine vigor about the next few years. He had insisted that the questions about Charlie and the *Observer* allegations be kept until the end—he didn't want those whores in the production gallery welching on their promise to keep that to ten minutes. Anyway, he wanted to be well into his stride. After forty-five minutes discussing the national interest and its bright future, surely any fair-minded man would find the questions simply mean and irrelevant?

Sarah was smiling encouragingly from a seat at the edge of the studio floor as they went into the final commercial break. He blew a kiss at her as the floor manager waved his arms to let them know they were about to go back on air.

"Prime Minister, for the final few minutes of our program, I'd like to turn to the allegations printed in the *Observer* last week about your brother, Charles, and the implication of possible improper share dealing."

Collingridge nodded, his face serious, unflinching.

"I understand that earlier this week Downing Street issued a statement denying that your family had any connection with the matter, and suggesting that there may have been a case of mistaken identity. Is that correct?"

"No connection, no. Not at all. There may have been some confusion with another Charles Collingridge for all I know, but I'm really not in a position to explain the extraordinary *Observer* story. All I can tell you is that none of my family has had anything whatsoever to do with Renox shares. You have my word of honor on that." He spoke the words slowly, leaning forward, looking directly at the presenter.

"I understand that your brother denies ever having opened an accommodation address in a Paddington tobacconist's."

"Absolutely," Collingridge confirmed. "It's well known he's not in the best of shape right now but—"

"Forgive me for interrupting, Prime Minister, our time is very short. Earlier this week one of our reporters addressed an envelope to himself, care of Charles Collingridge, at the same address in Paddington used to open the bank account. It was a vivid red envelope to make sure it stood out clearly. Then yesterday he went to reclaim it. We filmed him. I'd like you to look at the monitor. I apologize for the poor quality but I'm afraid we had to use a concealed camera because the proprietor of the shop seemed very reluctant to cooperate."

The presenter swiveled his chair so that he, along with the audience, could see the grainy but still discernible video that was being shown on the large screen behind him. Collingridge flashed a look of concern at Sarah before cautiously turning his own chair. He watched as the reporter approached the counter, pulled out various pieces of plastic and paper from his wallet to identify himself, and explained to the shopkeeper that a letter was waiting for him in the care of Charles Collingridge who used this address for his own post. The shopkeeper, the same overweight and habitually offensive man who had served Penny several months before, explained that he wasn't going to release letters except to someone who could produce a proper receipt. "Lots of important letters come here," he sniffed. "Can't go handing them out to just anyone."

"But look, it's there. The red envelope. I can see it from here."

With a scratch at his belly and a frown of uncertainty, the shopkeeper turned and extracted the envelopes from a numbered pigeonhole behind him. There were three of them. He placed the red envelope on the counter in front of the reporter, with the other two envelopes to one side. He was trying to confirm that the name on the envelope, c/o Charles Collingridge, matched that of the reporter's identity cards, when the camera zoomed in on the other envelopes. It took a few seconds to focus before the markings on the envelopes came clearly into view. Both were addressed to Charles Collingridge. One bore the imprint of the Union Bank of Turkey. The other had been sent from the Party's Sales and Literature Office at Smith Square.

The presenter turned once more to his adversary. The Christian had been cornered.

"The first envelope from the Union Bank of Turkey seems to confirm that this address was used to buy and sell shares in the Renox Chemical Company. But we were puzzled about the letter from your own Party Headquarters. So we called your Sales and Literature Office, pretending to be a supplier with an order for Charles Collingridge but with an indecipherable address."

Collingridge knew what he must do. He must stop this rape of his brother's reputation and denounce the immoral and underhand methods used by the program, but his mouth had turned to desert sand and, while he struggled to find the words, the studio filled to the recorded sound of the telephone call.

"...so could you just confirm what address we should have for Mr. Collingridge and then we can get the goods off to him straight away."

"Just one minute, please," an eager young voice said. "I'll call it up on the screen."

There was the sound of a keyboard being tapped.

"Ah, here it is. Charles Collingridge, 216 Praed Street, Paddington, London W2."

"Thank you. Very much indeed. You have been most helpful."

The presenter turned once again to Collingridge. "Do you want to comment, Prime Minister?"

The Prime Minister stared, silent, wondering if this was the moment he should walk out from the studio.

"Of course, we took seriously your explanation that it might be a case of mistaken identity, of confusion with another Charles Collingridge."

Collingridge wanted to shout that it wasn't *his* explanation, that it was nothing more than an off-hand remark made without prejudice by his press secretary, but already the presenter was continuing, cutting off any route of escape.

"Do you know how many other Charles Collingridges there are listed in the London telephone directory, Prime Minister?"

Collingridge offered no response, but sat looking grim and ashen faced.

"I wonder if you'd be interested to know that there are no other Charles Collingridges listed in the London telephone directory. In fact, sources at British Telecom tell us that there is only one Charles Collingridge listed throughout the United Kingdom. And that's your brother, Prime Minister."

Again a pause, inviting a response, but none was offered.

"Since this appears to be an abuse of insider information, we asked both the Renox Chemical Company and the Department of Health if they had a Mr. Charles Collingridge working for them. Renox tells us that neither they, nor their subsidiaries, have any Collingridge among their employees. The Department of Health's Press Office was rather more cagey, promising to get back to us but they never did. However, their trade union office was much more cooperative. They, too, confirmed that there is no Collingridge listed as working at any of the Department's 508 offices throughout the country." The presenter shuffled his notes. "Apparently they did have a Minnie Collingridge who worked at their Coventry office until two years ago, but she went back to Jamaica." The lion smiled as he closed his jaws.

At the side of the stage Collingridge could see Sarah. Tears were running down her cheeks.

"Prime Minister, we've almost come to the end of our program. Is there anything you wish to say?"

Collingridge sat staring at Sarah, wanting to run to her and embrace her and lie to her that there was no need for tears, that everything would be all right. He was still sitting motionless in his chair as the eerie silence that had settled in the studio was broken by the program's theme music.

It was the end.

❖ ❖ ❖

On his return to Downing Street Collingridge went straight to the Cabinet Room. He entered stiffly, looking slowly and with an exhausted eye around the room. He walked slowly around the Cabinet table, so eloquently shaped like a coffin, trailing his fingers on the brown baize cloth, stopping at its far end, where he had first sat as the Cabinet's most junior member. It seemed so much longer than ten years ago, almost another lifetime.

When he reached his own chair, in the middle of the room, beneath the gaze of that great survivor Walpole, he reached for the single telephone that stood beside his blotter. The Downing Street switchboard was a legendary institution, simply known as "Switch," its female operators seeming to be endowed with powers of witchcraft that enabled them to reach anyone at any time. "Get me the Chancellor of the Exchequer. Please."

It took less than a minute before the Chancellor was on the line.

"Colin, did you see it? How badly will the markets react?"

The Chancellor gave an embarrassed but honest opinion.

"Bloody, eh? Well, we'll see. I'll be in touch."

Collingridge then spoke to the Foreign Secretary. "What damage, Patrick?"

"What's *not* damaged, Henry? We've been trying to stuff our brothers in Brussels for years. Now they're laughing at us."

"Is it recoverable?"

Collingridge got a prolonged silence in answer.

"Bad as that, eh?"

"Sorry, Henry."

And, for a fleeting moment, Collingridge thought the other man meant it.

Next it was the turn of the Party Chairman. Williams was ancient, filled with experience, had seen sad times before. He knew such occasions were best dressed in formality rather than friendship. "Prime Minister," he began, because he was speaking to the office rather than the man, "within the last hour I have had calls from seven of our eleven regional chairmen. Without exception, I am sorry to say, they believe the situation is quite disastrous for the Party. They feel that we are beyond the point of no return."

"No, Teddy," Collingridge contradicted wearily, "they feel that *I* am beyond the point of no return. There's a difference."

He made one more phone call. It was to his private secretary asking him to seek an appointment at the Palace around lunchtime the following day. The secretary rang back four minutes later to say Her Majesty would be available to see him at one o'clock.

And with that it was done.

He was supposed to feel relieved, a great burden lifted from his shoulders, but every muscle in his body hurt, as though he'd been kicked for hours by soccer thugs. He gazed up into the stern features of Walpole. "Oh, yes, you'd have fought the bastards, to the very end. You'd probably have won. But this office has already ruined my brother and now it is ruining me. I won't let it ruin Sarah's happiness, too," he whispered. "Better let her know."

A little while later he left the room in search of his wife, after he had dried his face.

PART THREE
THE DEAL

TWENTY-FOUR

The time for change is when it can no longer be resisted. In other words, when you have a man by the balls and are pulling hard, he will invariably follow in your footsteps.

Monday, October 25

The day after the disastrous outing on *Weekend Watch*, and shortly before ten o'clock, the members of the Cabinet assembled around the baize-covered table. They had been called individually to Downing Street rather than as a formal Cabinet, which was normally held on a Thursday, and most had been surprised to discover their colleagues also gathered. There was an air of tension. They dragged with them the contents of the newspapers and their explosive editorials, and the conversation around the table was unusually muffled while they waited for their Prime Minister.

As the tones of Big Ben striking the hour seeped into the room, the door opened and Collingridge walked in.

"Good morning, ladies and gentlemen." His voice was unusually soft. "I'm grateful to see you all here. I won't detain you long."

He took his seat, the only chair in the room with arms,

and extracted a single sheet of paper from the leather bound file he was carrying. He laid it carefully on the table in front of him and then looked slowly around at his colleagues. His eyes were raw, sleepless. There wasn't a sound to be heard in the room.

"I'm sorry I wasn't able to inform you that this morning's meeting was to be one of the full Cabinet. I wanted to ensure that you could all be assembled without creating undue attention and speculation." He looked around the table to see if he could read anything in their faces, in search of Barabbas. "I'm going to read to you a short statement that I'll be issuing later today. At one o'clock I shall be going to the Palace to convey the contents formally to Her Majesty. I must ask all of you, on your oaths of office, not to divulge the contents of this message to anyone before it's released officially. I must ensure Her Majesty hears it from me and not through the press. It's a matter of courtesy to the Sovereign. I would also ask it of each one of you as a personal favor to me."

He picked up the sheet of paper and began to read in a slow, matter-of-fact voice. "Recently there has been a spate of allegations in the media about the business affairs of both me and my family. These allegations show no sign of abating. I have consistently stated, and repeat today, that I have done nothing of which I should be ashamed. I have adhered strictly to the rules and conventions relating to the conduct of the Prime Minister."

He ran his tongue around dried lips. The paper he was holding trembled.

"The implied allegation made against me is one of the most serious kind for any holder of public office, that I have used my office to enrich my family. I cannot explain the extraordinary circumstances referred to by the media that have given rise to these allegations, so I have asked the Cabinet Secretary to undertake a formal independent investigation into them. I am confident that the official investigation by the Cabinet

Secretary will eventually establish the full facts of the matter and my complete exoneration."

He blinked, rubbed an exhausted eye.

"This investigation will inevitably take some time to complete. In the meantime the doubts and insinuations are doing real harm to the normal business of Government, and to my Party, and also to those I love. The time and attention of the Government should be devoted to implementing the program on which we were so recently re-elected, but this is not proving possible. The integrity of the office of Prime Minister has been brought into question, and it is my first duty to protect that office."

He cleared his throat, a sound of feathered thunder.

"Therefore, to re-establish and preserve that unquestioned integrity, I have today asked the permission of Her Majesty the Queen to relinquish the office of Prime Minister as soon as a successor can be chosen."

The silence was profound. Hearts had momentarily stopped beating.

"I have devoted my entire adult life to the pursuit of my political ideals," he continued, "and it goes against every bone in my body to leave office in this fashion. I am not running away from the allegations but rather ensuring that they can be cleared up as quickly and expeditiously as possible. I also want to bring a little peace back to my family. I believe history will show that I have made the right judgment."

Collingridge replaced the piece of paper in his folder. "Ladies and gentlemen, thank you," he said curtly, and, before anyone could sigh, let alone respond, he strode out of the door and was gone.

TWENTY-FIVE

All members of a Cabinet are referred to as Right Honorable Gentlemen. There are only three things wrong with such a title...

Urquhart sat at the end of the Cabinet table transfixed. As the murmuring and gasps of surprise broke out around him he would not, could not, join in. He gazed for a long time at the Prime Minister's empty chair.

He had done this. Alone. Had destroyed the most powerful man in the country. While the others around the table erupted in a babble of confusion, his mind turned to a memory forty years old, when as a raw military recruit he had prepared to make his first parachute jump 2,500 feet above the fields of Lincolnshire. Sitting in the open hatchway of a twin engine Islander, his feet dangling in the slipstream, gazing down at the landscape a million miles below. Jumping was an act of faith, of trust in one's destiny, showing contempt for acts that terrified others. But the view from up there had been worth the danger. As he and the others had jumped the wind had picked up, knocking them aside; one had broken a leg, another a shoulder, but Urquhart had wanted to go straight back up and do it all over again.

Now, as he gazed at the empty chair, he felt just the same. He gave an inner cry of joy while contriving outwardly to look as shocked as those around him.

❖ ❖ ❖

While others lingered, milling around in confusion, Urquhart walked the few yards back to the Chief Whip's office in 12 Downing Street. He locked himself in his private room and by 10:20 a.m. he had made two phone calls.

Ten minutes later Roger O'Neill called a meeting of the entire Press Office at Party Headquarters. "You guys are going to have to cancel all your lunch arrangements today. I've had word that shortly after one o'clock this afternoon we can expect a very important statement from Downing Street. It's absolutely confidential, I can't tell you what it's about, but we have to be ready to handle it. Push everything else aside."

Within the hour five lobby correspondents had been contacted with apologies to cancel lunch. Two of them were sworn to secrecy and told that "something big was going on in Downing Street." It didn't take a *Brain of Britain* winner to conclude that it was likely to have something to do with "the Collingridge Affair."

One of those facing the prospect of a canceled lunch was the PA's Manny Goodchild. Instead of twiddling his thumbs, he used the formidable range of contacts and favors he had built up over the years to ascertain that every single member of the Cabinet had canceled engagements in order to be at Downing Street that morning, although the Number Ten Press Office refused to confirm it. He was a wise and experienced old hound and he smelled blood, so on a hunch he phoned the Buckingham Palace Press Office. That, too, like Downing Street, had nothing to say—at least officially. But the deputy press secretary had worked with Goodchild many years before on the *Manchester Evening News* and confirmed, entirely off the record and totally unattributably, that Collingridge had asked for an audience at 1:00 p.m.

By 11:25 a.m. the PA tape was carrying the story of the secret Cabinet meeting and the unscheduled audience expected to take place at the Palace. It was an entirely factual report. By midday IRN was feeding local radio with a sensationalized lead item that the Prime Minister "will soon be on his way for a secret meeting with Her Majesty the Queen. Speculation has exploded in Westminster during the last hour that either he's going to sack several of his leading Ministers and inform the Queen of a major Cabinet reshuffle, or he's going to admit his guilt to recent charges of insider trading with his brother. There are even rumors that she has been advised to exercise her constitutional prerogative and sack him."

Downing Street filled with the press pack, jostling, eager. The far side of the street from the famous black door became obscured by a forest of cameras and hastily erected television lights. At 12:45 Collingridge walked out onto the doorstep of Number Ten. He knew the presence of the crowd denoted treachery. Someone had betrayed him, again. He felt as though nails had been driven through his feet. He ignored the screams of the press corps, didn't look up, wouldn't give them the satisfaction. He drove off into Whitehall, pursued by camera cars. Overhead he could hear a helicopter hovering, pursuing. Another crowd of photographers was waiting outside the gates of Buckingham Palace. His attempt at a dignified resignation had turned into a public crucifixion.

❖ ❖ ❖

The Prime Minister had asked not to be disturbed unless it was absolutely necessary. After returning from the Palace he had retired to the private apartment above Downing Street, wanting to be alone with his wife for a few hours, yet once again his wishes counted for nothing.

"I'm terribly sorry, Prime Minister," his private secretary apologized, "but it's Dr. Christian. He says it's important."

The phone buzzed gently as the call was put through.

"Dr. Christian. How can I help you? And how is Charlie?"

"I'm afraid we have a problem," the doctor began, his tone apologetic. "You know we try to keep him isolated, away from the newspapers so that he won't be disturbed by all these allegations that are being thrown around. Normally we switch his television off and find something to divert him during news programs but…The fact is, we weren't expecting the unscheduled reports about your resignation. I'm so deeply sorry you've had to resign, Prime Minister, but Charles is my priority. I have to put his interests first, you understand."

"I do understand, Dr. Christian, and you have your priorities absolutely right."

"This morning he's heard everything. All these allegations about shares. And your resignation. He's deeply upset, it's come as a great shock. He believes he's to blame for all that's happened and I'm sorry to tell you but he's talking about doing harm to himself. I'd hoped we were on the verge of making real progress with him, but now I fear we're on the brink of a real crisis. I don't wish to alarm you unduly but he needs your help. Very badly."

Sarah saw the look of anguish that had stretched across her husband's face. She sat beside him and held his hand. It was trembling.

"Doctor, what can I do? I'll do anything, anything you want."

"We need to find some way of reassuring him. He's desperately confused."

"May I talk to him, doctor? Now? Before this thing goes any further."

There was a wait of several minutes as his brother was brought to the telephone. Collingridge could hear the sound of protest and gentle confusion down the line.

"Charlie, how are you old boy?" Henry said softly.

"Hal, what have I done?"

"Nothing, Charlie, absolutely nothing."

"I've ruined you, destroyed everything!" The voice sounded strangely old, hoarse with panic.

"Charlie, it's not you who's hurt me."

"But I've seen it on the television. You going off to the Queen to resign. They said it was because of me and some shares. I don't understand it, Hal, I've screwed everything up. I don't deserve to be your brother. There's no point in anything anymore." There was a huge, gulping sob on the end of the phone.

"Charlie, I want you to listen to me very carefully. Are you listening?"

Another sob filled with mucus and tears and grief.

"You have no need to ask my pardon. I'm the one who should be down on my knees begging for forgiveness. From you, Charlie."

"Don't be stupid—"

"No, you listen, Charlie! We've always got through our problems together, as family. Remember when I was running the business—the year we nearly went bust? We were going down, Charlie, and it was my fault. Too tied up in my politics. And who brought in that new client, that order which saved us? Oh, I know it wasn't the biggest order we'd ever had but it couldn't have come at a more vital time. You saved the company, Charlie, and you saved me. Just like you did when I was a bloody fool and got caught drink-driving that Christmas."

"I didn't do anything really…"

"The local police sergeant, the one who was a golfing friend of yours, somehow you persuaded him to fix the breath test at the station. If I'd lost my license I'd never have been selected for my constituency. I'd never have set foot in Downing Street. Don't you see, you silly bugger, far from ruining it for me you made it all possible. You and me, we've always faced things together. And that's just how it's going to stay."

"I don't deserve—"

"No, you don't deserve, Charlie, not a brother like me. You were always around when I needed help but what did I do in return? I got too busy for you. When Mary left, I knew how much you were hurting. I should've been there, of course I should. You needed me but there always seemed other things to do. I was always going to come and see you tomorrow. Always tomorrow, Charlie, always tomorrow." The emotion was cracking Collingridge's voice. "I've had my moment of glory, I've done the things that I wanted to do. While I watched you become an alcoholic and practically kill yourself."

It was the first time that either of them had spoken that truth. Charles had always been under the weather, or overtired, or suffering from nerves—never uncontrollably, alcoholically drunk. There were no secrets any longer, no going back.

"You know something, Charlie? I'll walk out of Downing Street and be able to say bloody good riddance, screw the lot of them—if only I know I still have my brother. I'm just terrified that it's too late, that I've neglected you too badly to be able to ask for your forgiveness—that you've been alone so long you don't see the point in getting better."

There were tears of exquisite anguish at both ends of the phone. Sarah was hugging her husband as though he were about to be swept overboard by the storm.

"Charlie, unless you can forgive me, what's been the bloody point? It will all have been for nothing."

There was silence.

"Say something, Charlie!" he said in desperation.

"Bloody idiot, you are," Charlie blurted. "You're the best bruv any man could have."

"I'll come and see you tomorrow. Promise. We'll both have a lot more time for each other now, eh?"

"Sorry about all the fuss."

"To tell you the truth, I haven't felt this good in years."

TWENTY-SIX

*The shadows of infidelity should always lurk at the door;
otherwise, a marriage grows stale.*

Mattie, I'm surprised," Urquhart said as he opened his
front door to find her standing beneath the lamp.
"You've been avoiding me."

"You know that's not true, Mr. Urquhart. It's you who's been
avoiding me. You practically ran away from me every time I
tried to get near you at the conference."

"Well, they were a hectic few days in Bournemouth. And
you are from the *Chronicle*. I have to admit that it wouldn't have
been"—he searched for a word—"*proper* for me to have been
seen talking to one of their journalists, particularly one who
is—how can I put this?—as blond as you."

His eyes were dancing in merriment and yet again she hesitated, as she had done so many times when she'd picked up
the phone to call him but held back. She wasn't entirely sure
why. This man was dangerous, she knew that, made her feel
things she shouldn't, yet when she was with him she tingled
with excitement right down to her toes.

"People might have misunderstood, seeing you and me huddled in some dark corner, Mattie," he continued, more serious

now. "And that front page of yours did mortal damage to my Prime Minister."

"Whoever leaked the poll did the damage, not me."

"Well, timing is everything. And now you're here once again. To ask me questions."

"It's what I do, Mr. Urquhart."

"And there's an early chill for the time of year, I think." He gazed along the street as though to check the weather, and who might be watching. "Why don't you come in?"

He took her coat, sat her down in a large leather chair in his study, found them both whiskey.

"I hope this isn't improper, too," she ventured.

"Unlike Bournemouth there are no prying eyes."

"Mrs. Urquhart…"

"Is at the opera with a friend. Won't be back for some time. If at all."

And in a few words he had thrown a cloak of conspiracy around them that she found nestled so comfortably on her shoulders.

"It's been quite a day," she said, sipping.

"It isn't every day that a comet appears in the sky and burns so spectacularly."

"Can I talk to you frankly, Mr. Urquhart, not even on lobby terms?"

"Then you'd better call me Francis."

"I'll try—Francis. It's just that…My father was a strong character. Clear blue eyes, clear mind. In some ways you remind me of him."

"Of your father?" he said, a little startled.

"I need your advice. To understand things."

"As a father?"

"No. Not even as a Chief Whip. As a…friend?"

He smiled.

"Is it all coincidence?"

"Is what coincidence?"

"These leaks. The opinion poll. It was put under my door, you know."

"Extraordinary."

"Then the Renox shares. I can't help feeling that someone's behind it all."

"A plot to get rid of Henry Collingridge? But, Mattie, how could that be?"

"Sounds silly, perhaps, but…"

"Leaks are a part of the trade, Mattie. There are some politicians who can't pass the doors of the *Guardian* without going inside and turning on the taps."

"You don't destroy a prime minister by accident."

"Mattie, Henry Collingridge wasn't destroyed by his opponents but by his brother's apparent fiddling of the Renox shares. Cock-up, not conspiracy."

"But, Francis, I've met Charlie Collingridge. Spent several hours with him at the Party conference. He struck me as being a pleasant and straightforward drunk who didn't look as if he had two hundred pounds to put together, let alone being able to raise tens of thousands to start speculating in shares."

"He's an alcoholic."

"Would he have jeopardized his brother's career for a few thousand pounds' profit on the Stock Market?"

"Alcoholics are rarely responsible."

"But Henry Collingridge isn't an alcoholic. Do you really think he'd stoop to feeding his brother insider share tips to finance his boozing?"

"I take your point. But is it any more credible to believe there's some form of high-level plot involving senior party figures to cause total chaos?"

She pursed her lips and a frown crept across her brow. "I don't know," she conceded. "It's possible," she added stubbornly.

"You may be right. I'll bear that in mind." He finished his drink, the moment was over. He found her coat, escorted her to the door. He had his hand on the lock but didn't open it. They were close together. "Look, Mattie, it's possible your fears are correct."

"I don't fear it, Francis," she corrected him.

"In any event the next few weeks are going to be tumultuous. Can we do this again, discuss these ideas, whatever twists and turns we discover—just you and me? Entirely privately?"

She smiled. "You know, I was going to ask you much the same."

"Mrs. Urquhart doesn't spend the entire week in London. She's often away or involved with her other activities. Tuesday and Wednesday nights I'm usually here on my own. Please feel free to drop round."

His gaze was steady, penetrating, left her stirred and with a sense of danger.

"Thank you," she said softly. "I will."

He opened the door. She was down the step when she turned. "Are you going to stand, Francis?"

"Me? But I'm the Chief Whip, not even a full member of the Cabinet."

"You're strong, you understand power. And you're a little bit dangerous."

"That's kind of you—I think. But, no, I won't be standing."

"I think you should."

She took another step but he called after her.

"Did you get on with your father, Mattie?"

"I loved him," she said before finally slipping into the night.

❖ ❖ ❖

He settled himself back in his chair with a fresh whiskey, his mind alive with the events of the day, and of the hour just past. Mattie Storin was exceptionally bright and beautiful, and had made it clear she was available. But for what, precisely? The possibilities seemed as endless as they were attractive. He was musing contentedly on the matter when the phone rang.

"Frankie?"

"Ben, excellent to hear from you, even at this late hour."

Landless ignored the sarcasm. "Interesting times, Frankie, interesting times. Isn't that what they say in China?"

"I believe it's a curse."

"I guess old Harry Collingridge would agree!"

"I was sitting here thinking much the same."

"Frankie, you haven't got time to sit on your backside. Game on. You up for it?"

"Up for what, Ben?"

"Don't be so—what's the word?"

"Obtuse?"

"Yeah, up your arse. I need you to be right out in the open with me, Frankie."

"About what?"

"Do you want to stand?" Landless pressed impatiently.

"For the leadership? I'm merely the Chief Whip. I don't appear on stage, I sit in the wings and prompt the players."

"Sure, sure, but do you want it? Because if you do, old son, I can be very helpful to you."

"Me? Prime Minister?"

"Frankie, we're playing a new game now, bigger balls. And your balls are almost as big as mine. I like what you do and the way you do it. You understand how to use power. So do you want to play?"

Urquhart didn't immediately reply. His eye went to an oil that hung on his wall in an ornate gilded frame, of a stag at bay surrounded by baying hounds. Did he have the stomach for it? The words came slowly. They took him by surprise. "I would like to play very, very much."

It was the first time he had confessed his ambition to anyone other than himself, yet with a man like Landless who exposed his naked desires with every chime of the clock, he felt no embarrassment.

"That's good, Frankie. That's great! So let's start from there. I'm going to tell you what the *Chronicle's* running tomorrow. It's an analysis piece by our political correspondent, Mattie Storin. Pretty blond girl with long legs and great tits—you know who I mean?"

"I think so."

"She's going to say it's an open race, everybody's hand dipped in Collingridge's blood, lots more chaos to come."

"I believe she is right."

"Chaos. I like chaos. Sells newspapers. So who is your money on?"

"Well, let's see…These things normally only last a couple of weeks. So the slick Willies, the flashy television performers, they're the ones who will gain the best start. The tide is every-thing; if it's with you it will sweep you home."

"Which slick Willy in particular?"

"Try Michael Samuel."

"Mmm, young, impressive, principled, seems intelligent—not at all to my liking. He wants to interfere all the time, rebuild the world. Too much conscience, not enough experience."

"So what do you suggest, Ben?"

"Frankie, tides turn. One minute you're swimming for the shore, the next you're by an outfall pipe just after I've flushed my toilet."

Urquhart heard the other man swilling drink around a goblet and taking a huge draught before he continued.

"Frankie, I'm going to tell you something. This afternoon I instructed a small and extremely confidential team at the *Chronicle* to start contacting as many of your party's MPs as they can get hold of to ask which way they're going to vote. Wednesday we're going to publish—which I confidently pre-dict will show young Mickey Samuel with a small but clear lead over the rest of the field."

"What? How do you know this? The poll hasn't even been

finished yet." A sigh of understanding, "Oh, Ben, I'm being naive, aren't I?"

"Ring-a-ding-ding, Frankie. You're on the ball. That's why I like you. I know what the fucking poll is going to say because I'm the fucking publisher."

"You mean you've fixed it. But why are you pushing Samuel?"

"First one to get to the sewage pipe. Oh, you'll be there somewhere, Frankie, toward the back of the field but not in bad shape for a Chief Whip. But young Mickey will be out in front, so everyone else has a target, the man they most want to beat. I reckon in a couple of weeks' time he's going to be amazed at the number of bad friends he's got."

"So where do I fit into this great plan?"

"You come from behind, as the actress said to the archbishop. The compromise candidate. While all those other bastards are drowning each other, you slip quietly through as the man they all hate least."

"When all the other trees have been blown down, even a bush can stand tall."

"What?"

"Nothing. Can I trust you?"

"Trust me?" He sounded horrified. "I'm a newspaperman, Francis."

Urquhart burst into dark laughter. It was the first time the proprietor had called him by his proper name. Landless was serious.

"So aren't you going to ask me what I want out of all this?" the proprietor asked.

"I think I already know, Ben."

"And what's that?"

"A friend. A friend in Downing Street. A very good friend. A friend just like me."

TWENTY-SEVEN

A politician should never spend too much time thinking. It distracts attention from guarding his back.

Tuesday, October 26

The Prime Minister's private office, his inner sanctum. Urquhart found him at his desk signing a thick pile of letters. He was wearing reading glasses, something he rarely did with others around. Even more unusual, there wasn't a single newspaper in sight.

"Henry, I haven't had a chance to speak with you since yesterday. I can't tell you how shocked—devastated I was."

"No sympathy, Francis, no sackcloth and ashes. I feel strangely content with the situation. A burden lifted. And all those other clichés."

"As I listened to you I felt as if I were…falling out of the sky, quite literally."

"Happy landings." The Prime Minister cast his spectacles aside and rose from his desk, leading Urquhart over to two well-stuffed armchairs overlooking the park. "Anyhow I don't have time for self-pity. Humphrey Newlands is on his way over so we can get the leadership election under way. Then I'm off to spend the rest of the day with Charlie. It's marvelous to have time for such things."

Urquhart was astonished to see he meant every word of it.

"You wanted a private chat, Francis?"

"Yes, Henry. Look, I know you're not going to support any particular candidate in the election, not publicly at least…"

"It would be most improper."

"Yes, but that doesn't stop you taking a keen academic interest. We both know you've been badly let down by some of your colleagues recently."

"The term 'ungrateful bastards' does somehow spring to mind."

"You have a right—I would argue you even have a duty—to make sure you leave the Party in safe hands. Now as Chief Whip I'm not going to stand myself, of course. Entirely neutral. But that wouldn't stop me keeping you informed of what's going on."

They both knew that a prime minister in his last days still had influence—political followers and personal friends, as well as the not inconsiderable matter of his nominations for the Resignation Honors List with its peerages and knighthoods that every retiring prime minister was allowed. For many senior members of the Party this would be their last chance to rise above the mob and achieve the social status their wives had so long aspired to.

Collingridge scratched his chin. "You're right, Francis. I haven't worked all these years simply to watch someone throw everything away. So tell me, how do things look?"

"Early days, difficult to tell. I think most of the press is right to suggest it's an open race. But I'd expect things to develop quickly once they get going."

"No front runners, then?"

"Well…" Urquhart wobbled his head from side to side, just as Jhabwala had done.

"Come on, Francis. Your gut feeling is good enough for me."

"My nose tells me Michael Samuel has something of a head start."

"Michael? Why so?"

"In a short and furious race there's no time for developing solid arguments. It's all about image. Michael's good on television."

"A media man."

"And inevitably he'll have the subtle support of Teddy and Party Headquarters."

Collingridge's face clouded. "Yes, I see what you mean." He drummed his fingers loudly on the arm of his chair, weighing his words carefully. "Francis, it's not my intention to interfere but neither can I play the innocent. If the Party is to have a free and fair contest, we can't have Party Headquarters messing about with things. Not after their recent performance; the wretched election, all those leaks, not to mention that bloody opinion poll." He spat out the last words. For all his protestations of contentment there was still a tempest raging inside. "And one thing above all the others I won't forgive. You know, someone leaked the news of my visit to the Palace yesterday. I'm told that came out of the back door at Smith Square. How dare they? How did I become the clown in a media circus!" His fist smacked down on the arm of his chair.

"You were owed a little dignity, Henry."

"It's not just me; it's Sarah, too. She doesn't deserve that." He was breathing more strenuously, in anger. "No, I won't bloody-well stand for it. I will not have Teddy's merry men interfering in this fucking election!" He leaned toward Urquhart. "I don't suppose you have much love for Teddy, either, not after he did such a hatchet job on your reshuffle proposals. I'm sure you guessed that at the time."

Urquhart nodded, glad to have his suspicions confirmed.

"What can I do, Francis? How can I make sure this election is run properly?"

"My interests are like yours, I simply want to ensure fair play. People need time to think, not to be swept along in a rush to judgment."

"So?"

"So give them a little longer to make their choice. Slow the pace down. Enjoy your last few weeks in office. I've got nothing against Michael but you should make sure you hand over to a successor chosen by the Party, not the media."

"And least of all by that old goat Teddy."

"You might say that, as Prime Minister, but as Chief Whip I couldn't possibly comment."

Collingridge chuckled. "I don't want to extend the period of uncertainty any longer than necessary but I suppose an extra week or so couldn't do any great harm."

"Under the rules, the timing is entirely in your hands, Henry."

Collingridge glanced at his watch. "Look, Humphrey will be outside. Better not keep him waiting any longer. He'll offer his advice and I shall listen to it most attentively, although I suspect his expertise is more in the area of beach resorts than leadership races. I'll stew on it overnight, let you know in the morning what I decide. You'll be the first to know, Francis." He led the Chief Whip toward the door. "I'm so grateful to you. I can't tell you how comforting it is to have someone like you around, someone with no ax to grind."

❖ ❖ ❖

They had come back to her apartment, kicked the door closed, laughed as they had ripped off their clothes, stumbled across the floor, hadn't even made it as far as the bedroom. Now Mattie and Krajewski lay in a cat's cradle of limbs. He thought he had never been happier, tangled together on her sofa; her mind was already elsewhere.

"Collingridge?" he muttered, removing his hand from her unblemished breast.

She didn't seem to notice the edge of disappointment. "I've been thinking, Johnnie. About Charlie Collingridge."

"I lie sweating between your thighs and you're thinking of another man," he protested, half joking.

"I know he's an alcoholic and everything," she continued, oblivious, "and they're often not responsible for their actions."

"I'm not sure *I* am when I'm with you."

"But it's all too simple."

"Does life have to be complicated?" he begged, pressing himself into the small of her back.

"I just can't believe Charlie Collingridge was capable of it, let alone had the means."

"There's only one man who knows," Krajewski muttered, "and he's locked away in some clinic or other."

She turned to face him. "Where?"

He sighed as he felt his passion subside. "I think it's supposed to be a closely guarded family secret."

"I want to find him."

"And how does our Reporter of the Year propose to do that?"

She pushed herself away from him, wrapped herself in a blanket and disappeared into the kitchen. He went in search of his boxer shorts, found them behind the television, and reluctantly slipped into them as she returned with two glasses of wine. They arranged themselves on the rug in front of the empty fireplace.

"When was the last time anyone saw Charles Collingridge?" she asked.

"Why, er…When he was driven away from his home over a week ago."

"Who was he with?"

"Sarah Collingridge."

"And…?"

"A driver."

"Exactly. So who was the driver, Johnnie?"

"Damned if I know."

"But it's a place to start." Once again she prised herself away from him and crawled over to her television, which was surrounded by a scattering of videotapes. "It's here somewhere," she said, making the mess still worse. She found the tape she was looking for and soon the TV screen was a blizzard of images as she fast-forwarded through a compilation of news programs. She was so engrossed that she failed to notice the blanket had slipped from her shoulders. Krajewski sat, lost in nipple awe and stretching excitement. He was considering picking up the television and throwing it out of the window when, through the blizzard, Charles Collingridge appeared, huddled in the back of the fleeing car, and the blanket was back around her shoulders.

"Look, Johnnie!"

He moaned as she pressed yet another button to run the program back to the start. And there, for less than a second, as the car swept out into the main road, they could see the face of the driver through the windscreen. She pressed the pause button and they found themselves staring at a balding and bespectacled face.

"And who the hell is he?" Krajewski muttered.

"Let's figure out who he's not," Mattie said. "He's not a Government driver—it's not a Government car and the drivers' pool is very gossipy, so we would have heard something. He's not a political figure or we would have recognized him…" She turned from the screen and faced him, failing to recognize his scowl of disgust. "Johnnie, where were they going?"

He felt himself torn between his own journalistic curiosity and his desire to throw himself at her. Damn, grow up, Krajewski, he scolded himself. "OK, not to Downing Street. And not to some hotel or other public place." He pondered the options. "To the clinic, I suppose."

"Precisely! That man is from the clinic. If we can find out who he is, we'll know where they've taken Charlie!"

"I suppose I could get a hard copy of the face off the video tape and show it around. We could try Freddie, our old staff photographer. He's got an excellent memory for faces and he's also an alcoholic who dried out a couple of years ago. Still goes every week to Alcoholics Anonymous. Might be able to put us on the right track. There aren't that many treatment centers. We should be able to make some progress."

"You're the best, Johnnie."

And for the first time that evening, he felt she meant it.

"I'm a mercenary bastard. I require payment," he ventured. "Mattie, can I stay the night?"

Her eyes filled with regret, she shook her head. "Johnnie, remember our ground rules."

"No romance. Right. Well, if you've got what you want from me I suppose I'd better be going," he snapped, eaten away with what he called "nipple rage." He sprang to his feet and dressed hurriedly, but as he was halfway toward the door his shoulders sagged in defeat. "Sorry, Mattie," he said. "It's just that…you're someone very special for me. I live in hope."

He was at the door. He turned. "Is there anyone else, Mattie?"

"No, Johnnie, of course there isn't," she said. "That's not what this is about."

But as he closed the door behind him, she wondered if she was being honest with him. How could she be? She wasn't sure she was being honest with herself. It wasn't the sort of conversation nice girls had.

TWENTY-EIGHT

Some political campaigns hit the ground running. Others simply hit the ground.

Wednesday, October 27

Daily Chronicle. Page 1: Samuel Ahead. Takes Shock Lead.

———◆———

Michael Samuel, the youthful Environment Secretary, was last night emerging as the front runner in the race to become Prime Minister.

In an exclusive poll conducted during the last two days by the Chronicle *among almost two-thirds of Government MPs, 24 percent nominated him as their first choice, well ahead of other potential candidates.*

Samuel is expected to announce his candidacy within days. In a bitter blow to his rivals, he is expected to get the backing of influential party figures such as Lord Williams, the Party Chairman. Sources predict such support could be crucial.

No other name attracted more than 16 percent. Five potential candidates obtained between 10 percent and 16 percent. These were Patrick Woolton (Foreign Secretary), Arnold

*Dollis (Home Secretary), Harold Earle (Education), Paul
McKenzie (Health), and Francis Urquhart, the Chief Whip.*

*Urquhart's inclusion in the list at 12 percent caused
surprise at Westminster. He is not even a full member of
the Cabinet but as Chief Whip has a strong base in the
Parliamentary party. Observers say he could prove a strong
outside candidate. However, sources close to Urquhart last
night emphasized he had made no decision to enter the contest,
and is expected to clarify his position sometime today…"*

❖   ❖   ❖

The Prime Minister had changed his mind. He read all the
newspapers that morning. The commentaries which a week
before had been ripping his flesh off in strips were now, in
their fickle and inconstant fashion, praising his self-sacrifice
that would enable the Government to make a fresh start—
"although he must still resolve many outstanding personal and
family issues to the public's satisfaction," thundered *The Times.*
As always, the press had no shame in sleeping on both sides of
the bed, like tarts.

He read the *Chronicle* particularly carefully, as clearly had
others. A consensus seemed to be emerging: it was an open
race but Samuel was the front runner. Collingridge cast the
paper into a corner, where it flapped like a dying swan, and
summoned his political secretary.

"Grahame. An instruction to Lord Williams, copy to
Humphrey Newlands. He is to issue a press release at twelve-
thirty this afternoon for the lunchtime news. Nominations for
leadership election will close in three weeks' time on Thursday,
November 18, with the first ballot to take place on the following Tuesday, November 23. If a second ballot is required it
will be held as prescribed by the Party's rules on the following
Tuesday, November 30, with any final run-off ballot two days
later. Have you got that?"

"Yes, Prime Minister." The secretary nodded but hid his eyes. It was the first time since his resignation announcement that they had been alone and able to talk.

"You know what that means, Grahame? In exactly six weeks and one day, you and I will be out of a job. I haven't always found time to thank you properly these past years, but I want you to know how bloody grateful I am."

The aide shuffled with embarrassment.

"You must start thinking about your own future. There will be my Resignation Honors List. You'll be on it. As will several newly knighted gentlemen in the City who will be happy to make you a generous offer. I'll make sure of it. Think about what you want, let me know. I still have a few favors to cash in."

The secretary raised eyes filled with regret and gratitude.

"By the way, Grahame, it's possible Teddy Williams might want to get hold of me and encourage me to shorten the election process. I will not be available. You are to make it clear to him that these are instructions, not terms for negotiation, and they are to be issued without fail by twelve-thirty."

There was a short pause.

"Otherwise, tell him, I shall be forced to leak them myself."

❖ ❖ ❖

The tide waits for no man and it was already ebbing for Michael Samuel. Almost as soon as Collingridge had announced his resignation he had consulted his mentor, Teddy Williams.

"Patience, Michael," the elder statesman had advised. "You will almost certainly be the youngest candidate. They'll try to say you are too callow, too inexperienced, and too ambitious. So don't look too much as if you want the job. Show a little restraint and let them come to you."

Which was to prove excellent advice but entirely irrelevant to the circumstances. No sooner had the *Chronicle* hit the streets promoting Samuel's name than Urquhart appeared in front of television cameras to confirm that he had no intention of standing. "I'm flattered, of course, that my name should even be mentioned but I feel it would be in the Party's best interests if I, as Chief Whip, remain entirely impartial in this contest," he said, adding a self-deprecatory nod before disappearing, pursued by the shouted but unanswered questions of the mob.

The search was on for Samuel, and the release later that morning of the detailed election timetable added fuel to the fervor. By the time the breathless inquisitors of the mob had tracked him down to the Intercontinental Hotel off Hyde Park, just before an early lunch meeting, they were in no mood to accept conditional answers. Samuel couldn't say no, they wouldn't accept maybe, not when they discovered that he had already appointed the nucleus of a campaigning team. So, after considerable harassment, he was forced into making an announcement on the steps of the hotel, surrounded by a chaos of baggage and raised umbrellas, that he would indeed be running.

The one o'clock news offered a clear contrast between Urquhart, the dignified and elder statesman declining to run, and the apparently eager Samuel holding an impromptu press conference on the street and launching himself as the first official candidate nearly a month before the first ballot was to be held.

Urquhart was watching the proceedings with considerable satisfaction when the telephone rang. He heard the sound of a toilet flushing, which faded into the unmistakable sound of Ben Landless laughing before the line went dead.

TWENTY-NINE

*Some political careers are like a book that has been misfiled
in the British Library. It's a small mistake, as mistakes go,
but the result is perpetual oblivion.*

Friday, October 29—Saturday, October 30

T his what you want?"
Krajewski's tone still carried the hurt of their last
encounter. He'd been avoiding Mattie in the newsroom since then but now he was leaning over her shoulder,
careful not to get too close, clutching a large manila envelope
in his hand. He let it drop in front of her, and from it she withdrew a 10x12 color photograph. The face of the driver stared
at her, grainy and distorted but with reasonable clarity.

"Freddie came up trumps," Krajewski continued. "He took
this along to his AA meeting last night and the group leader
recognized it immediately. The name is Dr. Robert Christian,
who's a well-known authority on the treatment of drug and
alcohol addiction. Runs a treatment center in a large private
house near the south coast in Kent. Find Dr. Christian, and my
bet is you've found your Charlie."

"Johnnie, I don't know how to thank you," she said excitedly.
But already he had gone.

❖ ❖ ❖

The following day, Saturday, wasn't a working one for Mattie. Immediately after an early lunch she climbed into her old BMW, filled it with petrol, and pointed it in the direction of Dover. The traffic was heavy as she barged her way through the shopping crowds of Greenwich before she emerged onto the A2, the old Roman road which pointed the way from London into the heart of Kent. It took her past the cathedral town of Canterbury and a few miles beyond she turned off at the picturesque village of Barham. Her road map wasn't particularly helpful in finding the even smaller village of Norbington nearby but with the help of several locals she found herself some while later outside a large Victorian house, bearing a subdued sign in the shrubbery that declared itself to be the Fellowship Treatment Center.

There were several cars in the leafy driveway and the front door was open. She was surprised to see people wandering around with apparent freedom, and no sign of the formidable white-coated nurses she had expected to find patrolling the grounds for potential escapees. She parked her car on the road and, sucking a mint for courage, walked cautiously up the drive.

A large, tweed-suited gentleman with a white military mustache approached and her heart sank. This was surely the security patrol in pursuit of intruders.

"Excuse me, my dear," he said in a clipped accent as he intercepted her by the front door. "Have you seen any member of staff about? They like to keep out of the way on family visiting days, but you ought to be able to find one when you need them."

Mattie offered her apologies and smiled in relief. Fortune had followed her and she had struck the best possible day to avoid awkward questions. The place had the atmosphere of a fashionable country retreat rather than an institution; no strait-jackets, no restraints, no locks on the doors, no institutional smells. She found a fire safety map on the wall of the hallway with a detailed plan of the house, which Mattie used to guide herself around the premises in search of her quarry. She found him outside on a garden bench, staring out across the valley in the last of the October sun. Her discovery gave her no joy. She had come to deceive.

"Why, Charlie!" she exclaimed, sitting herself down beside him. "What a surprise to find you here."

He looked at her with a total lack of comprehension. He seemed worn down, his reactions slow, as though his mind was in some faraway place. "I...I'm sorry," he mumbled. "I don't recognize..."

"Mattie Storin. You remember, of course you do. We spent a thoroughly enjoyable evening together in Bournemouth a couple of weeks ago."

"Oh, I'm sorry, Miss Storin. I don't remember. You see, I'm an alcoholic, that's why I'm here, and I'm afraid I was in no condition a few weeks ago to remember very much at all."

She was taken aback by his frankness while he smiled serenely.

"Please don't be embarrassed, my dear," he said, patting her hand like an elderly uncle. "I'm an addict. Trying to cure myself. Had a million ways of hiding it from everyone but only managed to fool myself. Want to get better. That's what this treatment center is all about."

Mattie blushed deeply. She had intruded into the private world of a sick man and felt ashamed.

"Charlie, if you don't remember who I am, then you won't remember I'm a journalist."

The hand was withdrawn, the smile disappeared, replaced by a look of resignation. "Bugger. And you look such a nice girl. Suppose it had to happen sometime, although Henry was hoping I could be left alone here quietly..."

"Charlie, please believe me, I haven't come here to make life difficult for you. I want to help."

"They all say that, don't they?"

"Don't say anything for the moment, just let me talk a little."

"Oh, all right. Not as if I'm going anywhere."

"Your brother, the Prime Minister, has been forced to resign because of allegations that he helped you buy and sell shares to make a quick profit."

He started waving his hand to bring her to a halt but she brushed his protest aside.

"Charlie, none of this makes any sense to me. It just doesn't add up. I think someone was deliberately trying to undermine your brother by accusing you."

"Really?" His old oyster eyes began to wobble with interest. "Who would do that?"

"I don't know. I only have suspicions. I came to see if you could point me toward something more solid."

"Miss Storin—Mattie, may I call you that? You said we were old friends…I'm a drunk. I can't even remember meeting you. So how can I be of help? My word carries no weight whatsoever."

"I'm neither a judge nor a prosecutor, Charlie. I'm just trying to piece together a puzzle from a thousand scattered shards."

His weary eyes searched beyond the hills toward Dover and the Channel, as though a different world lay out there. "Mattie, I've tried so hard to remember, believe me. The thought that I have disgraced Henry and forced him to resign is almost more than I can bear. But I don't know what the truth is. I can't help you. Can't even help myself."

"Wouldn't you remember something about buying so many shares?"

"I've been very sick. And very drunk. There are many things I have absolutely no recollection of."

"Wouldn't you have remembered where you got the money from, or what you did with the proceeds?"

"It does seem unlikely I would have had a small fortune lying around without my remembering it or, more likely, spending it on alcohol. And I've no idea where the money could have gone. Even *I* can't drink away £50,000 in just a few weeks."

"What about the false address in Paddington?"

"Yes, they mentioned something about that. A complete mystery. I don't even know where Praed Street in Paddington is when I'm sober, so it is preposterous to suppose I would have found my way there drunk. It's the other side of London from where I live."

"But you used it—so they say—for your bank and subscription to the Party's literature service."

Charles Collingridge suddenly roared with laughter, so violently that tears began gathering at the corners of his eyes. "Mattie, my dear, you're beginning to restore my faith in myself. No matter how drunk I was, I could never have shown any interest in political propaganda. I object when the stuff is pushed through my letterbox at election time; having to pay for it every month would be an insult!"

"No literature?"

"Never!"

Autumn leaves scuttled across the lawn. The sun was settling lower and a warm, red glow filled the sky, lighting up his face. He seemed to be visibly returning to health, and to be content.

"I can't prove a thing. But on my word as a gentleman, I don't believe I am guilty of the things they say I have done." He took her hand once more and squeezed it. "Mattie, it would mean a lot to me if you believed that, too."

"I do, Charlie, very much. And I'm going to try to prove it for you." She rose to leave.

"I've enjoyed your visit, Mattie. Now that we are such old friends, please come again."

"I shall. But in the meantime, I've got a bit of digging to do."

❖ ❖ ❖

It was late by the time she got back to London that evening. The first editions of the Sunday newspapers were already on the streets. She bought a heavy pile of them and, with magazines and inserts slipping from her laden arms, threw them on the back seat of her car. It was then she noticed the *Sunday Times* headline.

The Education Secretary, Harold Earle, not a noted Greenpeace lover, had just announced his intention to stand for the leadership and launched his campaign with a speech entitled "Clean Up Our Country."

"We have talked endlessly about the problems of our inner cities, yet they continue to decline, and the impoverished state of our inner cities has been matched by the degeneration of our countryside," the *Sunday Times* reported him as saying. "For too long we have neglected such issues. Recycled expressions of concern are no substitute for positive action. It's time we backed our fine words with fine deeds. The opinion polls show that the environment is an issue on which the voters say we have failed. After more than twelve years in office, they are right to say that this is unacceptable, and we must wake up to these concerns."

"Now why is the Education Secretary making such a fuss about environmental matters?" she asked herself as she came to the end of his thunderous speech. "Silly me. I'm getting slow in my old age. Can't decipher the code. Which Cabinet Minister is supposed to be responsible for environmental matters, and therefore responsible for this mess?"

The public fight to eliminate Michael Samuel had begun.

THIRTY

There is no form of wickedness in which a politician can't indulge and a journalist won't inflate. Hysterical exaggeration is the hallmark of them both.

Wednesday, November 3

Mattie tried many times during the following week to get hold of Kevin Spence. Despite the repeated assurances of his gushingly polite secretary, he never returned her calls, so she waited until well beyond the time that secretaries usually have left for home before she called again. The night security guard put her straight through.

"Miss Storin, no, of course I haven't been avoiding you," Spence lied. "I've been very busy. These are distracting times."

"Kevin, I need your help again."

There was a pause. He was braver and more focused when he wasn't looking into her eyes. "I remember the last time I gave you my help. You said you were going to write a piece on opinion polls. Instead you wrote a story slandering the Prime Minister. Now he's gone." He spoke with a quiet sadness. "He was always very decent to me, very kind. I think you and the rest of the press have been unspeakably cruel."

"Kevin, that wasn't my story, I give you my word. My copy was hijacked, my byline wasn't on it. I was even more furious than you must have been."

"I'm afraid I have been very naive. Good night, Miss Storin." He was about to put the phone down.

"Kevin, give me just a moment. Please! There's something strange about Mr. Collingridge's resignation."

And he was still there.

"Personally I don't believe what's being said about him and his brother. I'd like to be able to clear his name."

"I can't see how I could assist you," Spence said in a distrusting tone. "Anyway, nobody outside the Press Office is allowed to have contact with the media during the leadership campaign. Chairman's strictest orders."

"Kevin, there's a lot at stake here. Not just the leadership of the Party and whether you are going to win the next election. There's something much more personal, about whether history is going to regard Henry Collingridge as a crook or whether he's going to get a chance to put the record straight. Don't we owe him that?"

Another cautious pause, then: "If I could help, what would you want?"

"Something very simple. Do you understand the computer system at Party Headquarters?"

"Yes, of course. I use it all the time."

"I think your computer system has been tampered with."

"Tampered with? That's impossible. We have the highest security. Nobody from outside can access it."

"Not outside, Kevin. Inside."

The silence from the other end of the phone was more prolonged this time.

"Think about it, Kevin. Your opinion poll was leaked from the inside. Only explanation. Dropped you right in it."

She heard Spence whisper a mild curse as he battled with his doubts.

"Look, I'm working at the House of Commons. I can be with you in less than ten minutes and I guess the building is very quiet at this time of night. No one will notice, Kevin. I'm on my way over."

"Come in through the car park," he muttered. "For God's sake don't use the main reception."

She was with him less than seven minutes later.

They sat in his small garret office, penned in by the mountains of files that tumbled over every available flat surface and onto the floor. A glowing green screen dominated his desk and they were sitting close beside each other in front of it. She had unfastened a button on her blouse; he had noticed. Mattie decided she would scold herself later.

"Kevin, Charles Collingridge ordered material from the Party's sales and literature service and asked them to be delivered to an address in Paddington. Right?"

"Correct. I checked it as soon as I heard, but it's there all right. Look."

He tapped a few characters on the keyboard, and up came the incriminating evidence on the screen. "Chas Collingridge Esq 216 Praed St. Paddington London W2—001A/ 01.0091."

"What do these other hieroglyphics mean?"

"The first set simply means that he subscribes to our comprehensive literature service. The second shows when his subscription expires. It's our way of knowing what he wants—everything, or just the main publications, or if he was a member of our specialist book club, that sort of thing. Each one of our marketing programs has a different set of reference numbers. It also shows how he pays, if he's up-to-date or behind on subscription."

"And Charles?"

"Was fully paid up from the beginning of the year."

"Even though he's an alcoholic with no money who can't even read when closing time has come."

Spence shifted uneasily in his chair.

"This information, can you bring it up on all the monitors in the building?"

"Yes. It's not information we regard as particularly confidential."

"So tell me this, Kevin." She leaned forward a little, breathed deep; men were pathetic, it worked all the time. "If you felt like bending the rules a little, wanted to make me a subscriber to your comprehensive literature service, could you do that? Enter my details from this terminal?"

"Why…yes." Spence was beginning to follow her line of inquiry. "You think that Charles Collingridge's details were hacked or invented. It could be done. Look."

His fingers flew like a concert pianist's and within a few seconds the screen was showing a comprehensive literature subscription in the name of "M Mouse Esq, 99 Disneyland Miami."

"But that's not enough, Mattie. You couldn't get away with backdating it to the beginning of the year because…What a fool I am! Of course!" he exploded and started thrashing away once more at the keyboard. "If you really know what you're doing, which very few people in this building do, you can tap into the main frame subdirectory…"

His words were almost drowned in the clattering of the keys.

"You see, that gives access to the financial data. So I can check the exact date when the account was paid, whether it was paid by check or credit card, when the subscription was first started…"

The monitor screen started glowing.

"You can only do it if you've got the right password and— oh, my giddy aunt!" He pushed himself away from the screen as if it had insulted him. Then he stared once more.

"Mattie, you're not going to believe this…"

"Whatever it is, I think I just might."

"According to the accounting record, Charles Collingridge has never paid for the literature service, this month or any month. His details only appear on the distribution file, not the payment file."

"Kevin, can you tell me when his name first appeared on the distribution file?" she asked, very softly.

A few more keystrokes, this time cautious, deliberate affairs.

"Jesus. Exactly two weeks ago today."

"Let me make sure I understand, Kevin. I want to be clear. Someone in this building, not the accounts staff or anyone who understood computers very well, altered the file to include Charles Collingridge's name for the first time two weeks ago."

He nodded. His face had gone white.

"Can you tell me who altered the file, or from which terminal it was altered?"

"No. It could have been done from any terminal in this building. The computer program trusts us…" He shook his head as if he had failed the most crucial test of his life.

"Don't worry, Kevin, you've been brilliant." She turned from the screen to face him, leaned toward him. "We're on the trail. But it's very important you don't utter a word of this to anyone. I want to catch whoever did this and if he knows we're looking he will cover his trail. Please, will you help me, keep this quiet until we've something more to go on?"

His eyes met hers. "Who on earth would believe me, anyway?" he murmured.

THIRTY-ONE

Beauty is in the eye of the beholder. Truth lies in the hands of its editor.

Monday, November 8—Friday, November 12

The weekend newspapers hadn't even tried to hide their irritation. Samuel and Earle, and the Cabinet ministers who were expected to run, had all behaved themselves, no outright personal attacks on their rivals, so the press did it for them.

The *Observer* declared that it had been "a disappointing and uninspiring campaign so far, still waiting for one of the candidates to breathe life back into the Party." The *Sunday Mirror* dismissed it as "irrelevant and irritating" while the *News of the World*, not to be outdone, described it in characteristic style as "flatulent, a passing breeze in the night." "Samuel and Earle?" the People said. "If that's the answer, it was a damned fool question."

These criticisms kicked the campaign to life early on Monday morning. Encouraged by the media view that the right contender still hadn't emerged, two further Cabinet Ministers threw their hats into the ring—Patrick Woolton, and Paul McKenzie, the Secretary of State for Health. Both were reckoned to have a reasonable chance of success. McKenzie had made a name for himself selling the popular hospital scheme and had managed to duck the blame for its postponement by pointing the finger at the Treasury and Downing Street. "I'm in!" he announced.

Ever since his conversation with Urquhart at the Party conference, Woolton had been running hard behind the scenes. He had lunched almost every editor in Fleet Street, taken drinks with leading backbenchers and slept with no one but his wife. He also thought he had an advantage, or at least a uniqueness, in his Northern roots, which he hoped would establish him as the "One Nation" candidate in contrast to the avocado and olive oil backgrounds of most of the other major contenders. Not that this was likely to impress the Scots, of course, who tended to view the whole affair as if it were an entirely foreign escapade. Woolton had been hoping to delay his formal entry into the race, wanting to see how his rivals' campaigns developed, but the weekend press had been like a call to arms and he decided he should delay no longer. He summoned a press conference at Manchester Airport to make the announcement on what he termed his "home ground," trusting that no one would notice he had flown up from London in order to be there.

The press criticism incited everyone to sharpen their edges. Earle repeated his environmentalist criticisms but this time chose to attack the record of Michael Samuel by name; no more coded messages. Samuel retorted that Earle's conduct was reprehensible and incompatible with his status as a Cabinet colleague, as well as being a rotten example for an Education Secretary to set for young people. Meanwhile, Woolton's loose language at Manchester concerning the need to "restore English values with an English candidate" was vigorously attacked by McKenzie, who was desperately trying to rediscover his lost Gaelic roots and claiming it was an insult to five million Scots. The *Sun* went further, interpreting Woolton's words as a vicious anti-Semitic attack on Samuel; Jewish activists swamped the air waves and letter columns with complaints while a rabbi in Samuel's home town called on the Race Relations Board to investigate what he called "the most atrocious outburst by a senior political figure since Mosley." Woolton wasn't entirely unhappy with this overreaction, declaring, but only in private, that "for the next two weeks everyone will be looking at the shape of Samuel's ears rather than listening to what he's saying."

By Wednesday afternoon Urquhart felt the situation had developed sufficiently well for him to issue a public call for "a return to the good manners and standards of personal conduct for which our Party is renowned." It was echoed loudly in the editorial columns, even as the front pages of the same newspapers were splashing the latest outburst of bad behavior.

When, therefore, on Friday afternoon Mattie walked into Preston's office telling him she had more, he shook his head in weariness. "It had better be different," he said, throwing Earle's latest press release into a corner.

"This is different," she warned.

He appeared to take little interest.

"Front page different," she said.

"So make my knees tremble."

She closed the door behind her, making sure they couldn't be overheard. "Collingridge resigned because of allegations that he or his brother had been fiddling share deals through a Paddington tobacconist and a Turkish secondary bank. I think we can prove that he was almost certainly set up every step of the way."

"What are you talking about?"

"He was framed."

"Can you prove it?"

"I think so."

His secretary put her head round the door but was brusquely waved away.

"Here's what we have, Grev." Patiently she explained that she had checked the computer files at Party Headquarters which revealed that the distribution file had been tampered with.

"Why would anyone do that?"

"So that the false address in Paddington could be tied directly to Charles Collingridge."

"Why do you think it was false?"

"Anyone could have opened that accommodation address. I don't believe Charles Collingridge ever went anywhere near Paddington. Somebody else did it in his name."

The door opened yet again; another interruption. "Fuck off!" Preston growled and the intruder scuttled away.

"So why would anyone open a false address in Charlie Collingridge's name?"

"Because they were trying to frame him. And his brother."

"Too complicated," Preston remarked, but was still listening.

"I went to Paddington myself this morning. I opened up an accommodation address at the same tobacconist shop in an entirely fictional name. I then got a taxi to Seven Sisters Road and the Union Bank of Turkey, where I opened up an account in the same fictional name—not with £50,000 but with just £100. The whole thing took less than three hours start to finish."

"Jesus…"

"So I can now start ordering pornographic magazines, paid for out of the new bank account and delivered to the Paddington address, which could do a hell of a lot of damage to the reputation of one completely innocent politician."

"Who?"

In response she placed a bank book and the tobacconist's receipt onto the editor's desk. He looked at them eagerly, then exploded.

"The Leader of the Opposition!" he shouted in alarm. "What the fuck have you done?"

"Nothing," she said with a smile suggesting victory. "Except to show that Charles Collingridge was almost certainly framed; that he probably never went near the tobacconist shop or the Union Bank of Turkey, and therefore he couldn't have bought those shares."

Preston was holding the documents at arm's length as if they might catch fire.

"Which means Henry Collingridge didn't tell his brother about Renox Chemicals…" Her inflexion suggested there was more.

"And? And?" Preston demanded.

"He's innocent. Didn't have to resign."

Preston sagged back in his chair. A bead of perspiration had begun to gather on his brow. He felt as if he were being torn in two. With one eye he could detect the makings of a superb story, yet that was the problem, for with his other eye he couldn't fail to see the enormous impact that such a story would make on the world of Westminster. It would turn everything upside down, perhaps even save Collingridge. Is that what they wanted? Landless had just instructed him that he had fresh fish to fry and that all major pieces affecting the leadership race were to be cleared with him before publication. Hard news was little more than a commodity for Landless. What he yearned for was influence, power. Preston didn't know which way his boss would jump, he needed to play for time.

"You've been very busy, young lady."

"It's a tremendous story, Grev."

"I don't recall you running this by me or asking permission to spend my money opening accommodation addresses."

His reticence took her by surprise. "It's called initiative, Grev."

"I don't deny you've done well…" His mind was charging through his Thesaurus of flannel, trying not to commit himself. It was a well-thumbed volume. Then he knew what he had to do and the book closed shut with a snap. "But what have we got here, Mattie? You've shown it's possible to go charging round London opening accounts in Collingridge's name, but that's not enough. You haven't proved it wasn't Charlie Collingridge himself. That's still the easiest explanation to accept."

"But the computer file, Grev. It was tampered with."

"Haven't you considered the possibility that the computer file was altered, not to incriminate Collingridge, but *by* him, or one of his friends, to provide him with an alibi. A hook to catch a little fish like you."

"You're kidding…"

"For all we know it wasn't the distribution file but the accounts file which was altered. Might have happened only minutes before you saw it."

"But only a handful of people have access to the accounts file," Mattie protested. "And how could Charlie Collingridge have done that when he's drying out in a treatment center?"

"His brother."

Mattie was incredulous. "You can't seriously believe that the Prime Minister took the incredible risk of ordering the Party Headquarters' computer file to be altered just to falsify the evidence—after he had already announced his resignation."

"Mattie, think back. Or are you too wet behind the ears to remember? Watergate. Files were burned and tapes erased—by the President. During the Irangate scandal, a secretary smuggled incriminating material out of the White House in her knickers."

"This isn't the Wild West…"

"OK, Jeremy Thorpe. Leader of the Liberal Party. Put on trial at the Old Bailey for attempted murder. John Stonehouse went to jail after faking his own suicide. Lloyd George sold peerages out of the back door of Downing Street while he was screwing his secretary on the Cabinet table. It's what happens in politics, Mattie, all the time." Preston was warming to his theme now. "Power is a drug, like a candle to a moth. They are drawn toward it, take no heed of the dangers. They'd rather risk everything, marriages, careers, reputations, even their lives. So it's still easier to believe the Collingridges got caught with their hands in the till and were trying to cover it up."

"You can't tell me you won't run it!" she accused sharply.

"Calm down, for God's sake. What I'm saying is you haven't got enough for the story to stand up. There's a lot of shit here and you need a much bigger shovel. You need to do more work on it."

If he had meant it as a dismissal and a return to a quiet life, he was going to be disappointed. Her hands thumped onto his desk, and she was leaning across it to look him in his shifty eyes.

"Grev. I know I'm a stupid bloody woman but just explain it to me so I can understand. Either somebody set the Collingridges up, or the Prime Minister is guilty by falsifying evidence. One way or the other, it's a huge story and we have enough to lead the paper for a week."

"But which is it? We have to be sure. Particularly in the middle of a leadership contest."

"It's because there's a leadership contest that we have to do it! What's the bloody point of waiting until after it's over and the damage has been done?"

Preston had struggled hard but had run out of logic. He took badly to being lectured by one of his most junior members of staff, particularly a woman. He had had enough.

"Look, get your tits off my table and your tanks off my lawn. You burst into my office with a story so fantastic but without a shred of concrete evidence. You haven't written a word of copy. How the devil can I tell whether you've got a great story or simply had a good lunch?"

Much to her own surprise, she didn't scream at him but lowered her voice, like a threat. "Fine, Grev. If that's what you want you'll have your copy in thirty minutes." She turned and walked out, barely able to resist the temptation to slam the door off its hinges.

It was nearer forty minutes when she walked back in, without knocking, six pages of double-spaced copy clutched in her hand. Without comment she dropped them on the desk, standing directly in front of Preston to make it clear she wouldn't budge until she had her answer.

He left her standing as he read slowly through the pages, trying to look as if he were struggling with an important decision. But it was a sham. The decision had already been made in a phone call he'd made moments after Mattie had left his office.

"She's determined, Ben. She knows she's got the makings of a great story and she won't take no for an answer."

"Who cares? We don't run it," Landless had told him. "That's not my agenda right now."

"What the hell do you want me to do?"

"Act like an editor, Grev. Persuade her she's wrong. Put her on the cookery page. Send her on holiday. Promote her. But keep her quiet!"

"It's not that simple. She's not only stubborn as hell, she's also one of the best political brains we've got."

"I'm really surprised I have to remind you but you've already got the best political brains in the business. Mine!"

"I didn't mean—"

"Look, we've only got a couple of weeks before this bloody leadership race is over. There are big things at stake here, not just the future of the country but my business—and your job. Do you understand me?"

He was about to say of course he understood him but already the phone had been slammed down. Now she was back in his office, the cause of all his woes. He continued to shuffle the pages of her copy, no longer reading them, concentrating instead on what he was about to say, unsure how he should handle her. Finally he put Mattie's story down and stretched back in his chair.

"We can't run it. Too risky. I'm not willing to blow the leadership contest apart on the basis of speculation."

It was what she had expected. She replied in a whisper that hit Preston like a boxing glove.

"I will not take no for an answer."

Dammit. Why didn't she just accept it, shrug it off, put it down to experience or just burst into tears like the others? The quiet insolence behind her words made him all the more determined.

"I'm not running your story. I'm your editor, that's my decision. You will accept it or…"

"Or what, Grev?"

"Or realize that you have no future on our political staff."

"You're firing me?" This did surprise her. How could he afford to let her go, particularly in the middle of the leadership contest?

"No, I'm moving you to women's features, starting right now. Frankly, I don't think you've developed the judgment for our political columns, not yet, maybe in a couple—"

She flew straight across him. "Who's nobbled you, Grev?"

"What the hell do you mean?"

"You normally have trouble making up your mind whether you wear Y-fronts or boxers. Deciding to fire me from this story is somebody else's decision, isn't it?"

"I'm not firing you! You're being transferred…"

He was beginning to lose much of his carefully maintained control. His complexion looked as if he had been holding his breath.

"You're not firing me?"

"No!"

"Then I quit."

His cheeks looked like a cherry farm. He had to keep her at the *Chronicle*, at least for a while; it was the only way to control her. But what the hell was he to do? He forced a smile and spread his hands wide in an attempt to imitate a gesture of generosity. "Look, Mattie, let's not be hasty. You're among friends here."

Her nostrils flared in contempt.

"I want you to get wider experience on the paper. You've got talent, no denying that, even if I think you haven't quite fitted in on the political side. We want to keep you here, so spend the weekend thinking over what other part of the paper you might like to work on."

He saw her eyes and knew it wasn't working.

"But if you really feel you must go, don't rush into anything. Sort out what you want to do, let me know, we'll try to support you and give you six months' salary to help you on your way. I don't want any hard feelings. Think about it."

"I've thought about it. And if you are not printing my story, I'm resigning. Here and now."

The soft words turned to steel. "In which case I remind you that you have a contract of employment, and that stipulates you have to give me three months' notice. It also stipulates that until that time has elapsed we retain exclusive rights over all your journalistic work. If you insist, we shall rigidly enforce that provision, in the courts if necessary, which would ruin your career once and for all. Face it, Mattie, your copy isn't going to get printed here or anywhere else. Wise up, accept the offer. It's the best one you are going to get."

Suddenly she saw the face of her grandfather, smiling down at her as she curled up at his feet in front of a winter fire. "You are a pest, my little Mattie, always asking questions, questions, questions."

"But I want to know, *Farfar.*"

So her granddad had told her about how he had set out from his fishing village on the Norwegian fjord, on his dash for freedom, leaving everything behind, knowing that once he started he could never turn back. "I knew what was waiting out there for me," he said. "Terrifying things. There were German patrol boats, mine fields, and nearly a thousand miles of stormy seas."

"So why did you do it?"

"Because also waiting for me was the most terrifying and wonderful thing of all. The future." And he had laughed and kissed her curls.

Now she gathered up the papers on Preston's desk, sorted them into a neat pile, then ripped them slowly in half before letting them flutter back into his lap.

"You can keep the words, Grev. But you don't own the truth. I'm not sure you would even recognize it."

This time she slammed the door.

THIRTY-TWO

Politicians are much like aging authors and older women. The dangerous phase in their lives is when they are no longer content with the respect of friends but demand the adulation of an audience.

Sunday, November 14—Monday, November 15

I n the immediate aftermath of the *Chronicle*'s devastating opinion poll and Collingridge's resignation, Urquhart had written to all his parliamentary colleagues in his capacity as Chief Whip.

During the course of the leadership election, you will undoubtedly be approached by newspapers and pollsters trying to obtain your view about which candidate you are likely to support. I would encourage you not to respond. At best these surveys can only serve to disrupt the proper conduct of what is supposed to be a confidential ballot. At worst they will be used to make mischief. We can do without lurid headlines and outlandish comment. The best interests of the Party are best served by refusing to cooperate with such activity.

The majority was more than happy to accept his advice, but at least a third of MPs are generally reckoned to be constitutionally incapable of keeping anything quiet, even state secrets. As a result, less than 40 percent of the 337 Government MPs with votes in the ballot responded to the pollsters' pestering telephone calls on behalf of two Sunday newspapers. It left the impression that the Parliamentary Party was still a long way from making up its collective mind. Moreover, the views of those who did respond weren't much help, either. Samuel was ahead, but only narrowly and to a degree that the pollsters emphasized was "not statistically significant." Woolton, McKenzie, and Earle followed in close order, with four other candidates who had put their heads above the parapet considerably further behind.

The conclusions to be drawn from such evidence, just four days before the close of nominations, were flimsy, but that didn't seem to bother those who wrote the headlines.

"SAMUEL SLIPPING—EARLY LEAD LOST," roared the *Mail* on Sunday, while the *Observer* was scarcely less restrained in declaring "PARTY IN TURMOIL AS POLL REVEALS UNCERTAINTY."

The inevitable consequence was a flurry of editorials criticizing both the quality of the candidates and their campaigns. "This country has a right to expect more of the governing Party than this ferrets-in-a-sack routine," the *Sunday Express* intoned. "We may be witnessing a governing Party which is finally running out of ideas and leadership after too long in power."

The following morning's edition of the *Chronicle* was intended to resolve all that. Just three days before the close of nominations, it put aside convention and for the first time in its history ran its editorial on the front page. Its print run was increased and a copy was hand delivered to the London addresses of all Government MPs. No punches were pulled in its determination to make its views heard throughout the corridors of Westminster.

This paper has consistently supported the Government, not through blind prejudice but because we felt they served the interests of the nation better than the alternatives. Throughout the Thatcher years our convictions were well supported by the progress which was made, but in recent months we began to feel that Henry Collingridge was not the best leader to write the next chapter. That was why we supported his decision to resign.

But the lack of judgment being shown by the present contenders for his job threatens a return to the bad old ways of weakness and indecisiveness which we hoped had been left behind for good.

Instead of the steadying hand which we need to consolidate the economic and social advances of recent years, we have been offered a choice between youthful inexperience, environmental upheaval, and injudicious outbursts bordering on racial intolerance. This choice isn't good enough. We need a leader who has maturity, a sense of discretion, and a proven capacity for working with all his colleagues.

There is at least one senior figure in the Party who enjoys all of these attributes and who in recent weeks has been almost unique in upholding the dignity of Government, showing himself capable of putting aside his own personal ambition for the wider interests of his Party.

He has announced that it is not his intention to seek election as Leader of the Party, but he still has time to reconsider before nominations close on Thursday. We believe it would be in the best interests of the Party if the Chief Whip, Francis Urquhart, were to stand. We believe it would be in the wider interests of the entire country if he were to be elected.

Such an endorsement was like a lifeboat cutting through troubled seas. By the time Urquhart emerged from his home in Cambridge Street at 8:10 that morning, there was wriggling media scrum waiting to greet him. He had been waiting inside to ensure that the timing of his exit enabled BBC radio's *Today* program and all breakfast television channels to take it live. Attracted by the scramble of newsmen, a host of passers-by and commuters from nearby Victoria Station had gathered to discover the cause for the commotion and the television images suggested a crowd of ordinary folk, "real people" as one commentator described them, who were showing considerable interest in the man who now emerged onto the doorstep.

The journalists shouted; he waved a hand to quiet them. The hand also contained a copy of that morning's *Chronicle*. He smiled, an expression that contained both intrigue and assurance.

"Ladies and Gentlemen, as Chief Whip I would like to think you had gathered here because of your interest in the details of the Government's forthcoming legislative program. But I suspect you have other things on your mind."

A gentle quip, an appreciative chuckle from the journalists; Urquhart was now firmly in control.

"I have read with considerable surprise and obvious interest this morning's edition of the *Chronicle*." He held it up again so that the cameras could get a clear shot. "I'm honored they should hold such a high opinion of my capabilities—one which goes far beyond my own judgment of the matter, I can assure you. As you know, I had made it clear that I had no intention of standing, that I thought it was in the Party's best interest that the Chief Whip should stand above this particular contest."

He cleared his throat; they waited, in silence, pencils poised, microphones thrust still further forward, straining at the leash.

"And generally that's still my view. However, the *Chronicle* raises important points which should be considered carefully. I know you'll forgive me if I don't come to an instant or snap judgment out here on the pavement, not even for you, ladies and gentlemen. I want to spend a little time consulting a few colleagues, weighing their opinions. I also intend to have a long and serious discussion with my wife, whose views will be most important of all. I shall then sleep upon it all and let you know tomorrow what decision I have reached. Nothing more till then, I'm afraid. Tomorrow!"

With one final wave of his hand, still clutching the newspaper and held for many seconds to satisfy the screaming photographers, Urquhart withdrew into his house and shut the door firmly behind him.

❖ ❖ ❖

Mattie was beginning to wonder whether she had been hasty in storming out of Preston's office. She had spent a lonely weekend trying to identify newspapers for which she would like to work, but as she did so she quickly realized that none of them had any obvious gaps in their political reporting teams. She had made many telephone calls but they had led to few appointments. She also began to discover that a rumor was spreading a story that she had stormed out in tears after Preston had questioned her judgment, and sensitive feminine outbursts don't generally commend themselves to the alpha males of the newspaper club. It didn't help her mood when the Bank of England pushed up interest rates to protect sterling from speculators during the period of uncertainty. Mortgage rates followed within hours. Mattie had a mortgage, a hefty one. Paying for it was difficult enough even with a salary. Without one, the hyenas would be soon at her door.

That afternoon she went to the Commons in search of Urquhart. His name was everywhere, the main dish of the day, but he proved elusive and he wasn't returning her calls. It was by chance that she almost bumped into him as she was walking down one of the finely carved circular staircases off the Central Lobby. He was striding up the marble steps with the vigor of a far younger man and she was caught so by surprise that she almost slipped. He reached out, grabbed her arm, steadied her, pulled her to one side.

"Why, Mattie, what a delight."

"I've been trying to get hold of you."

"I know. I've been avoiding you." He laughed at his own appalling honesty. "Don't be offended, I'm hiding from everyone. Keeping a low profile. For the moment."

"But will you stand? I think you ought to."

"I really couldn't possibly comment, Mattie, you know that, not even to you."

"Tonight? Can I come round?"

Their eyes met. They both knew the request wasn't entirely professional. Only at that point did he let go of her arm.

"Mrs. Urquhart will be there. I will need to spend some time with her."

"Of course."

"And I suspect you'll find dozens of photographers waiting to photograph every little coming and going."

"Sorry, silly of me."

"I'd better go, Mattie."

"I hope…" She bit her tongue.

"Yes, what do you hope, Mattie?"

"I hope you win."

"But I'm not even a candidate yet."

"You will be, Francis."

"How can you possibly tell?"

"Let's call it feminine intuition."

That long, penetrating look again, the one that wasn't entirely professional. "I'm a great admirer of such qualities, Mattie."

She held his stare.

"But I must rush. I look forward to our next encounter."

And he was gone.

❖ ❖ ❖

The tide was coming in at a rush and the wooden platform that formed part of Charing Cross pier bobbed in the current. It was early evening but already densely dark, with a chill breeze that had started its journey somewhere out in the North Sea beyond the estuary coming off the water and wrapping itself around her ankles. Mattie pulled her coat tight and stuffed her hands back into her pockets. She was relieved to see the *Chronicle*'s private river taxi coming into view. It shuttled employees between the newspaper's Docklands plant downstream and the more central reaches of the capital. It was the shuttle that Mattie had used to ferry her between the newspaper and Westminster. Now Krajewski had asked to meet her, with a message.

"Grev says you've got to come back," Krajewski said as he walked down the short gangway from the boat.

"I quit."

"He knows that. The whole bloody newsroom heard you. Didn't know you could slam a door that hard without the wall falling down." His tone was light, trying to humor her. "Anyway, he says he wants you back, even if it's only to work out your three months' notice."

"I'd rather freeze out here," she said, turning away.

"You will freeze if you're not working, Mattie." He took her sleeve to slow her down. "Work your notice out."

"On women's features!" she snorted in contempt.

"Use the paper as a base for finding something else. Grev says that's OK with him."

"He wants to control me."

"I want to see you."

His words sat between them, staring.

"Whatever way you want, Mattie. Take it slowly, let's see what happens. Unless you can't stand me, that is."

"No, Johnnie, that's not it."

"Then what is it…?"

She set off again, but not at speed. They strolled along the

Embankment, tracing the twisted, confusing curves of the river with the floodlit vistas of the Festival Hall and the Houses of Parliament beyond.

"So what do you make of all the Urquhart stuff?" he asked eventually, trying to find some ground they could share.

"It's extraordinary. And exciting."

"Like a Messiah on a white charger galloping to the rescue."

"Messiahs don't ride chargers, stupid; they do donkeys."

They both laughed, felt easier. He moved closer, she slipped her arm though his as they kicked a path through the wind-swept piles of leaves gathered beneath the plane trees.

"Why did the paper do it?" she asked.

"Don't know. Grev just came in late yesterday, not a word to anyone, turned the paper inside out and produced his front page editorial from out of his pocket. No warning; no explanation. Still, it seems to have caused quite a stir. Perhaps he got it right after all."

Mattie shook her head. "I don't think it was Grev. It takes balls to position the paper in that way and he's such a shrivel dick. No, it could only have come from one place: the desk of our—your!—beloved proprietor. Last time he stepped in he was dethroning Collingridge, now he's trying to hand the crown to someone else."

"But why? Why Urquhart? He comes across as something of a loner, aristocratic, patrician, old school tie, don't you think?"

"The strong, silent type."

"Not one of the boys, no great fan club."

"But maybe that's it, Johnnie. Low profile. No one hates him enough to campaign against him, not like they're doing with Samuel." She turned to face him, her breath forming swirls of mist in the evening air. "You know, he might just slip through the middle while the others are all killing themselves. Landless could have picked a winner."

"You think he'll stand, then?"

"Certain of it."

"How can you be?"

"I'm a political correspondent. The best. But…"

"Gets cold on the outside of the tent, doesn't it?"

"I've lost my job, Johnnie, not my curiosity. I think there's something bigger going on here than anyone can imagine. Bigger than Landless, much bigger than Shrivel Dick. And too big even for the *Chronicle*."

"What do you mean?"

"Woodward and Bernstein?"

"They had a newspaper to print their stuff, Mattie."

"They also wrote a book."

"You're going to write a book?"

"Maybe."

"You want me to tell Grev that?"

"Only if it really upsets him."

THIRTY-THREE

The higher up the tree a cat climbs, the farther it will fall.
It's the same for politicians, except politicians don't bounce.

Tuesday, November 16

Would he? Wouldn't he? The following day's news was dominated by speculation about whether Urquhart would run. The media had excited themselves to the point where they would feel badly let down if he didn't, yet by mid-afternoon he was still keeping his own counsel.

So was Roger O'Neill. The previous day Mattie had telephoned Party Headquarters wanting to get an official view about computers, literature sales, and accounting procedures, only to discover that Spence had been absolutely right about the ban on staff contact with the media for the duration of the campaign. She could talk only with the Press Office, yet no one in the Press Office seemed capable or willing to talk to her.

"Sounds as if you're investigating our expenses," a voice down the phone had suggested. "Literature sales? We're a bit busy drowning right now, Mattie. Call back in a couple of weeks."

So she had asked for O'Neill's office and been put through to Penny Guy.

"Hi, it's Mattie Storin, from the *Chronicle*," she said, feeling only a twinge of dishonesty. "We met a couple of times, at the conference, remember?"

"Yes, Mattie. How can I help?"

"I was wondering—I know it's short notice and everything—but I was wondering if I could come over tomorrow morning sometime and have a quick word with Roger."

"Oh, I'm sorry, Mattie, but he likes to keep his mornings free to clear his paperwork and for internal meetings." It was a lie, and one she was increasingly forced to use as O'Neill's time-keeping had become spectacularly erratic. He rarely came into the office before 1:00 p.m. nowadays.

"Damn, I was really hoping…"

"What's it about?"

"I've got some ideas I want to bounce off him. About Charles Collingridge's sudden love of political literature. And the Praed Street address."

There was a pause, a distraction, as if Penny might have dropped the phone. "I'll call you back," she said and cut the connection.

❖   ❖   ❖

Penny had expected her alarm at Mattie's call to be converted into a volcano of panic when she phoned O'Neill, yet he seemed surprisingly confident. "She's got nothing, Pen," he insisted. "I hear she's in trouble with her newspaper anyway. It's not a problem."

"But what does she know, Rog?"

"How the fuck should I know? Let's get her in and find out."

"Rog?"

"You think I can't still do my old body swerve, Pen? She's only a bloody girl!"

She had tried to insist that it was foolish, he should be cautious, but he didn't do caution. Neither did he do mornings anymore, so Mattie had been invited to see him the following afternoon.

Penny loved O'Neill but her feelings brought her too close to him. She thought he was stressed, working too hard, suffering; she didn't comprehend the mind-pulverizing effects of cocaine. It kept O'Neill hyperactive into the small hours, unable to sleep until a cascade of depressant drugs gradually overwhelmed the cocaine and forced him into an oblivion from which he rarely emerged before midday, or sometimes later. So she grew increasingly confused and embarrassed as Mattie sat waiting for O'Neill. He had promised he would be on time but as the clock on his wall ticked on remorselessly, Penny's ability to invent new excuses began to vanish beneath her bewilderment about his public bravado and his private remorse, his inexplicable behavior and the irrational outbursts. She brought Mattie yet another cup of coffee.

"Let me give him a call at home," she suggested. "Perhaps he's had to go back there. Something he forgot, or not feeling too well…"

She went into his office to make the call, away from Mattie. She sat on the corner of his desk, picked up the phone and punched the numbers. With some embarrassment she greeted Roger on the phone, explaining in a whispered voice that Mattie had been waiting for more than half an hour and… Out of sight of Mattie her face gradually began to crumple in concern as she listened. She tried to interrupt but it was useless. Her lip began to tremble; she bit it hard, until the point came when she couldn't stand it any longer. She dropped the phone and fled from the office, past Mattie, in tears.

Mattie's first instinct was to run after the distressed Penny; her second and stronger instinct was to find out what had upset her. The receiver was still swinging beside the desk where it had been abandoned. She put it to her ear.

The voice that was still coming out of the phone was unrecognizable as Roger O'Neill. The words were incoherent, indecipherable, slowed and slurred to the point where it sounded like a doll with the batteries almost dead. There were gasps, moans, long pauses, the sound of tears falling, the mad music of a man in emotional agony and tearing himself apart. She replaced the receiver gently in the cradle.

❖   ❖   ❖

Mattie found Penny in the washroom, choking into a paper towel. Mattie touched her consolingly on the shoulder. Penny turned in alarm, as though slapped, her eyes raw and swollen.

"How long has he been like that, Penny?"

"I can't say anything!" she blurted, her confusion mixed with excruciating pain.

"Look, Penny, he's obviously in a very bad way. I'm not going to print any of this, for goodness' sake. I think he needs help. I think maybe you need a hug."

Mattie stretched out her arms and Penny fell into them as though she were the loneliest woman on the planet. She stayed there, locked in Mattie's arms, until there were no more tears left. When she had recovered sufficiently to escape, she and Mattie went for a walk in nearby Victoria Gardens to refresh themselves in the crisp air blowing off the Thames, and where they could talk without interruption. The fight had gone from Penny. She asked Mattie for an assurance that none of what she said would be printed, and when Mattie agreed, it began to pour forth. She told of how the Prime Minister's resignation had put O'Neill in turmoil, how he had always been a little "emotionally extravagant" but had been growing worse. "I think the resignation had really brought him close to a breakdown."

"But why, Penny? Surely they weren't that close?"

"He liked to think he was close to the whole Collingridge

family. He was always arranging for flowers and special photographs to be sent to Mrs. Collingridge, doing little favors whenever he could. He loved it all."

Mattie sighed, took in the cold air, the same wind that had blown her grandfather on his journey across the sea. How would he have felt about what she was doing? She felt guilty; she knew she wasn't being simply a friend to Penny, but hadn't her grandfather left all his friends behind, even his family, for what he knew was right? She, like him, had to press on. "Roger's in trouble, isn't he? We both heard him just now, Penny. Something has really got to Roger, something that's eating away at him from the inside."

"I...I think he blamed himself so badly over the shares."

"The shares? You mean the Renox shares?" Mattie pressed, trying to hide a flush of alarm.

"Charlie Collingridge asked him to open the accommodation address because he wanted somewhere for his private mail. Roger and I went to Paddington in a taxi and he sent me in to do the paperwork. I knew he felt uneasy at the time, I think he sensed there was something wrong. And when he realized what it had been used for and how much trouble it had caused, he just began going to pieces."

"Why did Charlie Collingridge ask Roger to open the address and not do it himself?"

"I've no idea, it was just a silly favor Rog agreed to do for him. Perhaps Charlie felt guilty because of what he was going to use it for. Fiddling the shares."

They were leaning on the parapet, staring out over the gray, sluggish river. A seagull landed beside them and stared with menacing yellow eyes, hoping for food. Mattie stared back and the bird flapped its wings and disappeared, crying out in disappointment.

"I'm sure it was something like that," Penny continued, "something Charlie was ashamed of. He took advantage of us.

Roger just breezed into the office one day and said he'd got this little job to do, that it was terribly confidential and I had to keep quiet about it. As silent as if I were sucking a bishop, he said. You know Rog. Tries to be an Irish poet. Thinks he has a way with words."

"So you never saw Charlie Collingridge yourself?"

"No. I've never met him. Rog likes to handle all the important people himself."

"But you are sure it was Charlie Collingridge?"

"Of course, Rog said so. And who else could it have been?" A burst of November air sent dead autumn leaves scurrying around their ankles like rats and Penny shivered. "Oh, God, it's all such an awful mess."

"Penny, relax! It'll be all right. These things sort themselves out." Mattie linked her arm through Penny's and they began to walk on. "Why don't you take a couple of days off? Roger can survive without you for a little while."

"Can he? I wonder."

"He can't be that useless. Knows how to make tea and use the office computer, doesn't he?"

"He's strictly a coffee man and types with one finger."

"Slow but sure."

"No, just slow."

It made sense to Mattie. Whoever messed with the computer file was no expert. O'Neill was no expert. It didn't make them one and the same but it made sense. So many fingers were pointing at O'Neill.

They had arrived back at Smith Square in the shadow of the church.

"You know, they still use gaslight in this square," Mattie said, pointing to the ornate street lamp above their heads.

"Do they?" Penny looked up and shook her head in surprise. "You know, I've walked around this square every day and never noticed. You have a sharp eye."

"I try."

They were outside the headquarters building. Penny heaved a sigh as she contemplated going back inside to everything that waited for her there. She squeezed Mattie's hand. "I love him, you know. That's the problem."

"Love should never be a problem."

"And there was me thinking how wise you were!" Penny laughed, her strength having returned. "Thanks for listening. It's been great just to be able to talk."

"Call me. Any time. And take care of yourself."

"You, too."

Mattie walked slowly the few hundred yards back to the House of Commons, oblivious of the chill, warmed by thoughts that were on fire with impatience, and with one thought burning brighter than all the others. Why the hell had Roger O'Neill framed Charles and Henry Collingridge?

THIRTY-FOUR

Every politician has his principles. It's simply that some are on a wavelength so rare you would require a telescope at Jodrell Bank to locate them.

Tuesday, November 16—Wednesday, November 17

U rquhart declared his intention to run for the leadership at a press conference held in the House of Commons timed to catch the early evening news and the following day's first editions. This was no pavement scramble but an announcement backed by the historic atmosphere of the Palace of Westminster with its noble stone fireplaces, its dark oak paneling, and its atmosphere of ageless authority. It was dignified, restrained, almost humble. No one had accused Samuel, Woolton, and the others of such things. Mortima was by his side and he emphasized that this was a family decision. He gave the impression of a man who was being dragged reluctantly toward the seat of power, placing his duty to his colleagues and his country above his own personal interests. It was political theater, of course, from a carefully rehearsed script, but he did it so well.

The following day, on Wednesday morning, Landless also held a press conference, another piece of theater but with an entirely different atmosphere. He sat in one of the palatial reception rooms of the Ritz Hotel at a long table covered with microphones, facing the cameras and questions of the financial press. Alongside him and almost dwarfed by his bulging girth sat Marcus Frobisher, the Chairman of the United Newspapers Group who, although an industrial magnate in his own right, was clearly cast in a secondary role for this occasion. To one side a large video screen played some of the *Chronicle*'s better advertising material interspersed with cuts of Landless being greeted by workers, pulling levers to start the printing presses, and generally running his empire in a warm and personal manner. And there was the man himself, smiling for the cameras.

"Good morning, ladies and gentlemen." Landless called the throng to order in a voice which was considerably less common cockney than the one he adopted on private occasions. "Thank you for coming at such short notice. We have invited you here to tell you about one of the most exciting steps forward for the British communications industry since Julius Reuter established his telegraph service in London more than a hundred years ago." He shifted one of the microphones a little closer to allow a few moments for the sense of excitement to take hold. "Today we wish to make an historic announcement. We have decided to create the largest newspaper group in the United Kingdom, which will provide a platform for making this country once again the worldwide leader in information services." He smiled around the room, then at Frobisher. "Chronicle Newspapers has made an offer to purchase the full issued share capital of the United Newspapers Group at a price which values them at £1.4 billion. That's a premium of 40 percent above the current market price. And I am delighted to say that the board of the United Newspapers Group has unanimously accepted the bid." More smiles. Frobisher was smiling, too, but Landless had a magnetism and physical presence that dragged all attention in upon him, leaving others struggling in shade. "We have also agreed the terms for the future management of the combined group. I shall become Chairman and Chief Executive of the new company, and my good friend and former competitor, now colleague"—he stretched a huge paw to grasp the shoulder of Frobisher, stopping just short of his neck—"is to be our President."

Several wise heads around the room were nodding in understanding. They knew Landless, had no doubts he would be in sole charge of the new operation. Frobisher had been kicked upstairs so high that the only view anyone would get of him was his arse. He sat there trying hard to put on a good face.

"This is a huge step for the British newspaper industry, and for the country as a whole. The combined operation will control more national and major regional titles than any other newspaper group. The amalgamation of our international subsidiaries will make us the third largest newspaper group in the world. It will be a springboard for our ambition, which very simply is to become the biggest newspaper group on the planet. And based right here in Britain." He beamed, his huge face split with a vast predatory smile. "Now ain't that exciting!" he declared, reverting to his east London accent, and cameras flashed as though on his command. He let them have their few moments before once more taking the reins.

"Now I know you'll all be bursting with questions—so let's start!"

A hum of excitement swept around the room and a forest of hands shot up to catch his eye.

"I suppose to be fair I ought to take the first question from someone who won't be working for the group," Landless jested. "Can we find anyone unlucky enough to fit that description?" With theatrical exaggeration he shielded his eyes from the bright lights and searched the gathering for a suitable victim and they all laughed at his cheek.

"Mr. Landless," shouted the business editor of the *Sunday*

Times. "The Government have made it very clear in recent years that in their view the ownership of British newspapers is already concentrated in too few hands. They've made it clear they would consider using their monopolies and mergers powers to prevent any further consolidation. How on earth do you expect to get the necessary Government approval?"

Many heads around the room nodded in agreement. Good question. Landless appeared to agree.

"An excellent point," he said, spreading his arms wide as if to hug the question to his chest and slowly throttle it to death. "You're right, of course, the Government will need to make its mind up. Newspapers are part of the worldwide information industry. It's growing and changing every day. You all know that. Five years ago you lot worked in Fleet Street with old typewriters and printing presses that should've been scrapped when the Kaiser surrendered. Today the industry is modernized, it's decentralized, it's computerized."

"Shame!" cried a voice and the room burst into nostalgic laughter for the days of long liquid lunches at El Vino's wine bar and prolonged printers' strikes which allowed them weeks or sometimes months off, a time when they could write books or build boats and dream dreams, and all of it while still on full pay.

"You know that had to change. And we've got to keep on changing, we can't stand still. We have to face competition not just from each other but from satellite television, local radio, breakfast TV, and the rest. More people will be demanding information twenty-four hours a day, from all parts of the world. They won't be buying newspapers which arrive hours after the news has occurred and then covers them in filthy printing ink. If we are going to survive we've got to move from being parochial newspapers to being suppliers of information on a worldwide basis. And for that we need clout." He lifted his shoulders in an enormous shrug that subsided with the deftness of an avalanche. "So the Government has got to decide. Does it play the ostrich, bury its head while the British newspaper industry goes bust like the British car industry, dead inside ten years as the Americans, Japanese, and even Australians take over? Or will it be visionary and back the best of British? Simple proposition. Do we duck and decline? Or take on the rest of the world and beat it?"

A blitz of flash guns greeted him as he sat back in his chair while the journalists who still took shorthand scribbled furiously to catch up with him. The questioner turned to his neighbor. "What do you think? Will the old bastard get away with it?"

"The industrial logic is compelling, that's for sure, and there's something rather charming about a working class kid on the make, don't you think? But if I know our Ben, he won't be relying just on persuasive logic or passion. He's the sort of guy who's already prepared the ground, every inch of it, even the cracks. I think we'll soon see just how many politicians owe him favors."

❖   ❖   ❖

The answer seemed to be that a whole host of politicians owed Landless. With nominations closing the following day and the first ballot due in just a week, no one seemed keen to take him on and risk antagonizing the combined might of the Chronicle and United groups. There was a rush to endorse his idea that within hours had grown into a stampede among contenders as they struggled not to be left behind. Why, the man was surely not only enlightened but deeply patriotic. Once again, it seemed that Landless had discovered the way to tickle a politician's fancy. By teatime he was able to sit back with his usual mug of Bovril and snap his red braces in delight.

Not everyone was taken in, of course. The *Independent* couldn't resist the temptation to have a dig.

The Landless announcement burst like a grenade in the middle of the leadership race—which presumably was his intention. Not since the Profumo scandal have so many politicians been caught pulling their trousers down. It is not only undignified but a dangerous state for a politician to be caught in.

Not all the aspirants joined the stampede. Samuel was cautious, noncommittal—he had too many knife wounds in his back to stick his head above the parapet yet again. He said he wanted to consult the workforce of the two groups before reaching his decision and, even before Landless's Bovril had gone cold, union representatives were denouncing the plan. They noted there were no guarantees about job security and hadn't forgotten or forgiven a tactless Landless quip that he'd had to fire ten thousand people for every million he had made. In the face of opposition from the unions, Samuel realized it would be absurd for him now to endorse the deal, so sought refuge in silence.

Urquhart also stood out from the crowd. Within an hour of the announcement he was in front of cameras giving a thoroughly polished analysis of the global information market and its likely trends. His technical expertise far outshone his rivals', yet he was cautious. "While I have the highest respect for Benjamin Landless I think it would be wrong of me to jump to conclusions before I've had an opportunity to consider all the details. I think politicians should be careful; it gives politics a bad name if we all look as if we're dashing around trying to buy the support of the editorial columns. So to avoid any possible misinterpretation, I shan't be announcing my own views until the leadership contest is over. By which time, of course," he added modestly, "they may be of no interest anyway."

"If only all his colleagues could have taken the dignified and principled stand of the Chief Whip," the *Independent* commented, raining down on him in praise. "Urquhart is establishing a statesmanlike tone for his campaign which marks him out from the pack. It will do nothing to harm his chances." Other editorials echoed the line, not least the *Chronicle*.

> *We encouraged Francis Urquhart to stand for the leadership because of our respect for his independence of mind and his integrity. We were delighted when he accepted the challenge and we are still convinced that our recommendation was correct. His refusal to rush to judgment over the Chronicle–United newspaper merger is no less than we would expect.*
>
> *We still hope that after due deliberation he will wholeheartedly endorse the merger plans, but our view of Urquhart is based on much more than commercial interest. He is the only candidate who so far has demonstrated that he has that vital characteristic missing in so many—the quality of leadership.*

From around the corridors of Westminster it was possible to detect the sound of doors being slammed in frustration as ambitious politicians realized that, once again, Urquhart had stolen a march on them. A penthouse suite overlooking Hyde Park offered a different perspective. Landless gazed out across the treetops and the world he hoped would soon be his. "To you, Frankie boy," he muttered into his glass. "To us."

THIRTY-FIVE

For some it is the end of the rope. For others it is only the beginning.

Thursday, November 18

When nominations closed at noon on Thursday, the only surprise was the last-minute withdrawal of Peter Bearstead. He'd been the first to announce his intention to stand but already his race was run. "I've done what I set out to do, which was to get a proper election going," he announced punchily. "I know I haven't got a chance of winning, so let the others get on with it. I'll be there to help drag the bodies out of the arena."

He had meant to say he would "be there to help bind the wounds" but not for the first time his love of a sharp phrase had run away with his judgment. He immediately signed up with the *Daily Express* to write personal and indiscreet profiles of the candidates for the duration.

So now there were nine, an unprecedentedly large field, but the prevailing view was that only five of them were in with a serious chance—Samuel, Woolton, Earle, McKenzie, and Urquhart. With the list of combatants complete, pollsters redoubled their efforts to contact Government MPs and sniff which way the tide was running.

Paul McKenzie was determined to show the sharpest edge of his sword. The Secretary of State for Health was a frustrated man. He'd been in charge of the health service for more than five years and had hoped as ardently as Urquhart for a new challenge in a post-election reshuffle. The long years in charge of an unresponsive bureaucracy had left him feeling diminished. A few years previously he had been regarded as one of the rising stars of the Party, a man who could combine a tough intellect with a deep sense of caring. Many predicted he would go all the way. But the health service had proved to be a bureaucratic beast he was incapable of breaking let alone training, and his encounters with picket lines of protesting nurses and ambulance men had left his image deeply frayed. The postponement of the hospital expansion plan had been the last straw. He'd grown dispirited, had talked with his wife about quitting politics at the next election, so had greeted Collingridge's downfall like a drowning man discovers dry land. He entered the final five days before the first ballot overflowing with enthusiasm and energy, anxious to make an immediate impact, determined to get his head above the crowd. He had asked his staff to find a suitable photo-opportunity, some excuse to revive his tarnished image—but no bloody hospitals, he instructed. His fingers had been chewed off all too often. He'd spent the first three years of his time in the Ministry conscientiously visiting hospitals and trying to learn about patient care, only to be met on bad days by picket lines of nurses complaining about "slave wages," and on worse days by violent demonstrations from ancillary staff protesting about "savage cuts." He'd been nicknamed "Dr. Cut," although the unions had often painted an additional consonant onto their banners. Even the doctors' unions seemed to take the view that health budgets should be set by the level of noise rather than the level of need. At times, but only in private, it had reduced McKenzie to tears of frustration.

He almost never got to see the patients. Even when he tried to sneak into a hospital by a back entrance the demonstrators always seemed to know beforehand precisely where he would be, ready to throw their abuse at him just when the television camera crews had arrived. Being beaten up in public by an angel of mercy was never great for the image or his self-esteem. So McKenzie had simply stopped visiting hospitals. Rather than running a gauntlet of abuse, he opted out and stuck to safer venues. It was a matter of self-preservation.

So his plan was as simple as it was safe. Instead of a hospital—"it would be entirely wrong to use sick patients for my own political purposes"—his office had arranged for him to visit the Humanifit Laboratories at their headquarters just off the M4. Humanifit made a wide range of equipment for handi-capped people and had just developed a revolutionary wheel-chair operated by voice commands. Even paraplegics unable to move their limbs could use it. The combination of new British technology and enhanced care for the disabled was just what McKenzie was looking for and so, barely a couple of hours after nominations closed, the Secretary of State's car was hastening down the motorway in search of his salvation.

McKenzie had been careful. He didn't take the success of the visit for granted. Factories were all well and good but a spirited demo was a thousand times more attractive to the cameras. He had been ambushed too many times, so he was careful to ensure that his office informed the media only three hours before his impending arrival, soon enough to scramble their camera crews but not enough to get rent-a-mob out and active. As he approached the Humanifit facility, he nestled back in his leather seat, practiced his smile, and congratulated himself on his caution. It was all going to work very well.

Unfortunately for McKenzie, his staff had been too efficient.

Governments need to know where their Ministers are at all times; like all other MPs they have to be available if at all possible in the event of an emergency or in case of a sudden vote in the House of Commons. So, on the previous Friday, following her standing instructions to the letter, McKenzie's diary secretary had sent a full list of his forthcoming engagements to the office of the government's coordinating authority—otherwise known as the Chief Whip.

As he was driven the final few hundred yards down the country road to the factory's green-field site, McKenzie combed his hair and prepared himself. The ministerial car passed alongside the red brick wall that curved around the site and, as the Minister in the rear seat made sure his tie was straight, it swept in through the front gates.

No sooner was it through than the driver jammed on the brakes, throwing McKenzie against the front seat, spilling papers on the floor and ruining his careful preparations. Before he had a chance to curse the driver and demand an explanation, the cause of the problem confronted and swirled around him. It was a sight beyond his wildest nightmare.

The tiny car park in front of the factory's reception office was jammed with a throng of seething protesters, all dressed in nurse's uniform and hurling abuse, with every angry word and action recorded by the three television cameras that had been dutifully summoned by McKenzie's press officer and placed in an ideal viewing position on top of the administration block. No sooner was the official car inside the gates than the crowd surged around, kicking the bodywork and banging placards on the roof. In a couple of seconds the aerial had gone and the windscreen wipers had also been wrenched off. The driver had the sense to press the panic button fitted to all Ministerial cars which automatically closed the windows and locked the doors, but not before someone had managed to spit directly into McKenzie's face. Fists and contorted faces were pressed hard up against the glass, all threatening violence on him; the car rocked as the crowd surged against it, smothering it, suffocating him, until he could see no sky, no trees, no help, nothing but hatred at close quarters.

"Get out! Get out!" he screamed, but the driver raised his hands in helplessness. The crowd had surrounded the car, blocking off any hope of retreat.

"Get out!" he continued to scream, overcome by claustrophobia, but to no avail. It wasn't a matter of judgment, more of fallible instinct as McKenzie, in despair and desperation, leaned forward and grabbed the automatic gear stick, throwing it into reverse. The car gave a judder and moved back barely a foot before the driver's foot hit the brake but too late. It had driven into the crowd. A wheelchair had been knocked over, a woman in nurse's uniform struck. She appeared to be in great pain.

The crowd parted and, seizing his opportunity, the driver reversed his vehicle out of the gates and onto the road, pulling off a spectacular hand-brake turn to bring the nose of the car round and effect a rapid escape. He sped away leaving large black rubber scars on the road surface.

McKenzie's political career was left on the road alongside the ugly burnt tire marks. It didn't matter that the wheelchair had been empty or the woman was not badly injured, or that she wasn't in fact a nurse but a full time union convener and an experienced hand at turning a picket line drama into a newsworthy crisis. No one bothered to inquire and why should they? They already had their story. The tide had turned against the drowning man and swept poor McKenzie once more out to sea.

THIRTY-SIX

*It was once said that all political careers end in failure.
That's why politicians have a front side and a back side. It
makes them easier to stack.*

Friday, November 19

It had been a difficult week for Mattie. The pace of activity in the leadership race had picked up sharply yet she found herself treading water, feeling left behind by events. Nothing had come of her few job interviews. It became clear to her that she had been blacked by all the newspapers in the expanding Landless empire and none of his remaining competitors seemed particularly keen to antagonize him. The word had gotten around, she was "difficult." And on Friday morning the mortgage rate had gone up.

But the worst of it was her frustration with herself. While she had gathered more pieces of the jigsaw, still she could find no pattern in them. Nothing seemed to fit. It left a dull, throbbing ache in her temples that had been with her for days, so she had hauled her running gear out of the wardrobe and began pounding her way around the leaf-covered tracks and pathways of Holland Park, hoping that the much needed physical exercise would purge both body and mind. Instead it seemed only to add to her pains as her lungs and legs began to complain. She was running out of ideas, stamina, and time. The first ballot was just four days away and all she was doing was scattering squirrels.

In the fading evening light she ran along the sweeping avenue of chestnut trees that towered magnificent and leafless above her; down Lime Tree Walk where in daylight the sparrows were as tame as house pets, past the red bricked ruins of old Holland House, burned to the ground half a century ago, leaving itself wrapped in brooding memories of past glories. In the days before London had grown into a voracious urban sprawl, Holland House had been the country seat of Charles James Fox, the legendary eighteenth century radical who had spent a lifetime pursuing revolutionary causes and plotting the downfall of the prime minister. It had always been in vain. Yet who had succeeded where he had failed?

She went over the ground again, the field of battle on which Collingridge had fallen, the election campaign, the leaks, the scandals, and the personalities that had been sucked into the mire—not just Collingridge and his brother Charlie but Williams, O'Neill, Bearstead, McKenzie, Sir Jasper Grainger, and Landless, of course. That was it. That was all she had. So where did she go from here? As she climbed the slope toward the highest part of the wooded park, digging into the soft earth, she bounced the alternatives to see if any would fly.

"Collingridge isn't giving interviews. Williams will only talk through his Press Office. O'Neill doesn't seem capable of answering questions, and Landless wouldn't stop for me on a pedestrian crossing. Which leaves…" She came to a sudden halt, scattering dead leaves. "Why, you, Mr. Kendrick."

She started running once more, her feet lighter as she broke the top of the hill and began stretching out on the long downhill slope that led toward her home. She felt better now. She had gotten her second wind.

Saturday, November 20

As Harold Earle clambered gently out of bed so as not to disturb his wife and headed for the shower, he felt content with his week's work. He'd been nominated as one of the five "most likely" candidates, then watched as Samuel's bandwagon failed to roll and McKenzie's derailed. There was the Chief Whip's creditable showing, of course, but Earle couldn't believe Urquhart could succeed; he had no senior Cabinet experience of running any great Department of State, and at the end of the day experience counted. Particularly experience like Earle's.

He'd started his climb many years before as Maggie Thatcher's Parliamentary Private Secretary, a post of no formal power but whose position close to the eternal flame left others in awe. His promotion to the Cabinet had been rapid and he'd held several important portfolios including, for the last two years under Collingridge, responsibility for the Government's extensive school reforms as Secretary of State for Education. Unlike some of his predecessors he had managed to find common ground with the teaching profession, although there were those who accused him of being unable to take really tough decisions and of being a conciliator.

But didn't the Party in its present mood need a touch of conciliation? The infighting around Collingridge had left scars and the growing abrasiveness of the campaign for his successor was doing little but rub salt in the wounds. Woolton in particular was proving a pain with his attempts to rekindle memories of his early rough and tumble North Country political style; calling a spade a bloody shovel only antagonized the more traditional spirits in the Party. The time was right for Earle, exactly right.

Today, Saturday, would be a big day, a rally among the party faithful in his constituency to wave the flag, a brightly decked hall packed with supporters whom he could greet on first-name terms—in front of the cameras, of course. And he would announce a major policy initiative. He and his officials had been working on it for some time and with just a little fire under their fannies they would have it ready. The Government already offered school leavers without a job a guaranteed place on a training course, but now they would have the opportunity to complete that training in another Common Market country, which would provide practical skills and language training as well.

Earle was confident it would be well received. A speech that would glow with references to new horizons and youth opportunity and brighter futures and every other kind of cliché he could squeeze within an inch of its life.

And the *coup de grâce*. He would call it that, use the French, entirely appropriate. He'd got the bureaucrats in Brussels to pay for the whole thing. He could already feel the tumultuous applause that would wash over him, carrying him all the way to Downing Street.

A large crowd of cheering supporters was waiting for him outside the Essex village hall when he arrived. They were waving little Union Jacks and old election posters proclaiming him as "The Earle of Essex," which had been brought out to give the occasion all the atmosphere of the campaign trail. There was even a brass band that struck up as he came through the doors of the hall, proceeding down the aisle shaking hands on all sides. The local mayor led him up onto the low wooden platform as the cameramen and lighting crews maneuvered to find the best angle. He climbed the steps, kissed his wife, gazed out over the crowd, shielded his eyes from the lights, waved to their applause even as the mayor was trying to herald him as "the man who needs no introduction, not to you—and soon not to anyone in the country!" At that moment Harold Earle felt as if he was on the brink of the greatest personal triumph of his life.

And that was the moment he saw him. Standing in the front row, squashed between the other cheering supporters, waving and applauding with the rest of them. Simon. The one person in the world he had hoped he would never see or hear from again.

They had met in a railway carriage, late one night as Earle had been coming back from a rally in the Northwest. They had been alone, Earle had been drunk, and Simon had been very, very friendly. And handsome. Appealed to a side of Earle he had been struggling since university to forget. As the train thundered through the night he and Simon had entered a world cut off from the bright lights and responsibilities they had just left. Earle had discovered himself committing acts that would have made him liable to a prison sentence several years before and which were still only legal between consenting adults in private and certainly not in a British Rail carriage twenty minutes out of Birmingham.

Earle had staggered from the train at Euston, thrust two twenties into Simon's hand, and spent the night at his club. He couldn't face going back home.

He hadn't seen Simon for another six months until out of the blue he'd turned up in the Central Lobby of the Houses of Parliament asking the police attendants if he could see him. When the panic-stricken Minister arrived the youth hadn't made a public fuss, had explained how he had recognized Earle from a recent party political broadcast, had asked for the money in a very gentle fashion. Earle had paid him some "expenses" for his trip to London and wished him well.

Simon had turned up again a few weeks later and Earle knew there would be no respite. He had instructed Simon to wait. Then he had sought sanctuary in the corner of the Chamber, spent ten minutes looking over the scene he had grown to love, knowing that the youth outside threatened everything he treasured in his life. Finding no answer himself he had dragged himself to the Chief Whip's Office and spilled the lot. There was a youth sitting in the Central Lobby blackmailing him for a brief and stupid fling they'd had many months before. He was finished.

"Bit of a bugger's muddle," Urquhart had suggested before apologizing for the inappropriate metaphor. "But not to worry, Harold, worse things happened on the retreat from Dunkirk, not to mention the Upper Corridor Committee Room. Just point the little shit out to me."

Urquhart had been as good as his word, bloody magnificent, in fact. He had introduced himself to the boy and assured him that if he were not off the premises in five minutes the police would be called and he would be arrested for blackmail. "Oh, don't think you're the first," Urquhart had assured him. "Happens remarkably often. It's simply that in such sordid cases the arrest and subsequent trial are held with desperately little publicity. No one will hear who you've been trying to blackmail, and very few people will even get to know how long you've been sent down for. Perhaps only your poor mother."

Without further inducement the youth had come to the conclusion he had made a terrible mistake and should vanish from the premises and from Harold Earle's life as quickly as possible, but Urquhart had taken the precaution of taking down the details from Simon's driving license, just in case he were to continue to cause trouble.

And now he was back, squashed into a seat in the front row, ready to make unknown demands about which Earle's fevered imagination could only torment itself. The torment went on throughout the speech, which ended as a considerable disappointment to his followers. The content was there, printed in large type on his small pages of recycled paper, but the fire was gone. He stumbled through his officials' tired prose, sweat dripping from his nose even on a cold November day, his mind seeming elsewhere even as he was delivering the lines. The faithful still clapped and applauded enthusiastically when he was finished, but it didn't help. The mayor almost had to drag him into the pit of the hall to satisfy the clamor of the crowd for one last handshake and the chance personally to wish their favorite son well. As they cheered him and pummeled him on the back he was drawn ever closer to Simon's youthful, penetrating, knowing eyes. It was as if he were being dragged toward the gates of Hell itself. But Simon caused no scene, did nothing but shake his clammy hand and smile while toying nervously with the medallion that swung ostentatiously around his neck. Then he was gone, just another face left behind in the crowd.

❖ ❖ ❖

When Earle arrived back home, two men were standing outside in the cold street waiting.

"Evening, Mr. Earle, Mrs. Earle. Simmonds and Peters from the *Mirror*. Interesting rally you had. We've got the press handout, the words, but we need a bit of color for our readers. Like how the audience reacted. Got anything to say about your audience, Mr. Earle?"

He rushed inside without a word, dragging his wife and slamming the door behind him. He watched through a curtained window as they shrugged their shoulders and retreated to the estate car parked on the other side of the street. They pulled out a book and a thermos flask, and settled down for the long night ahead.

THIRTY-SEVEN

The nature of ambition is that it requires casualties.

Sunday, November 21

They were still there the following morning just after dawn when Earle looked out. One was asleep, napping under a trilby hat pulled down over his eyes, the other was rifling through the Sunday newspapers. They bore little resemblance to the previous week's editions. A leadership campaign that had been dead in the water had now, with Urquhart's intervention and McKenzie's catastrophe, sprung into life.

What was more, the pollsters were beginning to wear down the MPs' resistance. "ALL SQUARE!" declared the *Observer*, announcing that the 60 percent of the Parliamentary Party they had managed to cajole into giving a view were now evenly split between the three leading candidates—Samuel, Earle, and Woolton, with Urquhart close behind. McKenzie had disappeared without trace, as had the small lead that Samuel had previously enjoyed.

The news would give no joy to Earle. He had spent a sleepless night, pacing the floors and fending off the questions of his increasingly worried wife. He had tried to find comfort but could see only Simon's face. The presence of the two journalists had kept nagging at him. How much did they know? Why were they squatting on his doorstep? As the first fingers of dawn began to spread cold and gray in the November sky, he found himself drained. He could resist no longer. He had to know.

Peters nudged Simmonds awake as the unshaven figure of Earle, his silk dressing gown wrapped tight around him, emerged from the front door of his house and made toward them.

"Works like a dream every time," Peters said. "Like a mouse after cheese. Let's see what he has to say for himself, Alf—and turn that bloody tape machine on."

"Good morning, Mr. Earle," Peters shouted as Earle approached. "Don't stand out there in the cold, come sit inside. Care for a cup of coffee?"

"What do you want? Why are you spying on me?" Earle demanded, ignoring the offer.

"Spying, Mr. Earle? Don't be silly, we're just looking for a bit of color. You're a leading candidate to become Prime Minister. Seen the newspapers yet? You're all over them. People are bound to take more interest in you—about your hobbies, what you do. Who your friends are."

"I have nothing to say!"

"Could we interview your wife, perhaps?" Simmonds asked.

"What are you implying?" Earle demanded in a contorted, high pitched voice.

"My goodness me nothing at all, sir. By the way, have you seen the photos of your rally yesterday? They're very good, really clear. We're thinking of using one on our front page tomorrow. Here, have a look."

A hand thrust a large glossy photograph out of the window and waved it under Earle's nose. He grabbed it, then he gasped. It showed him gripping the hand and looking straight into the eyes of a smiling, simpering Simon. The details were awesomely clear. It almost looked as if some hidden hand had added a trace of eyeliner around Simon's large eyes and his fleshy, petulant lips appeared to have grown darker, more prominent. The fingers playing with the medallion around his neck were beautifully manicured.

"Know this gentleman well, do you, sir?" Simmonds asked.

"One of your close supporters, is he? And how precisely does he support you, Mr. Earle?" Peters joined in.

Earle's hand was trembling. He threw the photograph back through the car window. "What are you trying to do? I deny everything. I shall report your harassment to your editor!"

"Editor, sir? Why, bless me, it's him what sent us."

THIRTY-EIGHT

It's all very well volunteering to lead an army, but that's the point that the enemy aims at first. Better just a few steps behind, give yourself time to pick your way through the piles of bodies.

Monday, November 22

The Members' Lobby that is the main entrance to the Chamber is dominated by large bronze figures of Churchill and Attlee and Lloyd George. The toecaps of the statues are bright from the brushing fingers of MPs hoping to share in their greatness. The Lobby has two solid oak doors that protect the Chamber and on which Black Rod knocks to summon MPs for the State Opening of Parliament. The door is set in a battered stone arch that still bears the scars of the destruction of the original Chamber in the bombing of 1941. When the Chamber had been rebuilt, Churchill had asked for the disfigured and scorched arch to be retained. "To remind us."

The Lobby is also where Members collect messages.

"Hello, Mr. Kendrick."

He looked up from his inspection of various pieces of paper to find Mattie at his elbow. He smiled. "You're…"

"Mattie Storin."

"Yes, of course you are." His eyes wandered before returning to her face. "And what can I do for you, Mattie?"

"I'd like to ask you a few questions, if that's all right."

"My pleasure. But not now, I'm afraid," he said, glancing at his watch. "How about tea? My place? Four-thirty? I'll have plenty of time for you then."

Kendrick was an Opposition backbencher and his office was a small single room in Norman Shaw North, the red brick building made famous in countless aging black and white films as New Scotland Yard, the headquarters of the Metropolitan Police. The forces of law and order had long since moved to a gray concrete fortress in Victoria Street, and the parliamentary authorities had been delighted to snap up the vacant, albeit dilapidated, space just across the road from the Houses of Parliament to provide much needed additional office space. Kendrick jumped up from his desk as she walked in.

"Mattie, come into my home and invade my personal space. It's got as much charm as a monk's cell, hasn't it?"

"Wouldn't know. I don't do monks," she replied.

He helped her out of her coat, his eyes appreciative rather than predatory, her woolen sweater deliberately tight, her skirt short enough to show her knees. She needed his attention and she was getting it.

"Tea, or…" he inquired, lifting an eyebrow.

"Or," she said.

He pulled a bottle of chardonnay from a small refrigerator that stood in a corner and pulled down two glasses from a bookshelf. She sat on the small sofa while he poured.

"Home," she said, raising her glass in salute.

"This is nothing like bloody home and I never want it to be," he growled. "How the hell we're expected to run a faded empire from broom closets, God only knows. But I'll drink to it with you, anyway."

"You can't hate it so much. You spent years struggling to get into the place."

"Ungrateful sod, aren't I?" he said and burst into a fetching smile.

"And you've managed to make your mark very quickly."

"Flattery, eh? And legs. You must want something very badly." He looked at her with steady, understanding eyes. It was her turn to smile.

"Mr. Kendrick—"

"Oh, bloody hell, we're way past the Mr. Kendrick stage, I hope."

"Stephen, I'm looking at a piece on how Parliament works and how politics can be so full of surprises. And when it comes to surprises, yours was one of the biggest."

Kendrick chuckled. "I'm still amazed at how my reputation was built on such a—well, what would you call it? Stroke of luck? Throw of the dice? Guesswork?"

"Are you trying to tell me you didn't actually know the hospital scheme had been shelved, that you were guessing?" she asked, her tone incredulous.

"You don't believe that?"

"Let me put it this way. I'm a cynic with a smile."

"Well, so long as you're smiling, Mattie…" He poured another glass for her. "Let me put it this way. I wasn't absolutely certain. I took a risk."

"So what did you know?"

"Off the record?"

"Way off, if you like."

"I've never really told the full story before to anyone…" He glanced down to where Mattie was rubbing her ankles, as if to relieve sore shins. "But I like your interrogation technique. And I suppose there's no harm in telling you a little of the background." He pondered a second to decide how far he should go. "I found out that the Government—or rather their Party

Headquarters—had planned a massive publicity campaign to promote the new hospital plan. They'd worked hard at it, spent a lot of money on the preparations—well, you would, wouldn't you, with a plan like that? But at the last minute they canceled the whole bloody thing. Just pulled the plug on it. I thought about it for a long while, and the more I thought the only explanation that made any sense was that they weren't pulling the plug just on the publicity campaign but on the policy itself. So I decided to challenge the Prime Minister—and he fell for it! I couldn't have been more surprised myself."

"I don't remember any discussion at the time about a publicity campaign."

"They wanted the element of surprise. I think all the planning of it was highly confidential."

"You obviously have confidential sources."

"And that's exactly how they're going to stay, even for you. Confidential! It's the sort of thing I wouldn't even tell my ex."

"You're…"

"Divorced. Very single."

Mattie suspected he was offering a deal but, as attractive as he was, she wasn't willing to pay that sort of price. Her life was already complicated enough.

"I know how valuable sources are," she said, getting the conversation back on track, "but can you give me a little guidance? The leak could only have come from one of two sources, Party or Government, yes…?"

"Insight as well as ankles."

"There's been bad blood between Party Headquarters and Downing Street since the election. You said it was a party publicity drive, so it would be logical to suspect the information came out of Party Headquarters."

"You're very good, Mattie. But you didn't get that from me, OK? And I'm not saying any more about my source." His tone had lost its gaiety, he was now in business mode and cautious.

"No need to worry. Roger's secret is safe with me."

Kendrick was halfway through a mouthful of wine. He let it dribble back into his glass. The eyes, when they came up to meet hers, were like unhammered steel. "You think I'm shallow enough to turn on an old friend just because you flash your tits at me?"

An old friend? The pieces of this part of the jigsaw were beginning to fit together. "I know it was Roger. I don't need you to confirm it. And I'm not on an inquisition. He's got enough on his plate without this. This won't appear in the press."

"So why are you here?"

"Information. Understanding."

"And there was me beginning to like you. I think it's time for you to leave, Mattie."

✧ ✧ ✧

The men from the *Mirror* were there at lunchtime and still there in the evening, reading, picking their teeth, watching. They had been waiting for Earle in their sordid little car almost continuously for forty-eight hours, witnessing every flicker of the curtain, photographing everyone who called including the postman and the milkman. And his wife, of course. He found only a crumb of comfort that she had left early to visit her sister. Sweet, blind woman that she was, she'd assumed the journalists were lurking outside her front door because of the leadership campaign—which, in a way, they were.

Earle had no one to turn to, no one with whom to share his misery or seek wise counsel. He was a lonely figure, a sincere and even devout man who had made one mistake for which one day he knew he would pay.

They had grown tired with waiting. They knocked on the door. "Sorry to bother you, Mr. Earle. Simmonds and Peters again. Just a quick question our editor wanted us to ask. How long have you known him?"

Into his face was thrust another photograph of Simon, this time taken not at a public rally but in a photographer's studio, and dressed from head to foot in black leather slashed by zip fasteners. The jacket was open to the waist, exposing a slender, tapering body, while from his right hand there trailed a long bullwhip.

"Go away. Go away. Please—go away!" he screamed, so loudly that neighbors came to the window to investigate.

"If it's inconvenient, we'll come back some other time, sir." Silently they filed back to their car and resumed the watch.

THIRTY-NINE

Those who wish to climb the tallest trees must accept the consequence that it is likely to expose their most vulnerable parts.

Tuesday, November 23

They were still there the following morning, waiting for him. Earle had no emotional resources left. He sat weeping gently in an armchair in the study, his fingernails, or what was left of them, buried deep into the arm. He had worked so hard, deserved so much, yet it had all come to this.

He knew he must finish it. There was no point in going on. He no longer believed in himself and knew he had forfeited the right to have others believe in him. Through misty eyes he reached into the drawer of his desk, fumbled as he took out his private phone book. He touched the numbers on the phone as if he were dipping his fingers in the cruelest acid. He fought hard to control his voice throughout the brief conversation. Then it was finished, and he could weep again.

❖ ❖ ❖

The news that Earle had pulled out of the race left everyone aghast as it flashed through Westminster later on Tuesday morning. It had happened so unexpectedly that there was no time to alter the printed ballot papers except with an ignominious scratching through of his name with a pen. Sir Humphrey was not best pleased that his carefully laid preparations should have been thrown into chaos at the last minute and had rough words to use for anyone who was willing to listen, but on the stroke of 10:00 a.m. Committee Room Number 14, which had been set aside for the ballot, opened its doors and the first of the 335 Government MPs who were going to vote began to file through. There would be two prominent absentees—the Prime Minister, who had announced he would not vote, and Harold Earle.

Mattie's intention had been to spend the day at the House of Commons chatting to MPs and gauging their sentiment. Most appeared to think that Earle's withdrawal would tend to help Samuel: "the conciliators tend to stick with the conscience merchants," one old buffer had explained, "so Earle's supporters will drift toward young Disraeli. They haven't got the imagination to do anything more positive." Disraeli. The Jew. The campaign was taking a more unpleasant personal edge.

She was in the press gallery cafeteria spilling coffee with other correspondents when the Tannoy system announced there was a call for her. She hoped it might be a job offer, that someone had changed their mind; she deserted her coffee and went to the nearest phone. The shock that hit her when she heard the voice was even greater than the news of Earle's withdrawal.

"Hello, Mattie. I understand you were looking for me last week. Sorry you missed me, I was out of the office. Touch of gastric flu. Do you still want to get together?"

Roger O'Neill's voice sounded so friendly and enthusiastic that she had trouble connecting it with the voice she had heard dribbling down the phone a few days earlier. It sounded like a completely different man.

"If you're still interested, why not come across to Smith Square later today?" he offered.

It left Mattie wondering what chaotic circus ride O'Neill was on. Yet her reaction was nothing compared to that of Urquhart a little earlier. He had telephoned to instruct O'Neill to make the appropriate arrangements for Simon to attend Earle's weekend meeting, and also to ensure that the *Mirror* was anonymously informed about the connections between the two men. Instead, like Mattie and Penny, he had discovered O'Neill sliding steadily into his cocaine-induced oblivion and losing touch with events outside his increasingly narrow, kaleidoscopic world. There had been a confrontation. Urquhart couldn't afford to lose O'Neill's services, but neither could he afford to have loose ends unraveling.

"One week, Roger, one more week and you can take a break, forget all of this for a while. Come back to that knighthood you've always wanted. It will change everything for you. With a 'K' they'll never be able to look down their noses at you again. And I can arrange it, you know I can. But you let me down now, you lose control, and by God I'll make sure you regret it for the rest of your life. Damn you, get a grip on yourself. You've got nothing to fear. Just hold on for a few more days!"

O'Neill wasn't entirely sure what Urquhart was going on about. Hold on? Of course he could hold on. To be sure he'd been a little unwell but his befuddled brain was in denial and still refused to accept there was any major problem with his behavior. He could handle it. Everything. There was no room in his life for doubts, especially about himself. He could cope with it all, particularly with a little more help, just a little…Only a few more days, pull a few strings, a few more sidesteps, and wipe the condescending smiles off their faces. Arise, Sir Roger! It would be worth a little extra effort.

"Of course, Francis. Not a problem. I promise."

"Don't get this wrong, Roger. Don't you dare."

And O'Neill had laughed, even as his eyes flowed and his nose dribbled like an old man's on a windy day.

When at last he had wiped himself down sufficiently to return to his office, Penny had told him of Mattie's visit, that she was asking questions about the Paddington accommodation address.

"No worries, Pen. I'll deal with it," he exclaimed, burying the instantaneous flicker of alarm, falling back on the swaggering confidence of years of salesmanship. Why, hadn't they said that he could sell snow to Siberia, that old ladies would cross the street to be kissed by him? All it needed was passion, a little self-belief. Mattie was nothing but a witless woman, no heavy shit.

So when she arrived in his office after lunch, he was bright, alert, those strange eyes of his still amazingly animated but seemingly anxious to help.

"It was just a stomach upset," he explained. "Sorry I had to stand you up but whatever it was the doctor gave me really got to me, gave me a right kicking." He smiled, so full of Irish charm. "Better now. So Pen tells me you were asking about Mr. Collingridge's accommodation address."

"That's right. It was Charles Collingridge's address?"

"Sure it was."

"But he didn't open it himself."

O'Neill's eyes were in a renewed frenzy, like objects trying to escape the pull of gravity, but the confident smile remained fixed. And Mattie was desperate to cover her source, Penny, so she invented on the spot.

"The shopkeeper has never met Collingridge, doesn't recognize his photograph, swears he's never been in the shop," she continued.

"A friend, then," O'Neill said, scrabbling for a cigarette.

"Who?"

"Well, it certainly wasn't bloody me!" O'Neill chortled, emerging from beneath a haze of tobacco smoke. "Look, Mattie, if you're looking for something on the record, you know I'll have to say that Mr. Collingridge's personal affairs are his own, and there won't be any point in your staying even to finish your tea." He leaned closer to her, across his desk. "But if you want to talk, off the record, not for reporting…"

"I'm enjoying the tea," she replied.

He lit the cigarette, drew on it deep, filling his lungs, swelling his confidence. "OK. Even off the record you'll know there's a limit to how much I can say, but you know how unwell Charlie has been recently. He's not been—how can I put it?—'fully responsible' for his actions." He curled his fingers to emphasize the quotation marks. "It would be a terrible pity if you were to go out of your way to rake through all this and punish him still further. His life is in ruins. Whatever he's done wrong, hasn't he suffered enough? For pity's sake, Mattie, give the man a chance to rebuild his life."

Mattie's humor began to curdle inside as she watched the passing of guilt onto innocent shoulders dressed up as self-less charity, but nevertheless she smiled encouragingly. "Fair enough, Roger. Nothing to be gained from further harassment. So let me turn to a different point."

And she saw his eyes grow steady for a second, the smile relax. He thought he'd won. Beaten this simple girl at her own game. Another sidestep, another swerve, and he was free. God, Roger, you're good!

"Let's talk about leaks," she continued. "So many of them in recent months. The Prime Minister is supposed to blame Smith Square for much of his troubles."

"I doubt whether that is fair, but it is not a state secret that relations between him and the Party Chairman have been very strained."

"Strained enough for that opinion poll we published during party conference to have been deliberately leaked from inside Party Headquarters?"

The eyes began wobbling once again. "People always want someone to blame. Someone else. I guess that's partly what we're here for." He laughed in self-mockery. "It's so easy to point the finger but I think that assumption is very difficult to justify. Apart from the Party Chairman there are only—what, five people in this building who get sent those full opinion polls. I'm one of those five, and I can tell you we take their confidentiality damned seriously." He lit another cigarette. Time to think. "But they also get sent to every Cabinet minister, all twenty-two of them, either at the House of Commons where they might first go through the hands of a gossipy secretary, or to their departments, and they're often a nest of vipers, civil servants who have no love for this Government. If you're looking for leaks, they're the obvious places to start."

"OK, but the papers were leaked at the headquarters hotel in Bournemouth. Secretaries or unfriendly civil servants don't go to the Party conference or roam around the headquarters hotel."

"Well, who knows, Mattie? It's still much more likely to have come from a source like that. For the love of God, can you imagine Lord Williams down on his hands and knees outside hotel room doors?"

He laughed loudly to show how ridiculous it was, and Mattie joined him. But O'Neill had just admitted he knew the manner in which the opinion poll had been leaked. He could only have known that for one reason. His overconfidence was tightening like a noose around his neck.

"Let me turn to another leak, then, the one on the hospital scheme. I'm told that you were planning a major publicity drive that had to be scrapped at the last minute because of the change of plan."

"Really? Who on earth told you that?" O'Neill asked, his mind in hyper-drive and coming to settle on his old friend Kendrick. Stupid bastard, always had a weakness for a pretty woman. "Never mind, I won't push you, I know you won't reveal your sources. But they sound exaggerated to me. The Publicity Department here is always ready to support Government policy, that's what we do. If the scheme had gone ahead then certainly we'd have wanted to help promote it, for sure, but we had no specific campaign in mind."

"I was told you had to scrap a big publicity push which had been carefully planned and was ready to go."

The limp ash from his cigarette gave up its struggle to defy the laws of gravity and cascaded down his tie; O'Neill ignored it, his brows knitted in concentration. "If that's what you've heard, Mattie, you've been misinformed. Sounds to me like someone with his own ax to grind. Are you sure he's in a position to know all the facts? Maybe he's got his own angle to sell?"

With a broad grin, O'Neill tried to smother Kendrick as a reliable source. The smile grew more rigid when he realized he'd talked about the source as "he," but there was no way this slip of a girl could have picked up on such a gentle stumble. Yet she was asking too many questions; O'Neill was beginning to feel uncomfortable. He felt a gut-wrenching need for more substantial support than a cigarette could give him, no matter what Urquhart had said.

"Mattie, I've got a busy day, what with the result of the ballot later this evening and everything. Could we finish it here?"

"Thanks for your time, Roger. I've found it immensely helpful."

"I haven't told you anything."

"But you do it so persuasively."

"Any time I can help," he said as he guided her toward the door. As they did so, they passed by the computer terminal stationed in the corner of his crowded office. She bent down to inspect it and her blouse fell forward a couple of inches. He drew closer, delighted at the excuse.

"Your Party is well ahead of the others in the technology game. I suppose all the terminals in this building are linked through the central computer?"

He straightened, alarm bells ringing from somewhere deep inside and loud enough to distract him for the curve of her breasts. "I…guess so," he said. He placed a hand in the small of her back and pushed her gently toward the door.

"I'm afraid I'm a bit of a moron with computers. Maybe sometime you could give me a few lessons, Roger."

"You'd have to be desperate to ask me," he joked.

"You seem like a man who could handle most things."

"We all get put through a training course but I'm scarcely capable of switching the wretched thing on," he said. "Barely use it myself. Just for internal mail, that sort of thing." His eyes were flickering violently, he was no longer in control. "Sorry, got to rush," he muttered, and fled from his own office.

❖ ❖ ❖

At 5:00 p.m. the doors to Commons Committee Room 14 were ceremoniously shut to bar any further attempts to lodge votes. The gesture was an entirely empty one because the last of the 335 votes had been cast ten minutes earlier. Behind the locked doors and beneath huge oil paintings and flock wallpaper of the deepest hue, Sir Humphrey and his small team of scrutineers gathered, content that the day had gone smoothly in spite of the appalling start given to their preparations by Earle. A bottle of whiskey did the rounds while they fortified themselves for the count. In different rooms within the Palace, the eight candidates waited in various states of excitement and sobriety for the summons that would change their lives.

Big Ben had struck the quarter after six before the call went out, by half past six the doors to the committee room were unlocked and a swarm of MPs swept in to witness a moment of history. There were too many of them to be accommodated on the long school-like desks and even in standing room, so the doors were left open and the throng spilled into the corridor outside. Substantial sums were being wagered as Members made last-minute calculations as to the likely outcome; in the corridor among the overspill, the men from the media tried to soak up every whisper.

Sir Humphrey was enjoying his moment. He was in the twilight of his career, long since past his parliamentary heyday, and even the small misunderstanding over his holiday in the West Indies had helped bring him greater recognition around the Westminster circuit than he'd enjoyed for many years. "'Tis an ill wind that blows up no skirt," he had been heard quipping in the Smoking Room. Now he sat on the raised dais of the Committee Room flanked by his lieutenants, smoothing his mustache and calling the meeting to order.

"Since there has been such an unprecedentedly large number of names on the ballot paper, I propose to read the results out in alphabetical order," he began.

This was unwelcome news for David Adams, the foppish former Leader of the House who had been banished to exile on the backbenches by Collingridge's first reshuffle after claiming too publicly that he spent more time with the Queen than did the Prime Minister. He had hoped for a respectable showing in order to establish his claim for a return to Cabinet. His silk pocket handkerchief seemed to droop in dismay as Newlands announced he had received only twelve votes. He'd been promised much more as he had poured decent claret down so many of his colleagues' throats. "Bitches!" he was heard to mumble.

Sir Humphrey continued with his roll call. None of the next four names, including McKenzie's, could muster more than twenty of their colleagues. Paul Goddard, the maverick Catholic who had stood on the single issue of banning all forms of legalized abortion, received but three. He shook his head defiantly; his rewards were not to be of the earthly kind.

Sir Humphrey had only three more names to announce— Samuel, Urquhart, and Woolton—and a total of 281 votes to distribute. The level of tension in the packed room soared. A minimum of 169 votes was required for success on the first ballot. A couple of huge side bets were hurriedly concluded in one corner as two Honorable Members wagered whether there would, after all, be a result on the first round.

"Michael Samuel," intoned the chairman, gazing round the room like a Hamlet at the grave. "Ninety-nine votes."

The room was in dead silence until a tug on its way up the Thames blew its klaxon three times. A ripple of amusement covered the tension and Samuel muttered that it was a pity tug masters didn't have a vote. He was clearly disappointed to be such a long way from the winning line.

"Francis Urquhart—ninety-one votes."

He had been given a seat on one of the long desks at the front; he offered a silent nod of gratitude.

"Patrick Woolton—ninety-one votes."

And it was done. The room erupted. No one was paying attention to Newlands any longer. He tried to struggle through. "Since no candidate has been elected, there will be a second round a week today. I would remind everyone that those wishing to offer themselves for the second ballot must resubmit their nominations to me by Thursday. I declare this meeting closed!"

But no one was paying the slightest attention to him any longer.

FORTY

Political friendships are only impressions, easily rubbed away.

U rquhart's office was overflowing with colleagues and alcohol. Celebration was in full swing. It was one of the finest offices available to a Member with a gracious window offering a fine view across the river to the Archbishop of Canterbury's ancient Gothic palace at Lambeth. "Different sides," as he would occasionally reflect. He stood dispensing drinks as still more newcomers pressed his hand and offered their congratulations. It was the first time during the campaign he had seen some of these faces but that did not matter. New faces were new votes.

"Quite splendid, Francis. Absolutely excellent result. Do you think you can go on to win?" inquired one of his senior parliamentary colleagues.

"I believe so," Urquhart responded with quiet confidence. "I have as good a chance as anyone."

"I think you're right, you know," his colleague said, gushing as he quenched some inner fire with a huge gulp of something white. "Young Samuel may be ahead but his campaign is going backwards. It's between the experienced hands now, you and

Patrick. And, Francis, I want you to know you have my whole-hearted support."

Which, of course, you will want me to remember when I have my hands on all that Prime Ministerial patronage, Urquhart thought to himself, chuckling as he offered his gratitude and Mortima, who was gliding seraphically around the room despite the crush, refreshed the depleted glass and offered an endearing smile.

One of his younger supporters had produced a box of lapel badges and was pushing his way through the room sticking them on jackets. The badges simply proclaimed "FU." The young politician, who was Napoleonic in stature and flushed in face, found himself standing in front of Mortima. Excitedly he thrust one of the badges in the general direction of her chest. His eyes were endearing but, as his hand approached her bosom, increasingly uncertain. Then they met hers and he blanched as though whipped. "Oh, God. Sorry. I think this belongs else-where," he blurted and disappeared back into the crowd.

"Where do you get these people from?" she whispered in mock awe into her husband's ears.

"When he grows up he might be a great man."

"If he grows up, send him to me. I'll let you know."

New arrivals were still pouring into the room.

"Where have they all come from?" Mortima asked, worried they might run out of refreshment.

"Oh, some of them have been very busy," he replied. "They'll already have made brief but prominent appearances at both Samuel's and Woolton's receptions, on the basis that we can never be too sure. And you can't, can you, my dear? Be too sure?"

"I like to know where I stand with those around me, Francis."

"Of course, my dear. That's why I have a friendly Whip in both Michael's and Patrick's parties, counting heads, collecting faces. Making sure."

They stared into each other's face, oblivious for the moment of the crush around them.

"Whatever it takes, Francis."

"Will you want to know?"

She shook her head. "No, any more than you want to know, my love." She turned and pressed on with her duties.

In the background the telephone had been ringing persistently with messages of congratulation and inquiry. Urquhart's secretary had been fielding the calls in between opening bottles and providing small talk, yet now she was at Urquhart's side, a frown creasing her face. "It's for you," she whispered urgently. "Roger O'Neill."

"Tell him I'm busy and that I will call him later," he instructed.

"But he called earlier. He sounds very anxious. Asked me to tell you it was 'very bloody hot,' to quote his exact words."

With an impatient curse he withdrew from his guests to the window, where his desk gave him a little shelter from the press of celebration. "Roger?" His tone was gentle as he cast a bright face around the room at his guests, not wanting them to know the irritation he felt inside. "Is this really necessary? I've got a room full of people."

"She's on to us, Francis. That bloody bitch—she knows, I'm sure. She knows it's me and she'll be on to you next, the cow. I haven't told her a thing but she's got hold of it and God knows how but…"

"Roger, listen carefully. Pull yourself together." Urquhart's tone remained controlled but he turned to the window, away from lip readers.

But O'Neill was gabbling, his conversation running away like a driverless express.

Urquhart interrupted, "Roger, tell me slowly and clearly what all this is about."

Yet the gabbling began again and Urquhart was forced to listen, trying to make sense of the chaotic mixture of words, splutters and sneezes. "She came over to see me, the cow from the press lobby. I don't know how, Francis, it's not me and I told her nothing. I fobbed her off—think she went away happy. But somehow she's got onto it. Everything, Francis. The Paddington address, the computer. Even that bloody leaked opinion poll. And that bastard Kendrick must've shot his mouth off. Jesus, Francis. I mean, what if she doesn't believe me?"

"Hold your tongue for a second," Urquhart seethed as he smiled. "Who, Roger? Who are we talking about?"

"Storin. Mattie Storin. And she said…"

"Did she have any firm evidence? Or is she just guessing?"

O'Neill paused for the briefest of moments. "Nothing firm, I think. Just guesswork. Except…"

"Except what?"

"She's been told I had something to do with opening that Paddington address."

"How on earth—?"

"I don't know, Francis, I don't bloody know. But it's all right, no need to worry, she thinks I did it for Collingridge."

"Roger I could happily—"

"Look, it's me who's done all the dirty jobs for you, taken all the risks. You've got nothing to worry about while I'm in it up to my neck. Oh, Francis, I need help, I'm scared! I've done too many things for you that I shouldn't have touched, but I didn't ask questions and just did what you said. You've got to get me out of this, I can't take much more—and I won't take much more. You've got to protect me, Francis. Do you hear? Oh, God, please, you've got to help me!"

"Roger, calm yourself," he said quietly into the receiver, cupping it with both hands. "She has absolutely no proof and you have nothing to fear. We are in this together, you understand? And we shall get through it together, all the way to Downing Street."

Nothing but uncontrollable sobbing came from the other end of the phone.

"I want you to do two things, Roger. I want you to keep remembering that knighthood. It's just a few days away now."

Urquhart thought he could detect a stumbling expression of gratitude.

"And in the meantime, Roger, I want you to keep well away from Miss Storin. Do you understand?"

"But—"

"Keep away!"

"Whatever you say, Francis."

"I will deal with her," Urquhart whispered and cut the connection.

He stood, his shoulders braced, looking out of the window, letting his emotions wash over him. From behind him came the hubbub of the powerful men who would propel him into Downing Street. To the front he gazed across the centuries-old view of the river that had inspired so many great men. And he had just put the phone down on the only man who could ruin it all for him.

FORTY-ONE

What does a politician end up saying to St. Peter when at last they meet? Complain about the number of spoiled ballot papers? Plead that if only the polling stations had stayed open a little longer everything would be different?

I have my own plan. I intend to look him in the eye and tell the old bastard he's fired.

He had called her later that evening. "Mattie, would you care to come round?"

"Francis, I'd love to, really love to, but won't there be a scrum outside your house?"

"Make it late. They will all have gone."

"And…Mrs. Urquhart? I wouldn't want to disturb her."

"Already returned to the country for several days."

It was nearly midnight when she slipped quietly through the front door in Cambridge Street, making sure no one was watching. She felt somehow devious, yet expectant.

He took off her coat, very slowly, was looking closely at her. She felt awkward and suddenly kissed him on the cheek.

"Sorry," she blushed. "It's just…congratulations. Bit unprofessional, I suppose."

"You might say that, Mattie. But I'm not going to complain." And he started laughing.

Soon they were seated in his study with its close, almost conspiratorial cracked-leather atmosphere, whiskey in hands.

"Mattie, you've been rather naughty, I hear."

"What have you heard?" she asked in alarm.

"Among other things, that you've upset Greville Preston."

"Oh, that. I'm afraid I have."

"Afraid?"

"Grev won't print anything of mine. I've been banished. On gardening duty."

"That could be rather attractive."

"Not when the whole world is changing and I'm not part of it. Not when…" She hesitated.

"When what, Mattie? I can tell something's bothering you."

"When something truly wicked is going on."

"That's politics for you."

"No, this isn't just politics. It's far worse."

"Tell me everything—if you'd like to. Treat me as a father confessor."

"No, I could never do that, Francis."

"I thought you said I reminded you of your father."

"Only in your strength."

Her cheeks brightened a little, she seemed bashful; he smiled. And suddenly for Mattie the room was filled with a swirl of colors—the crystal blue of his eyes, the swirling amber of the whiskey, the deep dark hues of the old leather, the rug of Persian purples. She could hear her heart beating in the womb-like silence. She held out her glass as he refilled it, knowing that she had started something by coming here that she would have to finish.

"I think someone deliberately targeted Collingridge."

"I'm fascinated."

"The leaked polls, leaked information. I think the Paddington address was a set-up, which means…"

"What does it mean?"

"The share dealing was a set-up, too."

Urquhart looked startled, as if someone had pinched his cheek. "But why?"

"To get rid of the Prime Minister, of course!" she exclaimed, frustrated that he was being so slow to see what she had now clearly understood.

"But…but…who, Mattie? Who?"

"Roger O'Neill's part of it."

"Roger O'Neill?" Urquhart burst into mocking laughter. "But what on earth could he possibly have to gain from all this?"

"I don't know!" She pounded the leather sofa with her fist, her frustration boiling over.

Urquhart rose from his own chair and came to sit by her. He took her hand, slowly unfurled each of her fingers, rubbed the palm with his thumb. "You're upset."

"Of course I'm upset. I'm a journalist sitting on the biggest bloody story of the century and no one will print it."

"And I think you're too upset to think clearly."

"What do you mean?" she said, affronted.

"Roger O'Neill," he repeated, his tone full of scorn. "The man can't control his own habits let alone juggle the parts of a complicated plot."

"I've noticed."

"So…?" he prodded, encouraging her.

"He must be acting with someone else. Someone more significant, more powerful. Someone who could benefit from the change of leadership."

He nodded in agreement. "There has to be another figure in there somewhere, pulling O'Neill's strings." He was pushing her down a dangerous trail but he knew she would get there eventually under her own steam. Better to hold her hand.

"So we're looking for a mystery man with both means and the motive. In a position to control O'Neill. With access to sensitive political information."

He looked at her with growing admiration. She was not only beautiful but, once she got going, made her way along the path with surprising skill. She gasped as she reached the end of the trail and suddenly saw the view.

"Someone who'd been engaged in a bitter battle with the Prime Minister."

"There are plenty of those."

"No! No! Don't you see? There's only one man who fits that whole bill." She was panting with the excitement of discovery. "Only one. Teddy Williams."

He sat back on the sofa, his jaw sagging. "Dear God. This is appalling."

It was her turn to take his hand, squeezing it. "Now can you understand why I'm so frustrated. This extraordinary story, but Grev won't touch it."

"Why?"

"Because I can't prove it. There's no hard evidence. So I'm stuffed. I just don't know what to do, Francis."

"That's one of the reasons I asked you round here tonight, Mattie. You're going through a difficult time. I think I might be able to help."

"Really?"

"You need something else to offer Preston, something he'll be unable to resist."

"What's that?"

"The inside story of the Urquhart campaign. Who knows, I might even win. And if I do, afterwards those who have favored access would be in a very powerful position in Fleet Street. And I can assure you, Mattie, that if I win, you will have particularly favorable access."

"You're serious, Francis? You would do that for me?"

"Most certainly."

"But why?"

"Because!" His eyes lit up in amusement, then became serious once again, looking deep inside her. "Because you are quite brilliant at your job, Mattie. Because you are exquisitely beautiful—am I allowed to venture that opinion?"

She smiled coquettishly. "You are very much allowed to say that. I couldn't possibly comment."

"And because, Mattie, I like you. Very much."

"Thank you, Francis." She leaned forward, kissed him, not on the cheek this time but on the lips. She drew back. "I'm sorry, I shouldn't have done that."

He hadn't moved, steady, like a rock. She kissed him again.

❖　❖　❖

It was much later that evening, well after one, after Mattie had returned to her home, that Urquhart left his house and went back to his room in the Commons. His secretary had already emptied the ashtrays, cleared the glasses, straightened the cushions. It had still been boiling with noise when he had left but now it was a silent as the dead. He closed the door behind him, locked it carefully. He crossed to the four-drawer filing cabinet with its stout security bar and combination lock. He twirled the dial four times, back and forth, until there was a gentle click and the security bar fell away into his hands. He removed it and bent down to open the bottom drawer.

The drawer creaked as it came open. It was stuffed full of files, each with the name of a different MP, each containing embarrassing and even incriminating material he had carefully withdrawn from the safe in the Whips' Office. It had taken him nearly three years to amass these secrets, these acts of utter stupidity.

He knelt on the floor while he sorted through the files. He found what he was looking for, a padded envelope, already addressed and sealed. He put it to one side, then he closed the drawer and secured the filing cabinet, testing as he always did to make sure the lock and security bar had caught properly.

He didn't drive straight home. Instead he drove to one of the twenty-four-hour motorcycle messenger services that flourish among the seedier basements of Soho. He dropped the envelope off and paid in cash for it to be delivered to its destination. It would have been easier, of course, for him to have posted it in the House of Commons where they have one of the most efficient post offices in the country. But he didn't want a House of Commons postmark anywhere near this envelope.

FORTY-TWO

Cruelty of any kind is unforgivable. That's why there is no point at all in being cruel in half-measure.

Wednesday, November 24

The letters and newspapers arrived almost simultaneously with a dull thud on Woolton's Chelsea doormat. Hearing the early-morning clatter, he came downstairs in his dressing gown and gathered them up, spreading the newspapers across the kitchen table while he left the post on a small antique bench in the hallway. He received more than three hundred letters a week from his constituents and other correspondents and had long since given up trying to read them all. So he left them for his wife, who was also his constituency secretary and for whom he got a generous secretarial allowance from the parliamentary authorities to supplement his Cabinet minister's stipend.

Inevitably, the newspapers were dominated by the leadership election. The headlines seemed to have been written by journalists moonlighting from the *Sporting Life* and phrases such as "Neck and Neck," "Three Horse Race," and "Photo Finish" were splashed across the front pages. Inside, the less feverish commentaries explained that it was difficult to predict which of the three leading contenders was now best placed. He bent over the analysis in the *Guardian*, not normally his first port of call. It often hopped around uselessly on its left leg but, since it wouldn't end up supporting any of the candidates at the next election, it was arguably more measured and objective about the outcome.

> *The Party is now presented with a clear choice. Michael Samuel is by far the most popular and polished of the three, with a clear record of being able to pursue a political career without throwing out his social conscience. The fact that he has been attacked by some elements of the Party as being "too liberal by half" is a badge he should wear with pride.*
>
> *Patrick Woolton is an altogether different politician. Immensely proud of his Northern origins, he poses as a man who could unite the two halves of the country. Whether his robust style of politics could unite the two halves of his own Party is altogether more debatable. Despite his time in the Foreign Office, he professes to have little patience with diplomacy and plays his politics as if he were still hooking for his old rugby league club. The Leader of the Opposition once described him as a man wandering the streets of Westminster in search of a fight, and not particularly both-ered with whom.*

Woolton let out a muffled roar of appreciation, demolished half a slice of toast and rustled the paper once more.

> *Francis Urquhart is more difficult to assess. The least experienced and well known of the three, nevertheless his performance in the first round ballot was remarkable. Three reasons seem to explain his success. First, as Chief Whip he knows the Parliamentary Party extremely well, and they*

*him. Since it is his colleagues in the Parliamentary Party
and not the electorate at large who will decide this election,
his low public profile is less of a disadvantage than many
perhaps assumed.*

*Second, he has conducted his campaign in a dignified
style which sets him apart from the verbal fisticuffs and
misfortunes of the other contenders. What is known of his
politics suggests he holds firm to the traditionalist line, some-
what patrician and authoritarian perhaps, but sufficiently
ill-defined for him not to have antagonized either wing of
the Party.*

*Finally, perhaps his greatest asset is that he is neither
of the other two. Many MPs have certainly supported him
in the first round rather than commit themselves to one of
the more contentious candidates. He is the obvious choice
for those who wish to sit on the fence. But it is that which
could ultimately derail his campaign. As the pressure for a
clear decision grows, Urquhart is the candidate who could
suffer most.*

*So the choice is clear. Those who wish to air their social
consciences will support Samuel. Those who thirst for blood-
and-thunder politics will support Woolton. Those who cannot
make up their minds have an obvious choice in Urquhart.
Whichever way they decide, they will inevitably deserve what
they get.*

Woolton chuckled as he finished off the last of the toast
and his wife arrived to join him, her arms laden with the
morning's post.

"What do they say?" she said, nodding at the newspapers.

"That I'm Maggie Thatcher without the tits," he said. "Home
and bloody dry."

She replenished his mug of tea and sighed as she sat beside
the pile of mail and began sifting through it. She had gotten

the process down to a fine art. Her word processor was carefully programmed with a series of standard responses that, with only the barest brush of a keyboard, would make a reply seem personalized. Then they would be signed with the help of a little autograph machine he had brought back from the States. Even though many of the letters were from the usual bunch of discontents, lobbyists, professional whingers, and nutters who wrote in green ink, they would all get an answer. She wouldn't risk losing her husband even a single vote by failing to offer some form of reply even to the most abusive.

She left the padded brown envelope until last. It had been hand-delivered and was firmly stapled down; she had to struggle to open it, risking her manicure in the process. As she pulled out the last tenacious staple a cassette tape fell into her lap. There was nothing else in the envelope, no letter, no compliments slip, no label on the tape to indicate where it had come from or what it contained.

"Fools. How on earth do they expect us to reply to that?"

"It's probably a recording of last weekend's speech or a tape of a recent interview," he suggested distractedly, not bothering to look up from his newspaper. "Give us some more tea, lass, and let's give it a whirl." He waved broadly in the general direction of the stereo unit.

His wife, dutiful as ever, did as he bade. He was slurping his tea, his attention fixed to the editorial in the *Sun*, when with a burst of red light the playback meter on the tape deck began to show it was reading something. There was a series of low hisses and crackles, it was clearly not a professional recording.

"Turn the bloody thing up, then, love," he instructed, "let the fox hear the chicken."

The sound of a girl's laughter filled the room. It was followed, moments later, by her low, deep gasp. The noise hypnotized the Wooltons, rooting them to the spot. No tea was supped and no paper turned for several minutes as through the

speakers came many noises: heavy breaths, low curses, a complaining mattress, a grunt of happiness, the rhythmic banging
of a headboard against a wall. The tape left little to the imagination. The woman's sighs became shorter and more shrill, only
pausing to gasp for breath before they climbed ever higher.

Then, with mutual cries of ascension and fulfillment, it was
done. A woman's giggles mixed with the deep bass panting of
her companion.

"Oh, my, that was bloody marvelous," the man gasped.

"Not bad for an oldie."

"That's what you get with age. Stamina!"

"Can we do it again, then?"

"Not if you're going to wake up the whole of bloody
Bournemouth," an unmistakable Lancashire accent said.

Neither Woolton nor his wife had moved since the tape
had begun but now she stepped slowly across the room and
switched it off. A soft, gentle tear fell down one cheek as she
turned to look at her husband. He couldn't return her gaze.

"What can I say? I'm sorry, love," he whispered. "I'll not lie
and tell you it's bogus. But I am sorry, truly. I never meant to
hurt you."

She made no reply. The look of sorrow on her face cut him
far more deeply than any angry word.

"What do you want me to do?" he asked gently.

She turned on him, her face flooded with pain. She had to
dig her nails deep into her palm to retain control. "Pat, I have
turned many a blind eye over the last twenty-three years and
I'm not so stupid as to think this is the only time. You could
at least have had the decency to keep it away from me and to
make sure my face wasn't rubbed in it. You owed me that."

He hung his head. She let her anger sink into him before
she continued.

"But one thing my pride will not tolerate is having a tart like
that trying to break up my marriage and make a fool of me. I'll

not stand for it. Find out whatever the blackmailing little bitch wants, buy her off or go to the police if necessary. But get rid of her. And get rid of this!" She flung the tape at him; it bounced off his chest. "It doesn't belong in my house. And neither will you if I have to listen to that filth again!"

He looked at her with tears in his own eyes. "I'll sort it out. I promise. You'll hear no more about it."

FORTY-THREE

Love reaches a man's heart. Fear, on the other hand, gets to his more persuadable parts.

Thursday, November 25

Penny cast an unwelcoming frown in the direction of the solid steel sky and, muffled in wool, she stepped carefully onto the pavement from the Earl's Court mansion block in which she lived. The weathermen had been talking for days about the possibility of a sudden cold snap and now it had arrived, intent on getting on with its job. As she picked her way over frozen puddles she regretted her decision to wear heels instead of boots. She was moving slowly along the edge of the pavement, blowing hot breath on her fingers, as a car door swung open, blocking her path.

She bent low to tell the driver to be more bloody careful when she saw Woolton at the wheel. She beamed at him but he didn't return her warmth. He was looking straight ahead, not at her as she obeyed his clipped instruction and slipped into the passenger seat.

"What is it you want?" he demanded in a voice as hard as the morning air.

"What are you offering?" She smiled, but an edge of uncertainty was already creeping in as she saw his eyes. They were soulless.

The lips were thin, curled, exposing his teeth as he spoke.

"Did you have to go and send that tape to me at home? That was a damned cruel thing to do. My wife heard it. It was also extremely stupid because she knows about it now so you can't blackmail me. No newspaper or radio station will touch it, the potential libel damages will have them all running for cover, so there's not much use you can make of it."

It wasn't the truth. The tape could still do immense damage to him in the wrong hands but he hoped she would be too stupid to see all that. His bluff seemed to have worked as he watched her face fill with alarm.

"Pat, what on earth are you talking about?"

"The bloody tape you sent me, you silly trollop. Don't you go coy on me!"

"I…I sent you no tape. I haven't the slightest idea what you're talking about."

The unexpected assault on her feelings had come as a considerable shock and she began to sob and gasp for breath. He grabbed her arm ferociously and tears of real pain began to flow.

"The tape! The tape! You sent me the tape!"

"What tape, Pat? Why are you hurting me…?"

The trickle of tears had become a torrent. The street outside began to disappear behind misted windows and she was locked in a world of madness.

"Look at me and tell me you didn't send me a tape of us in Bournemouth."

"No. No. What tape?" Suddenly she gasped and the tears died in horror. "There's a tape of us in Bournemouth? Pat, that's vile. But who?"

He released her arm and his head sank slowly onto the steering wheel. "Oh, my God, this is worse than I thought," he muttered.

"Pat, I don't understand."

His face was gray, suddenly aged, his skin stretched like old parchment across his cheeks. "Yesterday a cassette tape arrived at my home. It was a recording of us in bed at the Party conference."

"And you thought that *I* had sent it? Why, you miserable shit!"

"I hoped it was you, Pen."

"Why? Why me?" she shouted in disgust.

He gripped the steering wheel, knuckles white, looking ahead, but not at the road. "I hoped it was you, Pen, because if it's not you then I haven't the faintest idea who's doing this. And it can't be any type of coincidence that it's arrived now, so many weeks after it was made. They're not trying to blackmail me for money. They want me out of the leadership race." His voice faded to a whisper. "As far as next Tuesday goes, I'm toast."

❖ ❖ ❖

Woolton spent the rest of the morning trying to think constructively. He had no shred of doubt it was the leadership race that had caused the sudden appearance of the tape. He threw a dozen ideas against the wall as to who was behind it, even the Russians, but nothing stuck. He had nowhere else to go. He called his wife—he owed her that, and more—then he called a press conference.

Faced with such a problem, some men might have decided to fade gently from the scene and pray that their quiet retirement would not be disturbed, but Woolton wasn't some men. He was the type who would rather go down fighting, trying to salvage whatever he could from the wreckage of his dreams. He had nothing to lose.

He was in a determined mood by the time the press conference gathered shortly after lunch. With no time to make more formal arrangements he had summoned the media to meet him on the Albert Embankment, on the south side of the river directly opposite the Houses of Parliament. He needed a

344 ❖ MICHAEL DOBBS

dramatic backdrop and the gingerbread palace with the tower of Big Ben would provide it. As soon as the cameramen were ready, he began.

"Good afternoon. I've got a short statement to make and I'm sorry I'll not have time afterwards for questions. But I don't think you're going to be disappointed."

He waited as another camera crew arrived and heaved their equipment into position.

"Following the ballot on Tuesday, it seems as if only three candidates have any realistic chance of success. In fact, I understand that all the others have already announced they'll not be standing in the second round. So, as you gentlemen have put it, this is a three-horse race."

He paused. Bugger it, but this was hard. He hoped they were all freezing, too.

"Of course, I'm delighted to be one of those three, honored, but three can be an unlucky number. There aren't really three alternatives in this election, only two. Either the Party can stick to the practical approach to politics that's proved so successful and kept us in power for over a decade. Or it can develop a new raft of policies, sometimes called conscience politics, which will get Government much more deeply involved—some would say trapped—in trying to sort out every problem in the world. Big Brother it's called, and as you all know that's never been my brand of tea."

The reporters stirred. Everyone knew there were divisions within the Party but it was rare for them to be given such a public airing.

"However well intentioned, I don't believe that a new emphasis on conscience politics would be appropriate—fact is, I think it would be a disaster for the Party and the country. I reckon that's also the view of the clear majority within the Party. Yet that is just the way we could end up drifting if that majority gets divided between two candidates. The two candidates who support pragmatic policies are Francis Urquhart and myself. Now I am a practical man. I don't want my personal ambitions to stand in the way of achieving those policies in which I've always believed. But that's just what might happen."

Despite the cold air his words were catching fire, sending spirals into the air.

"That place"—he cocked a thumb at the Parliament building behind him—"means too much to me. I want to make sure the right man is running it with the right policies in place. So, ladies and gentlemen"—he gave one last look around at the mass of cameras and bodies that pressed around him, toying with them for a second more—"I'm not going to take any risks. Too much is at stake. So I am withdrawing from the race. I shall be casting my own vote for Francis Urquhart, who I sincerely hope will be our next Prime Minister. I have nothing more to say."

His last words were almost lost in the clatter of a hundred camera shutters. He didn't wait but began striding up the riverside steps toward his waiting car. A few gave chase, running after him, but were able to get no more than the sight of him being driven off across Westminster Bridge. The rest stood in a state of bewilderment. He had left them no time for questions, no opportunity to develop theories or detect hidden meanings behind his words. They had only what he had given them so they would have to report it straight—which is precisely what Woolton intended.

He drove home, where his wife stood waiting on the doorstep, no less confused. He was smiling ruefully as they went inside; she allowed him a kiss on her cheek, he made the tea.

"You decided to spend more time with your family, Pat?" she asked, skeptical, as they sat on opposite sides of the kitchen table.

"Would do no harm, would it?"

"But. There's always a 'but' somewhere with you. I understand why you had to back out and I suppose that's going to have to be punishment enough."

"You'll stick with me, love? That's more important than anything, you know that."

She chose her words carefully, not wanting to let him slip so freely off the hook. "I shall go on *supporting* you, as I always have. But…"

"That bloody word again."

"But why on earth did you decide to support Francis Urquhart? I never knew you two were that close."

"That superior bugger? We're not close. I don't even like him!"

"Then why?"

"Because I'm fifty-five and Michael Samuel is forty-eight, which means that he could be in Downing Street for twenty years until I'm dead and buried. Francis Urquhart, on the other hand, is almost sixty-two. He's not likely to be in office more than five years. So with Urquhart, there's a chance of another leadership race before I'm reduced to dog meat. In the meantime, if I can find out who's behind that tape, or they suffer some really brutal and horribly painful accident, as I sincerely hope they will, then I'm in with a second chance."

His pipe was hurling thick blue smoke at the ceiling as he worked on his logic.

"In any event, I've nothing to gain from remaining neutral. Samuel would never tolerate me in his Cabinet. So instead I've handed the election to Urquhart on a plate and he'll have to show some public gratitude for that."

He looked at his wife, forced a smile for the first time since they had heard the tape.

"Hell, it could be worse. How do you fancy being the Chancellor of the Exchequer's wife for the next couple of years?"

FORTY-FOUR

To lie about one's strength is the mark of leadership; to lie about one's faults, the mark of politics.

Friday, November 26

The following morning's weather was still well below freezing, but a new front had passed over the capital bringing crystal skies to replace the leaden cloud of the previous day. It felt like a fresh start. From the window of his office Urquhart gazed out at what seemed for him to be a future as bright as the sky. After Woolton's endorsement he felt invulnerable. He was almost home.

Then the door burst open with the sound of an exploding shell and from the rubble emerged the tattered figure of Roger O'Neill. Even before Urquhart could demand to know what on earth he was doing, the babbling commenced. The words were fired like bullets, being hurled at Urquhart as if to overwhelm him by force.

"They know, Francis. They've discovered the file is missing. The locks were bent and one of the secretaries noticed and the Chairman's called us all in. I'm sure he suspects me. What are we going to do? What are we going to do?"

Urquhart was shaking him to stop the incomprehensible gabble. "Roger, for God's sake shut up!"

He pushed him bodily into a chair and slapped his face. Only then did O'Neill pause for breath.

"Now slowly, Roger. Take it slowly. What are you trying to say?"

"The files, Francis. The confidential party files on Samuel you asked me to send to the Sunday newspapers." He was panting from both physical and nervous exhaustion. The pupils of his eyes were dilated, the rims as raw as open wounds, the face the color of ashes. "You see, I was able to use my pass key to get into the basement without any trouble, that's where all the storage rooms are, but the files are in locked cabinets. I had to force the lock, Francis. I'm sorry but I had no choice. Not very much but it bent a little. There's so much dust and cobwebs around that it looked as if no one had been in there since the Boer War, but yesterday some bitch of a secretary decided to go in there and noticed the bent lock. Now they've gone through the whole lot and discovered that Samuel's file is missing."

"You sent them the original file?" Urquhart asked, aghast. "You didn't just copy the interesting bits as I told you?"

"Francis, the file was as thick as my arm, it would have taken hours to copy. I didn't know which bits they'd be most interested in, so—I sent them the lot. It could have been years before anyone noticed the file was missing, and then they'd have thought it was simply misplaced."

"You absolute bloody fool, you…"

"Francis, don't shout at me!" O'Neill screamed. "It's me who's taken all the risks, not you. The Chairman's personally interrogating everyone with a pass key and there are only nine of us. He's asked to see me this afternoon. I'm sure he suspects. And I'm not going to take the blame all on my own. Why should I? I only did what you told me…" He was weeping.

"Francis, I can't go on lying. I simply can't stand it anymore. I'll go to pieces!"

Urquhart froze as he realized the truth behind O'Neill's desperate words. This quivering man in front of him had neither resistance nor judgment left; he was beginning to crumble like an old wall without foundations. Not even for a week, not even for this week of all weeks, could O'Neill control himself. He was on the edge of his own personal disaster, the slightest wind would send him hurtling down toward destruction. And he would take Urquhart with him.

When he spoke his voice was firm but conciliatory. "Roger, you are over-anxious. You have nothing to fear, no one can prove anything and you must remember that I'm on your side. You are not alone in this. Look, don't go back to the office, call in sick and go home. The Chairman can wait till Monday. And tomorrow I would like you to come and be my house guest in Hampshire. Come for lunch and stay overnight while we talk the whole thing through—together, just the two of us. How does that sound to you?"

O'Neill gripped Urquhart's hand like a cripple clinging to his crutch. "Just you and me, Francis…" he wept.

"But you mustn't tell anyone you're coming to visit me. It would be very embarrassing if the press were to find out that a senior party official was my house guest just before the final leadership ballot—it wouldn't look right for either of us. So this must be strictly between the two of us. Not even your secretary must know."

O'Neill tried to mutter words of gratitude but was cut short by three enormous sneezes that had Urquhart reeling in disgust. O'Neill didn't seem to notice as he wiped his face and smiled with the newfound eagerness of a spaniel.

"I'll be there, Francis. You can trust me."

"Can I, Roger?"

"Course you can. Even if it kills me, I'll be there."

Saturday, November 27

Urquhart slipped from his bed before dawn. He hadn't slept but wasn't tired. He was alone, his wife away for the weekend, he wasn't entirely sure where, but it was his choice, he had asked her for a little time alone. She had searched his face carefully, trying to spot the reflection in his eye of some lover or inappropriate entanglement. He wouldn't be so stupid, of course, not on the weekend before such a week, yet men had the capacity to be so inexplicably stupid.

"No, Mortima," he had whispered, understanding her concern. "I need a while to reflect, walk a little, read a little Burke."

"Whatever it takes, Francis," she had replied, and left.

It was early, even before the first light of morning was breaking above the New Forest moors. He dressed in his favorite hunting jacket, pulled on his boots, and walked out into the freezing morning air along a bridle path that led across Emery Down toward Lyndhurst. The ground mist clung closely to the hedgerows, discouraging the birds and damping down all sound, a cocoon in which only he and his thoughts had any existence. He had walked nearly three miles before he began a long, slow climb up the southern face of a hill, and slowly the fog began to clear as the rising sun cut through the damp air. He had just emerged from a bank of swirling mist when he saw the stag across the patch of sun-cleared hillside, browsing among the damp gorse. He slipped gently behind a low bush, waiting.

He wasn't prone to introspection but there were moments when he needed to dig inside himself, and in that inner space he found his father, or elements of him. It was on a patch of moor similar to this, but in the Highlands of Scotland, beneath a bush of yellow flowering gorse, that they had found his body. Beside him had been his favorite twenty-bore Purdy, handed down from his own father, only one cartridge used. That was all it had taken to blow off half his head. A stupid man, weak.

Brought shame upon the name of Urquhart that still made the son twist inside and feel somehow lessened.

The stag, a fallow deer, had his head high, sniffing the morning air, his broad oar-like antlers catching the young sun, a scar on his mottled flank suggesting he might have fought a recent rut and lost. This was a young buck, he would have another day, but Urquhart knew he wouldn't be so fortunate. The fight in which he was engaged would be his last, his time wouldn't come round again.

The stag edged closer as it continued to browse, oblivious of his presence, the rich chestnut coat shining in the light, its short tail twitching. It was a sight that when he was younger he might have watched for hours, yet he couldn't sit here now, not with his father. Urquhart stood, not thirty yards in front of the buck. It froze in confusion, sensing it should already be dead. Then it leaped to one side and in an instant was gone. Urquhart's laughter followed it into the mist.

When he returned home he walked straight to his study, without changing, and picked up the phone. He called the editors of the four leading Sunday newspapers. He discovered that two of them were writing editorials supporting, one was waving the flag for Samuel and the other was noncommittal. However, all four were in varying degrees confident that he had a clear advantage, a conclusion confirmed by the *Observer*'s pollsters who by now had succeeded in contacting a substantial majority of the Parliamentary Party. The survey predicted that Urquhart would win comfortably with 60 percent of the vote.

"It seems it would take an earthquake to stop you winning now," the editor had said.

"Or the truth," Urquhart whispered, after he had put down the receiver.

Urquhart was still sitting in his study when he heard O'Neill's car draw up sharply on the gravel driveway outside. The Irishman parked carelessly and clambered out wearily.

As he stepped into the hallway, Urquhart couldn't help but note that his guest was almost unrecognizable as the man he had taken to lunch in his club less than six months before. The casual elegance had turned into outright scruffiness, the hair that was once informal was now unkempt, the clothes were creased, the collar unbuttoned and crumpled. The once suave and fashionable communicator now appeared like a common tramp and those deep, twinkling eyes, the features which both women and clients had found so captivating, had sunk without trace, replaced by two wild, staring orbs that flashed around the hallway in constant pursuit of something they could never find.

Urquhart led O'Neill to one of the second floor guest rooms. He said little as they climbed the stairs, every space in time filled by O'Neill's babbling and breathless commentary. The guest showed little interest in the fine views across the New Forest afforded by the room; he threw his overnight bag carelessly on the bed. They retraced their way down two flights of stairs until Urquhart led him through an old, battered oak door into his book-lined study.

"Francis, this is beautiful, truly beautiful," O'Neill said, gazing at the collection of leather-bound books, paintings covering a range of traditional topics from ships under full sail in heavy seas to clansmen in a distinctive green tartan, and a pair of antique globes. It wasn't beautiful, that was typical exaggeration, but it was intimate and entirely Urquhart. Cut crystal glasses surrounded two decanters that stood in an alcove in the dark wooden bookcase.

"Help yourself, Roger," Urquhart invited. "There is a rare Speyside and an island whiskey full of peat and seaweed. You choose." He watched with clinical concentration as O'Neill overfilled a tumbler with whiskey and began draining it.

"Oh, can I get one for you, Francis?" O'Neill spluttered, finally remembering his manners.

"My dear Roger, not *just* at this moment. I must keep a clear head, you understand. But please feel free."

O'Neill poured another enormous glass and slumped into a chair. And as they talked the alcohol began to do battle with whatever else was inside his system and the raging in his eyes became a touch less frenetic even as his tongue became thicker and his conversation increasingly lost its coherence. Depressant fought stimulant, never achieving peace or balance, always leaving him on the point of toppling into the abyss.

"Roger," Urquhart was saying, "it looks as though we shall be in Downing Street by the end of the week. I've been doing some thinking about what I'll need. I thought we might talk about what *you* wanted."

O'Neill took another gulp before answering.

"Francis, I'm drenched in gratitude that you should be thinking of me. You're going to be a class act as Prime Minister, Francis, really you are. As it happens, I've also been giving some thought to it all, and I was wondering whether you could use someone like me in Downing Street—you know, as an adviser or even your press spokesman. You're going to need a lot of help and we seem to have worked so well together and I was thinking..."

Urquhart waved his hand for silence. "Roger, there are scores of civil servants to take on those responsibilities, people who are already doing that work. What I need is someone just like you in charge of the political side of things, who can be trusted to avoid all those wretched mistakes that the Party organization has been making in recent months. I'd very much like you to stay at Party Headquarters—under a new Chairman, of course."

A look of concern furrowed O'Neill's brow. The same meaningless job, watching from the sidelines as the civil service ran the show? Wasn't that what he'd been doing these last years? "But to do something like that effectively, Francis, I shall need support, some special status. I thought we'd mentioned a knighthood."

"Yes, indeed, Roger. That would be no more than you deserve. You've been absolutely indispensable to me and you must understand how grateful I am. But I've been making inquiries. That sort of recognition may not be possible, at least in the short term. There are so many who are already in line to be honored when a Prime Minister retires and there's a limit on the number of honors a new Prime Minister can hand out. I'm afraid it could take a while…"

O'Neill had been slumped in his chair, slipping forward on the leather seat, but now he pulled himself up straight, confused, indignant. "Francis, that's not what we said."

Urquhart was determined to test O'Neill, to bully him, prod him, stick a finger in his eye or up his arse, shower him in offense and disappointment, put him to a little of the pressure he would inevitably come under in the next few months. He wanted to see how far O'Neill could be pushed before reaching the limit. He hadn't a moment longer to wait.

"No, that's not what we fucking said, Francis. You promised! That was part of the deal! You gave your word and now you're telling me it's not on. No job. No knighthood. Not now, not soon, not ever! You've got what you wanted and now you think you can get rid of me. Well, think again! I've lied, I've cheated, I've forged, and I've stolen for you. Now you treat me just like all the rest. I'm not going to have people laughing at me behind my back anymore and looking down their noses as if I were some smelly Irish peasant. I deserve that knighthood— and I demand it!"

The tumbler was empty and O'Neill, shaking with emotion, hauled himself from the chair to refill it from the decanter. He chose the second decanter, not caring what was in it, spilling the dark malty liquid over the rim of the glass. He slurped a huge mouthful before turning to Urquhart and resuming his avalanche of outrage.

"We've been through all of this together, as a team, Francis.

Everything I've done has been for you and you wouldn't have gotten anywhere near Downing Street without me. We succeed together—or we get fucked together. If I'm going to end up on the shit heap, Francis, I'm damned if I'm going there on my own. You can't afford that, not with what I know. You owe me!" He was trembling, spilling more whiskey. The pupils of his eyes were like pinpricks. He was dribbling.

The words had been spoken, the threat made. Urquhart had offered O'Neill a gauntlet of provocation that, almost without pause for breath, had been picked up and slapped into Urquhart's face. It was clear it was no longer a matter of whether O'Neill would lose control, but how quickly, and it had taken no time at all. There was little point in continuing to test him. Urquhart brought the moment to a rapid conclusion with a broad smile and shake of the head.

"Roger, my dear friend. You misunderstand me entirely. I'm only saying that it will be difficult this time around, in the New Year's Honors List. But there's another one in the spring, for the Queen's Birthday. Just a few weeks away, really. I'm only asking you to wait until then." He laid his hand on O'Neill's trembling shoulder. "And if you want a job in Downing Street, then we shall find you one. We work as a team, you and I. You've deserved it. On my word of honor, Roger, I will not forget what you deserve."

O'Neill was unable to respond beyond a murmur. His passion had been spent, the alcohol burrowing its way inside, his emotions torn to pieces and now pasted back together. He fell back into his chair, ashen, exhausted.

"Look, have a sleep before lunch. We can sort out the details of what you want later," Urquhart suggested, refilling O'Neill's glass himself.

Without another word, O'Neill closed his eyes. He drained the glass yet again and within seconds his breathing had slowed, yet even asleep his eyes still flickered beneath their lids in constant turmoil. Wherever O'Neill's mind was wandering, it had found no peace.

Urquhart sat looking at the shrunken figure. Mucus was dripping from O'Neill's nose. The sight reminded Urquhart yet again of his childhood, and of a Labrador that had been with him through years of faithful service as a gun dog and constant companion. One day the gillie had come and explained that the dog had suffered a stroke; it must be put down. Urquhart had been devastated. He had rushed to the stable where it slept and was greeted with the pitiful sight of an animal that had lost control of itself. The rear legs were paralyzed, it had fouled itself, and its nose and mouth, like O'Neill's, were dribbling uncontrollably. It was as much as it could do to raise a whimper of greeting. There was a tear in the old gillie's eye as he fondled its ear. "There'll be no more chasing o' rabbits for you, old fella," he had whispered. He had turned to the young Urquhart. "Time for you to go, Master Francis."

But Urquhart had refused. "I know what is needed," he had said.

So together they had dug the grave at the back of the orchard near a thick hedge of yew, had lifted the dog to a bright spot nearby where it could feel the warmth of an autumn sun. Then Urquhart had shot it. Put an end to its suffering. As he stared now at O'Neill, he remembered the tears he had shed, the times he had visited the spot where he had buried it, and wondered why some men deserved less pity than dumb animals.

He left O'Neill in the library and made his way quietly toward the kitchen. Under the sink he found a pair of rubber kitchen gloves and stuffed them, along with a teaspoon, into his pocket before proceeding through the back door toward the outhouse. The old wooden door groaned on rusty hinges as he entered the potting shed. The mustiness hit him. He used this place rarely but he knew precisely what he was looking for. High on the far wall stood an ancient, battered kitchen cupboard that had been thrown out of the old scullery many years before and which now served as a home for half-used tins of paint, stray cans of oil, and a vigorous army of woodworm. At the back, behind the other cans, he found a tightly sealed tin. He put on the rubber gloves before taking it from its shelf and walking back toward the house, holding the can as if he were carrying a flaming torch.

Once back in the house he checked on O'Neill, who was still profoundly asleep and snoring like a distant storm. He made his way quietly upstairs to the guest room and was relieved to discover that O'Neill hadn't locked his overnight case. He found what he was looking for in the toilet bag, crammed alongside the toothpaste and shaving gear. It was a tin of men's talcum powder, the head of which came away from the shoulders when he gave it a slight wrench. Inside there was no talcum but a small self-sealing polyethylene bag with the equivalent of a large tablespoonful of white powder. He took the bag to the polished mahogany writing desk that stood in the bay window and extracted three large sheets of blue writing paper from the drawer. He placed one sheet flat and poured the contents of the bag into a small mound on top of it. He placed a second sheet beside it and, still in his rubber gloves, opened the tin he had brought from the potting shed and spooned out another similarly sized pile of white powder. Using the flat end of the spoon as a spatula he proceeded with the greatest care to divide both mounds of white powder into two equal halves, scraping one half of each onto the third page of writing paper that he had creased down its middle. The grains were of an almost identical color and consistency, and he mixed the two halves together to hide the fact that they had ever been anything but one. With the aid of the crease along the middle of the paper, he prepared to pour the mixture back into the polyethylene bag.

He stared at the sheet of paper, and his hand. It had a gentle tremble. Was that nerves, age, indecision? Something he had inherited from his father? No, never that. Whatever it took, never that! The powder slipped unprotesting into the polyethylene bag, which he then resealed. It looked as if it had never been touched.

Five minutes later, in a corner of the garden near the weeping willow, where his gardener always had a small pile of garden rubbish ready to burn, he lit a fire. The tin was now empty, its contents flushed away, and he buried it in the midst of the blaze along with the blue writing paper and the rubber gloves. Urquhart watched the flames as they flared, then smoked, until there was little left but a battered old can covered in ash.

He returned to the house, poured himself a large whiskey, swallowed it almost as greedily as had O'Neill, and only then did he relax.

It was done.

FORTY-FIVE

It was that wise old sailor of stormy seas, Francis Drake,
who remarked that the wings of opportunity are fledged with
the feathers of death. Someone else's death, for preference.

O'Neill had been asleep for three hours when he
was roused by someone shaking him fiercely by
the shoulder. Slowly he focused his eyes and saw
Urquhart leaning over him, instructing him to wake up.

"Roger, there's been a change of plan. I've just had a call from
the BBC asking if they can send a film crew over here to shoot
some footage for their coverage on Tuesday. Samuel has apparently already agreed, so I felt I had little choice but to say yes.
They'll be here for some time. It's just what we didn't want. If
they find you here it'll start all sorts of speculation about how
Party Headquarters is interfering in the leadership race. Best
to avoid confusion. I'm sorry, but I think it best that you leave
right away."

O'Neill was still trying to find second gear on his tongue as
Urquhart poured some coffee past it, explaining once again
how sorry he was about the weekend but how glad he was they
had cleared up any confusion between them.

"Remember, Roger. A knighthood next Whitsun, and we can

sort out the job you want next week. I'm so happy you were able to come. I really am so grateful," Urquhart was saying as he tipped O'Neill into his car.

He watched as O'Neill edged his way with practiced caution down the driveway and out through the gates.

"Good-bye, Roger," he whispered.

FORTY-SIX

Lust broadens the horizon. Love narrows it to the point of blindness.

Sunday, November 28

The dawn chorus of the quality Sundays made sweet music for the Chief Whip and his supporters.

"URQUHART AHEAD," the *Sunday Times* declared on its front page, supplementing that with the endorsement of its editorial columns. Both the *Telegraph* and the *Express* openly backed Urquhart while the *Mail on Sunday* tried uncomfortably to straddle the fence. Only the *Observer* gave editorial backing to Samuel yet even this was qualified by its report that Urquhart had a clear lead.

It took one of the more lurid newspapers, the *Sunday Inquirer*, to give the campaign a real shake. In an interview conducted with Samuel about "the early years," it quoted him as acknowledging a passing involvement in many different university clubs. When pressed he had admitted that until the age of twenty he had been a sympathizer with a number of fashionable causes that, thirty years later, seemed naive and misplaced. Only when the reporter had insisted the paper had documentary evidence to suggest that these causes included the Campaign for Nuclear Disarmament and republicanism had Samuel suspected he was being set up.

"Not that old nonsense again," Samuel had responded testily. He thought he'd finished with those wild charges twenty years ago when he had first stood for Parliament. An opponent had sent a letter of accusation to Party Headquarters; the allegations had been fully investigated by the Party's Standing Committee on Candidates and he had been given a clean bill of health. But here they were again, risen from the dead after all these years, just a few days before the final ballot.

"I did all the things that an eighteen-year-old college student in those days did. I went on two CND marches and was even persuaded to take out a regular subscription to a student newspaper which I later found was run by republicans." He had tried to raise a chuckle at the memory, determined not to give any impression that he had something to hide. "I was also quite a strong supporter of the anti-apartheid movement and to this day I actively oppose apartheid," he had told the journalist. "Regrets? No, I have no real regrets about those early involvements; they weren't so much youthful mistakes as an excellent testing ground for the opinions I now hold. I know how foolish CND is—I've been there. And I love my Queen!"

That was not the line the *Inquirer* chose to emphasize. "SAMUEL WAS A COMMIE!" it screamed over half its front page, declaring in "shocking revelations" it claimed were "exclusive" that Samuel had been an active left-winger while at university. Samuel could scarcely believe the manner in which his remarks had been interpreted; he wondered for a moment whether it was actually libelous. Yet underneath the headline, the article got even worse.

Last night Samuel admitted he had marched through the streets of London for the Russians in his days as a CND

member in the 1960s when ban-the-bomb marches fre-
quently ended in violence and disruption.

He was also a financial supporter of a militant anti-
monarchy group, making regular monthly payments to the
Cambridge Republican Movement some of whose leaders
actively voiced support for the IRA.

Samuel's early left-wing involvement has long been a
source of concern to party leaders. In 1970 at the age of
twenty-seven years old, he applied to fight as an official
party candidate in the general election. The Party Chairman
was sufficiently concerned to write to him demanding an
explanation of "the frequency with which your name was
associated at university with causes that have no sympathy
for our Party." He managed to pass the test and got himself
elected. But last night Samuel was still defiant.

"I have no regrets," he said, adding that he still sympa-
thized strongly with some of those left-wing movements
he used to support…

The rest of the day was filled with fluster and commotion.
Nobody truly believed he was a closet Communist; it was
another of those silly, sensationalist pieces intended to raise
circulation rather than the public's consciousness, but it had to
be checked out. The inevitable result was confusion at a time
when Samuel was trying desperately to reassure his supporters
and refocus attention on the serious issues of the campaign.

By midday Lord Williams had issued a stinging denun-
ciation of the newspaper for using confidential documents
that he claimed had been stolen. The *Inquirer* immediately
responded that, while the Party itself seemed to be unforgiv-
ably incompetent with safeguarding its confidential material,
the newspaper was happy to fulfill its public obligations and
return the folder in its possession to its rightful owners at
Party Headquarters—which they did later that day in time to

catch the television news and give the story yet another lease
of life.

Nobody took the story as having deep meaning. Most
dismissed it as being as much about the typical incompe-
tence of Party Headquarters as Samuel himself. But his campaign had run into misfortune since it began. Napoleon had
asked for lucky generals and Britain could demand no less.
None of it was reassuring for someone who claimed to be
on top of events. It wasn't the way to spend the final hours
before battle.

❖ ❖ ❖

He had called Mattie. "I need you. Can you come round?"

She had all but run to him, at his home in Cambridge Street,
and the moment he had closed the door against the outside
world he was on her, over her, soon inside her. He seemed to
have extraordinary energy, a man in desperate need of release.
He had cried out as he had finished, a lonely sound that for a
moment she mistook for anguish, or was it guilt? The pursuit
of power raised many passions that didn't always sit comfortably with each other. She knew that herself.

When they had finished and she had eased her body off
his, they lay silently beside each other for a while, lost in
their thoughts.

"Why did you call me, Francis?" she asked eventually.

"I needed you, Mattie. I was feeling suddenly very lonely."

"You'll soon be surrounded by the entire world. You won't
have a moment to yourself."

"I think that was partly it. I'm a little frightened. I need someone I can trust. I can trust you, can't I, Mattie?"

"You know you can." She kissed him. "This won't last forever, I know that, but when you've finished with me I'll understand more about myself and everything I'm interested in."

"Which is?"

"Power. Its limits. The compromises it requires. The deceits."

"Have I made you so cynical?"

"I want to be the best political correspondent in the country, perhaps in the entire world."

"You're using me!" he chuckled.

"I hope so."

"We are different in so many ways, you and I, Mattie, but somehow I feel that if I can be certain of your"—he searched for a suitable word—"loyalty, then for a while the entire world might follow in your footsteps."

She ran a soft finger across his lips. "I think it's more than loyalty, Francis."

"We can't get too deep, Mattie. The world won't let us."

"But there's only you and me here, Francis." She slipped on top of him once more and this time he didn't cry out in anguish.

FORTY-SEVEN

Sometimes I hate myself for my inadequacies. But I find it easier to hate others more.

Monday, November 29

The janitor found the body soon after he had clocked on at 4:30 on a dark, frost-kissed morning for his shift at the Rownhams service area, located on the M27 outside Southampton. He was cleaning the toilets when he discovered that one of the cubicle doors wouldn't open. He was nearing his sixty-eighth birthday and cursed as he lowered his old bones in order to peer under the door. He had difficulty making it all the way down but eventually spotted two shoes. Since socks and feet were attached to the shoes he needed nothing more to satisfy his curiosity. There was a man inside the cubicle and whether he was drunk, diseased, or dying it was going to knock hell out of the cleaning schedule. The elderly man cursed as he staggered off to fetch his supervisor.

The supervisor used a screwdriver in an attempt to open the lock from the outside but it appeared that the man's knees were wedged firmly up against the door, and push as hard as he might he couldn't force it open more than a few inches. The supervisor bent his hand around the door in an attempt to shift the man's knees but instead grabbed a dangling hand that was as cold as ice. He recoiled in horror and insisted on washing his hands meticulously before he stumbled off to call the police and an ambulance, while the cleaner stood guard.

The police arrived shortly after 5:00 a.m. and, with rather more experience in such matters than the janitor and supervisor, had the cubicle door off its hinges in seconds. O'Neill's body, fully clothed, was slumped against the wall. His face was drained of color and stretched into a leering death mask exposing his teeth. The eyes were staring wide open. In his lap the police found two halves of an empty tin of talc, and on the floor beside him they discovered a small polyethylene bag containing a few grains of white powder and a briefcase stuffed with political pamphlets. They found other small white granules of powder still clinging to the leather cover of the briefcase, which had evidently been placed on O'Neill's lap to provide a flat surface. From one clenched fist they managed to prise a twisted £20 note that had been fashioned into a tube before being crumpled by O'Neill's death fit. His other arm was stretched aloft over his head, as if the grinning corpse was giving one final, hideous salute of farewell.

"Another druggie taking his last flaming fix," the police sergeant muttered to his younger colleague. "It's more usual to find them with a needle up their arm but this one looks as if he did his dying swan routine on cocaine."

"Didn't realize that was lethal," the constable said.

"Might have been too much for his heart. Or maybe the stuff was adulterated. There's a lot of it pushed around these motorway service stations and the junkies never know what they're buying. Sometimes they get unlucky." He started rummaging through O'Neill's pockets for clues to his identity. "Let's get on with it, laddie, and call the ruddy photographers to capture this sordid little scene. No use us standing here guessing about...

Mr. Roger O'Neill," he announced as he found a wallet bearing a few credit cards. "Wonder who he is? Or was."

It was 7:20 by the time the coroner's representative had authorized the removal of the body. Ambulance men were struggling to get the contorted body out from the cubicle and onto their stretcher when the call came over the radio. The body not only had a name but also a track record.

"Hell," the sergeant told the radio controller, "that'll put the pussies among the pigeons. We'll have CID inspectors, superintendents, even the chief constable arriving to get a gander at this one." He scratched his chin as he turned to the fresh-faced constable. "Got ourselves a prize one here, we have. Seems our boy beneath the blanket was a senior political figure with his fingers in Downing Street. You better make sure you write a damned good report, laddie. Dotted *I*'s and crossed *T*'s. Going to make a bit of a bestseller, is my guess."

❖ ❖ ❖

Mattie was in the shower, washing away the last traces of the previous evening, when her phone rang. It was Krajewski, calling from the *Chronicle*'s newsroom.

"It's a little damned early, Johnnie," she began complaining before he cut her off.

"You need to know this. Another of your impossible coincidences. It's just come over the tape. Seems the Southampton police found your Roger O'Neill dead in a public lavatory just a couple of hours ago."

She stood naked, dripping over her carpet but oblivious to the mess that was spreading around her. "Tell me this is simply your tasteless way of saying good morning, Johnnie. Please."

"Seems I'm destined always to be a disappointment to you, Mattie. It's for real. I've already sent a reporter down to the scene but it appears the local police have called in the Drug Squad. Word is he may have overdosed."

Mattie trembled as one of the pieces fell into place like the slamming of a cell door. "So that was it. An addict. No wonder he was all over the place."

"Not the sort of guy you'd want sitting beside the plane's emergency exit, that's for sure," he responded, but even as he did so a wail of misery and frustration poured down the phone.

"Mattie, what on earth…?"

"He was our man. The only one we know for certain was involved in all the dirty tricks, who left his prints over everything. The man who could unlock the whole bloody mystery for us. Now he's disappeared from the scene the day before they elect a new Prime Minister, leaving us with a big fat zero. Don't you see, Johnnie?"

"What?"

"This can't be coincidence. It's bloody murder!"

❖ ❖ ❖

As soon as she had thrown on some clothes and even without drying her hair, Mattie rushed off in search of Penny Guy, yet it seemed a futile chase. She rang the bell of Penny's mansion block continuously for several minutes with no response until a young resident in a hurry left the door ajar and Mattie slipped inside. She took the creaking lift to the third floor and found Penny's apartment. She knocked on it for several further minutes before she heard a scuffling from inside and the latch was thrown. The door opened slowly. At first there was no sign of Penny, but when Mattie walked inside she found Penny sitting quietly on the sofa, curtains drawn, staring into emptiness.

"You know," Mattie whispered.

The agony that had run lines through Penny's face was answer enough.

Mattie sat down beside her and held her. Slowly Penny's fingers tightened around Mattie's hand as a drowning woman clings to driftwood.

When at last Penny spoke, her voice was faltering, soaked in misery. "He didn't deserve to die. He was a weak man, maybe, but not an evil one. He was very kind."

"What was he doing in Southampton?"

"Spending the weekend with someone. Wouldn't say who. It was one of his silly secrets."

"Any idea?"

Penny shook her head stiffly, by fractions.

"Do you know why he died?" Mattie asked.

Penny turned to face her with eyes that burned in accusation. "You're not interested in him, are you? Only in his death."

"I'm sorry he died, Penny. I'm also sorry because I think Roger will be blamed for a lot of bad things that have happened recently. And I don't think that's fair."

Penny blinked slowly, like a simpleton struggling with a matter of advanced physics. "But why would they blame Roger?"

"I think he's been set up. Someone has been using Roger, twisting him and bending him in a dirty little political game— until Roger snapped."

Penny considered this for several long moments. "He's not the only one who's been set up," she said.

"What do you mean?"

"Pat. He was sent a tape. He thought I'd done it."

"Pat who?"

"Patrick Woolton. He thought I'd made a tape of us in bed together so that I could blackmail him. But it was someone else. It wasn't me."

"So that's why he quit!" Mattie gasped in a rush of understanding. "But...who could have made such a tape, Penny?"

"Don't know. Almost anybody at the Party conference I suppose. Anyone in Bournemouth, anyone at the hotel."

"Penny, that can't be right! Whoever blackmailed Patrick Woolton would have to know you were sleeping with him."

"Rog knew. But he would never...Would he?" she pleaded,

suddenly desperate for reassurance. Doubts were beginning to close in on her.

"Someone was blackmailing Roger, too. Someone who must have known he was on drugs. Someone who forced him to leak opinion polls and alter computer files and do all those other things. Someone who…"

"Killed him?"

"I think so, Penny," she said softly.

"Why…?" Penny wailed.

"To cover his tracks."

"Will you find him for me, Mattie?"

"I'll try," she said. "I just don't know where to start."

❖ ❖ ❖

The weather had grown bitterly cold but Mattie seemed unaware. Her mind had become like her laundry basket, overflowing with cast off ideas, and in the attempt to sort through them she had spent the day punishing herself. She had gone for a long run through the park, had attacked the masses of cleaning that had piled up in every corner of her flat, even got to ironing her underwear, but nothing helped. O'Neill's death had slammed the door on every thought in her head. It was evening before she called Krajewski.

"Come over, Johnnie. Please."

"You must be desperate."

Her silence did nothing to make him feel any better.

"But it's bloody snowing outside," he protested.

"Is it?"

"Twenty minutes," he muttered before putting the phone down.

It was nearer forty. He arrived clutching a large box of pizza.

"Is that for me?" she asked as she opened her door. "How sweet."

"No, it's for me, actually. I assumed you'd eaten." He sighed.

"But I guess there's enough for two." He was determined not to give her an easy time. She didn't deserve it.

They finished the pizza with their backs propped against her living room wall, crumbs scattered around them, the box discarded, her newly cleaned floor once more a mess.

"Did you tell Grev I was writing a book?" she asked.

He wiped his fingers on some kitchen towel. "Decided not to. I didn't think it was a great idea to let him know I was still in contact. You're not exactly flavor of the month at the *Chronicle*, Mattie. Anyway," he added, the touch of sourness back in his voice, "everyone would assume I was shagging you."

"I've hurt you, haven't I?"

"Yup."

"Sorry."

"There's always the chance I might make a footnote in that bloody book, I suppose."

"The story just gets bigger and bigger, Johnnie, but I haven't got the ending, the missing piece."

"Which is?"

"Who killed O'Neill."

"What?" he spluttered in alarm.

"It's the only thing that makes sense," she said, earnest and animated once more. "None of what's been going on was coincidence. I've found out that Woolton was deliberately blackmailed out of the leadership race. Somebody got rid of him, just as they got rid of Collingridge, and McKenzie, and Earle, I suspect. And O'Neill."

"Do you have any idea what you're saying? The stupid sod overdosed! This isn't the KGB we're dealing with."

"As far as O'Neill is concerned it might just as well have been."

"Jesus!"

"Johnnie, there is someone out there who will stop at nothing."

"But who? Why?"

"That's the bloody trouble. I don't know! Everything leads

back to O'Neill and now he's gone!" She kicked the empty pizza box in frustration.

"Look, isn't it much easier to suppose that any nonsense was down to O'Neill himself?"

"But why would he have gotten involved?"

"I don't know. Blackmail. Money for his drugs, maybe. Perhaps a power thing. Addicts never know when to stop. He got too deeply involved—and got scared. Lost control and killed himself."

"Who kills themselves in a public lavatory?" she said scornfully.

"His mind was blown!"

"And whoever killed him took advantage of that!"

They were both panting in frustration, shoulder to shoulder yet a world apart.

"Back to basics," Krajewski said doggedly, trying once more. "All the leaks. Let's play motive and opportunity."

"Money wasn't the motive. There's no sign of that."

"So it must be some dirty little power game."

"Agreed. Which means O'Neill wasn't the man behind it."

"He had the opportunity, though."

"Not for all the leaks. Some of them were from Government, not from the Party. Highly confidential stuff that wouldn't have been available even to every member of the Cabinet, let alone a party official."

"Not even Teddy Williams?"

"He would scarcely need to burgle his own files, would he? Least of all files that dropped his chum Samuel into the sewage system."

"So…"

"Government. It has to be someone in government."

Krajewski found a morsel of pizza stuck in his cheek and moved it around with his tongue while he thought. "You got a list of Cabinet ministers?"

"In a drawer somewhere."

"Then get off that sensational arse of yours and find it."

After a little rummaging that exposed the profound limitations of her efforts to clean up, she discovered the list among a pile of papers and handed it to him. He went to her work table and with his arm swept the piles of books and assorted debris to one side, exposing the smooth, laminated white work surface. The whiteness of the desk was like an open notepad waiting to be filled. He grabbed an artist's pen and began scrawling down all twenty-two names.

"OK. Who could have been responsible for the leaks? Come on, Mattie. Think!"

She paced the room as she concentrated, trying to find her way through the bureaucratic maze. "There were two leaks which could only have come from inside the Cabinet," she said at last. "The Territorial Army cuts and the Renox drug approval. And at a guess I think we can add the cancellation of the hospital program; I never bought into the idea that O'Neill and the Party were deeply involved."

"So who in Government would have known about those?"

"Whoever was on the relevant Cabinet committee."

"Ready to play when you are," he said, pen poised.

Slowly she began reciting the members of the various ministerial groups that would have had early knowledge of the decisions. "Right, the TA cuts," she began. "There's the Defense Secretary, the Financial Secretary, the Chancellor possibly." The membership of Cabinet committees was supposed to be confidential but was the subject of informed gossip among everyone in the lobby. "And of course the Prime Minister." She was counting off on her fingers. "Then there's the Employment Secretary and the Foreign Secretary, too."

He ticked the names on the list.

"The hospital scheme would have been an entirely different committee. Health Secretary, Treasury Ministers, Trade and Industry, Education, Environment. I think that's it."

More ticks.

"But the Renox drug approval…Damn it, Johnnie, that wouldn't have gone to any Cabinet committee. It was a departmental thing, would've been handled by the Health Secretary and his Ministers. The Prime Minister's office would have heard about it, of course. I can't think of anyone else."

Now she was at his side, both leaning over the table, staring at his handiwork. As she searched the list, her shoulders sagged.

"We seem to have screwed up," Krajewski muttered quietly.

There was only one name with three ticks beside it, one man with access to all three bits of leaked information, one man who they could pronounce guilty.

Henry Collingridge. The man who had been the victim of these leaks. Their efforts had led them to the most absurd conclusion of all.

"Fuck!" she exclaimed bitterly and turned away, kicking the battered pizza box yet again and sending more crumbs flying. Then her frustration turned to quiet tears that began sliding down her cheek and onto her breast.

He put his arms around her. "Sorry, Mattie," he whispered, "I guess it was just Roger all along." He kissed her cheeks, tasting the salt, then he kissed her lips in a manner that was intended to take her far away from her sorrows. She pulled back sharply.

"What's wrong, Mattie?" he asked, hurt. "Sometimes we're so close and then…"

She wouldn't answer, shed more tears; he decided to give it one more chance.

"Can I stay the night?"

She shook her head.

"On the sofa?"

Another shake.

"It's snowing like bloody Alaska outside," he pleaded.

She raised her eyes, whispered. "I'm sorry, Johnnie."

"There is someone else, isn't there?"

Again no answer.

He slammed the door behind him with such force that more papers scattered around the floor.

FORTY-EIGHT

Westminster is a zoo. There you will find great beasts on display, penned in behind bars, their strength drained, their spirits slowly crushed, objects of derision for those of small minds and profound disinterest for those of great thoughts.
I prefer the jungle.

Tuesday, November 30

The morning newspapers fell onto the doormats of a million homes like a death knell for Samuel's candidacy. One by one, editor by editor, they lined up behind Urquhart, not just the titles that Landless had his fingers on but most of the others, too. Sometimes even editors like to play safe, swim with the tide, and it was flowing inexorably in Urquhart's direction.

Only two newspapers among the quality press swam on their own, the *Guardian* because it was bloody minded and insisted on backing Samuel, and the *Independent* because it had too many minds and so refused to endorse any one.

The mood was reflected in the two camps, Urquhart's supporters finding it difficult to hide their air of confidence, Samuel's already working on excuses.

Even before the appointed hour of 10:00 a.m. a large group of MPs had gathered outside the oak doors of Committee Room 14, each hoping to be the first to cast a vote and qualify for a footnote in history. The thickening snow that was beginning to blanket Westminster gave the proceedings a surrealistic calm. It would be Christmas soon, the lights had already been switched on in Oxford Street. Peace on earth. In a few hours the battle would be over, with public handshakes and congratulations all round when the result was announced, even as in private the victors planned their recriminations and the losers plotted revenge.

❖   ❖   ❖

Mattie hadn't managed any sleep. She felt overwhelmed, there were too many ideas wrestling with each other inside her head. Why was she treating Johnnie so badly? Why was she falling for a man like Urquhart she could never have? Why couldn't she see the pattern in what was going on around her? Too many dead ends. They made her feel a failure.

She had spent the morning trudging heedlessly through the snow searching for inspiration but ending up soaked, her feet frozen with her hair left in damp strings. It was early afternoon before she turned up at Westminster. The snow had stopped falling and the skies were clearing to blue crystal, leaving the capital looking like a scene from a Victorian Christmas card. The Houses of Parliament appeared particularly resplendent, like some wondrous gingerbread cake covered in white icing. The Union flag on Victoria Tower stretched proudly as Concorde flew overhead on its flight path to Heathrow. In the churchyard of St. Margaret's, nestling under the wing of the great medieval Abbey, carol singers filled the air with song and rattled collecting tins at tourists. None of this she noticed.

Celebrations were already under way in various parts of the House of Commons. As she made her way beneath the shadow of Big Ben, one of her colleagues from the press gallery rushed over to share the latest news. "About eighty percent of them have already voted. Urquhart's home and dry. It looks like a landslide." He cast a curious eye at her. "Christ, Mattie, you look awful," he said, before scurrying on.

Mattie felt a flutter of excitement. With Francis in Downing Street she had a chance of rebuilding her life. Yet even as she thought of such things a cold hand of doubt closed around her. She didn't deserve it. Foolishly, early that morning, she had walked toward his house in Cambridge Street, drawn to him, desperate for his wisdom, only to see him on his distant doorstep kissing his wife Mortima for the benefit of cameras. Mattie had put her head down and hurried quickly away, ashamed of herself.

Yet her doubts, and her needs, had grown. Some wickedness, some outrage was taking place but the world seemed stubbornly blind to it. Surely Francis would understand, know what to do. She knew she would never be with him on her own again, not once he was in Downing Street surrounded by body guards and diary secretaries. If she were to get to him, it had to be now. Her only chance.

Urquhart wasn't in his room, nor in any of the bars or restaurants of the Palace of Westminster. She asked in vain around the corridors but no one seemed able to help. She was about to conclude that he had left the premises, for lunch or interviews, when one of the friendly Palace bobbies told her he'd seen Urquhart not ten minutes earlier headed in the direction of the roof garden. She had no idea that such a place existed, or even where it was.

"That's right, miss," he laughed, "there aren't many who do know about our roof garden. Only the staff, really, not the politicians. We like to keep quiet about it in case they all rush up there and spoil it for us. But Mr. Urquhart, he's different, seems to know every corner of this place."

"Where is it? Will you tell me?"

"It's directly above the Chamber itself. A roof terrace where we've put some tables and chairs so that in summer the staff can catch a little sun, take sandwiches and a flask of coffee. It'll be empty this time of year, though. Except for Mr. Urquhart, that is. I guess he wants to do a bit of pondering on his own. Chosen the right place for it, he has. Now don't you go disturbing him or after tomorrow I'll have to arrest you!"

She had smiled, he had succumbed, and now she was following his directions, using the stairs past the Strangers' Gallery and up again until she had passed the paneled dressing room reserved for the Palace doorkeepers. Then she saw a fire door that had been left ajar. As she stepped through it she emerged onto the roof, bathed in sunlight, and let out a gasp of awe. The view was magnificent. Directly in front of her, towering into the cloudless sky and made brilliant in the sunshine and snow, was the honey-drenched tower of Big Ben. Every detail of the beautifully crafted stone stood out with stunning clarity and she could see the tremor of the great clock hands as the ancient mechanism pursued its remorseless course. To her left she found the vastness of the tiled roof of Westminster Hall, the oldest part of the Palace, survivor of fire, war, bomb, riot, and revolution; to her right the irrepressible Thames ebbed and eddied in its own timeless fashion.

There were fresh footsteps in the snow. He was standing by the balustrade at the far end of the terrace, looking out beyond the rooftops of Whitehall to the white stone walls of the Home Office. Behind it lay Buckingham Palace where, later that evening, he would be driven in triumph.

She trod in his footsteps, for comfort. He turned suddenly, startled, when he heard the creaking of her step.

"Mattie!" he exclaimed. "This is a surprise."

She advanced toward him, reaching out, but something in his eyes told her this was neither the time nor the place. Her arms fell to her side.

"I had to see you, Francis."

"But of course. What is it you want, Mattie?"

"I'm not entirely sure. To say good-bye, perhaps. I don't think we're going to get much chance to see each other any-more, not like…"

"Our time the other night? I think you may be right, Mattie. But we will always share that memory. And you will always have my friendship."

"I also wanted to warn you."

"About what?"

"Something evil is going on."

"Where?"

"All around us—around you."

"I don't understand."

"There have been so many leaks."

"Politics is a soggy business."

"Patrick Woolton was blackmailed."

"Really?" He looked at her in sudden alarm, as though he had been slapped.

"The Collingridges were set up over the Renox shares."

He was silent now.

"And I think someone killed Roger O'Neill." She looked at the incredulity bubbling up in his eyes. "You think I'm mad?"

"No, not at all. You looked distressed, not mad. But that's a very serious allegation, Mattie. Do you have any sort of proof?"

"A little. Not enough. Not yet."

"So who is behind it all?"

"I don't know. For a while I thought it might be Teddy Williams, it might still be, but I can't do this on my own, Francis. I don't even have a newspaper to write for any more. I was hoping you might help."

"And how would you like me to help, Mattie?"

"I believe one man was behind it all. He used Roger O'Neill, then got rid of him. If we can find one link in the chain, just one, perhaps the shares, then it will lead to the others, and everything will come out, it always does, and we can—"

She was babbling as it all tumbled forth. He stepped toward her and held her arms, squeezing them gently, forcing her to stop.

"You look tired, Mattie. You're very upset."

"You don't believe me."

"Far from it. You may have stepped upon the greatest story you will ever write. Westminster is a dark and sometimes dirty corner where men trade their principles for a few years in power. It's a very old game. But it's also a dangerous game. You must be very careful, Mattie. If you're right and someone has been responsible for Roger O'Neill's death, that places you in the line of fire, too."

"What should I do, Francis?"

"Will you allow me to take charge of this for you, for a little while? With luck by tomorrow I shall be in a position to ask all sorts of questions, put a few ferrets down the rabbit holes. Let's see what comes up."

"Would you?"

"For you I'd do just about anything, Mattie, surely you must know that."

Her head fell forward onto his chest in gratitude and release. "You are a very special man, Francis. Better than all the rest."

"*You* might say that, Mattie."

"There are many people who are saying that."

"But you know I couldn't possibly comment."

He smiled, their faces only inches apart.

"You must trust me completely on this, Mattie. Will you? Not a word to anyone else."

"Of course."

"And one weekend, very soon, during the Christmas break, perhaps you can come to my country house. I'll make some excuse about needing to clear some papers from it. My wife will be listening to Wagner in some corner of the continent. You and I can be alone again. Sort this out."

"Are you sure?"

"The New Forest can be beautiful at that time of the year."

"You live in the New Forest?"

"Near Lyndhurst."

"Just off the M27?"

"That's right."

"But that's where Roger O'Neill died."

"Is it?"

"Probably no more than half a dozen miles."

He was looking at her strangely now. She stepped away from him, feeling weak, dizzy, leaned against the balustrade for support. And the pieces of the jigsaw moved about in her mind and suddenly fitted precisely together.

"Your name wasn't on the list," she whispered.

"What list?"

"Of Cabinet members. Because the Chief Whip isn't a full member of the Cabinet. But because you're responsible for discipline in the party they'd be bound to consult you about canceling the hospital program. And the TA cuts. So that you can—what is it you say?—*put a bit of stick about*."

"This is very silly of you, Mattie."

"And every Government department has a junior whip attached to it to make sure there's proper coordination. Fingers on the pulse, ears to the ground, all that sort of thing. Your men, Francis, who report back to you. And because you are the Chief Whip you know all about their little foibles, who is off his head with cocaine, who is sleeping with who, where to put the tape recorder…"

His face had gone pale, the glow in his cheeks drained, like an alabaster mask, except for the eyes.

"Opportunity. And motive," she whispered, aghast. "From nowhere to Prime Minister in just a couple of months. How on earth did I miss it?" She shook her head in self-mockery. "I missed it because I think I love you, Francis."

"Which doesn't make you particularly objective. As you said, Mattie, you don't have a single shred of proof."

"But I will get it, Francis."

"Is there any joy in the pursuit of such truth, Mattie?"

A solitary snowflake fell from the sky. As he watched it he remembered something an old embittered colleague had told him when he had first entered the House, that a life in politics was as pointless as nailing your ambition to a snowflake. A thing of beauty. Then it was gone.

"How did you kill Roger?" she asked.

A fire had taken hold of her, a flame of understanding that glowed fierce. He knew there was no point in prevarication.

"I didn't kill him. He killed himself. I did no more than hand him the pistol. A little rat poison mixed with his cocaine. He was an addict, driven to self-destruction. Such a weak man."

"No one deserves to die, Francis."

"You told me yourself the other night, I remember your words clearly. I remember everything about the other night, Mattie. You said you wanted to understand power. The compromises it requires, the deceits it entails."

"But not this."

"If you understand power, you will know that sometimes sacrifice is necessary. If you understand me, you will know that I have the potential to make an exceptional leader, one who could be great." There was a rising passion in his voice. "And if you understand love, Mattie, you of all people will give me that chance. Otherwise…"

"What, Francis?"

He stood very still, his lips grown thin, the cheeks gaunt. "Did you know my father killed himself?" he asked, his voice so soft it all but carried away in the winter air.

"No, I didn't."

"Is that what you want of me?"

"No!"

"Expect of me?"

"Never!"

"Then why do you pursue me?" He was gripping her arms tightly, his face contorted. "There are choices we have to make in life, Mattie, desperately difficult choices, ones we may hate ourselves for but which become inevitable. You and I, Mattie, we must choose. Both of us."

"Francis, I love you, really I do, but—"

And with that tiny, sharp-edged conjunction, he broke. The chaos within him suddenly froze, his eyes stared at her, melting in sorrow like the flake of snow that had fallen from the crystal Westminster sky. He let forth a desperate sob of despair, an animal in unbearable pain. Then he lifted her and threw her over the balustrade.

She cried as she fell, more in surprise than alarm. The cries stopped as she hit the cobbles below and lay still.

❖ ❖ ❖

She was a strange girl. I think she was infatuated with me. That sometimes happens, sadly, to people in public positions. She turned up on my doorstep once, late at night, completely out of the blue.

Disturbed? Well, you might say that but it's not for me to comment, although I do know she had recently left her job at the Chronicle *and had been unable to find new employment. I can't tell you whether she resigned or was fired. She lived on her own, apparently. A sad case.*

When she approached me on the roof she seemed distressed and rather disheveled. A number of people including a newspaper colleague and one of our policemen in the Palace can attest to that. She asked me for a job. I told her that wouldn't be possible, but she persisted, pestered, grew hysterical. I tried to calm her but she only grew worse. We were standing by the balustrade and she threatened to throw herself off. I moved to grab her but she seemed to slip on the ice, the conditions were quite treacherous, and before I knew it or could stop her she had disappeared. Was it deliberate on her part? I hope not. Such a tragic waste of a young life.

It's not the best way to start a premiership, of course it's not. I wondered for a while if I should step aside rather than carry this burden forward. Instead I intend to take a close interest in the issue of mental illness among the young. We must do more. I will never forget the sadness of that moment on the rooftop. It may sound strange but I believe that young lady's suffering will give me strength, something to live up to. You understand that, don't you?

I start my time in Downing Street with a renewed determination to bring our people together, to put an end to the constant drip of cynicism that has eroded so much of our national life and to devote myself to our country's cause. I shall make sure that Miss Storin's death will not have been in vain.

And now, if you will excuse me, I have work to do.

THE END

AFTERWORD

It was a most glorious, splendiferous, monumental cock-up that took place twenty-five years ago. It completely changed my life. It was this book, *House of Cards*.

I was on the tiny island of Gozo and in a sore mood. I started complaining about everything—the sun, the sea, and in particular the latest bestseller. Soon my partner was fed up. "Stop being so bloody pompous," she said. "If you think you can do any better, for God's sake, go and do it. I haven't come on holiday to listen to you moaning about that wretched book!"

Spurred on by her encouragement, I took myself down to the pool. I'd never thought of writing a book, but now I was armed with a pad, a pen, and a bottle of wine, everything I needed to become a writer—except, of course, for those irksome details known as Character and Plot. What could I possibly write about? My mind wandered back a few weeks, to the reason I was sulking and feeling so sore.

Conservative Party headquarters, 1987. A week before Election Day. I was Margaret Thatcher's chief of staff. She was about to win a record third election but Maggie had been persuaded by a combination of rogue opinion polls and uncharacteristic nervousness that she might lose. She hadn't slept properly for days, had a raging toothache, and insisted that someone else should suffer. That someone was me. On a day that became known as "Wobble Thursday," she stormed, she blew up a tempest, she was brutally unfair. Her metaphorical handbag swung at me time and again. I was about to become another footnote in history.

When we left the room, that wise old owl and Deputy Prime Minister, Willie Whitelaw, rolled his eyes and declared: "That is a woman who will never fight another election." He'd spotted the seeds of self-destruction that all too soon would become apparent to the entire world.

As I sat beside my swimming pool, Willie's words were still ringing in my ear. I reached for my pen and my bottle of wine. Three bottles later I thought I had found my character— his initials would be FU—and a plot. About getting rid of a Prime Minister. So Francis Urquhart and *House of Cards* was born.

I had no thought of getting it published—for me it was no more than a little private therapy—but through glorious and entirely unplanned good fortune soon it was a bestseller and the BBC was transforming it into an award-winning drama series with the magnificent Ian Richardson. I retired hurt from active politics and became a full-time writer. Now, twenty-five years after the book was published, FU is changing my life again. Step forward Kevin Spacey with his sensational new TV series. My house of cards has been rebuilt.

To mark this new lease of life for FU, I've taken the opportunity of reworking the novel—no great changes, no one who read the original will think it a different book, but the narrative is a little tighter, the characters more colorful, and the dialogue perhaps crisper. I've revisited it in order to repay some of the pleasure that *House of Cards* has given me during all these years. What has remained constant is the novel's unashamed wickedness. Bathe in it. Enjoy.

So was it worth that drubbing by Maggie Thatcher? Well, what's that phrase? You might say that, but I couldn't possibly comment.

Michael Dobbs
Lord Dobbs of Wylye
www.michaeldobbs.com
@dobbs_michael

ABOUT THE AUTHOR

Michael Dobbs is also Lord Dobbs of Wylye, a member of the British House of Lords. He is Britain's leading political novelist and has been a senior adviser to Prime Ministers Margaret Thatcher, John Major, and David Cameron. His bestselling books include *House of Cards*, which currently airs on Netflix, as well as *To Play the King*, *The Final Cut*, *Churchill's Triumph*, *Churchill's Hour*, *Never Surrender*, and *Winston's War*. Read more on his website, www.michaeldobbs.com.